Design Flaws

of the
Human Condition

Design Flaws

of the
Human Condition

Paul S. Schmidtberger

Broadway Books, New York

PUBLISHED BY BROADWAY BOOKS

Published in the United States by Broadway Books, an imprint of
The Doubleday Broadway Publishing Group, a division of Random House, Inc.,
New York.
www.broadwaybooks.com

BROADWAY BOOKS and its logo, a letter B bisected on the diagonal, are
trademarks of Random House, Inc.

Book design by rlf design

LIBRARY OF CONGRESS CATALOGING-IN-PUBLICATION DATA
Schmidtberger, Paul.
    Design flaws of the human condition / Paul Schmidtberger.—1st ed.
        p.   cm.
    1. Gay men—Fiction. 2. Businesswomen—Fiction. 3. Anger—Treatment—
Fiction. 4. Gay men—Relations with heterosexual women—Fiction.
5. Manhattan (New York, N.Y.)—Fiction. I. Title.

    PS3619.C4463D47 2007
    811'.6—dc22
    2006034834

ISBN 978-0-7679-2675-1

PRINTED IN THE UNITED STATES OF AMERICA

10 9 8 7 6 5 4 3 2 1

FIRST EDITION

For my mother, Mary,

gratia plena

All is not well;
I doubt some foul play.

—William Shakespeare

Design Flaws
of the
Human Condition

Prologue. In Which the Peace and Tranquility of Manhattan Are Disturbed by an Unusual Meteorological Phenomenon

Helvetica Carlyle, née Fahrtstaller, had never gotten a cab that quickly in her entire life, and Helvetica Carlyle, it has to be said, was an extremely demanding woman.

Was being the operative word.

At thirty-two feet per second, it took only about 3.8 seconds for her body to plunge from the seventeenth floor of her Park Avenue co-op down onto—or more precisely, *through*—the roof of the taxi that had just pulled up to the awning outside the building. The cab driver, one of three Bangladeshi brothers who shared a single studio apartment, a single driver's license, and a single counterfeit green card, panicked and clawed his way out of the car, leaving the passengers, a well-dressed elderly couple, sitting face-to-face with the corpse. They exchanged a long look before the wife finally sighed, leaned forward, bent back what remained of one of Helvetica's ears and peered behind it.

"Oh, that lying little such and such," she said. "She *did* have work done."

Chapter One. In Which Ken's "Really Great Day," as Preordained by a Starbucks Employee, Fails to Materialize

"Have a *really* great day."

Ken Connelly never treated himself to anything from Starbucks except on those rare occasions when he worked all three of his jobs on the same day, and this was one of those days. Ken started off in the morning as Professor Connelly, since his real job, as he liked to think of it, was as an adjunct professor of English at City College where he taught composition. He taught two different sections, which was enough to require his presence at City College almost every day of the week. Unfortunately, it wasn't enough to qualify him for a permanent position on the faculty or for any kind of health insurance, which was too bad given that he'd started to develop a strange headache that appeared every time the words "faculty" and "meeting" passed into each other's orbits and wound up anywhere near each other.

Job number two was at the reference desk in Cohen Library, the main library at City College. Taking that job had raised a few eyebrows in the English Department, but a person has to eat, and Ken's two composition sections didn't pay diddly-squat, so he applied and became a part-time reference librarian, sans benefits, naturally. Still, it was a pretty good gig because nobody ever asked the reference librarians for anything other than change for the photocopiers.

For eleven months out of the year, the job was entirely

benign, the only exception being January when *Sports Illustrated* released its Swimsuit Issue, which went directly from the cataloging service to the reference desk where, along with anything else that was likely to be stolen, you had to leave ID to borrow it. On some level it was a little amusing that Ken Connelly served as the gatekeeper to the Swimsuit Issue since he had relatively little interest in sports and absolutely no interest in photos of scantily clad women. Yes, the rumors were true—Professor Connelly was gay. Stage direction: *gasp.*

Job number three was totally off-the-wall, but, for all its flaws, it paid better than the other two combined *and* it provided benefits: Ken Connelly was a night proofreader at the law firm of Leighton, Fennell & Lowe. Leighton Fennell was one of those huge New York law firms that's so big that they have everything: their own cafeteria; their own travel agency; a battalion of wordprocessors who typed away twenty-four hours a day, seven days a week downstairs in the basement; and, tucked away in a room just off Word Processing, a team of proofreaders.

The job of the proofreaders was to take documents that Word Processing had just finished and compare the new version with the old version to be sure that the word processors, who typed at warp speed and barely had time to breathe, let alone think, didn't make any errors. Which is impossible, and which is why the firm employed proofreaders to go through the documents line by line, page by page, to catch stray errors and correct them. Occasionally an attorney would ask the proofreaders to read an entire document all on its own just to be sure there weren't any mistakes in it, which was tedious, but nowhere near as bad as the attorneys who came downstairs to *hover* and get in the way of anything ever getting finished. Generally speaking, though, the attorneys stayed upstairs in their own world, their canopy of treetops far above the jungle floor, where they could shriek and throw tantrums and fling feces at one another to their hearts' content.

Ken got the job when he was still a starving PhD candidate up at Columbia, thinking, incorrectly, that he'd quit the minute he finished defending his thesis and he'd walk right out of Leighton Fennell's door and right into a plum tenure-track position in some name-brand English department at a university that had a "faculty-only hour" three times a week in their glitteringly clean, Olympic-sized swimming pool. His lackluster brown hair would turn blond from the chlorine, and he'd trade in his otherwise unremarkable chest for a set of those "pectoral muscles" that suddenly seemed to be all the rage.

Well, *that* didn't happen.

So all these years later, Ken was still going downtown to Leighton Fennell five evenings a week—five-thirty to midnight—where he'd pick up a project from the wire basket at the front counter as he came in, go over to his cubicle, and start proofing. Well, he'd start proofing after he adjusted the little photo frame on his desk. It was this nifty triangular Lucite photo frame that the day proofreader, Maeve, had bought, *sort of* as a joke, for all three people who shared that particular cubicle: day shift, swing shift, night shift. Each of them had a photo on his or her side of the triangle, and the whole thing spun around like a lazy Susan in a high-end Chinese restaurant. Ken twirled it around so that he could gaze, time permitting, upon the picture of Brett, his beloved.

Maeve wrote poetry and performed at open-mike nights all over New York, and the photo on her side of the frame was this very artsy, very dramatic shot of her and her poet boyfriend embracing. The photo for the graveyard shift showed this handsome guy and his equally handsome boyfriend who were flashing all fifty-six of their gleamingly white teeth. Hugged between them, there was a big, bouncy yellow Labrador, the kind of dog that gets to sleep in an expensive, L.L. Bean doggie bed.

And then one afternoon Ken came to work only to find that the boyfriend's head had been covered up with a Post-it. That lasted for about a week until Ken came in and found that the Post-it—along with the boyfriend's head—had disappeared altogether. And *that* lasted for about a month before the dog got ripped out of the picture too, meaning that somewhere in Manhattan, a graveyard shift proofreader had just lost a gay canine-custody battle.

In any event, Ken arrived at work for the third time that day—the Friday of Labor Day weekend—and he swiveled the picture frame around so he could see Brett smiling at him from out at Jones Beach where they'd taken the photo, and then he got down to brass tacks. Or tried to, rather. Unfortunately, there was an almost palpable sense of tension coming from the bunkers in Word Processing and Ken guessed, correctly, that one of the lawyers had found his way downstairs to screw everything up. He went over to the counter at the front of the office to see what the deal was, and it wasn't pretty.

Dina, the evening supervisor for both WP and Proofreading, was standing on one side of a cubicle, and Crayton Reed, ostrich-faced partner and asshole of truly pharaonic proportions, was standing on the other side. And in the middle, poor little Bonnie Grohs was trying to make sense of Crayton Reed's pile of gibberish. Bonnie would finish a page of corrections, and as she took it off her little easel, Crayton would snatch it out of her hands and plunk himself down at the empty cubicle next to her and stare at it with his ostrich face and swear under his breath and then start re-changing things and trying to shove the paper back onto the easel. Crayton, it would seem, was about to wet his pants.

Apparently, they were working on a prospectus for an initial public offering worth hundreds of millions of dollars, which sounds complicated, but a prospectus is really just a description of what's being put up for sale. Only it's a description that's several hundred pages long and written in terms carefully designed to say absolutely nothing.

Unfortunately, Crayton Reed had turned this relatively simple exercise into a long, slow, secretarial death march. He had crossed out huge parts and then changed his mind and jammed them back in. He had riders and attachments all over the place. He had clutter. And above all, he had horrible handwriting. He had *horrendous* handwriting. Plus he kept trying to read over Bonnie's shoulder as she typed each letter, and when Dina chased him away, he'd pace around the room wringing his hands and screaming into the telephone at some group of junior nobodies whom he was apparently holding hostage upstairs in a conference room. He kept telling anyone who'd listen that the client was on a plane and she wanted this thing waiting for her when the plane landed. "Do you understand that? Do you understand what a plane is? Am I the only person here who is capable of *grasping* the fact that the *client* is on a *plane* and that she is *waiting* for this fucking document the second it *lands*?"

And then he spotted Ken. "What's *he* doing?" he asked Dina, so Ken grabbed the first interoffice envelope out of the wire basket and beat it back to his cubicle. Only he didn't even have time to open the envelope because Dina was suddenly right in front of him, taking it back out of his hands. "Sweetie," she whispered, "don't give me a hard time about this, but he doesn't want you working on anything else. He wants you to be ready for his document when it comes out."

"He *what*?" Ken said.

"He doesn't want you working on anything else. He wants you ready to proof the document the second—that's what he said—the *second* it comes out of the printer."

"You're kidding," Ken said.

"Do I look like I'm kidding?"

"No, I guess you don't," Ken said. "But if you're okay with me sitting here doing nothing, it's definitely okay with me."

Dina was in the middle of saying thanks and that she hoped it would all blow over soon enough when they suddenly heard the sound of a chair scraping against the floor in Word Processing followed by a sharply drawn breath, and then the sound of five separate, utterly distinct words: *"Gee! Zus! Fuh! King! Christ!"*

"Gotta go!" Dina said, racing off.

As Bonnie worked her way through the pile of changes, Crayton made her start printing the earlier parts of the document so Ken could proof them in real time. Crayton conscripted one of his lowly associates from the conference room upstairs to come ferry the pages back and forth, which was a relief for everyone since the associate served as a much more convenient lightning rod for Crayton. "Is that what they taught you in law school?" Ken could hear Crayton shouting. "They taught you to be stupid? They teach Stupid 101 in law school these days?"

So Bonnie typed while Dina coaxed actual responses out of Crayton as to what his scribbling might possibly mean, and the lowly associate walked the pages over to Ken, who checked them, and then walked them back to Crayton, and in the end, they got it done and everything got back to normal.

Until one of the interoffice pages showed up at around nine o'clock, and instead of dumping his interoffice envelope into the little wire basket, he whispered something to Dina who pointed out Ken to him. He came over and handed Ken an envelope. "What's this?" Ken asked.

"I don't know, but Mr. Reed says I'm supposed to wait here for a reply."

Inside there was a note from Crayton scrawled on a page of yellow legal paper. It said that the client had received the draft prospectus, no thanks to certain elements in this firm who remain steadfastly devoted to *not* getting things done. But in any event, the client was pleased with the *legal* analysis and the *legal* services provided by Leighton, Fennell & Lowe; indeed, her only criticism was a particular sentence on page eighty-seven, which begins—quite incorrectly—with the word "and."

"So why's he telling me this?" Ken thought.

"As a *proofreader*"—the note went on, underlining the word "proofreader" twice—"it is *your* responsibility to catch these kinds of errors *before* they reach our clients. I am not prepared to tolerate *your* dereliction of *your* duties, particularly when they compromise *our* clients' interests." Despite himself, Ken felt his face turning red. "Please see to it that this does not happen again," the note finished.

He looked up at the interoffice page. "Is this some sort of joke?"

"Nope."

"And he's waiting for a response?"

"That's what he said."

"There's nothing to respond to," Ken said. "He chewed me out and that's that. Tell him that I got the note. No wait, tell him *thanks* for the note. And then tell him I read it and that's that."

"There's no way I'm getting involved," the page said. "I'm not telling him nothing."

"Oh, fine," Ken said. He took the piece of yellow paper and flipped it over and wrote: "Dear Mr. Reed, I'm sorry the client wasn't entirely satisfied with your draft prospectus. However, even sticklers for grammar are divided over the question as to whether it is necessarily incorrect to begin a sentence with the word 'and.' I hope that allays your concerns."

"That's it?" the page said. He didn't seem to relish the idea of going back upstairs to see Mr. Reed.

"That's it."

No more than ten minutes later, the lowly associate walked in, this time with a typewritten memo for Ken. "First of all," Crayton wrote, "the client was dissatisfied with *our* draft prospectus, not with *my* draft prospectus. The sole error in that prospectus was a grammatical error and as our proofreader—or at least as someone who is *paid* to sit there and *act* as if he's proofreading—*you* should have corrected it. You did not, and when I pointed this out to you, you tried to sidestep the issue with the nonsensical argument that *everyone's* making that mistake these days."

"Now don't tell me," Ken said. "Let me guess. He's waiting for a response, right?"

"Yes he is."

"I told you not to tell me," Ken said, looking around for Dina. Unfortunately, she was upstairs out on the sidewalk teaching Bonnie how to smoke.

"Why doesn't this jerk just go home?" Ken asked. "I mean, the prospectus is done, and whoever this client is—and she sounds like a real piece of work—she's got to be happy because she pointed out only one ridiculous error, if you can even call it an error. Besides, all I do is check his changes; I don't draft any of this stuff myself."

But the associate just shrugged, so Ken turned the memo over and wrote: "Again, I'm sorry that the client was not satisfied. However, norms of usage can and do change."

That held Crayton for all of five minutes, after which the lowly associate came back and handed Ken a memo that had "Formal Warning" typed onto the re: line and was copied to Dina, to the day supervisor, and to the head of personnel. It said: "The firm's client has legitimately complained about *your* use of the word 'and' to begin a sentence. This usage is incorrect. It has always been incorrect, it will always be incorrect, and any document that includes this error is unacceptable."

"Understood," Ken replied on the back of the memo. "But please permit me to cite an excerpt from a document which, I trust you will agree, was drafted with the same high standards and commitment to quality in mind as *our* prospectus." He let his mind drift back to his first year as an adjunct at City College when he'd somehow gotten corralled into acting as the faculty advisor for a ghastly, avant-garde production of the nativity play. For some reason, Mary and Joseph wore leathery World War II–era gas masks, and the three kings pushed their gifts along in shopping carts. Still, every single word came back to him as if it had been yesterday— "*And* it came to pass that Joseph went up from Galilee, out of the city of Nazareth, into Judaea, unto the city of David, which is called Bethlehem, to be taxed with Mary, his espoused wife, being great with child. *And* so it was that, while they were there, the days were accomplished that she should be delivered. *And* she brought forth her firstborn son, and wrapped him in swaddling clothes and laid him in a manger because there was no room for them in the inn."

Paul Schmidtberger

"And *that*," Ken thought, "means you can go soak your head." He handed the memo back to the lowly associate and went upstairs to the cafeteria for his break, smiling to himself and thinking about the not entirely discouraging review the play had gotten the following day in *The Campus*: "An insult to the word 'pablum.'"

When he got back downstairs, though, all hell had broken loose. Nobody was even pretending to work anymore, and all eyes were collectively glued to the door of Dina's little office behind which a violent argument was unfolding. Dina's voice kept telling Crayton Reed's voice to calm down and think this through, which, judging from the string of invective unleashed by Crayton, was an argument that didn't particularly *resonate* with him.

Everyone in the whole clerical netherworld heard Crayton screaming the word "Now!" and then a muffled response from Dina.

"No, *now*!"

"Crayton, this is *my* department," Dina said.

Crayton picked up her phone and dialed Security. "Should I have them escort you out too?" he asked.

"No," Dina said. "I would not like to lose my job over this. All I'm saying is—"

"Good," Crayton said. He told Security to get their asses downstairs and remove a former employee from the premises, and then he went back upstairs to settle down and do his time sheets. He billed his unpleasant conversation with Dina to the client, which totaled zero point one hours, so he rounded it up to an even half hour and called it "Attention to administration of file."

Ken knew it was all over before Dina even came out of her office and over to his cubicle. "I'm sorry," she said.

"You're letting me go?" he asked.

"*They're* letting you go. Or rather, that asshole's letting you go. Ken, you know that, don't you? I did what I could."

"Dina, I've worked here for nine years. I was here when you got here, remember?"

"I know," she said.

"And besides, we don't correct the content. You told him that? That it's not our job? I mean, Jesus, if I could correct the content, I wouldn't worry whether sentences started with the word 'and'; I'd make it all less boring."

That made Dina crack a sad little smile, and Ken realized how close to tears she was, so he got up and hugged her and told her that everything was going to be all right.

"What are you going to do?" she asked.

"That I don't know."

"Well, at least you know where you can get a glowing recommendation," she said. "Give them my direct line."

"Oh, Dina, I don't know. I mean, I definitely will, you know, give them your number, and I appreciate it, but I don't know that I want to find another job proofreading or coding documents or anything along those lines."

"I know, sweetheart. It's just something to bear in mind." Dina cast a glance around Ken's cubicle, looking for something to help Ken pack up, but there was just so little to begin with. "You know," she said, "if that asshole ever leaves—*Mister* Reed—I'll take you right back. No questions asked. He leaves and we'll arrange it so that you can cross paths with him upstairs in the lobby. How about that?" Another sad, wry smile.

"I appreciate it, Dina. But I don't think people like that ever leave," Ken said.

Dina had to admit defeat on that point. The clerical netherworld had long been aware of the first principle of law firm dynamics: the bigger the asshole, the lower the likelihood that he'll ever leave.

When not one, but two security guards eventually turned up, Dina kept them at bay while Ken made the brief rounds to say good-bye. He told Dina to say "Hey" to anyone he'd missed, and then he was officially ejected from the premises of Leighton, Fennell & Lowe.

Out on the sidewalk, he saw the line of car service cars that Leighton Fennell kept on permanent call for lawyers who left late at night, and he thought, "Well, what are they going to do, fire me?" and he climbed into the first one and settled back into the leathery luxury as they drove north, consoling himself with the thought that at least he'd get to see Brett awake for once. Except that the driver's radio doodad eventually crackled to life and he answered it and listened to some incomprehensible static and then replied with the address that Ken had given him: "345 West Seventieth Street." More crackling, and then the driver hung up.

And ten seconds later the driver's cell phone rang and he answered it, and for some reason Ken thought he could hear Crayton's voice leaking out of the cell phone. The driver was answering in monosyllables—"yes," "yes," "but," "yes." And then he said, "*What?*"

Screechy, scratchy, belligerent Crayton.

"Go, go, go!" thought Ken, willing the car to make it through the traffic light on Fifty-seventh Street where the West Side Highway stops being a street and starts being a highway—as in a road where there's no way to stop.

"*What?*" the driver asked again. The light turned yellow and the driver seemed to hesitate for a moment, and then instinct took over. He floored it and the big, boxy Lincoln shot through the intersection and up the ramp.

"I can't stop here," the driver said into the phone. "I'm on the West Side Highway. There's no place to stop!"

The phone unleashed a series of ungodly noises, and all Ken could think of was one of those machines that shut-ins use to mimic hysterically barking dogs to scare off prowlers. Suddenly the driver slammed on the brakes and the Lincoln screeched and then fishtailed and then came to a stop in the right lane. A horn—seemingly disassociated from any sort of moving vehicle—shrieked by, inches away. "He says that you have to get out," the driver said.

"*Here?*" Ken shouted. "I'm not getting out here. What the hell's the matter with you? You're going to get us both killed!" Another horn screamed by.

"That's what I told him, but he said I have to stop right where I am and let you out or he'll have me—" And before the driver finished, another horn shrieked in their ears and the driver's side-view mirror got itself blasted to kingdom come.

"Oh, Jesus," Ken thought. "This is what it's like to be dead. I'm dead and I died on the West Side Highway and I'll be on the news tonight unless something more interesting happens."

But just then Ken heard the sound of wheels desperately spinning and then gripping the pavement and then the Lincoln shot forward and picked up speed and a truck came right up to their back window and let fly with a long, bellowing blast of horn, but they were finally safe. Safe enough for the driver to roll down his window and give the truck driver the finger.

"Holy shit," Ken said. "Are you all right?"

"Yeah, I guess so," the driver said. "What the fuck did you do to those people anyway?"

"Nothing! That's just it, I didn't do a thing."

"Well, you sure as shit didn't do nothing, that's for sure."

"Yes, I did do nothing," Ken said. "As a matter of fact."

"Do you know how much trouble I'm going to get into?"

"Well, do you know how much trouble I'm already in?" Ken replied.

The driver chewed it all over for a while and then neatly summarized his assessment of the situation. "Shit," he said. "Shit, shit, shit, shit, *shit!*"

He exited at Seventy-second Street and took Ken all the way to his building, the intrepid little Santa Monica tucked away at the end of Seventieth Street. They went through the motions of exchanging numbers and addresses—just in case—although the driver couldn't really see declaring this incident on his insurance since that would involve actually *having* insurance, a little matter he'd let slide ever since he'd incurred the extra expense of underwriting his new girlfriend's cocaine habit.

Ken went upstairs and let himself into the apartment as quietly as possible. He left his briefcase and his sad box of Leighton Fennell junk right by the door so Brett wouldn't spot them right away and guess what'd happened and ruin the rarity of a night in together. He tiptoed down the hallway to the living room which was empty and quiet, although their stereo was still turned on and shedding a pale green glow over its tiny little corner of the universe—evidence that Brett had let the CD play itself out, probably while reading in bed.

Ken tiptoed up to the door of the bedroom, paused, and then pushed it open. And there was Brett, his beloved, in bed. With somebody else. Although *on* the bed would probably be more accurate, since they were very much on top of the covers as opposed to under the covers, a somewhat unconventional choice for two men who were stark naked.

What the . . . ?

Ken's mind spun, desperately trying to latch onto something—anything. He was in the wrong apartment. Wrong floor. Wrong building. Wrong block. Bad dream. Bad practical joke.

He pulled the door shut and stood there, devoid of any idea as to what to do other than to stand there with his hand on the knob. Had they seen him? For some reason his heart was pounding up in his ears instead of inside his chest, and he felt dizzy. This isn't happening, he thought. This is not happening in *our* bed.

And then he remembered to breathe. Breathe in, breathe out. Repeat as necessary.

The ringing, rhythmic pounding sound in his ears slowly subsided and was replaced by a muffled, rhythmic thumping sound emanating from the other side of the door. "I guess that means they didn't see me," Ken thought, and before he had time to really decide what to do, he banged the door open and switched on the lights. Two heads snapped over toward him at the same moment. The face of the stranger bore a dull, faintly curious expression as to the source of the interruption, whereas Brett's eyes met Ken's for a moment before looking away. And then and only then—as Ken noted for the record—did they actually stop screwing.

"You'll be leaving now," Ken finally said.

"No problem, man," a stranger's voice answered.

"No," Ken said. "I meant both of you."

Paul Schmidtberger

Chapter Two. In Which Iris Unwisely Disregards the Captain's Advice to Sit Back, Relax, and Enjoy the Flight

Things hadn't been going very well for Iris. In the first place, she'd been marooned in California—correction, in hideous Costa Mesa in hideous Orange County—for the last five days, and now all she was trying to do was *leave*, and the people at the ticket counter just couldn't seem to get that through their heads. "Let me see if I can break it down for you," Iris imagined herself lecturing the gate agent who'd summarily bounced her off to the side and out of the way of more deserving customers. "I want you to catapult me up into the air, heading east, and I want you to fling me hard enough so that when I come back down, I'm in New York. Do you understand that? I don't care how you do it, just make it happen."

"That would've taught him a thing or two," Iris thought.

Instead, the jerk had just repossessed her ticket and told Iris to wait.

It wasn't supposed to be like this. In the first place, Iris was supposed to be a high-powered businesswoman. She was supposed to be a killer businesswoman. She worked for Hamilton-Styron Marketing, and when she got on a plane, she was supposed to stride down the jetway, settle into her business-class seat, and then crack open her sleek laptop and punch in ideas and bits of inspiration before they evaporated and escaped from her clutches.

Unfortunately, the reality was that Iris didn't really care.

Yes, she was clawing her way to the top of the corporate ladder, and yes, she'd been named a senior analyst at Hamilton-Styron at the tender age of thirty-two, but the truth of the matter was that she was beginning to find six a.m. conference calls and two-hundred-page "summaries" all a little bit ridiculous.

For the moment, though, she just wanted to get back home to New York and to Jeremy, her love. The trip to Costa Mesa was supposed to have been an overnighter; instead, it had stretched into three days, and then four, and then when it looked like they were going to go on indefinitely, Iris managed to slip out and buy some extra clothes at this positively humongous mall, which she hated to do because she was planning to lose a little weight and wouldn't get very much wear out of the new clothes. But she cheered herself up by getting Jeremy a gorgeous ivory shirt that would go perfectly with the schoolboy mop of wheat-colored curls that still looked great on him even though he hadn't been a schoolboy for a good long time.

And now she was finally on her way home. The gate agent called her name—"Iris Steegers!"—and handed her back her ticket with a boarding pass, saying, "There you go." Iris looked at the boarding pass and said that row 43 didn't sound like business class to her, and he told her that they couldn't upgrade her to business.

"But I have the miles," she said.

And he said, "It's not a question of having the miles. Only a certain number of seats are allocated to upgrades, and *those* seats have been filled."

"So what you're saying is that there are *other* seats in business class that aren't filled, right?"

"I guess so."

"Well, then put me in one of those." Iris's ticket, which was fully refundable, fully changeable, fully this-, that-, and the other thing-able, had cost her company well over three thousand dollars. Iris told the gate agent as much, and he looked back at his computer and studied the blinking gibberish for a long time and then finally chose a target—one of the weak or elderly keys on the keyboard, Iris imagined—and then stabbed at it until the computer finally gave in and coughed up a different screen of blinking green gibberish.

"Sorry, but no can do," he said. Some nonsense about how crowded things always were as Labor Day weekend got under way.

At the top of the jetway, they made Iris check her little wheelie bag even though she'd put it in the overhead compartment a million times before. And when she got to the door of the plane itself, some old battle-ax told her that she couldn't take on three different carry-on bags, and Iris said, "I don't have three carry-on bags. This is my briefcase and this is a laptop and this is my purse."

And the battle-ax called her ma'am. "Ma'am," she said, "you're only permitted *one* carry-on bag and one personal item. Now if you'd like assistance in checking any *other* baggage, then . . ." But Iris was already stuffing her laptop and her purse into her briefcase. They easily fit in there. "There," she said brightly. "Now I only have one bag."

"All I'm saying is that the rule is—"

"Thanks," Iris said, cutting the battle-ax off. "I appreciate your *concern*."

Not only did Iris have to suffer the indignity of walking through business class on the way to her seat in the back of the plane, but she got stuck in a human traffic jam there and got treated to a good, long look at all the empty seats plus the few lucky individuals occupying the other seats, sipping the champagne and orange juice that rightfully should have been Iris's. She looked at a bony wrist with clunky gold jewelry on it lifting a glass of Perrier to its owner's lips, and Iris felt a wave of intense hatred for the woman who owned those lips. Iris would've liked to wear clunky jewelry to accentuate bony wrists, but Iris's build was oh, how to put it, a little too *imposing* for that.

Row 43 was the very last row, and Iris settled herself in and waited for them to shut the *bleeping* doors and to *bleeping* cross-check them, whatever that meant, a little exercise that was delayed by the arrival of a couple who had the two seats directly in front of her and needed quite a bit of time to stow their two wheelie suit-cases, several different shopping bags, her purse, his backpack, and a *huge* collapsible stroller. Sadly, Iris thought, they didn't stow their baby, who was turning raspberry red from screaming.

Then the captain got on and announced a delay and handed the mike over to some stewardess who read a long list of irrelevant in-formation plus a few points of order, including the fact that the plane was equipped with eight restrooms, two in first class, two in business class, and four in the main cabin, and everyone was called upon to mutually respect this arrangement.

About an hour later, they finally pushed back and the captain added his welcome to everyone else's and gave them a step-by-step explanation of their trajectory even though he could've said they'd be flying via Uzbekistan for all that anybody was listening. And then the captain repeated the same odd bit about the cabins: "Once we're airborne," he said, "the cabins will be separated by curtains, and passengers are asked to confine themselves to their own cabin and, when seated, to keep their seatbelts securely fas-tened, just as a measure of extra security. After all," he said, "you never know when you're going to encounter some unexpected turbulence."

"True enough," Iris thought, reflexively tightening her seatbelt.

"We're number twenty-six for takeoff," the captain said, clicking his microphone off.

When they finally got off the ground, the copilot got into the act and read off still more boilerplate stuff—snacks and drinks once they'd reached their cruising altitude, SkyPhone service with any major credit card available in the back of the plane, beer and wine for this much, cocktails and spirits for that much.

"Spirits," Iris thought. "What a lovely word. And so versatile, too."

Iris hadn't realized how hungry she was until the flight atten-dants started fiddling around in the galley right behind her, appar-ently chiseling ice sculptures out of blocks of ice. Worse, their carts eventually sailed right by her and up to the front of economy, which meant that not only would they never get to her, but *while* they were not getting to her, she'd be watching them serve everyone else.

And then, in the middle of all this, Iris suffered an unexpected assault on the rear guard of her sensibilities—a moderately high-pitched female and unmistakably New York voice somewhere behind her had swiped a major credit card through the SkyPhone and was now being put through to an office somewhere. From where Iris was sitting, the acoustics were amazing—the loudmouth could just as well have held the receiver up to one of Iris's ears and shouted straight through Iris's head.

Iris heard a set of well manicured nails tapping against the plastic SkyPhone, and then a faint, disembodied and disarmingly soothing receptionist's voice on the other end of the line announce: "Leighton, Fennell and Lowe."

"Crayton Reed," Iris's tormentress bellowed. No "please."

"Thank you," the tiny little voice said, followed by a click.

A pause. And then the line clicked to life and another disembodied woman's voice announced, "Mr. Reed's office."

"Yes, it's Helvie Carlyle calling for Crayton."

Some sort of muffled response.

"Oh, I'm sorry, I'm calling from a plane," Helvie shouted. Another mumbly pause, which was completely unproductive from the point of view of the caller, but gave Iris a second to steel herself. "I said *I'm calling from a plane!*"

Iris turned all the way around in her seat to launch her most withering glare and saw that it was the woman with the bony wrists and clunky jewelry from business class—well, *that's* just great—but Iris's scathing glare didn't even scratch the surface of the woman's demeanor. Instead, Helvie gave Iris a look that said: If you don't mind, this is a private conversation.

"No, he can't call me back because, as I believe I *already* mentioned, I am calling from a *plane*. An *airplane*." A long, long pause. And then an exasperated, "Fine, I'll call back."

Then Iris heard the *schwiiiiiip* sound of the credit card slicing its way through the innards of the SkyPhone and this time Helvie left a message on somebody's machine—apparently somebody named "darling"—and accepted darling's invitation to some reception somewhere. Helvie said that she was just thrilled to be able to make it.

Schwiiiiiip and the dialing started up again. Crayton Reed still wasn't available, and Helvie let loose with a loud, disapproving sigh. Iris could hear Crayton's secretary frantically assuring Helvie that Crayton was there, he was *somewhere* in the building, but they couldn't figure out where, and yes, she'd looked in the men's room, but no, he wasn't in there and not to worry, they'd find him and they'd find him pronto.

"Fine," Helvie said, hanging up. She headed back up the aisle to the sanctuary of business class and to Iris's stupefaction, the flight attendants backed their carts up out of her way rather than holding their ground and making her wait, as if Helvie exuded some sort of strange, invisible force field that was incompatible with food destined for human consumption.

The next time that Helvie came back to use the phone, Crayton's secretary Lannie—Iris felt like she was on a first name basis with her—tried to tell her that they were still looking for Crayton and that he didn't usually just disappear like that, but Helvie cut her off. "I want that prospectus," she said, "and I want it waiting for me at the airport when I land. I want it finished, printed, messengered, and waiting for me when I land, and I want it handed directly to me when I step off the plane, is that clear?"

"Yes, but—"

"There are no buts about it, *Lannie*."

"I just—"

"And no justs either. Am I making myself clear?"

"Yes."

"Good," Helvie said, clicking off.

By the next time Helvie called, all of six minutes later, Lannie had finally found Crayton right where he *wasn't* supposed to be, namely downstairs annoying Dina Marghosian and her evening crew of freaks and misfits. He took the call in Word Processing where he was able to assure Helvie that he was personally supervising each and every page as it came off the printer and that as far as he could see, the deal was full steam ahead. It was as good as done. It was all systems go. It was . . .

"Oh, Lord," Iris thought. Even though Crayton Reed was just a thin, scratchy voice overheard from a basement two thousand miles away, she could just tell that he was short. She could feel it in her bones. But it didn't stop him from plowing straight ahead.

"It was a *slam dunk*," he told Helvie.

"That's what I wanted to hear," she said. "I'll call you back in a bit."

When Helvie started calling again, Iris found herself trapped behind the detritus of her food tray, which the flight attendants showed no interest in removing. Lannie had just put Helvie on hold and Helvie had just muttered "imbecile" when Iris decided that she'd had about enough. She pushed her little stewardess button and the battle-ax appeared out of nowhere and Iris asked her if she wouldn't mind telling the woman who was monopolizing the SkyPhone to finish her call and take her seat.

"Beg pardon?" Battle asked.

"I said, would you mind asking that woman, there, the one who is monopolizing the telephone, to please finish her call, as quickly as possible, and leave."

"I don't understand, you're waiting to use the phone?"

"No, I'm not, I'm waiting for her to *stop* using the phone."

Battle just gave Iris a long, unblinking stare and then leaned over her, as if she were a child, to undo the stewardess call button so that Iris would understand that this conversation was going to be very brief. "And why would that be?"

"Because it's annoying," Iris said. "Because I can hear every word as if she were shouting in my ear, and because it's not reasonable to ask me to sit here and listen to her shriek at people when all I want to have is a little peace and quiet. That's why."

"Well, unfortunately, not all the planes in our fleet have phones at every seat," Battle said. "*Some* of them only have SkyPhones which, as you can see, are only located in the rear of the cabin."

Something tugged at the back of Iris's mind. "Well, then why doesn't she go use the phone in the back of *business* class? That's where she came from."

"There aren't any," Battle said. "This plane is only equipped with SkyPhones in the rear of the—"

"Wait a second," Iris said. "You said that we were supposed to stay in our own cabins. You said it at least twice! You said—"

"I said no such thing," Battle said.

"No, not *you* you, but you the airline, you the crew. You said it when we got on. You said that the plane was divided into different cabins and we were supposed to *respect* that arrangement and then the captain repeated it. He said it too. He said it in plain English."

"That announcement is made with regard to the bathrooms," Battle said.

"Well, that's your interpretation, *Miss*, but what you and your captain said was that we had to stay in our own cabins," Iris said. "And I would be very grateful if you would invite that woman there to *respect* that arrangement and return to her cabin."

"There's no point in getting agitated—"

"I'm not agitated," Iris said. "I'm asking you a simple question. I'm asking if you're planning to enforce the rule that you read to us, twice, when we got on."

"And I'm telling you that it's none of your business what goes on in business class. We're here to ensure *your* safety, number one, and I don't have the time to get involved in a debate about—"

"So basically, when you said that the plane was divided into separate cabins and we were supposed to *respect* that arrangement, what you really meant was that we can't crap in the business-class toilets, but they can come back here and shout on our phone?" Iris could barely believe her derring-do.

"I'll thank you to watch your language, and I'm not planning to warn—"

"So let me ask you this. Can they *crap* in our toilets too?"

And Battle turned on her heel and walked away.

Ah, the sweet sight of a vanquished enemy, punctuated only by the sound of Helvetica Carlyle telling her secretary to make sure that the car waiting for her at the airport had a reading light—a reading light that *works* this time—and no, she didn't get the confirmation number down because some cow in coach had been throwing a fit.

Unfortunately, there are two sides to every coin, and what Iris considered as a moral victory, the airline considered as interference with a flight crew, which, the captain informed her, was a federal offense. He'd come down the aisle followed by Battle and some other guy in a copilotish jacket and tie, followed by a clique of gawking flyboys. And all Iris could think was, *"Who's flying the plane?"*

And there wasn't going to be any arguing, Iris quickly deduced. Battle's version of events—that Iris had been belligerent and offensive—was immediately adopted as the official version. Then the captain told Iris that she had a choice: she could either sit there like a good girl and not say a word for the rest of the trip and they could deal with this when they landed, or they could tie her up and gag her and she could sit there like a good girl and not say a word for the rest of the trip. Which was it going to be?

"The former," Iris said. "The one without the restraints, please."

When they were about twenty minutes away from landing, the copilotish guy came down the aisle and squatted down next to Iris and told her that she was to remain where she was, seated and silent, while the rest of the passengers disembarked. She couldn't believe they were actually going to go through with this, that they were actually going to get her into trouble at Newark. And that's just what they did. The plane landed and it taxied around for a while and Battle, sounding surprisingly carefree and winsome, welcomed them to New Jersey's Liberty International Airport. She said she knew that people had a choice of airlines while flying— which brought the grand total of things she knew up to exactly one—and she thanked everyone for choosing hers.

Once all the passengers were gone, Iris hoped that they might give her a stern talking-to and let her go, but then the captain and his copilot and their ilk disappeared and Iris just sat there while a gang of Ecuadorians started coming through the plane shoveling an unbelievable quantity of trash into big green garbage bags. Then the back doors opened with a whoosh of warm, ripe New Jersey night air and some other people started banging around with all the metal food carts. And then, finally, a black woman with a graying collection of loosely tied braids got on, looked around, and then walked to the back of the plane. "Iris Steegers?"

"Yes?"

"Would you come with me please?"

"Certainly. Can I take my luggage?" Iris asked, thinking of the once lovingly wrapped shirt for Jeremy that was now smushed at the bottom of her briefcase-slash-laptop-slash-purse.

"Of course you can."

"And can I ask you one other thing?" Iris said. "I've actually been on the plane for quite some time and I didn't actually have a chance to, uh . . ."

"Use the bathroom?" the woman asked.

"Exactly. Will there be one where I'm, uh, where you're taking me . . . or . . . ?"

"Oh, just use the one right here," the woman said. "I can wait."

"Thanks a million," Iris said. Being arrested was *much* better than flying coach.

They brought her to a miniature Port Authority police station and instead of tossing her in a cell, they just told her to take a seat on one of the banged-up, molded plastic chairs lining a hallway. She could have been waiting to get her license renewed at the DMV.

The lady with the intricate graying braids sat at a desk and typed—hunt and peck—and Iris hoped that she'd get booked by her since she seemed so nice. Instead, some bald guy with zero external indicia that he was an officer of the law—no badge, no nametag, no head-busting billy club, no nothing—called her name and had her take a seat in front of his desk.

"Coffee?" he said, instead of *"Why'd ja do it?"*

He asked her only easy, objective questions: what was her name; where did she live; where did she work; was she planning on traveling outside the United States anytime soon? Iris said that she traveled frequently for work, but never outside the USA, and he seemed perfectly satisfied. Then he started asking about the flight, but it was the exact same thing—all his questions were utterly neutral: when did she buy her ticket; did she have a record of the purchase; had she been drinking before boarding (no); what had she had to drink on the flight (a vodka tonic); just one (yes); and then, oddly, could she recall what she'd paid for the vodka tonic with (what do you mean?); a five, a ten, a twenty (oh, a twenty); was she taking any medication (no); would she agree to a blood-alcohol test (sure, why not).

The guy typed it all in and then hit print and a form spit itself out of the computer. He dialed some number and talked with someone for a while and then told Iris that they couldn't do the blood test because the entire medical staff was on their thirty-first hour of waiting for a suspected drug mule who'd arrived on a flight from Caracas to give in and take a dump. "So we'll have to forget about the blood test," he said, "but we can give you a Breathalyzer instead." He went over to a cupboard and got something that looked like a high-school science project and made Iris breathe, as hard as she could, into one end. "Okeydokey," he said, tearing up the form he'd printed before, changing something on the computer, and then reprinting it all over again. He stamped both copies and signed both, and then pushed them across the desk to Iris and told her to sign and date both at the bottom.

"What is it?"

"Your release and your promise to appear in court on, let's see, September fifteenth."

"You're letting me go?"

"Well, you still have to go to court; you do realize that?"

"That's what I'm hearing," Iris said. "But I didn't do anything wrong. And if I did, why would you be releasing me? Can't we just forget this?"

"That's what you'll have to ask the judge to do," Officer No-Badge said. "I wish I could help you"—and he sounded like he truly meant it—"but I can't."

"But I'm free to go now?"

"Absolutely."

"But wait a second," Iris said. "How come I don't have to pay any bail?"

"I don't know," the officer said. He just shrugged.

"Could I say that I've been released on my own recognizance?" Iris asked.

"If you want."

Iris thought this was all quite fantastic. She'd never been released on her own recognizance before.

Iris got on the bus heading toward the parking lot and considered her options. Yes, she was facing criminal charges, but, by the same token, they were (a) ridiculous, and (b) nobody knew about them. Then she remembered all the people gawking at her on the plane and she slightly revised her thoughts: nobody that she cared about knew anything about this. And things were going to stay that way. Generally speaking, she didn't like the idea of keeping things from Jeremy, but if she told him everything that had happened, he'd be sympathetic and understanding—that was her Jeremy—but he'd *also* want to know why Iris hadn't stood up for herself and gotten everything sorted out right then and there. And since Iris didn't have an answer to that question, she decided to keep the whole thing quiet for the moment.

She got off the bus and found her car and decided that she'd just tell Jeremy that the plane was late. No wait, Jeremy might have called some toll-free number to find out when the plane was arriving—that'd be very much like Jeremy—so she decided to tell him that they'd lost her bags and she'd had to stand around forever when suddenly, just when all hope was lost, they'd found her bag right before it was about to be loaded onto a commuter flight to Allentown, Pennsylvania. No wait, to Chicago. No wait, to Malaysia. *That's* why she was so late.

A criminal, yes. But a good liar, no. Lying had never been Iris's strong suit.

She kissed the little pendant hanging from the rearview mirror—a picture of her and Jeremy in an antique silver locket that Iris had cleverly coated with a thick coat of clear nail polish to make it look cheap and plasticky so nobody would smash her window and steal it—and she blasted out of Newark airport and sailed over the Pulaski Skyway toward civilization. Adios, amigos! She came out of the Lincoln Tunnel, swung back around on Forty-second, and then headed over to the river and turned up toward home. Stuck at the last light right before the West Side Slow-way became the West Side Highway, she suddenly realized that she should've called Jeremy. She dug her cell phone out of her bag, hit the speed dial for home, and as the light changed, she stepped on the gas.

Riiing.

"*What the . . . ?*" Iris wrenched the steering wheel to the left and caught, just out of the corner of her eye, the sickening sight of the locket swinging violently up toward the roof of the car and she thought, "Well, this is it." She shrank her shoulders in toward her body as if that would somehow make her car thinner, thin enough to squeeze by the *asshole parked in the right lane of a major highway*, and she held her breath and—*smash!*

A pause.

Riiing.

Another pause.

Iris was still alive! She was still traveling north. And her car was still alive, and *it* was still traveling north too! She'd squeaked by. She'd clipped that guy's mirror, that's all. She'd . . .

"Hello?" Jeremy answered the phone.

Huh?

"Hello-oh?" Jeremy said.

"Oh, hey Jeremy, it's me."

"What's wrong? You sound upset."

"No, just a little stressed and a lot glad to be home."

"Speaking of," Jeremy said. "Where are you? I thought you'd be here at least an hour ago."

"I'm on the West Side Highway," Iris said.

"Oh, good," Jeremy said. "I left dinner in the oven. Was the plane late or what? What took you so long?"

And all Iris could feel was a gush of relief. She wouldn't have to lie to Jeremy, not *really* anyway. "It was nothing," she said. "I had a little accident."

"An *accident*? Jesus, are you all right?"

"I'm fine, I'm fine—it was just a little fender bender," Iris said. "I'll tell you all about it."

Chapter Three. In Which Ken Resolves to Organize His Thoughts, but Falls Short of the Mark

This is what Ken was thinking as he sat barricaded inside the little reference fortress in Cohen Library. He thought, "They should never have gotten rid of detachable collars. Nowadays, when you buy a shirt, it comes with a collar whereas *before*, the collar and the shirt were two different things. You starched and ironed the collar and then you attached it to your dress shirt and, if you were in a cartoon or an early slapstick movie, the nice, stiff collar would always come undone at some incredibly inopportune moment with an unmistakable *boing!*"

And everyone would laugh.

Ken sighed. Nothing seemed very funny to him these days.

Right after he'd caught Brett with the other guy, he'd gone into the kitchen and pulled the slatted wooden door shut behind him even though they never shut it except when something in the oven set off the smoke alarm in the front hall. "This is what I'm supposed to do," he thought. "I'm supposed to sit here out of the way while Brett gets dressed and gets rid of whoever that guy is, and then he's supposed to come over and knock softly and tentatively slide open the slatted wooden door so we can tearfully have it out."

Except that's not what happened. He heard the muffled sounds of two people getting dressed, the front door opening and shutting, very gently, and then . . . nothing. Not a sound. "He didn't?" Ken thought.

Oh, but he did. Brett left with the guy! There wasn't going

to be a scene that night. Nobody was going to get hit with a rolling pin—and theirs, bought with Ken's money, was made out of marble—and nobody was going to get hit with a waffle iron. Or with an electric juicer. Or with their countertop television. Ken wasn't really the type of person to have a TV in his kitchen, much less one in the living room and another one in the bedroom, but they'd bought the TV with the justification that Brett could study his craft—he was an actor—while cooking or chopping, which made a lot of sense if you put aside the fact that Brett never cooked.

Nor did he do the shopping. Quite the contrary, it was Ken who used to run to the A&P up on West End when there used to be an A&P up on West End. And when they finished building the Trump monstrosities right next door on the old rail yards and the neighborhood was suddenly infested with grossly overfed SUVs driven by grossly underfed trophy wives, Ken started going to the Trump Market instead.

When you think about it, Brett didn't really do much at all. He had an agent and he went out on auditions from time to time, but mostly he took acting classes. He took classes everywhere—at the New School, at the Learning Annex, at the West Side Y, with private instructors, in groups, in workshops. He was always signing up for something or heading off to a seminar or just coming back from a panel discussion. He had a perfectly active life that was perfectly well divorced, 99 percent of the time, from earning any income.

Way back when, Ken had thought that he and Brett were such a good fit. He was, or was hoping to be, after all, a professor of English. The tricks of his trade were words, and, more particularly, that rare alchemy that transforms certain combinations of words from primordial alphabet soup into literature. Brett, meanwhile, was studying to be an actor, and what do actors do? They recite words. They take words from a page and they breathe life into them on the stage or on the silver screen or, as in Brett's greatest success to date, on the set of a commercial for a pair of those wildly colorful sneakers—sorry, *running shoes*—that the whole world suddenly woke up one morning and decided to start wearing.

In that commercial, Brett plays this clean-cut businessman who gets out of his stuffy downtown job on an exquisite summer evening and then encounters a series of obstacles while trying to reach this swanky, sultry cocktail party on a roof somewhere uptown (that's called the plot). There's an elaborate garden on the roof with gorgeous teak patio furniture that hasn't turned chalky and gray from the pollution (that's called the suspension of disbelief), and there are all these glamorous, tanned women who are lolling around waiting for something exciting to spice up their party.

And after vanquishing every imaginable obstacle, we see Brett climb over the ledge of the roof and approach this beautiful woman sitting on a chaise longue. For some reason, though, she doesn't look particularly pleased to see him. Brett glances at the bar. She looks like she's hot, like she's bored, but mostly she looks like she doesn't need another asshole with questionable intentions drooling over her and plying her with demon alcohol. She purses her lips. Rejection is imminent.

And what does Brett do? He opens his briefcase and produces—ta-dah!—an ice-cream cone! She breaks into a smile and nods toward the empty chaise longue next to her, and as the camera draws away, we see the two of them chatting and laughing. And as the camera pulls back farther, we see that despite the suit and tie, our little Brett has been wearing those sporty, wildly colored running shoes all along. He winks at the camera and the company's universally recognized logo appears on the screen along with their slogan, which an off-screen voice—not Brett's—reads: *"Just Get With It!"*

Brett made a lot of money on that commercial. It was wonderfully successful everywhere in the United States except Los Angeles, where focus groups hated it, and it was even more popular abroad, so much so that long after it had disappeared from the airwaves in the States, Brett continued to get a steady stream of residuals.

Really, the only fly in the ointment in terms of the whole commercial was the voice-over. Originally, Brett was supposed to do the voice-over himself; that way the producers would only have to pay one actor. The problem was that Brett's voice didn't test particularly well. People responded well to the cleft chin and the beautiful teeth and his floppy jet-black hair. And people *loved* the look he gives the camera at the beginning of the commercial, the one that says, "Well, what are we going to do to solve these problems?" Audiences consistently thought that it "drew them into the action" or that it "made them want to know what was going to happen next."

But the voice, that didn't work. It didn't make people "more likely than not" to try the product. It left them "neutral," or at least that's what Brett's agent told him. And when everything was said and done, they just went out and got someone else to do the voice-over: a four-hundred-pound grade school librarian who was out on disability because he couldn't bend down low enough to re-shelve the books where the "little shits" could get at them, but had a wonderfully rich, deeply resonant voice. And he did it to everyone's satisfaction except Brett's, because Brett thought that they weren't being very straightforward with him. Brett thought that they weren't calling a spade a spade. Brett's opinion was that they thought his voice sounded a little too gay, and *that's* why they didn't want it in the commercial.

On the plus side, the commercial confirmed for Brett the wisdom of sinking most of his spare time into working out at the gym. He got that spot, he'd said on more than one occasion, because he was in such great shape. He said that people don't really care what you have on your feet—it could be loafers or bedroom slippers for all they care. The reason they cough up all that money to buy those colorful, sporty shoes is because they want to be like you. They want to be beautiful and have a high-paying job downtown and not get pissed off when the subway's busted again and, not inconsequentially, have that lovely body that's just discernible beneath the suit.

So, much like watching tremendous quantities of TV whenever he was home, Brett considered it a professional obligation to stay in shape, and to do so, he belonged to *Sweat!* And not only was *Sweat!* fantastically expensive, but it was all the way down on Twenty-third Street in Chelsea, whereas Ken and Brett lived all the way up at Seventieth Street. Be that as it may, Brett just had to go there and he had to go there at least four times a week, lugging this gigantic sports bag that contained the tight, stretchy gym garments to which Brett was partial. On those rare occasions when Ken would meet Brett at *Sweat!* after a workout, he'd get there early and watch the people coming and going and just be amazed that people who wore such tiny, little, . . . uh . . . *minimalist* clothing could still carry, every last one of them, such truly enormous gym bags.

And despite the presence of an estimated two million non-invalid females in the City of New York, *Sweat!* was virtually all men. Gay men, in fact. *Sweat!* was a gay gym. Thus Brett, who was otherwise a perfectly logical person, was capable of taking an acting class at the West Side Y—which was, among other things, a gym—and then turn around and go all the way down to Chelsea to go to *Sweat!*—also a gym—before turning around and heading all the way back home. It didn't make a lot of sense, but that's the way things were.

Actually, aside from not making any sense, the real problem with *Sweat!*, as far as Ken was concerned, was how perfectly put together Brett always seemed after a workout. Perfectly shaven, not a hair out of place. Basically, Brett walked out of there looking like a million bucks. And *that*, in turn, had led Ken to the unpleasant conclusion that Brett probably spent a *little too much time in the locker room.*

Still, the undeniable fact of the matter was that Brett really was beautiful. He'd been born with more than his share of luck—the fine bone structure, the six-foot-plus-change height, the floppy jet-black hair. And like any wise investor, he'd taken those natural gifts and with meticulous care, a little cosmetic dentistry, and a lot of time at *Sweat!*, he'd parlayed them to the point where he was, for lack of a better word, a knockout. And he was bright, too. He read books; he had his own idea for a play simmering on the back burner; and he genuinely understood the art of theater. In short, Brett had been perfect for the role of Ken's boyfriend.

Indeed, little Maxine, the English Department secretary, just loved Brett and always made sure that he was invited to any function to which faculty husbands and wives were invited. In fact, she sometimes invited Brett along even when faculty husbands and wives *weren't* invited. And she did it not just because Brett could talk drama, literature, and poetry as well as the rest of them, but because she genuinely liked him. Maxine, by the way, had nursed and mothered the morons in the English Department for more than twenty-five years, and she'd seen her share of unsuitable husbands, unsuitable wives, and unsuitable partners over the years. Maxine comforted those denied tenure and practiced shuttle diplomacy between warring factions on the faculty. She had her own special box of "Financial Aid" Kleenex in her bottom desk drawer reserved for graduate students on pecuniary life support, and she was even rumored to have disguised herself and defended a thesis years and years ago for a graduate student who was then in the first few weeks of what would turn out to be a decades-long psychotic break. And her defense of the thesis—"Reading Between the Lines: The Overlooked Undercurrents of Loneliness, Solitude, and the Inexorable March Towards Death in *Anne of Green Gables*"—was actually successful.

So how come someone like Brett could fool someone like Maxine? That was the question on Ken's mind as he sat there in his little reference fortress. He'd racked up exactly zero requests for reference assistance all afternoon and hadn't even bothered to shelve the two reference items that had been borrowed on somebody else's shift. He'd pulled one out of the return bin about an hour earlier, but since then it had only gotten as far as his lap. "I either have to get up off this stool and put this book back where it belongs," he thought, "or sit on this stool for the rest of my life."

"Or something in between the two," he added. He hated sloppy thinking.

And he hated the fact that he was now going to have to go back to people like Maxine—who'd bent over backward to make Brett feel as welcome and as real and as equal as anybody else—and tell them that Brett was now, uh, *out of the picture*. Plus he was going to have to find a way to do it without going into the details. It was just too humiliating.

Worse, the truth was that this had been his last go at it.

What people didn't know was that when Ken met Brett, Ken had already given up on love. They'd met when Ken was only thirty-four—in human years, which is as old as dirt in gay years. Ken had already been around the block and seen what was out there and how it worked, or, more accurately, how it *didn't* work, and he'd given up. No more dates, no more disappointments. He'd thought, "I'm willing to go out with Mr. Right when he walks down to the end of Seventieth Street and straight in the door of the Santa Monica and knocks on my door."

And that's essentially what happened with Brett, only with a scream instead of the knocking part.

Brett had been subletting from the hedge-fund guy who lived down the hall from Ken, down on the side of the building right next to the Trump construction site with all the Trump dynamiting, the Trump strip-mining, and the Trump carpet-bombing. One evening a blood-curdling scream came out of the apartment and Ken sat bolt upright on the couch, placed the remote control gently down on a coaster, and flung his glass of wine at the TV.

Ah, *shit*.

He went out to investigate and found Brett standing down at the end of the hall. "Sorry about the theatrics," Brett said. "But I'm having a little emergency here."

"So I gathered," Ken said.

It turned out that the guy—"I'm Brett," he'd said, shaking Ken's hand—had been making dinner and he'd decided to make macaroni & cheese and there hadn't been any clean pots, which wasn't his fault because he'd been really busy recently and in any event, the point wasn't *why* there weren't any clean pots, the point was that there *weren't* any, period, so he'd had to wash one of the dirty ones that had been soaking in the sink. Only when he'd gone up to the sink to deal with it, there was a blurry brown blob floating in one of the pots, and he couldn't remember making anything that would bloat itself up into a blurry brown blob once it'd soaked for a while. He'd made Stove Top Stuffing the day before, and that *might* have resulted in a blurry brown *layer*, but this was a blurry brown *blob*, not a layer, and besides, he remembered eating every last bit of the Stove Top Stuffing because (a) he'd been starving; and (b) people don't just *forget* about an entire serving of carbohydrates—not in this day and age they don't.

"And so . . ." Ken prompted.

And so Brett had peered in closely at the unidentified object and just as he did, the brown blob suddenly moved and twisted and flopped out a prehistoric, webbed wing and scared the holy living bejesus out of Brett.

"A wing?" Ken asked.

"A wing," Brett said. "There's a bat in my sink. And it's alive."

Their options were not numerous. It definitely didn't amount to a 911 emergency, that much was obvious, Brett said, but bats carried horrible diseases and rabies. . . .

"Horrible diseases *including* rabies," Ken found himself gently correcting Brett in his head. Then he said, "Hold on a second," and ran back to his own apartment. He came back with a pair of quilted oven mitts, silently cursing the day that he'd said to himself—"Oh, why *not*?"—and bought oven mitts with a Minnie Mouse motif. Then he had an even better idea and he made another round-trip and this time he came back wearing his long winter overcoat. "That way," he said, "there's less of me it can bite."

Paul Schmidtberger

He went into the apartment with Brett right behind him and they crept down the hallway until they reached the kitchen and Ken saw the hideous brown blob for himself. Was it dead now? Was it trapped? Or was it taking a bath? Do bats take baths? Were bats really that fastidious?

"Colander," Ken said, leaning back and whispering the word to Brett.

"In the cupboard up on the left," Brett whispered from somewhere very close to the back of Ken's neck. Ken started to tiptoe toward the cupboard but something was holding him back. He craned his neck back toward Brett until Brett realized what he was doing and took his hands off Ken's shoulders. Ken tiptoed across the kitchen and opened the cupboard as if he were defusing a bomb and pulled out the colander. And then, in one lightning burst of bravado—God only knows where *that* came from—he pounced at the sink and clamped the colander upside down over the pot. "Window!" he shouted. "Open the window!"

Brett flung the kitchen window open while Ken kept the bat trapped between the colander and the pot, holding it out in front of him as far as he could. The bat struggled furiously while disgusting, bat-contaminated water poured out the holes in the colander.

Fuck, there were bars on the kitchen window!

Brett ran into the living room and flung that window all the way open and Ken carried the offending houseguest over to the window and stuck his arms out, and then Brett lowered the sash almost all the way so that Ken looked like one of those super-high-precision scientists who works behind a glass hood. Ken swung his hands apart and the bat dropped straight down toward the sidewalk and out of view, and as Ken scrambled to pull his hands inside before the bat decided to get itself some revenge, Brett smoothly opened the window wide enough to readmit the pots and pans and the oven-mitted hands and then slammed it down again.

Homos, one. Blood-sucking harbingers of death, zero.

. . .

Neither of them had eaten yet—that had been the whole point of the aborted pot-washing exercise in the first place—so they agreed to regroup in ten minutes and go out to eat. Ken washed his face and hands and brushed his teeth, and when he went back out into the hallway, Brett had completely transformed himself: nice shirt, very nice pants that were neither jeans nor khakis, and a hint of cologne. Andirons by Bô, if Ken wasn't mistaken. Almost like a date, Ken thought.

They went to the All State Café and talked about the Trump construction and how that probably was, or was not, related to the arrival of the bat. From there they started trading anecdotes about other unexpected encounters with nature they'd had in the city and Ken got to tell his story about getting stung by a bee while riding the F train between East Broadway and Delancey Street (northbound) and how he usually got very little sympathy for that story because so few people believed that it was actually possible to get stung by a bee while riding the F train. Whereas Ken would be happy to reassure you that it was. You know, very much possible.

And as they talked, the subjects just kept piling up. Not only were there no awkward pauses, but they were actually running a subject matter surplus—What is it that you do? Where are you from? How do you like Manhattan? What's your favorite restaurant? Are you *single* single, or are you single as in you're involved in one of those insanely complex arrangements where you complain about your ex-boyfriend 99 percent of the time but occasionally sleep with him?

Brett was studying to be an actor, and before Ken could say to himself, "Oh, so *there's* the catch," Brett told him about getting a part in a commercial, an honest-to-goodness, paying, nationwide commercial. Brett told him what the commercial was all about and how divorced the shooting process was from the *methodologies* he'd been studying in his classes, and Ken couldn't believe he was having dinner with a bright-eyed knockout who used words like "methodologies." Dinner turned into dessert and dessert turned into after-dinner drinks, and when they arrived back at the fourth floor of the Santa Monica, Brett wrapped his arms around Ken's neck and kissed him at the top of the stairs.

And that's how it started. They dated and that was that, and when the hedge-fund guy who owned Brett's apartment disappeared altogether and stopped paying the rent, Brett moved into Ken's place in what had to be, logistically speaking, the least difficult move of all time. The bank foreclosed on what used to be Brett's old apartment and it was eventually sold to a horrendous woman with a piercing voice and a cell phone permanently screwed into the bones of her skull. She hung around the building for two years and then married her fiancé—*she* has a fiancé?—and the apartment sat empty again, but this time only for a few weeks before it got snapped up by someone involved in one of the first Trump Tower divorce cases, the one who'd lost the Trump Tower apartment in the divorce but wanted to stay in the neighborhood because he'd won the Trump Tower parking spot down in the basement. Not to mention joint custody of their brat.

Brett and Ken had watched all this, this ebb and flow, this demonstration of the inexhaustible ability of humans to make each other happy and/or miserable, all from the window of the fourth floor of the Santa Monica, and now Brett had gone and shot the whole thing to hell. Thrown it all away.

This wasn't getting Ken anywhere. "You know, if I'm going to be perfectly honest with myself," Ken thought, "then I should have seen this coming." Before he fell in love with Brett—before the word "methodologies" came out of Brett's beautiful lips and left Ken no choice but to fall in love with him—Brett had been shooting a commercial and his prospects had seemed so solid and bright. Everything about that commercial had gone swimmingly, *except* they decided not to use Brett's voice, and opinions differed as to how and why that had happened. But Brett was full of shit, Ken thought. It didn't have anything to do with sounding gay or not sounding gay; the fact of the matter was that Brett didn't sound trustworthy. And he didn't sound trustworthy for a very good reason—because he *wasn't*. Random people had picked up on that. Random people in focus groups had picked up on that while Ken had missed it. Imagine that—people who'd been recruited into focus groups solely because they were willing to trade an hour of their lives in exchange for a dinner voucher at a participating Chili's Restaurant had watched the commercial and they'd picked right up on it—Brett didn't sound trustworthy. And Ken had missed it. What a world!

Ken looked over at the clock in the library and thought, "One more hour and then I can finally clear out of here." He opened the book that was still sitting in his lap and looked at the little sticker on the inside cover which read: "Reference Material—Does Not Circulate." A little thought crept into his head and he just couldn't help himself. He took out his mechanical pencil and clicked it a few times to rev it up and then added: "But Brett Manikin does." And that gave him a little chuckle.

He re-shelved that book and pulled the other one out of the return bin and edited its sticker too. And then he looked around his dusty little reference fortress and back at the clock and pulled a handful of books off the shelf. "Only an hour left," he thought. "I'd better get busy."

Chapter Four. In Which Iris Swears to Tell the Truth, the Whole Truth, and Nothing but the Truth, or Something Along Those Lines

It wasn't easy being a criminal, Iris thought. There were just too many places where you could get tripped up. Yes, she'd taken a day off work for her court appearance, but no, she hadn't breathed a word about it to Jeremy. Obviously not. She'd gotten up and dressed and left the house when she normally did, but then she had to bum around town killing time until her 1:30 p.m. arraignment, or whatever it was called, down at the Federal Courthouse. Plus she was going to have to tell Jeremy all about a boring day at work, which she hadn't actually endured, while there were a million interesting things happening all around her.

The courthouse had a fabulous stone staircase outside that seemed perfect for trudging up all weary and harassed on your way into court with nothing more than a briefcase in your hand and your faith in the law in your heart, and then bounding down later once you'd been exonerated. "Miss Steegers!" the reporters would yell, jostling each other and jockeying for space. "How does it feel to be free?"

Inside, though, was a different story. They made her go through a metal detector and it beeped but nobody cared, and then it took forever to find the right courtroom, and once she did, it was a mob scene. There was a harried-looking, nine-month-plus pregnant woman up just below the bench, and, judging from the looks of things, you were supposed to go and argue with her. Iris got in line to argue with her, but it turned out to be more of an informal check-in. "Who's your lawyer?" the pregnant lady wanted to know.

"Lawyer?" Iris said faintly. The thought hadn't even crossed her mind. Why would she need a lawyer? "Um, I don't have one."

"All-righty," the pregnant woman said, checking something off on a list. There, problem solved. She said that Iris's case would be about the thirtieth case to be called.

"Is there anyone here from the airline?" Iris asked. She'd kept an eye out for Battle, but so far, so good.

"What airline?"

"It's what the case is about," Iris said. "This whole misunderstanding is about something that happened, well, something that *didn't* happen on a plane."

"Well, I don't know what happened or didn't happen and I don't care. There's no airline in this case."

"Well, who is there then?" Iris wanted to know.

"The United States," the lady said. "It's the United States versus Iris Steegers."

Eventually people settled down a bit and then a door in the back opened and the pregnant lady metamorphosed into a pregnant drill sergeant and she barked, "All rise!" and the judge strode in and swept up onto the bench in his black robe. A stenographer took a seat near the pregnant lady who stood up, kneaded her back, and announced that court was now in session.

Her job was to call out a case and then, while the lawyers and the parties were falling all over other people's briefcases and coming up to the two podiums, she would hand the file up to the judge who looked at it over his half-glasses. He'd say what the case was and what the specific issue was, and then he'd let the lawyers argue. He didn't seem like a particularly mean man. Impatient, clearly, but not mean.

There weren't any witnesses or anything like that; instead, it was as if all the people who were involved in various cases had questions and today was the day that they got to come to the judge to have those questions answered.

Should so-and-so's bail be reduced? (Nope.)

Could somebody else *please* have a new trial because the jury in the old one had been tainted? (Nope.)

Could somebody's frivolous complaint be dismissed? (Yup.) Iris pricked up her ears at that. That sounded promising. That sounded like just the ticket.

During some of the criminal matters, this sheriffy-looking person would go to a door in the back and lead a prisoner out who'd confer with his lawyer for about ten seconds, and then the lawyers would have their argument and the prisoner would invariably get taken back to the room in the back by the sheriffy-looking guy who'd lock the door and stand guard until they needed a new or better prisoner.

Then Iris heard the pregnant lady calling her case and she went up to her favorite podium—the one that'd been winning more than the other—but some horrible guy in a suit made her move over to the other podium saying that she was the *defendant*. He, it turns out, was the prosecutor. Iris had her very own prosecutor. And she was petrified.

The prosecutor barely looked up from this file he was holding with color-coded number stickers at the end of it—exactly like at the gynecologist's—and he launched into a spiel about making a motion for a trial date and how everything was in order and how they envisioned a half-day trial of, say, four hours max, including jury selection, and the judge filled something out on a form and was handing it and the rest of her file back to the pregnant lady when Iris heard herself saying, "Wait!"

All eyes were on her.

"I didn't do anything wrong," she said.

"I beg your pardon?" the judge asked.

"This is a *mistake*," Iris said. "This is nonsensical. This is—"

"*Those*," the judge said, "are questions for the jury to decide. Juries decide questions of fact, and I decide questions of law. That's the division of labor here."

"Well, isn't there a law that says that you can't have a trial if it's about something ridiculous? Something that's a mistake?"

"No, there isn't."

"But you dismissed that other case," Iris said. "The frivolous one. The one where the lawyer said that this was all frivolous. It was the lawyer with the striped blue tie that didn't go with his suit." She scanned the courtroom behind her but she couldn't find her guy anywhere.

"Your Honor," the prosecutor started to complain.

"So what you're saying is that you're making a motion to dismiss?" the judge asked.

"Yes," Iris said. "I'd like one of those."

He motioned to the pregnant lady who gave Iris the stink eye as she heaved herself up and handed Iris's file back to the judge who started skimming through it.

"Charge?" he asked, baffling Iris, but the prosecutor stepped up and announced, "Interference with a flight crew," and the judge went back to reading. There was no expression on his face, either good or bad. "Counselor," he finally said to the prosecutor, "you have an affidavit here from one, uh, Anne-Marie Wyatt that says that the defendant used foul and abusive language."

"That's right."

"Is that your only affidavit?"

"That's the only one necessary to support the charge."

"That's not what I asked you. I asked you how many affidavits you have. Which is a simple question that calls for a simple, *numerical* answer. So, how many affidavits do you have? Move your lips so that a *number* comes out of them."

"One, Your Honor. But it's all that's necessary to support the charges."

The judge sighed audibly. "Well, tell me this. As terms, 'foul' and 'abusive' are descriptions, correct? What was the actual language in question?"

"I'm not sure that I have an entire *glossary* of the foul and abusive language employed by Miss Steegers here in front of me," the prosecutor said.

"Well, then why don't you tell me what you *do* have in front of you," the judge said.

"It would seem that she said 'crap.' "

"What was that?"

" *'Crap,'* your honor."

"Anything else?"

"Not in this affidavit."

"Which is your only affidavit," the judge said. Then he turned toward Iris. "Miss Steegers," the judge said. "Did you say 'crap' on a flight from LAX to Newark on, let me see, on August thirty-first?"

"Yes sir, but—"

"And did you employ any other language that might give offense?"

"No sir."

"Priors?" the judge asked.

"I don't understand," Iris said.

"I'm asking if you've ever been in trouble with the law before. You know, prior offenses?"

"Oh, good heavens, no," Iris said. "Nothing. Nothing at all. Not so much as a traffic ticket."

"Counselor?" the judge asked the prosecutor, who shrugged and looked over at the useless probation person who was always rustling papers at a pace about two or three cases behind everyone else. The probation guy had the dirt on all the criminal defendants and was always trying to elbow his way into the action. He leafed through one of his files and then looked up at the judge and announced that Miss Steegers was correct. She was clean. She had no record. "Although," he added with a halfhearted stab at humor, "she has had a ticket for a moving violation in the past."

"What ticket?" Iris thought.

"Well, was it *paid*?" the judge asked.

"Yessiree," the probation guy said.

I've never gotten a ticket in my life, Iris thought. Everybody knows that.

"Listen, Counselor," the judge said. "I'm not setting this for trial. There's no way I'm going to haul twelve people out of their jobs and—"

And the prosecutor *interrupted* him. He said, "Interference with a flight crew is a felony and it carries a potential sentence of more than thirty-six months and we don't drop those cases."

"First of all," the judge said, "there's no way it's interference with a flight crew. The best you have is failure to follow crew instructions. And I don't see how you plan to prove that to the jury with what you've presented to me."

"That's for the jury to decide," the prosecutor said. "They could easily conclude that Miss Steegers is not a credible witness. She just lied right now about never having a ticket. I believe you'll find it right on the transcript, the part where she was just swearing that—"

"Oh, shut up," the judge said. "Would you take anger management?"

"I'd be willing to take it back to the U.S. Attorney's Office and run it by my superiors," the prosecutor said.

"I didn't *ask* you if you were willing to take it back to your office. I'm *asking* whether you'd accept it, and I'm *telling* you not to make me any madder than I already am."

"The people would be willing to accept anger management," the prosecutor said.

"Miss Steegers?" the judge asked.

"Yes?"

"Would you?"

"Would I what? I'm not following."

"This is what I'm proposing," the judge said. "The prosecutor is willing to drop all the charges against you if you're willing to take—and complete—a course in anger management. The kind of place where they can help you . . . where they could try to ensure that this sort of thing doesn't happen again."

"Is that better or worse than probation?" Iris asked.

"Oh, it's much better," the judge said. "It's not even criminal at all. You take the course and when we receive your certificate of completion, this whole thing is wiped off the slate. As if it never happened."

"Well, then it's fine with me," Iris said.

"Case dismissed without prejudice," the judge announced, and all the judicial machinery cranked itself back up. The prosecutor gave Iris a hateful look, and Iris went over to confer with the pregnant lady about the details of the anger management thingamabob. Then, instead of going outside to give a press conference on the grandiose steps, she sat in the back row and watched the proceedings to kill a little more time and to see what would happen next.

The ticket thing, though, was something else altogether. Where had *that* come from and how on earth did the pasty, horrible probation guy get his hands on that kind of misinformation? It was about a week later and Iris decided to do a little investigating to sort things out. She went down to the DMV at Thirty-fourth Street, and literally the second she walked in the door, some official-looking person "managing" the line screamed at her that they *didn't* do licenses for boats or snowmobiles. Worse, that was about as helpful as they ever got.

So Iris called her insurance company and asked them what this was all about, and after about thirty seconds on hold, a woman with a calm, even voice who sounded like she was sitting in a nice, clean office where everybody got tons of stuff done, told her that yes, there'd been a ticket for speeding last January in Yardley, Pennsylvania. "Let's see," the woman said, "it seems that you were clocked at eighty-one miles an hour."

"You can tell that just from where you're sitting?" Iris asked.

"Oh, yes," the calm lady said. "We've got the ticket on microfilm."

"And I was doing eighty, well, eighty-*plus* miles an hour in Yardley, Pennsylvania, on, when was it again?"

"Last January. The eighteenth." That didn't make any sense. Iris and Jeremy had been out to Bucks County only twice in their lives, and both times had been during the summer. It'd been really hot the time they did the galleries in New Hope, and it'd been *stinking* hot the time they went to Washington Crossing.

"Does it say anything else?" Iris asked.

"No, not really. There's the year, the make and model of the car, and there's the record of payment and—"

"Oh, what about that?" Iris asked.

"Let's see. It was paid on April eighteenth with a check which cleared on . . . uh . . . the twenty-seventh. Of April."

"Can you look at the check for me?" Iris asked.

"We can certainly try," she said, clicking things and concentrating on her end of the line. It must be wonderful, Iris thought, to have a job where people call you up and you answer their questions and that makes them happy and then they go away and they wish you a good day and tell you have a nice weekend, even though it's only Wednesday afternoon.

"Paid by check on April eighteenth by a Mr. Jeremy Curtis Eberle," she said. "In the amount of two hundred and twenty dollars."

"Ah," Iris said. "Jeremy." And then even though this was New York City in the twenty-first century, she felt compelled to clarify things anyway. Partner? Significant other? What was the proper term for someone capable of asking for your car but incapable of asking for your hand in marriage? "Jeremy's my boyfriend," she finally said.

"Ah," the calm lady said. "And this is the first you're hearing about this ticket?"

"Something like that," Iris said, laughing. It was as if they'd caught Jeremy planning a surprise party for Iris and now they'd still have to act surprised when the event rolled around. "There's one thing I don't quite get," Iris said. "The ticket was on January eighteenth and the payment was something like, what, three months later? How come Jeremy, or, actually, me, how come we didn't get in trouble for that?"

"Let's see," she said, going back and clicking around some more. "Oh, I see," she said. "You were flashed."

"Flashed?"

"Meaning you weren't stopped by an officer. You, well, your car got flashed by a camera doing eighty-one miles per hour in Yardley, and it sometimes takes them a while to track down the address from the license plate and send the driver the ticket. Especially if the plates are from out of state."

"So I got this ticket in the mail?"

"You did. And the payment came in by mail."

Strange, Iris thought. "But it's all settled now?" she asked.

"Completely. Just don't get another ticket before your next renewal with us or you could end up with higher premiums."

"Oh, I promise I'll be good!" Iris said, figuring that now was probably not the best time to bring up the fact that she'd recently banged up the right front corner of her car on the West Side Highway.

"And you should probably tell your friend to lighten up on the pedal," the woman said.

"Well, he'll be getting a little talking-to," Iris said, and they both laughed and wished each other well and hung up.

On a certain level, the ticket made sense because Jeremy loved to drive fast. Jeremy's view of driving was that the controls were essentially on/off switches—they were supposed to be *all* the way on or *all* the way off. The brakes. The gas. The radio. That's how it worked. In every other aspect of his life, Jeremy was usually the most conscientious person around. He could talk about how wasteful paper towels were, and then, in less than a minute, somehow connect the wasteful extravagance of the "quicker-picker-upper" to river blindness in Africa. He could explain how pesticides go from grass to cow to milk and then right into your cereal bowl. If Jeremy ever became a werewolf, he'd be the type of werewolf who carried around a plastic bag so he could pick up his own droppings and dispose of them properly. But behind the wheel of a car, all that careful awareness went right out the window and he drove as if West Seventieth Street were his own personal Autobahn.

What *didn't* make any sense was why Jeremy hadn't told Iris about any of this. Jeremy viewed cops as the enemy, and he would've worn his ticket like a badge of honor, telling all their friends hilarious stories about his own personal brush with the police state. Jeremy was opposed, in no particular order, to cops; the military-industrial complex; red meat; multinational corporations; greenhouse gases; and the past, current, and future administrations of the City of New York. Jeremy would've *relished* a ticket.

And yet he hadn't said a word about it, and if the calm lady at the insurance company was correct, then Jeremy had intercepted a ticket addressed to Iris and paid it, no questions asked.

The first thing Iris did that evening when she got home was to go through Jeremy's checkbook. She hated to do it, but there it was—two hundred and twenty dollars, made out to the Borough of Yardley. She put the checkbook back and scooted over to her own desk and rifled through the boxes underneath it until she found her daily minder from last year. She found the third week of January and there, among all her crossed-out and rescheduled business stuff, she saw that she'd gone out to dinner—drinks *and* dinner—with her college roommate Stephanie, and she never saw Steffy unless Jeremy wasn't around because Jeremy didn't particularly care for Steffy and vice versa. And now, rifling through last year's daily minder, Iris could recall that night out with Steffy perfectly. Steffy had asked after Jeremy, and Iris had said that Jeremy was away because his aunt had died and he'd gone up to Holyoke to help his family deal with all the details.

So there you have it. In version (a) of the world, Jeremy had been up in Holyoke, Massachusetts, that week to settle his aunt's estate. In version (b) though, Jeremy was out in Yardley, Pennsylvania, zooming around at eighty-one miles an hour. Iris's first reflex was to look for peaceful coexistence. Could Jeremy have done both? Couldn't he have gone out to help his mom settle the estate and then have taken the *super*-long way home? No, that would really be a stretch. Did Iris have the dates wrong? No, not that either; they were right in front of her.

Iris picked up the phone the next day at work and called the Bucks County Sheriff's office in Doylestown and spent a lifetime on hold and getting transferred until somebody finally took pity on her. The woman who took pity on her promised to go pull the file and call Iris back, but Iris said she'd rather just hold and the lady said, "Honeybunch, last January is in a whole other building. Now if you want me to get myself up and walk all the way over there, please don't tell me you want me to do it while you're waiting on the line."

And Iris believed her and gave the lady her number and they hung up and the lady went away and thirty minutes later Iris's phone rang and the lady said she'd found the file and there it was—speeding in Yardley. One hundred and ten for speeding, plain and simple, plus thirty for costs and fees, plus twenty for being more than ten miles an hour over the limit, plus sixty more for being more than fifteen over the limit."

"Do you have the photograph?" Iris asked in a tiny little voice.

"I beg your pardon?"

"The photo," Iris said. "My insurance said that the ticket was flashed, that it wasn't some co—, some actual person flagging down the car and making us stop while he wrote out a ticket. Do you still have the picture there?"

Some rustling came over the wire. "Sure, it's here," she said.

"Could I have it?" Iris asked.

"I don't see why not."

Iris gave the lady her work address and then thanked her for her time and for walking all the way over to the other building, and the lady laughed and said not to worry about it and that was that.

Except that when the photo came a few days later, Iris couldn't believe her eyes. It was grainy and blurry, and the only thing that was really, really clear on it was the front license plate itself—that practically glowed like a beacon through the fog. The rest of the picture was blurrier and grainier, but you could still make out what was going on. The flash of the camera was reflected off part of the windshield so it wasn't possible to see everything in the interior, but it was clearly Jeremy who was driving—his carriage, his bearing, his iron grip on the wheel. Everything about it said Jeremy.

The upper part of his face was blocked by the reflection from the flash, but the bottom part was smiling—his chin was jutting forward and his teeth shone white against the grainy gray background. There was a shadow to the left, which could've been either somebody in the passenger seat or just another shadowy blob in a photo, but that's not what Iris was looking at. Iris was looking at Jeremy's shoulder which, the more she looked at it, the more it seemed as if somebody had plunked a hand onto Jeremy's shoulder. It was a little hard to tell.

"That is a hand," Iris thought. "That glint there is the thumb and those are the fingers just cresting over the summit of Jeremy's shoulder blade." There was a signet ring on one of the fingers, but beyond that, the disembodied hand might as well have fallen out of the sky.

Iris put the photograph away in the top drawer of her desk and tried to get back to concentrating on her work. She made it right through the afternoon and she was *this close* to making it through the entire day when she suddenly had a horrible thought. She got up right in the middle of a budget meeting with clients and strode out the door, even though she could tell that her boss was trying to harpoon her with some sort of eyebrow gesture designed to reunite her butt with her seat and to do so ex post facto.

Paul Schmidtberger

But Iris just had to see. She was walking as fast as her pumps would let her and then she started running—who cares how undignified it was—until she'd reached her office and slammed the door shut behind her and then she tore the photo out of her top desk drawer. Her chest was heaving, and it was ludicrous because unless she calmed down, she wasn't going to be able to see what she was looking for. She steadied herself and held the picture with two hands and opened her eyes and it was all there—the spooky, glowing numbers suspended in thin air; the grainy, ghostly figure guiding Jeremy's shoulder through the night; the ring; and the chin jutting forward and smiling or grimacing, one or the other, but doing something that let Jeremy's white teeth show. It was all there. Everything except the pendant. The pendant that had been hanging from the rearview mirror since time immemorial. The antique silver pendant that Iris had cleverly coated with clear nail polish to make it look cheap and plasticky and not worth stealing. The antique silver pendant with the picture of her and Jeremy inside it. Jeremy had taken it down.

Iris couldn't believe her eyes.

"*Jeremy?*" she thought.

Maxine got wind of the problem before anybody else in the English Department. The chairman of the department, Professor John Scillat—pronounced to rhyme with the word "filet," and under no circumstance pronounced like "skillet," as in the kitchen implement of choice for cooking pancakes and caramelizing onions—had come in that morning in a hideously foul mood. Usually this was just a sign that he and his wife had either separated again or reconciled again, the wife being a fan of couples counseling because it was the only place where she could yell at her husband for fifty straight minutes and still get credit for an hour. But before Maxine could get a good look at Professor Scillat's ring finger, he'd stomped past her desk and into his own office, slamming the door behind him. He stewed in his own juices all morning, and apart from a call that she put through from the Provost—which Scillat surprised her by taking—nothing particularly interesting happened until he popped out of his office with no warning and asked the professors and grad students hanging around Maxine's desk if any of them had ever heard of a certain Brett Manikin.

"Uh-oh," Maxine thought, making a split-second decision to keep her mouth shut. "This couldn't be good."

None of the learned minds assembled there volunteered any information, but Professor Scillat kept his pale, neutral eyes trained on them until one of the ancient professors who'd been coasting along on nothing but fumes for years—despite the fact that Scillat was trying to *build a department*—finally cleared his throat and said that he thought he recalled reading an article by him. Quite the provocative article, if memory served. Or maybe it was just an abstract of his work.

"Whose work?" Scillat asked.

"Why, Brett Manikin's, of course."

"Morons," Professor Scillat muttered, going back into his office and slamming the door again. Everyone looked at each other with the same bewildered expression. Professor Scillat usually muttered "morons" *after* he slammed his door.

Maxine grabbed her phone and called Ken at home but only got his answering machine. "Hey Ken, it's Maxine," she said. "Could you give me a quick ring as soon as you get this? It's no big deal, but I'd like to talk to you, and I'd really like to do it sooner rather than later."

Before Maxine could think of what to do next, Professor Scillat came bursting back out of his office and told her to rally the troops. "We're having a faculty meeting this afternoon," he said. "And I want you to make sure that Ken Connelly is there."

Maxine drew up a meeting notice and put a copy in each of the mail slots out in the hallway. And not two minutes after she finished, Scillat told her that she would have to do it over again because he wanted the notice to mention that the Provost would be joining them, and, as a result, Scillat expected perfect attendance on the part of the members of the department. Then, as Maxine was printing out a billion copies of the new notice, Ken finally called in. "What's up?" he asked, uttering what would turn out to be the last two cheerful words he would utter that day.

"Scillat's on the warpath," Maxine said. "And it's got something to do with Brett."

"With *Brett*?"

"That's right."

"*Brett* Brett?" Ken asked, instead of saying, "*My* Brett?"

"That's the one," Maxine said. "Is there something you think you should tell me?"

By the time the meeting began, Ken knew his goose was cooked. It was abundantly clear that *somebody* was about to get into trouble, and the buzz was that it was going to be Ken Connelly. The atmosphere was positively festive.

Professor Scillat opened the meeting by thanking the Provost for coming and then he got right down to business. Somebody in the department, it seemed, had defaced City College property. Some *troubled* person, for reasons unknown, had scrawled graffiti in books in the library.

Ken felt his face go bright red.

"Sacrilege is not too strong a word," Scillat went on. "This act represents the *defiling* of everything we stand for as an institution of learning." He looked around the room. "And if it hadn't been for the Provost bringing this to my attention with the greatest of dispatch, this, uh, *situation* might have gone unnoticed for who knows how long."

"Speaking of which," Ken thought, "how did they nail me so quickly?"

Scillat went on with his speech, explaining that the Provost had borrowed a brand-new reference book that had only recently been catalogued, and once he'd discovered and complained about the vandalism, it had been relatively easy for the head librarian to find the other books, narrow down the list of suspects to exactly one person, and then confirm the Brett connection. "If the Provost hadn't borrowed that book—*Cocktails for Two: Getting to Know Your Alcoholic Inner Child*—then we'd be merrily going along without any knowledge of the problem among us," Scillat said. "We'd be merrily going along without any knowledge of the *cancer* among us."

"Cancer?" Ken thought, correctly sensing an upcoming metaphor about cancer and how a cancer has to be cut out for the organism to survive. "They're not going to fire me over this, are they?"

Professor Scillat wound up his speech and said that before they were forced to sink to the indignity of accusations, perhaps the person responsible would like to come clean all on his own. Ken cleared his throat and raised his hand and the bloodletting began.

Ken said that it was an error in judgment and that neither it, nor anything even remotely similar to it, would ever happen again. He said that he was going through a difficult time, in a personal sense, but he never should've let those personal distractions interfere with his judgment. He said he was sorry in every conceivable way—regret for the act itself, apologies for the disgrace he'd brought upon the department, shame for his conduct—but nothing could stop the onslaught. He said that his unwise remarks had been written in pencil and that he would erase them as soon as possible, and it was like politely telling a member of your firing squad that his shoe's untied. The inevitable response being, "Well, thanks for the information, but we're still going to execute you."

And Ken couldn't believe the fervor of the attack, the concerted violence of it, and the inexplicable fact that the department was actually unified on a given subject. Yes, he'd done something stupid. Very stupid, in fact—though still worth a chuckle, he thought privately—and it could be undone by erasing it, but from the way they were acting, you'd think that he'd gone and gotten his hands on Shakespeare's original manuscripts and dumped them into the Hudson River. Or the East River. Whichever one was grosser.

The fact of the matter was that this wasn't the worst thing that anyone had ever done in the English Department. Faculty members enthusiastically stole mail out of each other's mail slots. Faculty members quietly stole dictionaries from the supply room. And for a long stretch in the eighties, the department held a cocktail party every Friday night and that whole boozy era didn't come to an end because of the drunken driving or the drunken trysts; it came to an end when somebody stole the little refrigerator where they kept the hooch right out of the faculty lounge. So people can do that, Ken thought, but I'm the one getting pilloried here.

Worse, Ken had never been in trouble before. For anything. Well, true, he'd just been fired from his other job for "gross misconduct"—a term that turned up in a registered letter he'd received from Leighton Fennell a few days after his departure. The letter was signed "Leighton, Fennell & Lowe," as if the firm had suddenly decided to start writing people letters, but Ken could spot Crayton Reed's horrendous handwriting a mile away. But in any event, all that was just work. In terms of things that really mattered, things like school, Ken had never caused any problems, never made any waves.

In his entire scholastic career, he'd been sent to the principal's office exactly once, and the unfairness of it all still made his ears burn. It happened one day in his tenth-grade chemistry class, and what Ken *hadn't* known was that in the class before him, three different butter-fingered girls had dropped test tubes onto the floor, shattering them. And each time, Mr. Massiello had told the class to be more careful and for God's sake watch what they were doing and that test tubes didn't grow on trees!

And then the bell rang and the giggling, butter-fingered girls left. Mr. Massiello rinsed out the remaining test tubes and hung them on the pegs next to the door, all while pondering the distinctly *unpleasant* question of whether the girls were actually klutzy or whether they'd done that on purpose. And that's when Ken burst through the door, as usual, the first to get there. The door bounced back hard against the wall and rattled the glassware that Mr. Massiello had just finished washing, and Mr. Massiello said: "Jesus, Ken! Could you be a little more careful? Doors don't grow on trees!"

And Ken had stopped in his tracks and thought about it and said, "Well, yes they do."

And Massiello booted him out! Massiello said he could just take himself and his attitude straight down the hall to the principal's office.

It'd been so humiliating, and in school the next day he was just a shadow of his former self. He went to his classes and minded his business, and in chemistry class he tried this new trick where he looked up toward the teacher, but not directly, so that he wasn't paying rapt attention (which would be an invitation to be called on) or clearly spacing out (which would also be an invitation to be called on). He wasn't one or the other anymore.

And as Ken worked his way through the rest of high school, he consciously squished down the ebullience that had gotten him into such hot water in the first place. The problem, though, is that ebullience doesn't put up all that much of a fight. After you squish it down, it doesn't bounce right back to its regular size like the pieces of spongy white bread that Ken liked to compact down to the size of a molar. Apparently, ebullience is *less technologically advanced* than white bread because after you squeeze a person's spirit away for a while, it just stays squeezed away.

So Ken put his faith instead in the written word. His homework was always flawless and he got into his first choice of college and he slowly began to set his sights on joining the illustrious faculty of an institution of higher education.

Except the illustrious faculty of this particular institution was currently ripping Ken a brand-new asshole. Scillat had turned to those assembled and asked who had something to add, and old Professor Bozek started to say that he didn't see what the big hullabaloo was all about, but Scillat cut him right off. "Who has an idea of how this might best be resolved?" he asked.

"Well, that's my point exactly," Professor Bozek tried to say. "I was just saying that I think—"

"Who has some *practical* solutions to offer?" Scillat asked, and the results were as varied as they were vicious. But Professor Scillat evidently had something else in mind. "What we need to do," he said, "is to get at the root cause of the problem. It doesn't help to treat symptoms if one doesn't treat the *source* of those symptoms. What's the use," he boomed, "of going out and having a new pair of glasses made when the *reason* you can't see is because there's a tumor in your brain that's squishing the nerves and all the optical whatnot off to the side?"

"To see better?" Professor Bozek volunteered.

"What?"

"To see better," Professor Bozek repeated. "You just asked why people would go out and get new glasses and the answer is so they can see better. Especially if they're going to be driving back and forth to the doctor and to chemo and what have you."

Professor Scillat had a fleeting vision of his own funeral. They'd lower his casket into the cold, wet ground and before they could shovel the clods of dirt back in over him, a group of doddering old City College imbeciles would climb in there with him and ask him stupid questions for the rest of eternity. He stamped his heel on the floor and lobbed an exasperated sigh up into the air like one of those skeet-shooting machines that flings up clay pigeons. "The *point*, gentlemen—"

A loud, distinctly feminine stage cough.

"*And* ladies. The point is that you have to treat the *source* of the problem, not the symptoms, and the source of the problem is clearly our colleague's anger." Baffled looks all around. Everyone thought that Connelly got caught writing smutty notes in books or on bathroom walls. Who said anything about anger?

"What I would propose," Scillat said, "is that we strive to *help* our colleague."

"Oh, that's great," Ken thought. "*Thanks for nothing.*"

On the other hand, helping didn't sound like being fired, so there was hope.

"What I'm proposing," Scillat said, thinking of the misery he went through every week in couples counseling, "is that we ask our colleague to attend a course in anger management. I'm asking that we give him the *tools* he'll need to work through these kinds of problems on his own, without having to compromise either his, or our, professional integrity."

Ken gave the room one of his patented "I appear to be paying attention though I'm really somewhere else" looks, and the matter was settled. Ken would attend a course in anger management and City College would forget all about the whole thing. Which would make one of them.

Tragically, Ken couldn't just disappear right after the meeting because he had a makeup section for one of his composition classes that afternoon, so he was forced to hang around and act as if everything was just fine. Maxine came through like a trooper, trotting into the faculty lounge at one point waving a brown interoffice envelope at Ken and saying, "Connelly! You got a fax from the Modern Language Association!" even though the supposed fax was just some recipes that Maxine had printed off the Internet ("Wow Them with Zesty Clamato Dip!"). Still, she'd done a great job on the fake letterhead.

Walking into his section, he couldn't predict whether the students had already heard about his public shaming or not. They were all abuzz when Ken walked in the door—far more excited than undergraduates should be in an afternoon makeup section—and his heart sank when he distinctly heard the word "library" amid the chatter, but it turned out that it didn't have anything to do with him. The undergrads were all upset because the university had just implemented a new rule that forbade sleeping in Cohen Library.

"Sleeping in the library?" Ken asked. "Who does that?"

"No, not like unrolling a sleeping bag and, you know, *sleeping* there," one of the students said, this horrible, praying mantis of a girl named Aimee. "They made it illegal to just sleep, as in closing your eyes for a few minutes and going to sleep."

"I don't understand," Ken said. "It's now illegal, well, against the rules of the university, to close your eyes in the library?"

"No," Aimee said. "You can close your eyes, but you can't sleep. If you fall asleep, they come over and poke you in the ribs and make you wake up."

"Why on earth would they do that?"

"Because they wanted to make it illegal for bums and homeless people to come into the library and sleep where it's warm, but since they can't just make it illegal for bums, they have to make it illegal for *everybody*. You know, so that the law's fair."

"Well, if the rule is fair," Ken said, "then why would you object to it?"

"But it's *not* fair," Aimee said. "*We're* not homeless."

When Brett had walked out of their home on the night Ken got fired, Ken figured that Brett was just seeing whoever that guy was down to the lobby and that he'd be right back. And then he figured that Brett was seeing him all the way to the subway entrance at Seventy-second and Broadway even though no etiquette book on earth says that home-wreckers should be walked to the closest subway entrance. As the minutes ticked by, Ken just kept revising the explanation. Brett hit every single red light on the walk home. Brett stopped to buy flowers on the way home. Brett was trying to buy flowers but the line at the twenty-four-hour grocery was moving at a snail's pace because the checkout guy was distracted by some Korean game show on TV where the idea was to guess how much various Korean celebrities weighed, and if you guessed correctly, you got a prize.

Later, Ken thought that maybe Brett had gone for a walk to clear his head. A very, very long walk.

Or he'd gone over to one of their friend's houses to let things calm down. But by the time midnight rolled around without any sign of Brett, Ken went to bed and he put the chain on the door just to serve Brett right when he came slinking home. Which, of course, presupposed that Brett would come slinking home. Which he did not.

Ken barely slept that whole night, waiting for the sound of Brett's step out in the hallway, the jingle of his keys and then the abrupt smack of the door running into a taut brass chain, but those sounds never came. Instead it was perfectly quiet—by Manhattan standards—and as the sun came up the next morning, Ken had to face the facts. Brett was leaving him. It practically boggled his mind because Brett was the one in the wrong. Brett was the one who'd cheated on Ken, and yet it wasn't Ken who was leaving Brett, it was the other way around!

For the entire Labor Day weekend, Ken sat at home waiting for something, some sort of explanation or indication from Brett as to what was supposed to happen next, but nothing came. By Tuesday, Ken had gotten mad enough to decide to make Brett's departure a little more *streamlined*. He took Brett's suitcases and dumped everything important into them—Brett's checkbook, his head-shots, some of the clothes he wore most, his gym crap—and he dragged them into the front hallway to wait. And at about eight-thirty that night, when Ken normally would've been down at Leighton Fennell, he heard a key turn in the lock and the door gently opening and then there was a long, quiet pause. Ken, who was sitting in the living room, coughed quite distinctly, and then there was another long pause before the door softly shut and whoever it was went away. With the suitcases.

Ken took that to mean that Brett was more interested in collecting his stuff than in offering up some sort of explanation, let alone an apology, so he gathered the rest of Brett's stuff up for him. He pulled the rest of those pretty, expensive clothes out of the closet and stuffed them into shopping bags. He pulled Brett's books off the shelves in the living room and threw them into the eighty-metric-ton garbage bags that Ken once bought by accident. He went through the medicine cabinet and tipped one after another of Brett's potions and creams into a wonderfully sturdy shopping bag from Armani Exchange. He was very generous in his decisions as to what was Brett's and what was his, especially given the fact that he'd paid for virtually all of it. In the kitchen, for example, he gave all the utensils that Brett had lobbied for to Brett even though no philosopher in his right mind would accord Brett ownership rights over a handheld, chrome-plated potato masher that (1) Ken had bought; (2) with his own hard-earned money; and (3) that Brett had never touched, be it to prepare mashed potatoes or to clean up after someone else had crushed the spuds in question.

Still, Ken unhooked it from the pot rack over the stove and tossed it in the Brett pile.

He stacked it all up in the front hall and waited for another stealthy visit from Brett, but when that didn't happen, he lugged it outside into the hallway and left it there for a while. And then, as if the whole experience hadn't been unsettling enough, nobody stole it! Thousands of dollars worth of Brett's things just sat there in the hallway until Ken got tired of them and dragged the bags downstairs and then up Seventieth Street to the corner of Broadway. He took the lid from a John Lobb shoebox and wrote "Free Stuff" on the inside of it and then slit open the garbage bags and stepped back to watch the feeding frenzy. For a brief moment, nothing happened, so he took the bull by the horns. "Oh my Gawd," he yelled, pointing over at the bags. "Is that *free* Calvin Klein?"

Chapter Six. In Which Iris Enrolls in School and Is Pelted with Various Bits of Learning

"Public Speaking," Iris read, pausing before dismissing the idea along with all the others that had come before it. Opera Appreciation, Personal Accounting, Spanish, Advanced Spanish, Wine Tasting, Non-Lyric Poetry, and Bonsai, the ancient Japanese art of harassing an otherwise promising oak tree with nail clippers and eyebrow tweezers until it finally gives up and retreats into itself and turns into a tiny, little facsimile of an oak tree.

"Jeremy would never buy that," Iris thought, flipping to the next page in the catalog.

Iris had gotten a very official-looking letter at work saying that her anger management courses were going to be held at the West Side Y and that it was up to her to get herself registered. She was supposed to tell the teacher that she was there for something called a judicial diversion, and she was supposed to give the teacher the enclosed form and then bring it back to court after successfully completing the course. The form looked like it had been photocopied and re-photocopied about a thousand times, most of them during earthquakes.

The trick, Iris realized, would be to find some adult education course that met at about the same time in the evening as her anger management class, and then all she'd have to do would be to tell Jeremy that she'd decided to take a class in Pottery or Sign Language or something along those lines. It was ideal—Jeremy could even walk her to her classes at the Y or meet up with her afterward for the stroll home.

The choices, though, were endless. It would have to be something credible—probably not Wok Cooking for Singles—something that Iris might have decided to take all on her own, which was itself a tall order since Iris wasn't really the kind of person to take adult education classes.

The other trick was that whatever course she picked, she'd have to disguise the fact that she wasn't actually learning anything. It wouldn't help to take a class in, say, Spanish, only to have Jeremy do something very Jeremy-ish and go out and book a romantic surprise vacation for them in Acapulco only to find out that the only thing Iris knew was the Spanish word for margarita.

Great. Cancel that idea.

And then she saw it—Restaurant Critiquing. How perfect was that? She scanned the time that the class met and it wasn't dead on but it was hardly far off either. Restaurant Critiquing. Learning about the art *and* science of appraising a restaurant—the food, the service, the décor—and then communicating that evaluation to others in a succinct, readable, and engaging manner. Iris couldn't believe her good fortune. All she had to do was casually mention to Jeremy that she'd decided to take an evening class in Restaurant Critiquing over at the Y and Jeremy would believe her. Everyone would believe her. Everyone would believe her because the simple fact of the matter was that Iris just *loved* to eat.

More than that, though, this class would mesh perfectly with the dynamics of their relationship. Which is to say that of the two of them, Jeremy was the more sociable one, the more outgoing one; it was no surprise that he worked—very well and very convincingly—in fund-raising consulting. Whenever they went out to dinner with friends, Jeremy was the one who organized it, and the party never got off the ground until Jeremy got there and captivated everybody with his stories. Now with this class, Iris wouldn't simply slip into the shadows while Jeremy held court; Iris would be there to take notes on the place and officially observe the goings-on. Now Iris would have a specialty too.

It'd been their dynamic from the beginning. Iris was retiring while Jeremy was outgoing. Iris tended to see two sides to everything while Jeremy was much more decisive. Jeremy used to say that if it weren't for his taking matters into his own hands, the two of them never would have met, and that's despite the fact that they met while they were *trapped in the same elevator*! And everyone around the table would always laugh and shake their heads in wonder.

And it was true, too. Jeremy and Iris had met while they were stuck in the elevator at the flagship Macy's on Thirty-fourth Street. Jeremy was there to buy a fleece jacket and Iris was trying to get somebody in Customer Service to do something about her nesting set of Rubbermaid microwave-safe tubs that were microwave-safe only in the sense that you could put them in the microwave without suffering any untoward results. You could not, however, turn the microwave *on*, because that made them quiver, and then pucker, and then collapse into a gooey, gutted, Dresden-ish version of their original selves.

What Iris and Jeremy *hadn't* known as they arrived at Macy's was that minutes earlier, yet another New Yorker had chosen the Hummel figurine display on the sixth floor as the perfect spot for his long-overdue nervous breakdown. Macy's had called the rescue squad, and the EMTs had commandeered the elevators and shut them down to prevent the newly minted nut from escaping even though by that point the guy was just patiently standing near a register watching a woman trying to return tinsel. Once they'd carted the guy away, though, Macy's forgot to turn the elevators back on, and Iris and about ten other dissatisfied customers just stood in the elevator uncomfortably while Jeremy slowly emerged as their leader.

"Punch the alarm button," Jeremy said, and the person next to the alarm executed the order. Then it was up to Jeremy to tell them how often they should punch which buttons and how much time to leave between rings of the alarm bell, which merely produced a distant, deserted-high-school-hallway ring. Iris caught herself staring at the take-charge guy and his halo of golden curls. Where had she seen him before?

Nothing happened for a while, but then Jeremy made everyone pile up their backpacks and shopping bags to make a seat for this one old lady even though she said she didn't need to sit down and it took forever to get her all folded up like a lawn chair and balanced on top of the pile.

"The Alco-hole!" Iris suddenly thought. *That's* where she'd seen him before, hanging around one of the Upper West Side's artsier bars, always the center of attention, always monopolizing the best table over near the pool table. Well, what do you know.

Jeremy took stock of their food situation and made everybody list what emergency supplies they had on them, and Iris—the same Iris who was usually in the background—was thrilled to see herself producing not just an unopened box of Chiclets, but a Twix bar as well.

And once he'd finished analyzing the food situation, Jeremy asked if there was a doctor among them and nobody answered. Was it Iris's imagination, or was Jeremy paying particular attention to her? "A nurse?" Jeremy asked. Silence. "Medical technician? Dentist? Dental hygienist?"

Nothing.

"You," he suddenly said, pointing at Iris. "What do you do?"

"Me?"

"Yes, you."

"Well, I'm in marketing."

"Oh," Jeremy said. He sounded vaguely disappointed, so Iris mumbled out a little extra detail—"For retirement plans."

"What's that you said?"

"Most of our clients are retirement plans and pension funds."

"Oh."

"And some HMOs."

That did the trick. "Oh, really?" Jeremy said. "As in health care organizations?"

"Exactly."

"Well that's perfect," he said. And then, turning to everyone else as if they *hadn't* just been listening to every single syllable, Jeremy announced that Iris worked in health care administration and from here on in, she was in charge of their medical issues.

"But . . ." Iris started to say, suddenly feeling her face go bright red, but then she changed her mind. After all, this Jeremy character seemed to know what he was doing.

When they eventually got sprung, Macy's was very apologetic and promised Jeremy—as their ringleader—that they'd review their safety procedures, but Iris was sorely disappointed that Jeremy didn't pass around a sheet of paper for everybody to leave their name and address so they could keep in touch and have reunions over the years (it had only been twenty-seven minutes of captivity). Still, Iris's curiosity was more than piqued and she found herself hanging around the Alco-hole more than she normally might have, and it took only four tries before she walked in one night and there was Jeremy, the take-charge elevator guy, standing at one of the drink wells at the bar and paying for the three or four beers in front of him. Iris told herself that it was absolutely ridiculous to be nervous, not that it helped, and then she took a deep breath and walked up to Jeremy and tapped him on the shoulder.

"Yes?" Jeremy's look was utterly blank. Nothing. Not the slightest flicker of recognition.

"It's me," Iris said. "From the elevator."

"What elevator?"

"At *Macy's*," Iris said. Good Lord, did this guy go around getting himself stuck in so many elevators that he couldn't keep track of them anymore? Was Iris that forgettable? Did . . .

And that's when Iris caught the glimmer in Jeremy's eye, the little smile he just couldn't keep pushed out of sight any longer. Jeremy winked and let himself laugh out loud and stuck out his hand. "I'm Jeremy," he said. "And I was hoping I might get to see you again."

Walking in the door of her classroom at the Y, Iris thought, "Well, welcome to a whole new world." It was immediately evident to her that this new world was divided into people who *had* to be there—they were the ones sullenly smushed up against the back wall of the classroom—and the ones who *wanted* to be there—the ones who'd staked out the seats in front and had fresh notebooks, pencils, and West Side Y catalogs with spiny, stegosaurus-like rows of Post-it tabs marking the million different things they were interested in. And as usual, Iris dithered. She stood there unable to choose one camp or the other and then, when she realized that she was beginning to attract unnecessary attention—defined as *any* attention in her book—she just slid into the first open seat. Right in the middle. She settled her things and then snuck a glance at the guy in the seat next to her. Late thirties or early forties. Glasses. No evident signs of uncontrollable anger about to be unleashed in the form of him choking her to death before the teacher got there. No wedding ring.

"What are you in for?" he asked.

"Interference with a flight crew," Iris said. He looked impressed. "And you?"

"Defacing public property," he said, just as the teacher strode into the room. "I'm Ken."

The teacher was a frizzy, blurry woman whose single most noticeable characteristic was that she was hard to keep track of. Was that a scarf or a shawl? Was the pile of hair on top of her head slowly working its way *out* of its loose braid or was it slowly being pulled and twisted *into* submission? Where did her knitty, layered clothes end and where did the artsy-crafty, wood and bead necklaces begin?

"Anger," she wrote on the blackboard, and then stepped back and contemplated the word. "I'm Lucinda," she said. "Lucinda Gross."

Lucinda passed out blank pieces of paper and told everybody to write out a definition of the word "anger." After a few minutes, she said "All right, pencils down," and had everyone pass their answers to the front so she could read a few of them at random.

"Anger," she read, leaving a very dramatic pause after the word and looking around the room. "Anger is when you get mad and can't stop being mad and don't particularly care if you can't stop being mad."

"Anger," she read, "is the absence of love."

"Anger made me want to punch my ex-wife's asshole psychiatrist new boyfriend's face in when I saw his asshole psychiatrist face in front of the Angelika where he was wasting space on the planet waiting in line for some stupid movie that only asshole psychiatrists would go see."

"Anger. Noun. A pronounced feeling of displeasure or belligerence aroused by a real or supposed wrong. Resentment. Exasperation. Indignation. Rage. Fury. As a verb, anger refers to the arousal of wrath. To vex, to irritate, to infuriate. Middle English, most likely from the Old Norse *angr*, referring to sorrow." Ken next door seemed pleased with himself.

"Anger is a poison."

"*My anger, my pain. Mine and mine alone. Wilting. Soaring. Breathing. Seething. My mother stitched my name into my underwear when I went away to camp, and when I saw those embroidered words forty-four fetid summers later, forty-four dead winters later— had I seen them in a dream?—they spelled A-N-G-E-R.*"

"Okay," Lucinda said. "And we're off!"

Lucinda gave them an overview of the schedule and passed around a fairly substantial syllabus—which Iris hadn't been counting on—but which seemed to arouse the interest of her neighbor. Then Lucinda explained that the hardest part of coming to terms with one's anger was actually *facing up to it*, which is why she'd written the word "anger" up on the board right in front of their faces and why she was planning to do that every class. Everybody looked back over at the word "anger" and then at Lucinda.

"All right," she said. "What we're going to do here first is to get to know each other." She had everyone in the room introduce themselves and say what they hoped to get out of the class, an assignment that resulted in the instantaneous appearance of a severe knot in Iris's stomach. Iris hated speaking in public. She'd hated it back when she was a little kid in school and she hated it to this day; Iris had never really cottoned to the idea of drawing attention to herself.

Hands shot up in the front of the room, and when they gave their spiels, there were a lot of abstractions: "I'm here to learn to get a grip on my anger before it destroys my ability to relate to others." Or "I'm hoping to learn the tools necessary to transform my anger, which is unproductive, into a form of energy that's *less* unproductive, which is to say, more productive."

In the back of the classroom, concrete goals were the order of the day: "I'm here because the custody and visitation order says I have to be." Or "I'm here to get my conviction for felony mischief wiped off my record because on account of if I don't, then it counts as a strike for three strikes, and I already have two other strikes."

One guy in the back stood up and announced that he was there "because he had a headache," and when he sat back down, Iris noticed that what she'd thought was just another weird fashion fad from the East Village was really a surveillance bracelet locked around the guy's ankle. "A *really* bad headache," he said.

Then one guy in the very back got up and launched into this unbelievably complicated story about getting into a fistfight in the checkout line at a D'Agostino's all over a quart of nonfat milk. There was no reining him in, and the story just wandered all over the place. He talked about the plastic bars that were supposed to separate his nonfat milk from the groceries after him; there was the fact that those separation bars weren't just bars anymore, but now had advertising stuck all over them, and the ad that day was for a carton of Pall Malls and was it, or was it not, contradictory to be buying nonfat milk because it's healthier for you and yet at the same time be reading ads about cheaper Pall Malls?

No one encouraged him but he just plowed right on. The whole point of the story seemed to hinge on the fact that the quantity of nonfat milk in question was a *quart*, not a *liter*, because the fact of the matter is, if we'd changed over to the metric system when we were *supposed* to way back when, then he'd never have gotten into a fistfight in line at the D'Agostino's over a quart of milk in the first place. Right?

"That's one way of looking at things," Lucinda said, earning herself points for bravery. "And you?" she asked Iris.

"I wasn't done yet," a voice from the back complained. Iris swiveled around. It was the nonfat milk guy.

"Well, why don't you try to sum things up then," Lucinda said.

"Okay," he said. "I also got in a fight at the checkout line at a Food Emporium."

"Is that it?"

"No, not really," he said. "But those are the only ones they know about."

When it was officially Iris's turn, she stood up and gave her version in the shortest, most neutral terms possible. She'd been on a plane; there'd been a misunderstanding; tempers had flared; and the entire incident was regrettable. She had to walk a fine line because after carefully watching all the other introductions, she'd noticed that Lucinda tended to react most favorably—judging by the slight increase in her jingly, jangly nods—whenever people acknowledged that some portion of the blame rested on their own shoulders. But by the same token, Iris hadn't done anything wrong. "The whole incident was definitely unfortunate," Iris heard herself summing up, "particularly since it seems that I'm the only one who has to pay the price."

"Meaning?" Lucinda asked.

"Meaning that I didn't get here on my own," Iris said. "Meaning that on some level one has to question why it is that *more* than one person can cause a problem, and yet only one person has to clean it up."

"I see," Lucinda said, directing her serene, studious gaze at Iris, who sat down and looked back, but no matter how carefully she watched Lucinda, nothing jingled and nothing jangled. Iris had let her down.

Ken, her next-door neighbor, on the other hand, seemed perfectly happy to take the floor. And he seemed very much at ease in addressing the room with this way he had of catching various people's eyes and drawing them back into what he was saying.

And what was he saying?

He was carefully, systematically trashing some guy named Brett Manikin. He said that Brett was his former partner—Iris pricked up her ears at that and thought, *"as in a lawyer?"*—but a minute later he referred to Brett as his former boyfriend, which was the end of any ambiguity and the beginning of some sarcastic noises from the back of the room. But Ken just raised his voice slightly and turned around and reined in the ringleader with nothing more than a very penetrating look and went on with his story. Brett had betrayed his trust. Brett had violated the sanctity of their home. Brett had lied to his face. Brett was a B-list actor whom everyone would be wise to steer clear of.

And then he said that *because* of all the trouble emanating from this Brett Manikin—that's spelled M-A-N-I-K-I-N—Ken had unwisely taken out his frustrations while on the job, meaning that he'd defaced public property before his better judgment caught up with his acts.

From there, things degenerated as the rest of the back of the room got their turn to tell their stories. Iris was genuinely shocked not just at what people apparently did to each other, but by the fact that they could do those kinds of things and all that happened to them was that they wound up in the same class that she did. There was a guy who beat up a bouncer at a bar even though, almost by definition, bouncers are simply not beat-up-able. There was another guy who mooned an agent in a token booth in the subway but claimed he didn't have an anger problem at all; he said he had a problem with getting drunk and mooning the clerks in token booths. Then he said that he never would've gotten caught if there hadn't been some stupid investigative journalist squeezed into the token booth one night who was doing a story about repetitive stress injury. The journalist went around filming people with boring jobs who got weird, arthritisy symptoms and then bitched about it high and low, and as far as he was concerned, repetitive stress injury might just as well be called repetitive stress bullshit. "All I have to see," he said, "is another report on TV about whiny assholes complaining about getting paid to do nothing and the only response I can think of is throwing a lamp through the TV."

Lucinda said that there was a big difference between *wanting* to throw a lamp through your TV and going through with it and actually *throwing* a lamp through your TV, and the guy just looked at her with this confused expression on his face. "Wouldn't you agree?" she said.

And he said, "Well, no. Who said anything about throwing a lamp through *my* TV?"

The last person was this gangly kid named Jeff. He said that he was—well, he *used* to be—a law student at St. John's, but they made him take an administrative leave and then transfer to Hofstra all on account of how he fractured a law professor's jaw.

He said that it wasn't actually *his* professor of criminal law, but a *different* professor of criminal law, so it's not as if he assaulted his own professor. Then he sat back down.

"But you broke his jaw?" Lucinda prodded.

"Yes. A compound fracture, actually."

"And that would've happened how?"

"Oh," he said. "It was this experiment thing that they do, but I didn't know about it. Obviously. What they do is you're sitting there in class learning about criminal law and how you have to read people their rights when they get arrested, and before you know what's happening, the doors to the amphitheater burst open and these guys come storming in and they scream—'Nobody move!'—and they've got guns and they grab the teacher and drag him out of the room."

"And?"

"And then people panic. Pandemonium. And that's when the doors open back up and there's all these security guards who aren't really security guards—they're just grad students dressed up as security guards—and they appear out of nowhere and start interviewing everybody about what happened and they take everybody's statement and the whole point of the exercise is that the teacher wasn't really kidnapped; it was all staged. They stage this strong-arm robbery and the idea is to show how inaccurate eyewitness testimony can be."

"And is it? Inaccurate, that is?" Lucinda was absolutely hooked.

"Well, yes and no. Some people give perfectly accurate accounts and others give totally worthless accounts."

"So the point is that you can't rely on eyewitness testimony?"

"I wouldn't say that," Jeff said. "I'm not entirely sure what the point is. I mean, as a *methodology*, I think the experiment demonstrates that in any given class, most of the students are average, a few are bright, and the rest are stupid."

Lucinda almost smiled in spite of herself. "And tell me," she asked, "how we got from there to here?"

"Oh, *that*," Jeff said. "Well, nobody told me that it wasn't for real. You know, that it was an experiment and that the thieves were all in on it. But in any event, I knew that it wasn't a real gun because I'm on, well, I *was* on a scholarship and I've had about a million part-time jobs, including working in the Toys "R" Us out in East Setauket. And since I knew it wasn't a real gun but I *thought* it was a real robbery, I tried to stop it."

"Tried how?"

"My laptop computer," Jeff said. "My former laptop computer. I didn't have time to think and I just winged it like a Frisbee at the guy with the gun and I nailed him right on the chin." The class was positively mesmerized. "I didn't really think it was possible," Jeff said, "but with four titanium rods and a spool of surgical wire, they actually shut a law professor up."

Chapter Seven. In Which Ken Defies Inertia and Indifference to Steer a Course Toward Friendship with Iris

Ken found himself doodling in the middle of his first anger management class even though he knew better than anyone that doodling was usually perfectly obvious to the teacher. It was funny how his students seemed to think that what they were doing was invisible to him. They doodled. They played cards on their computers. They leafed through catalogs. They put on makeup and solicited opinions regarding the desirable, undesirable, or neutral effect of the application. They took the makeup back off and tried over. Ad infinitum.

But here Ken was, doodling just the same, sketching the front door of the Santa Monica and imagining how he could improve the little archeological succession of signs out front. It started with NO PEDDLERS (1905); NO SOLICITING (1948); NO MENUS (1977); NO MENUS WITH MSG (1986); and he imagined getting the building to add a nice burnished brass plate that said: NO BRETT.

Besides, he didn't feel too bad about letting his mind wander right under the teacher's nose because Lucinda was actually quite well occupied. She'd finished up with everyone's personal story of how they'd gotten there, and she'd read out a list of rules before showing a movie. The rules were pretty straightforward: what happens in this classroom stays in this classroom; what—

"Question?"

"Yes?" Lucinda asked.

"Does that mean there's no homework?"

"No. There's going to be homework and I'll get to that in a second."

Lucinda explained that everything they said and did in the classroom was supposed to stay there. She explained that the classroom was supposed to be a safe place for people to get in touch with what's wrong, and, as a result, she wouldn't be tolerating any disrespectful, threatening, or inappropriate behavior on the part of anyone. "And," she added, "if you'd like to test me on that, go right ahead, because the first person who does will have his or her registration withdrawn.

"And some of you," she continued, "have some pretty important reasons for being here, so if you're removed from the class, then you'll just have to suffer the consequences. There won't be any second chances. For a number of you, this is *already* your second chance."

And that's when Ken realized that some of the people were there not just because they'd been railroaded into it like him—or were just a few cards short of a full deck like the people in the front—but because they had *the law* breathing down their backs. That's what Lucinda meant when she said that while the movie was playing, she'd be going around to those in the judicial diversion program to introduce herself personally and have them sign a sheet attesting to their presence.

The movie itself, while obviously a little scattered and touchy-feely, wasn't entirely without merit. First, it tried to show how violence has become trivialized in our society, and to prove the point, there was a montage of images from movies and TV programs that showed people being thrown through plate-glass windows, and the supply of these scenes was evidently endless. Every time there was a fistfight in a bar, somebody would get sucker punched in the jaw and would go flying through the plate-glass window in a glittering, sparkling shower of glass. Over and over, in westerns, in drama series, in murder mysteries, even in a commercial for a non-streak glass cleaner where the idea behind the commercial was that this seen-it-all, heard-it-all prop manager relied on such-and-such brand glass cleaner to get his plate-glass windows sparkling clean before the director yelled "Action!" and somebody else got thrown through one of his windows.

Then to show how trivialized and divorced from reality that stylized violence was, the movie showed what it would be like to throw a person through a *real* plate-glass window, as opposed to one that was designed to splinter into a dazzling explosion of crunchy bits of glass. Obviously they couldn't throw a real person through the glass, so they filled one of those snug rubbery scuba diver suits with wet sand, and then, on the count of three, heaved it through a real window.

The effect was actually quite jarring because there wasn't any of that immediately recognizable *smashing* noise; instead, there was a very flat *clank*—almost a metallic noise—which was followed by another dull, flat *clank* as a large shard of the broken glass cracked and fell out of the window frame. Compared to what Ken had expected, the real sound was so crude, so raw, so startlingly *un*realistic. And naturally enough, the wetsuit didn't get right up and dust itself off and jump back into the melee (the hero) or slink off into the night shaking his fist and vowing revenge (the hero's nemesis); it just lay there on the ground without a scratch anywhere on it except, when they turned it over, one long, deep gash running across one of its shoulder blades that revealed a deep—and deeply obscene—wound of wet sand.

Lucinda surprised Ken by stopping at the woman right next to him and crouching down to get her to fill out a judicial diversion form. "Judicial diversion," he said to himself, rolling the words around his mouth. It made him think of a bunch of old black-robed judges hanging out in somebody's basement rec room making prank phone calls. Lucinda whispered back and forth with Iris, the woman next to him, and they worked through the form pretty smoothly until they hit some sort of snag. Iris kept trying to explain her point of view but Lucinda wasn't following. People were starting to find their conversation more interesting than the movie, so Lucinda finally made a judgment call and marked something down and asked Iris if that was okay and Iris said fine and signed it.

After the film, they got to have a break and Lucinda warned everybody that they had to be back *and* in their seats at exactly eight-ten and then she explained where the restrooms and vending machines were and what the New York City and state regulations were governing the sale and consumption of tobacco and tobacco-related products, and while she did that there was a strange, fleeting reversal of roles as the front of the class seemed bored and distracted and the back paid rapt attention.

When the break started, Ken stayed in his seat for lack of any better ideas and his neighbor stayed in hers, and since it seemed impolite not to say anything, Ken asked her what she thought of the class so far and she said it wasn't as bad as she expected. And then she complimented Ken on what he'd said earlier.

"About?"

"About your friend, or your ex-friend anyway. The guy named Brett."

"Oh, him," Ken said. "Well, he definitely got me into a lot of trouble."

"It sure seems like it," Iris said. "But I guess you don't see him anymore or anything like that? Not that it's any of my business." Why was this Iris person fishing around for details about Brett?

"No," Ken said, a little too abruptly. "Not at all." Then he didn't want Iris to feel bad, so he softened things up a bit by saying that he'd asked around a little to see if he could get some information about what'd happened with Brett—they did have friends in common, after all—but beyond that, no, he hadn't talked to Brett since Brett had walked out the door, and he wasn't planning on talking to him anytime soon.

"Well, I think that what you did was very brave," Iris said. "That is, you know, not letting someone cheat on you and not just taking your lumps and not just letting bygones be bygones and . . . oh, I don't know."

"Well, thank you," Ken said, pausing to accept the compliment before moving on to some topic that didn't involve Brett or cheating spouses and certainly not the confluence of the two.

But Iris didn't move on. Iris stayed right where she was. Iris said, "In fact, I really don't know what I would do if I found out that *my* boyfriend was cheating on me." The way she said it, the way she said the words "my boyfriend" made it clear that as far as Iris was concerned, there was a species of living being out there in the world known as "a boyfriend," some of whom belonged to women and some of whom belonged to men. That simple. Ken felt a little smile spread across his face that knocked away some of those cluttery, unnecessary defenses. And just like that, there was a subtle shift in the dynamics of Lucinda Gross's anger management class—a bilateral accord had been formed between Ken and Iris. And all this was proposed, negotiated, and concluded without their ever discussing anything more elaborate than the fact that Ken was gay and he'd been railroaded into taking this course thanks to Brett's treachery, and that Iris was straight and she'd been railroaded into this class thanks to a horrible battle-ax of a stewardess. Two sides of the same coin. And, Iris added, her boyfriend didn't know about any of this and she intended to keep it that way.

"He's totally in the dark about this class?" Ken asked.

"Yup."

"Is there a way I can ask why without prying?" Ken said.

"Pry away."

"Well, why then?"

And Iris explained that she had her doubts. She said it was a long, long story, but if she was going to be perfectly honest, she'd have to say that she had her doubts.

"About your boyfriend?" Ken asked.

"That's right," Iris said. "About Jeremy."

. . .

It was so much fun to have a new friend! Ken found Iris thought-ful and well spoken and obviously interesting—that's the least you could say—and there were so many things to discuss. Where did she live? What did she do? When did she move to New York? And of course she was dying to know all about him. How long had he been with Brett before they broke up? Had he seen it coming? Did he think anyone else in the class was gay? Could he tell? Maybe that kid Jeff, the one who looks like Ichabod Crane? And how come Ken got roped into this anger management thing even though he hadn't been to court?

Ken explained about the English Department and the comfort-ing, cuddly way they had of gleefully stabbing one of their own in the back whenever he was down. And then Ken asked Iris about her court case, and she told him all about the hearing and the mean, podium-hogging prosecutor and how she hadn't even thought about getting a lawyer—and the two of them *really* bonded over how much they both hated lawyers—and how she got out of it when the judge actually looked through the folder and sent her here where all she had to do was mind her Ps and Qs and the whole thing would eventually get wiped off her record.

"It's unbelievable that they'd lump you in with this crowd," Ken said. "Speaking of which, what was that all about before?" Ken asked. "Not that I was *trying* to eavesdrop. It's just that I couldn't help overhearing."

"The thing with Lucinda?"

"Yeah. You had the least violent crime but she took the most time with you."

"That she did," Iris said. "It's so stupid you won't believe it."

"Try me."

"Well, the judicial diversion form asks all this official stuff about you, and right after your name, they ask if you've ever gone by any *other* name, and I've gone by another name."

"I don't get it," Ken said. "Were you once married or some-thing?"

"No, that's why it's so complicated. It's about my first name, which is Iris, only it wasn't *always* Iris."

"I still don't get it."

"Well, when I was born, my parents were totally torn between two different names: Iris and Clarice. And they just couldn't make a decision, even after I was born, and it was only when the hospital *made* them sign the birth certificate that they put in the name Iris. And everything was fine until I was about a year old when the two of them just sort of looked at each other one day and said—'You know, she really is more of a Clarice than an Iris'—and with that, they decided to get my name changed. They went into juvenile court and went through this long, complicated process and I became Clarice."

"Which doesn't seem to have stuck."

"Nope," Iris said. "They held on for about a year before they realized, *at a Tastee-Freez* no less, that they were actually right the first time. So they went back to court and went through the rigamarole all over again and I went back to being Iris and the judge told them that if they ever darkened his courtroom door again, he'd put them in jail and throw away the key. And that was that. The problem is that on forms they sometimes ask if you've ever gone by some other name, and I have to say yes, even though it was only for a year and I don't even *remember* it, but by the time I'm done explaining the situation, whoever I'm talking to thinks I'm nuts."

"I don't think it's nutty at all," Ken said. "It's *unusual*, but it's not all that nutty. And at least it means your parents were paying enough attention to actually wonder whether you might be more of a Clarice than an Iris, or vice versa, which is more than you can say about most parents these days." In fact, Ken said that the whole story made him want to meet Iris's parents, and Iris laughed and said to be careful what he wished for, but a moment later a little trace of a cloud passed across her face and she said, "You know, Jeremy doesn't see things that way."

"What way?" Ken asked.

"He doesn't think it's funny. The way you just said you do. He thinks I'm indecisive and that one of the *reasons* I'm indecisive is because my parents hemmed and hawed over my name and couldn't come to a decision that they could stick to."

"And do you agree with that?" Ken asked.

"Oh, *I don't know*," Iris joked. "I can't seem to make up my mind!" And they both laughed until they had tears in their eyes and the bell rang to end the break.

For someone who'd demonstrated such a firm grip on the present, Lucinda surprised Ken after the break by announcing that for their next exercise, the class was going to travel backward in time and pay a visit to the past.

Blank stares all around.

"And while we're there, we might adjust a few things," she said, passing out more paper.

The idea was for each person to think about the event that landed them in this class and then to write it down all the way to the right of their sheet of paper. "That represents the moment of truth," Lucinda said. "Whatever fight or eruption that brought you here, that goes on the right side of your papers. And all that beautiful, blank, empty space on the *rest* of the page is everything that happened *before* the event in question, okay? And what I want you to do is to sketch in all the events that you can recall that preceded it. So if we're talking about a dustup at the checkout counter of a D'Agostino's, then that goes over on the right and—"

"And at a Food Emporium."

"*And* at a Food Emporium," Lucinda repeated. "That goes to the right, and then you make a timeline of what preceded it. You know, I went to the bank. I watched TV. I got a telephone call with some bad news about a friend who's in the hospital."

"I don't have any friends in the hospital," the nonfat milk guy said. "And I can easily prove it."

"Well, that's just an example," Lucinda said. "And I'm not asking you to prove or disprove it. What I want you to do is to put in what actually happened. You know, in each of your individual cases. And once that's done, I want you to study your timelines carefully and then identify three places where you might have done something differently, something that *could*—I'm not saying it *would*—but something that *could've* avoided the final event. Okay?"

There was some shuffling and some rustling and then a brief groundswell of jealous disapproval at the kiss-ass up front who pulled a ruler out of her purse to make her timeline picture perfect and then didn't offer to lend the ruler to anyone else even though rulers aren't like pens or erasers—nobody's ruler ever got all *used up*.

Ken was a little put out because, for the second time in as many hours, the course that he was *assuming* would be a laughable waste of time—at best—and a ghoulish glimpse into pseudoscientific crap masquerading as real crap—at worst—was once again piquing his interest. He dutifully charted out his offense and then set up his timeline, only he was at a loss for anything he could've done differently. He knew what the answer was supposed to be. He was supposed to write everything down and, from that, he was supposed to see that what happened at the end was the result of a series of earlier, aggravating events. So if the end result was a driver getting a summons for flipping off a police horse, then the person has to look at the events that lead up to that. Did someone nick the paint on his car? Did he get held up for twenty minutes on a crosstown block because some imbecile in a bathrobe and curlers was arguing with the garbage men over whether they'd take something that *she* said was "just a planter"—you know, you put plants in it? Plants? *Green* things?—while the *garbage men* said it was clearly a lidless coffin filled with dirt.

The problem was that Ken just couldn't see where he'd gone wrong. Brett shouldn't have cheated on him. That was the whole problem. And that's obviously something Ken couldn't do anything about because Brett, like most cheaters, did it without Ken's knowledge.

"Hey, Ken." That would be Brett.

"Yes, sweetheart?"

"Can I borrow your Hermès tie?"

"Sure. What's the occasion?"

"Oh, I'm planning to cheat on you and I need to look my best."

And that's where Ken would say, "Oh, well, in *that* case, no, you may not borrow my tie." Pure fantasy; *everybody* knows that adjunct professors can't afford Hermès ties.

Ken sighed. Iris and the others were working away and Ken was getting nowhere. And not for lack of trying, either, because like he'd told Iris, he'd asked around and found out some scuttlebutt about Neil—ugh, *it* has a name—the home-wrecker who'd waltzed off with Brett. And no matter how he analyzed the situation, it didn't seem as if there was anything Ken could've done to stave off their whatever you want to call it, their liaison.

According to Ken's sources, Brett and Neil got to know each other while volunteering for an AIDS group that went around the Village late at night and talked people into participating in these very detailed interviews and questionnaires about their sex lives, which was actually a very helpful project on a variety of levels. First, it collected public health data that would never have gotten collected, and they did it for free. Who has engaged in which practices in the past ten days? Attach extra sheets if necessary. And as Brett used to say, data is never wrong. Data is just data, and you can't wage a war unless you know who the enemy is, and the better you know him, the more likely you are to win.

And Ken couldn't argue with that.

But beyond the public health benefits, there was another effect: just seeing the guys out there with their clipboards and their matching windbreakers and their cheeks all fresh from standing out on the corner of Christopher Street and Seventh Avenue tended to make people who viewed the whole question of protection as *depressing* look at it in a slightly more positive light. People *liked* it when good-looking guys with fresh cheeks took an interest in them and asked them a litany of personal questions and took the trouble to write their answers down on clipboards.

It's actually a great strategy. You go to bars and nobody talks to you all night—*at all*—and then suddenly there's this good-looking person who wants to talk to you. In fact, he wants nothing more than to talk to you. So you spill your guts. You tell him everything, and he writes it all down and gives you some free brochures and some condoms and that's that.

So that was how Brett met Neil. *More or less.* The truth was a little more delicate, because the truth of the matter was that Brett actually got Neil to join the group. Brett had stopped Neil on the street just like any other subject and got him to take the survey and asked him fifty million questions and carefully noted the responses, and they hit it off. Neil complimented Brett on his selfless devotion to the cause, and Brett demurred (and Brett had been schooled in the art of demurring by some of the finest drama coaches in Manhattan), and they got to talking and one thing led to another and eventually Neil joined the group too.

So to most people, it sounded as if Neil and Brett were just two more selfless souls out to do the world a little good. Just two more people out to make a difference. When in reality, Brett essentially had gone out and *interviewed* candidates—literally hundreds and hundreds of candidates—for the job of lover and then just picked the best one. Broadly speaking.

Ken didn't want to find himself in the undignified situation of getting an F from Lucinda, so he stuck a few obvious things into his timeline, like getting fired from Leighton Fennell shortly before the unfortunate events at the reference desk at Cohen Library. And then he added the words "financial strain," which seemed worth at least a C, but otherwise he couldn't focus. Ken couldn't focus on where he might have gone wrong because he *hadn't* gone wrong. He couldn't very well have prevented Brett from joining an AIDS group, particularly one that actually seemed to make a difference, could he? What kind of monster would do that? Besides, he'd been so proud of Brett for donating his time and energy, even if it was only two evenings a month, because it was still two evenings that he spent downtown in the freezing cold or in the blistering heat getting breathed on by total strangers, basket cases, freaks, losers, Wall Street jerks, New Jersey politicians, recovering gamble-aholics, fifty-year-old men in Keds sneakers, thirty-year-old men with canes, married men, illegal aliens, mean drunks, happy drunks, and the occasional melancholy drunk who'd burst into tears midway through the interview and when they'd ask him why he was crying he'd say, "Because I don't know what else to do."

In fact, Ken didn't just approve of what Brett and his group were doing; he himself felt energized. He felt a little bit less beaten up by the world, a little less likely to take things lying down, and that feeling spilled right over into all the other aspects of their daily lives. Take the time that Brett came home just before the sky started to lighten in June and they lay on top of the sheets talking until Brett noticed the two thick, creamy envelopes sitting on the desk and asked, "What are those?"

And Ken said, "They're wedding invitations."

"Invitation-*zuh*? As in two of them?"

"Yup."

"From Kara?" Kara was a friend of theirs who was engaged to a man who referred to himself as a Hollywood producer, even though he neither lived in Hollywood nor produced anything, let alone movies. "And why are there two of them?" Brett asked.

"Well, I'm going to go out on a limb here," Ken said, "but so that we'd both be invited to the wedding."

"Huh?"

"Let me see if I can make it even easier," Ken said. "Kara get married. Kara invite us. Kara—"

"That's not what I meant, Ken. What I meant is why are there two invitations instead of one invitation for the both of us?"

"That I don't know."

"Well, that makes a big difference," Brett said.

"Well, I hadn't thought about it," Ken said, but even as he said that he could tell Brett was right. The invitation should have been addressed to both of them. The two of them weren't going to just happen to leave the Santa Monica at the same time and then happen to go to the same wedding and then happen to get unwillingly drawn into the same conga line at the reception and then happen to go home together to methodically dissect the mother of the bride's tragic choice of contrasting piping for the seams of her suit, which, everyone agreed, made her look like a sofa. They were going to go to the wedding *together*. That was the difference.

He remembered falling asleep that night next to Brett and then crawling quietly out of bed the next morning to let Brett sleep— only this time with an idea in his head. He zipped out the door and bought a beautiful long oval copper-plated fish poaching dish from Williams & Sonoma, which cost a fortune, and then sawed it in half—lid and all. And then they had the two halves beautifully wrapped and delivered to the reception hall well in advance of Kara's wedding. You send separate invites, you get separate gifts— it's that simple. The thank-you notes—plural—were also simple: Kara tersely thanked each of them for the "thoughtful" gift, which they thought was hilarious since it was inadvertently truthful— they really *had* put a lot of thought into their gifts.

Now, though, sitting in a classroom at the West Side Y, Ken just couldn't reconcile the two different versions of Brett. There was the one who came home all hot and sooty and took a shower and talked to Ken on top of the sheets and spotted the wedding invitations and pointed out what was wrong with them—that *we* were a couple too—and then laughingly, gleefully helped Ken fix Kara's wagon. And then there was the Brett who slept with some stranger and did it in their bed, and did it despite the fact that Ken and Brett were a real couple and then *forgot* to plead for forgiveness and just left altogether. Which one was real and which was just a mistake? If one version was real, didn't the other one *have* to be a mistake?

Ken caught Iris's eye and she gave him a wan little smile that he normally would've interpreted as saying, "Hang in there." But Ken didn't have much confidence left in his interpretive skills. Not anymore. Not after everything he'd ever thought had turned out to be so wrong.

Chapter Eight. In Which Iris Searches Her Apartment and Discovers Cracks in the Foundation

Iris was sitting at her kitchen table doing her homework. Well, *trying* to do her homework. She'd set up her laptop and assembled a pad of paper and a number two pencil with an extra eraser next to it, just in case. Jeremy would probably be back within the hour and Iris wanted to get her homework out of the way before then. But nothing was coming.

Lucinda's assignment was relatively straightforward. Everyone was supposed to sit down at the end of every day and describe three instances in which they felt like they were about to lose their temper, but didn't. The idea was to describe the setting, the situation, the principal characters, and then to *slow* the sequence of events down as tempers started to flare and really *analyze* what was going on. How was it that a person could maintain control one day when on other days the same person might blow a fuse? What was different? What held them back?

Unfortunately, Iris was fresh out of ideas.

Worse, most of the people in the class seemed to have *tons* of opportunities to lose their tempers. Other than Ken and Jeff, the law-student-slash-superhero, the others were a bubbling cauldron of thick, acidic anger, and Iris just couldn't compete. In the back of the room, the students handed in essay after essay about all these concrete things that made them mad—people who tried to cut in lines; people who answered their cell phones in movie theaters; people who shushed *them*

for answering their cell phones in movie theaters; people who called them up with reminders about past-due payments for an Abdominizer bought on a payment plan with 16.5 percent interest; people who said, "Have a good one"; automatically renewable restraining orders; the cops; the fuzz; the heat; the Man . . .

And in the front of the room, it wasn't much better. It was more abstract, but those people were seething with anger too. In the front of the room, they wrote about eclipsed faith; clipped wings; smothered souls; the inevitable chasm between people that prevents real communication; tip jars at self-service restaurants; the ephemeral nature of love; the aching poetry of a child's first step; bitch secretaries who steal husbands; and the world's relentless hostility to their art.

Iris just didn't carry around that much bile. Sure, she had a demanding boss, but that was that. He was a jerk when she started and he was a jerk now and he'd probably be a jerk ten, fifteen, twenty years from now, but that didn't make that much of a difference to Iris. That was just life. You draw a hand, you play that hand. End of story. Her hand had an annoying, demanding boss in it, but that didn't make her "writhe in a passionate embrace with anger incarnate" (front of the class) or punch a hole through a DON'T WALK sign (back of the class) even though the DON'T WALK sign in question had been engineered in Taipei and tested outside Liverpool soccer matches to meet the sole and unique criterion that it be strong enough to withstand a human punch.

Iris tried to jazz up her demanding boss a little so she could come up with some scenarios in which she might've lost her temper, but it wasn't working. First she had him yell at her in a meeting, but he'd done that hundreds of times before and she'd never thought much of it other than to feel slightly sorry for him because he probably couldn't help it. Then she had him shake his fist at her in the hallway and threaten to fire her, but that wasn't credible because Iris was excellent at what she did, and no matter how obnoxious her boss was, he couldn't get by without her. So then she embellished a little more and had him give her a karate chop in the back of her neck as she was getting off an elevator. There. Then she added little touches to make it more believable, like how she'd been holding a stack of files for this hugely important Blue-Cross BlueShield account when he did it and she didn't want to drop them so she made a split-second decision and held onto the files and sacrificed herself and crashed face-first into the lobby floor.

Hmmm. Perhaps she'd need to give herself a black eye with one of her eyeliners before class.

And *that* gave her an idea. She went into the bathroom and rifled through her side of the cabinet until she found what she was looking for—the jar of Clinique Blended Face Powder that she'd felt obligated to buy after she'd been sprayed and captured one day on the ground floor of Lord & Taylor and forced to sit through a free makeover. And when exactly did department stores turn into game reserves where women like Iris got hunted for sport? No wait, forget that; try to stay focused. She brought the powder back to the kitchen and started dusting a fine layer of it over the blank pad of paper and then held it up to the light. Iris, it seems, had become very suspicious.

The pad, however, didn't seem particularly inclined to give up its secrets, so Iris had to blow a little excess foundation off in some places and add a thick, televangelist layer of extra foundation in other places, but in the end, she could put together bits and pieces of what had been written on the last sheet of paper on the pad before it'd been torn off and the evidence had been ripped to bits.

Let's see . . .

It was a bit of a mishmash, but toward the bottom there was some cryptic writing. Unfortunately, it didn't reveal any scheming on the part of Jeremy. Instead, it looked like the remnants of a shopping list—in Iris's handwriting—and all it did was remind her that it was probably time for her to buy some more Pringles. In short, the pad wasn't very much help at all.

· · ·

It had all started simply enough, this sleuthing thing. When Iris told Ken that she admired him for what he had done, for not putting up with Brett's philandering ways, she wasn't just moving her mouth around for the exercise—she meant it. And that was the problem, because if she meant it, then shouldn't she be getting to the bottom of Jeremy and the mysterious speeding ticket, the ticket that got dropped into Iris's life by a shadowy hand wearing a silvery signet ring?

She started by trying to keep a lookout for a signet ring amongst their friends and neighbors, but none turned up, which was actually kind of a relief because Iris didn't have a plan for what she was supposed to *do* once she spotted the offending piece of jewelry.

From there, though, things got a little more serious. She combed through their bank statements from back around the time of the aunt's funeral to see when and where any money was withdrawn, but there really wasn't anything untoward. There was a bigger than usual withdrawal from Citibank right before Jeremy left, but that would make sense irrespective of whether Jeremy was going to help his mom with his aunt's funeral in Holyoke or whether he was about to go gallivanting around Bucks County.

Jeremy's credit card statements, on the other hand, were much more interesting. Iris really didn't want to do it, but she went into Jeremy's files which, on the plus side, were exquisitely organized, though on the downside, Iris didn't really see how she could go back to the way things were with Jeremy after rifling through his files. She pushed that thought out of her head and pulled out Jeremy's credit card file and found what she was looking for. Right smack in the middle of the weekend in question, there was a charge posted from someplace called Holicong, Pennsylvania. Iris looked at a map and Holicong was just a hop, skip, and a jump away from Yardley, the place where Jeremy got caught with his chin jutting out into the flash of a police camera.

The charge was from something called the Covered Bridge, which was a lot better than, say, for example, someplace called The

Illicit Affair Inn. But whatever it was didn't really matter because the point was that there couldn't be any mistake—Jeremy had lied to her.

The phone rang and it was Ken. "What's the difference," he asked Iris, "between a white rhino and a black rhino?"

"What's the *what*?"

"The difference," he said. "You know, how is a white rhinoceros different from a black one?"

"Are you joking?"

"No, not at all."

"Well, let me see," Iris said. "I'm going to guess that the difference is that white rhinos are white whereas black rhinos are black."

"True enough," Ken said. "But there's a catch. All rhinos, black or white, spend their free time rolling around in dirt. It's got something to do with protecting themselves from mosquitoes or something like that, but the point is that they're always all dusty. So irrespective of their natural color, they all seem sort of gray, and there's no way to tell by just looking at them whether they're black or white underneath all that dirt and dust. It's only if you threw a bucket of water over them and scrubbed them down that you'd be able to see which was which."

"Why would anyone want to throw a bucket of water over a herd of rhinos?"

"Well, they wouldn't," Ken said. "That's not the point."

"It seems to me that you'd have to be pretty stupid to wander into a herd of rhinos and then, just because they *hadn't* gotten pissed off and trampled you to death, you push your luck a little further and throw a bucket of water over them and start a race riot."

"Actually, I don't think they have herds," Ken said.

"What's that?"

"Herds. You know, of rhinos. Like the way that cows come in herds and wolves come in packs and whales come in pods. I don't think they have *herds* of rhinos."

"Well, what do they have?"

"It's called a crash."

"A *crash*?"

"Yup."

"Well, just from the sound of it, I'd say that that's another reason for not wandering into their midst and upsetting everything by flinging buckets of water around."

"Well, I didn't say I was going to do it," Ken said. "I was just asking what the difference was between them."

"Wait a second," Iris said. "You wouldn't happen to be watching TV, would you?"

"I would." Ken said he was watching this totally absorbing nature program on Channel Thirteen about rhinos and how they roll around in dust all day and get gray and dingy.

"So hang on here," Iris said. "Did you know that the word for a bunch of rhinos was a crash *before* watching this program, or did you just learn it?"

A slight pause.

"Ah-ha!" Iris said, laughing. "Professor I-Know-Everything isn't quite as smart as he'd like us to believe!"

"Well," Ken said. "I knew that there was probably a special word for it; I just didn't know what it was."

"Who's in charge of those things anyway?" Iris asked. "I mean, who gets to sit around deciding that wolves come in packs and bumblebees come in this or that and that rhinos come in crashes?"

"I don't know," Ken said.

"And where do we complain if we don't like the name they choose?"

"I don't think we do."

"Well, that stinks."

"Indeed it does."

"Oh, and speaking of stinking," Iris said, "how are you doing with these nightly essays? I've been sitting here for an hour and I haven't even gotten one example down, let alone three, and I'm actually working on a deficit because I didn't do mine for yesterday yet."

"Well, you better not leave it for too long, because it seems like the kind of thing where it'd be pretty easy to let yourself get so far behind that you can't catch up."

"I know, but I can't even get one!"

"Well, I could sort of, you know, help you," Ken said. "I mean, only if you wanted me to."

"What do you mean?"

"I could give you a situation that'd make somebody mad and we'll say it happened to you, and Lucinda will never know the difference and everybody comes out ahead."

"Wouldn't that be . . . ?"

"Cheating?" Ken offered.

"Well, that's not actually the word I was looking for," Iris said. "I was thinking more along the lines of great. Fantastic. The bee's knees." Ken laughed. "A big, huge, bunch of bees' knees," Iris said.

Ken told her to hang on for a second and then he got back on the phone and rustled something around for a few moments. Then he said, "Oh, here we go!"

"Here we go what?"

"Here we go as in I've got a situation for you. We'll start with yesterday's first and then we'll get today's done. Do you have a pencil ready?"

"I do."

"Okay," Ken said. "Here goes—you're allergic to peanuts."

"But I'm not," Iris said.

"Yes, but Lucinda doesn't *know* that and Lucinda's never going to know it, so for all intents and purposes, you could be allergic to peanuts. And when I say you're allergic, what I mean is that with just one whiff of peanut, you could wind up in the emergency room or dead."

"Okay. Got it."

So Ken dictated and Iris took notes and the point was that Iris was highly allergic to peanuts and apparently this wasn't all that uncommon and restaurants were becoming more aware of this type of disability and the cafeteria at . . . "Hang on," Ken said. "Is there a cafeteria where you work?"

"Yup."

"Great. Okay, so the cafeteria is aware of the problem and they don't serve anything with peanuts in it so their employees don't just drop dead all the time instead of working and they take the whole thing really seriously and the cafeteria, no wait, the entire company, is supposed to be a peanut-free zone."

"A peanut-free zone?"

"Exactly. And even though you *thought* you were in a safe space, you snuck a bite of some leftover Thai takeout that your best friend brought to work in *your* freshness-guaranteed Tupperware, which she seems to have forgotten belongs to you, and the only reason she has it is because you used it to bring Jell-O shots to her party last week even though she didn't ask you to and it costs a lot more time and effort to make Jell-O shots than it does to just pick up a six-pack of beer on the way over and some of us don't really like beer all that much anyway." He paused. "Are you with me."

Iris repeated the last bits as she copied them down and told him to go ahead.

"Okay, so you snuck a bite of her leftover Thai takeout and you had to because your diet is killing you—by the way, you're on a diet—and it's not your fault that your diet is killing you because people aren't noticing that you've lost almost a pound and without the right kind of support, it's impossible to lose weight. I mean, people don't just *lose* weight like that. They don't just *misplace* it somewhere."

"Amen to that," Iris said.

"So you snuck a bite of her Thai takeout and the minute you tasted it, you knew there was peanut sauce in it and you didn't know what to do and you couldn't swallow it because you'd probably die so you had no choice and you had to spit it into your hand and then you ran to the ladies' room and everybody could probably tell that you had spit-up in your hand and they're probably *still* talking about it and none of this would've happened if your own best friend hadn't practically tried to kill you when she broke the rules about the peanut-free zone in the first place."

"Ken?" Iris asked.

"Yes?"

"Are you *reading* something?"

"What do you mean?"

"What do I mean? I *mean*, are you reading from something? What you just told me. Where'd you get that?"

"Uh . . ."

"Ken, did you give our anger management homework to your *students*?"

"Uh, is *'maybe'* one of the options?"

"No."

"Well, in that case, yes."

"Oh my God, that's brilliant!" Iris said. "What kind of stock are we looking at here?"

"Well, I had both sections do this as an assignment, and at twenty-five kids per section times three short essays per night, minus a certain number that are unusable, I'd say we're sitting pretty."

"That's great," Iris said. "So what was my best friend's name anyway?"

"Who?"

"The girl with the contraband Thai food."

"Oh, your ex-best friend. That's Lindsay."

"Lindsay," Iris said. "And what gets Lindsay mad?"

Iris could hear Ken shuffling some papers on the other end of the line, and then he came back on. "Everything," he said, whistling softly. "This is a gold mine."

By the middle of October, Ken and Iris had gotten into the habit of checking in with each other by telephone on the days between classes. At first Ken had been a little shy about it, and to a certain extent he preferred for Iris to call him rather than the other way around, because anyone who called his number automatically got him, whereas calling Iris meant there was a fifty-fifty chance of getting Jeremy, which wasn't what Ken was trying to do. He'd been briefed by Iris that the two of them were officially taking a class in restaurant criticism, and Ken found it a little weird how he always had to remind himself of that right before dialing Iris's number to make sure he didn't blurt the wrong thing out to Jeremy in the ten seconds it might take him to ask to speak to Iris. Lying, he thought, was essentially a full-time job.

From calling on the days between classes it wasn't very long before they started seeing each other between classes too, and the same unspoken rule applied: Jeremy wasn't invited. They talked about him a lot, though, and what was strange was that they fell into the habit of talking about Jeremy in the same tone of voice that they originally reserved for talking about Brett. And Brett, in theory anyway, was a totally different situation because Brett was guilty. Brett had been tried and convicted. Brett officially belonged to that group of people who go out and sabotage their relationships for no good reason. Brett was unnatural. If Brett were a bird, they'd concluded, he'd gladly foul his own nest.

So why do people screw up a good thing? Iris and Ken just didn't have the answer to that. It's one thing for a relationship to disintegrate—that's the kind of thing that happens—but it's another thing altogether for someone to have a fine, perfectly healthy relationship and then just go out and cheat and hope that he doesn't get caught. What kind of risk analysis is that? It was a lot easier to envision people who used infidelity to drive the last nail into the coffin of whatever relationship they were in but didn't have the guts to get out of. Okay, fine. But what about those people who were willing to risk a good thing just for some (undeterminable quantity of) extramarital sex?

Iris found herself thinking about a couple whose marriage had collapsed right under her nose. It was during her last year in college and she was living off campus in a room in a house with two comparative literature professors whose own kids had gone off to college, and Iris had her own bedroom with a beautiful Windsor chair thoughtfully placed next to the window for reading.

And then one day the dishwasher conked out and all hell broke loose. Iris heard a bitter argument a few nights later about how the husband professor just left his dishes in the sink because he didn't take the wife professor's career seriously, and how he blithely went through life thinking that if you leave a dirty dish in the sink, it would magically wash itself. *He*, on the other hand, said it was impossible to take her career seriously when all she had to talk about was dirty dishes. He said that dirty dishes weren't one of the subjects that *intellectually engaged people* gravitated to.

And she said, "Fuck you."

And from there it went downhill. The dishes piled up, and when the couple fought at night, the wife's refrain slowly changed from "You wrecked my career!" to "You wrecked my life!" It sounded like four distinct depth charges: You! Wrecked! My! Life!

And then the smell began. The kitchen started to stink to high heaven, and when Iris came home at night, the awful stench practically bowled her over as she walked in the door. She'd look over at the professors who were sitting in the living room, and they'd just look up at her as if nothing could be more natural than sitting in a cloud of homemade Agent Orange. "Hello, Iris," the wife would say, giving her husband a hateful, he-has-no-manners look, so he would say, "Hello, Iris," too.

Iris held out for two weeks before she broke the lease and moved in with Stephanie, and even though she was afraid of what the professors might do to her, nothing bad happened. Iris just said it was for some sort of made-up academic reason, and they didn't bother arguing with her. And that was the end of that.

Except it really wasn't. That was the end of Iris's involvement, but the story still had to play itself out. Whether or not Iris was there to witness it, there were still the shouting matches and there was still the decision to divorce, and then the blissfully unaware children (plus two, count them, two grandchildren!) had to be informed that their mother and father would be *reevaluating* some of the tenets governing their living arrangements. There were sides to be chosen and one of the professors had to move out and then there were the Self-Storage assholes to be dealt with who claimed that they couldn't take that much paper because it was a fire risk. And then there was the nest egg. The nest egg that had been *thirty-one years in the making*. The nest egg that would be seized on either end by two different divorce lawyers, and the only question in anybody's mind was which snake was going to swallow the other snake, because no matter what happened, the one thing for sure was that the egg itself was a goner.

"Ground control to Iris." A scratchy little version of Ken's voice hovered near her ear. Oh, Lord, caught with her head in the clouds again.

"I'm here," she said. "Where were we again?"

"*We* just finished your homework and I'm about to go to bed."

"Oh, is it that late?"

"Time and tides," Ken said.

"Well, thanks for the help—I owe you big for this."

"Pshaw!"

"Well, don't think it's not appreciated, because it is," Iris said.

"Double pshaw," Ken said. "And you're more than welcome. I guess I'll see you tomorrow?"

"It's a date!"

"Okay, talk to you—"

"Wait a second!" Iris cried. "You never told me what the difference was between black and white rhinos!"

"Oh, *right*," Ken laughed. "It was the weirdest thing, but on the show they said that whenever there was danger, one of them—black or white, I don't remember which—the mother runs ahead of her calf and he gets saved from the danger by trying to keep up with her, whereas with the other one, when there's danger, she runs *behind* her calf and keeps the pressure on him to run faster and that's how *he* gets away. Isn't that bizarre?"

"That's so strange. Does one work better than the other?"

"I don't know. I don't think they said."

"And is there some sort of lesson in there somewhere?"

"Probably. I just don't know what it is."

Iris hid her homework underneath some files in her briefcase, and then remembered that those files were in her briefcase precisely because she was supposed to study them, so she got them out, but she didn't even make it past the third or fourth page before she was too tired to go on. She pushed it aside and folded her arms on the table and the next thing she knew she was walking across the Serengeti under a brilliant blue sky. It was warm and the midday sunshine was glittering and Iris had just put her hand out absently to touch Jeremy's shoulder when a flock of birds that'd been hidden in the grass exploded up into the sky behind her. Iris whirled around.

Danger.

The wildebeests hesitated and for a split second there wasn't any sound at all, and then they took off and the churning, rumbling thunder of their hooves scared Iris even more and she could feel the panic flooding her system and she bolted. She flew across the plain—a strange, roaring, terrifying sound in her ears—and as she ran, wildly, blindly, she knew there was something wrong. *Jeremy*. Jeremy was supposed to be in front of her or Jeremy was supposed to be behind her and that was the key to the whole escape and they wouldn't get away unless she could remember how it was supposed to work but she couldn't.

"Iris?"

Oh, God. It was Jeremy's voice. Jeremy was safe!

"Iris? Did you fall asleep?"

Iris looked up, confused to be in the kitchen, which had mysteriously taken the place of the Serengeti. She rubbed her eyes.

"Iris, honey, what did you do to your face!" Iris put her hands up to her face and they came away with the dusky, dusty traces of her caked-on foundation. Jeremy trailed his finger along the pad and then across Iris's cheek and laughed. "What on earth have you been doing?" he asked. "Are you playing dress-up?"

And the sad thing, the heartbreaking thing about it, was that maybe it was true. Maybe that's all she'd been doing with Jeremy all along—playing dress-up. Playing house.

Chapter Nine. In Which Ken Offers to Scratch Iris's Back If She'll Scratch His, a Curious Proposal for Two Non-Itchy People

Normally, when Ken wanted to weasel his way out of doing something, he just said that he had a makeup session or some extra office hours and that was that. Unfortunately, that kind of excuse wasn't very helpful when it came to skipping a meeting of the English Department. Especially a meeting of the English Department that had been converted by His Scillatiness into an *Emergency Plenary Meeting of the English Department.*

The meeting was originally supposed to be one of those regular things where Scillat harangued the people who hadn't yet turned in their midterm grades and then berated anyone else in need of a good berating. Unfortunately, all that pleasure would have to wait for another day because this particular meeting had been hijacked by a pair of flip-flops. The great flip-flop debate had erupted when some naïve lecturer in the Applied Mathematics Department suggested, only half-jokingly, that students shouldn't wear flip-flops to her class. The students cried bloody murder, and now all the departments had been asked to weigh in on the issue.

Some people in the meeting thought that banning flip-flops was a good idea—purely from an olfactory point of view—while others offered complicated arguments that linked free expression with well-aired toes. Then someone asked why anyone would want to wear flip-flops as the weather got colder, but he got shouted down by a Virginia Woolf specialist who kept saying that Jesus wore sandals and *he* was born in the middle of winter. And from there, the debate only degenerated.

Ken was basically relieved that the department was hashing through this nonsense instead of taking care of regular business because it kept the focus off him. Ever since he'd been so thoroughly tarred and feathered by his colleagues at the last meeting, his appearances around the department had been very brief, and even today he'd felt his ears burning as he'd come in and taken his seat and watched his colleagues take notice of him—all the little gestures on their part that betrayed that they'd seen him and had briefly wondered why he'd been such a stranger recently and then remembered, *oh right*.

Or maybe it was all in his head.

Whatever the case, the great flip-flop debate was just what the doctor ordered.

Scillat wanted the English Department's position on casual footwear to be crystal clear. Unfortunately, there was very little by way of common ground. Some saw the whole episode as an example of insidious, Orwellian persecution, and others saw it as an example of insidious, Orwellian intolerance, and Professor Vicole, who was the resident Orwell specialist (and the author of the now out-of-print book *Orwellian Implications of the BetaMax Television Recording Device*) opened his mouth and everyone leaned toward him, but then he just shut it again without saying anything.

Maxine was taking down the minutes of the meeting, and Ken caught her eye and smiled, but even then he could still feel that same little flush of embarrassment. There wasn't any real reason to be embarrassed, especially with someone like Maxine, but the fact of the matter was that at any second the meeting could veer off track and right into his crimes and misdemeanors, particularly if he were foolish enough to wade into the debate, which he was not. It's a well-accepted fact that drowning men will grasp at straws. The lesser known corollary is that people losing (stupid) arguments in (stupid) faculty meetings will grasp at anything, and anything could include deflecting attention back onto Ken and his recent brush with the law.

"The trouble," he thought, looking around the room, "is that they know me and I know them."

And that's when it hit him. *Iris* doesn't know these people. At all. Iris exists in a completely different world, and the same thing is true in reverse, meaning that he didn't know *her* world at all. Take Jeremy, for example. Other than as a voice briefly heard on the phone, he didn't know Jeremy at all. Jeremy could be sitting right here in this meeting—well, that's a bad example—but let's say that Ken got on the subway and wound up sitting next to some guy, well that could turn out to be Jeremy and Jeremy wouldn't know it was Ken and Ken wouldn't know it was Jeremy. Suddenly Ken had an idea. Ken was going to recruit Iris to spy on Brett for him, and in turn, he was going to spy on Jeremy for her. Ken wanted to know exactly what was going on with Brett. He wanted to know whether Brett had ever really cared for him. He wanted to know how Brett could just walk right out the door on love the way that people walk out of the living room to get a snack during commercials for auto insurance at rock-bottom prices. Iris was going to get to the bottom of things for him and he'd do the same for her, and he exhaled and settled back in his seat feeling a little bit more anchored than he'd felt in ages.

"Professor Connelly!" Scillat's voice came out of nowhere. Ah, *nuts.* "We're not keeping you from something more important, are we?"

"No, sir."

"Well, then, is there a reason why you've chosen not to participate in a show of hands?" Oh, Lord. What the hell could they be voting on now? A motion to limit the debate to seventy-two more hours? A motion to invite a podiatrist as a guest speaker?

"No, sir."

"Well, then how do you vote?"

Ken let his eyes sweep slowly across the room, a gesture that looked *wonderfully* similar to the type of look that a person might give a crowd thirsting to hear his knowledge but which, in reality, was designed to catch a glimpse of the direction in which Maxine was slowly scratching her neck. She was scratching downward.

"No," Ken said confidently. "I vote no."

Ken told Iris all about his idea that night when Lucinda let the class take their break.

"You want me to do *what*?" she said.

"To spy for me," Ken said. "On my behalf. I want you to follow Brett around and figure out what the deal is with him and his home-wrecking friend Neil and whether they're really in love or whatever you want to call it, and in return, *I'll* spy on Jeremy for you."

"Oh."

What surprised Ken was that Iris was neither wholly in favor of the project nor wholly against it. Instead, Iris split the difference. Iris said that she'd be delighted to spy on Brett for Ken. No problemo. But as far as Jeremy was concerned, she felt a little more ambivalent.

"Why's that?" Ken asked. "If something's good for the goose, then it should be good for the *other* goose, right?"

"I guess so."

"You don't seem too convinced."

"No, it's not that," Iris said. "It's just that sometimes I guess a person would rather not know."

"And would you be one of those people?"

"That's the thing," Iris said. "I don't know!"

They went back into class after the break and found, to their great dismay, that they were going to have to act out some skits. Lucinda told everybody to divide themselves into groups of three, and Iris and Ken grabbed gangly Jeff before he could get conscripted into any other group. Lucinda had each group pick a slip of paper out of this colorful, floppy beach hat that looked exquisitely out of place in the late October classroom, and each slip of paper had a setting written on it plus the subject of a conflict. The idea was for the students to act out a scene demonstrating how that conflict could be avoided or defused. Ken was horrified to discover that their slip read: "Setting—The Meadowlands; Subject—spilled beer."

"I don't even have the slightest idea of what they play at the Meadowlands," Ken said.

"Well don't look at me," Jeff said.

"Boys," Iris said. "It's where the Giants play."

Blank looks.

"The *Giants*. As in football. They play football there, not to mention a bunch of other things. And not that any of that matters, because what matters here is the beer getting spilled in the stands."

Ken found himself looking curiously at Jeff while that last bit of their conversation seeped down to the part of his brain designed to be extra-absorbent to that particular kind of information. "Ah-ha," he thought, *"Jeff couldn't care less about sports."*

"Ken, what do you think?" Iris suddenly asked him.

"About what?"

"About the beer!" Iris cried. "We were trying to decide if the beer was spilled intentionally or whether it was just an accident." She looked around for Lucinda to see if she could get some clarification, but Lucinda was busy refereeing an argument that had broken out at the front of the room.

"Oh, I'd say we should probably make it accidental," Ken said. "I think if you intentionally spill beer on people at sporting matches they're probably allowed to kill you."

"How do you even *get* to the Meadowlands?" Jeff asked nobody in particular.

"You take the bus from the Port Authority or, if you're me, you hop in your car and peel out and you're there in ten seconds."

"You have wheels?" Jeff asked.

"I do indeed," Iris said, "but they're not going to get this skit written for us, so I'm taking over, and as of right now, you, Ken, you're the lout who spilled the beer, and you, Jeff, you're the lout who got the beer spilled all over him, okay?"

"And who do you get to be?" Jeff asked.

"I'm the beer lady," Iris said proudly. "And you, Ken, you're going to offer to buy Jeff a beer, just as a way to say you're sorry. Got it?"

"Got it." Ken couldn't quite put his finger on why, but he suddenly wasn't as put off by the idea of acting in a skit. He didn't care that it was supposed to be set in some violent stadium with a deceptively pastoral name. He didn't care that it was warm, watered-down domestic crap beer sold for the outrageous price of seven bucks a pop—seven bucks! He didn't care about any of that; instead, he gave himself over to the thespian pleasure of buying Jeff a beer.

Walking home later, Iris seemed to have a change of heart. She and Ken had said good-bye to Jeff and they were strolling slowly up Broadway dissecting their night of *thee-ate-er*, and after they'd dodged yet another one of those bossy jogging strollers that had been pressed into regular sidewalk service, Iris took Ken's arm as if to say, "I'm not moving any more. You're going to have to go around me."

Only what she said was, "I'll do it."

"You'll do what?"

"The spying!"

"You will?"

"Yup."

"Both ways, or . . . ?"

"Both ways," Iris said. "I guess in the end it's probably better to know."

"That depends on what you find out," Ken said.

"No," Iris said. "That depends on what *you* find out."

Iris met Ken right after work the next evening at the Warehouse— Ken chose the Upper West Side's only gay bar because of the statistically insignificant chance of running into Jeremy there—and Iris brought some pictures of their quarry. The first was a fresh, fun, outdoor shot of Jeremy on a tennis court. The picture had been taken in the middle of a doubles match, and he was up at the net waiting for his partner to serve behind him. Jeremy had his racquet in one hand and his other hand was tucked up behind his back, hidden away from his opponents' view, the way that doubles players sometimes signal each other when they're planning to poach. Only instead of giving a signal, Jeremy was giving his partner the finger, and from the bright, amused expression on his face, plus the fact that he was obviously aware of the photographer's presence, it was clear that this was all in jest. Jeremy, the picture seemed to indicate, could be a lot of *fun*.

Ken felt like he should probably say something, so he said, "He's good-looking."

"Well, thank you, I guess."

"Well, don't mention it, I guess!"

The second picture showed Iris and Jeremy together. They were at some sort of street fair, but the picture had been taken from relatively close, so it wasn't possible to see exactly what was going on behind them other than the fact that someone had strung some brightly colored pennants across the street and there was some appetizing, opaque smoke in one corner that looked like it might have originated directly underneath some tasty kielbasa. Beyond that, though, there were the same bright, interested eyes, this time trained directly on the photographer.

The third picture, on the other hand, was a horse of a different feather. The photo was printed on heavy, professional-looking paper and it was essentially a black-and-white shot of a license plate. The rest of it was all artsy and out of focus except for the part where Jeremy's face loomed up out of the blur, his chin jutting forward in some sort of weird, determined effort to rally the rest of his face and lead it into the picture.

"Oh," Ken said. "I bet there's a story behind that."

"That there is," Iris said. She told the bartender to keep the drinks coming—and she'd fantasized for *years* about telling a bar-tender to "keep 'em coming"—and then she sat Ken down and told him all about it.

As it would turn out, though, the pictures weren't necessary be-cause on the evening that Ken was planning to intercept Jeremy as he left work, Iris called him up to tell him that *she'd* just heard from Jeremy, and Jeremy wanted to meet Iris after work because he'd gotten extra tickets to some swanky fund-raiser down in the Singer Building—open bar with Grey Goose Vodka—so after all that fuss, all Ken needed to do was show up at the appointed time and wait to see who Iris met and walked off with. Easy as pie.

What was a little less easy was pretending not to know Iris. Ken had gotten to the posh building at 919 Third Avenue a few min-utes before Iris did—obviously the people at Jeremy's consulting firm didn't have things too bad these days—and he just settled himself against a broken newspaper vending machine while he waited. He spotted Iris coming down the street and had to stifle the urge to wave. And then what was *really* strange was that he ac-tually spotted Jeremy before Iris did. Ken had his eyes fixed on the revolving doors and he spotted someone about the right size push-ing his way through the door and popping out the other end and then *not* striding straight off to some pressing engagement, but pausing and shading his eyes with his hand instead. "Over there," Ken wanted to whisper. "She's *over there*."

Jeremy caught sight of Iris—who was mesmerized by the in-dustriousness of a bum methodically trying all the car doors on East Fifty-fifth Street—and his smile lit up. He set out toward Iris and made it almost all the way to his girlfriend before Iris turned around and spotted Jeremy and smiled in recognition. Ken re-minded himself that he was there on a mission and he tried to burn Jeremy's look, his height, his carriage—everything—into his mind, none of which was particularly difficult to do because Je-remy looked just like he did in the pictures. Iris and Jeremy de-scended into the subway at Fifty-first Street and Ken left them to their night out of rubbing elbows with the rich, the not so rich, and the fund-raisers who were there to even the score.

Spying, Ken soon discovered, took a lot of time. On TV, when you spied on people, you just crept up to their window, which was either on the ground floor or served by a well-developed network of ledges and gutters, and then you peered inside right at the moment when the bad guys saw fit to rehash the details of their diabolical plan.

In reality, Ken spent huge amounts of time simply waiting around, and when he wasn't waiting around, he was following Jeremy as he did banal, nonoffensive things like coming home from work; or stopping off at the store; or picking up the dry cleaning, including a plus-size suit that Ken recognized as belonging to Iris. Ken tended to keep a safe distance away except on those instances when Jeremy spoke on his cell phone. Then he'd crowd in as close as he could to listen, banking on the fact that people are supposed to be less attentive to their surroundings when they're blabbing on portable phones.

Restaurants were tricky, Ken discovered, because it was very hard to guarantee that you'd end up seated next to your prey, and even if you did, being a single person at the next table was far more conspicuous than being in a couple or a group. It was strange to think about. Generally speaking, in a crowded restaurant it's much better to have a single person at the table smushed up next to yours because single people take up less room. Plus, *un*like couples, single people won't bicker or, worse, feel the need to stare into each other's gooey, goopy eyes as if hoping—contrary to all prior evidence—to spot something actually going on inside the other person's head. Couples at the next table ruined dinners. Couples could caress, coo, hit a rough patch, pout, sulk, bicker, and then go back to cooing in a cycle that lasted about twenty, maybe twenty-five minutes, and putting up with it was torture. And despite all that, a single person who's just sitting there absorbed in a book still attracts more attention or, for Ken's purposes anyway, was simply more obtrusive, so for the moment, he found himself forgoing restaurants and following Jeremy into bars.

The first time he followed Jeremy into a bar, Ken took a table in the back next to all the flyers and free magazines and tried to make himself inconspicuous by pretending to read a Health Department brochure that featured an animated bear wearing an apron who was apparently going to have a pap smear. Ken realized that he was hideously ill prepared for spying because he didn't have so much as a notebook or a pen, let alone a spy camera hidden inside a paperclip or a stick of gum or something like that. It didn't matter, though, because Jeremy wasn't having a tête-à-tête where Ken would need to transcribe every illicit word; instead, someone arrived and they started chatting and then a few others arrived, and in the end it didn't seem like anything more insidious than the gang getting together to unwind after work. Jeremy went to get another pitcher for the table and apparently his companions were also in the fund-raising business with him, and all of them were in high spirits because they all kept coming back to the subject of some super-rich guy who'd finally given up the ghost after having made any number of huge charitable bequests in his will.

"Don't say anything until I get back!" Jeremy called over from the bar, and everyone laughed. But the subject was just too fresh, just too juicy to waste any more time, because the last thing Ken heard as he stood up and slipped off into the night was one of the friends sighing and then saying—"Oh, wait!"—as he remembered another detail. "Apparently," he said to the bright, expectant faces gathered around him, "his pacemaker was working so well that they couldn't even tell he was dead for the first half hour!"

The first time Ken hit pay dirt was more of an accident than anything else. He'd come to the neighborhood to see if Jeremy went anywhere during lunch, which he didn't, and then he ended up ducking into a Starbucks to wait out a shower, which, at first, had seemed like a nice, normal shower and then, more than a half hour later, seemed like some sort of busted celestial water main because it was pouring down from the sky and splattering up from the sidewalk and it didn't show any sign of letting up.

It didn't matter to Ken, though, because he'd gotten completely absorbed in this article in the paper about the effect of stress on a person's ability to think. These researchers had hooked volunteers up to various electrodes and then fed them a steady supply of simple mathematical questions. And as the subjects answered, the researchers kept a running tally of the correct response rate, which, given how easy the questions were, was something around 95 percent.

And then they blinked the lights on and off and shocked them. They sent a jolt of good, old-fashioned Consolidated Edison electricity coursing through their bodies. And then, as if nothing had happened, they went back to feeding the subjects simple questions. Five divided by five equals what? At 15 percent, what's the tip on a hundred-dollar dinner? As the subjects continued along and answered questions, the scientists would occasionally blink the lights, this time *without* the crippling shock, but the effect was the same. Every time they blinked the lights, the subjects *thought* they were about to get shocked and their scores would dip. Stress, therefore, cripples your judgment.

Fascinating, Ken thought, and on so many different levels. First that someone could take such a subjective, ethereal issue and cram it into such an objective, measurable test. And second, that the tip in the question was actually 15 percent even though Ken was willing to bet that the people at the dinner were jerks who ran their waitress around all night and kept asking her stupid, suspicious questions about whether their Bombay Sapphire Gin martinis were *really* made with Bombay Sapphire Gin, and then tried to stiff her on the tip.

Ken looked up from the paper and felt his heart leap up into his throat.

He was staring straight into Jeremy's eyes.

Quick, what's two plus two?

. . .

Jeremy folded up a dripping umbrella and then brushed away a few strands of wet hair that were plastered to his forehead, but throughout it all, he didn't once divert his steady, expectant gaze away from Ken's eyes. Ken was *thiiiissss* close to cracking and blurting out everything when he suddenly realized that Jeremy hadn't somehow gotten wise to Ken's nefarious doings and appeared out of the rain to bust his kneecaps; he just wanted the table next to Ken's which he couldn't properly claim until Ken removed the stray sections of his paper that were staking out little Arts & Leisure–sized bits of Manhattan real estate.

"Oh," he said, in spite of himself, and then he gathered up his paper and moved it across the fault line created where the two tables touched each other.

"Thanks," Jeremy said. Friendly. Open.

Ken gave a little, tight-lipped smile, one that he hoped would convey the sense that yes, he was polite enough to acknowledge gratitude for liberating table space under his dominion, but no, this was not to be interpreted as an invitation to enter into a discussion about the weather, even if in this case the weather actually was the most interesting thing going on.

Jeremy slid into his seat with this expert swoop of his shoulder that sent his little backpack in for a landing ahead of him. And then, to Ken's great consternation, he didn't do anything. He'd put some sort of elaborate coffee and whipped cream combination down on the table in front of him and then went about—who knows what the proper word for it is—*customizing* it with various chunks of brown sugar and clouds of cinnamon, all of which he thoughtfully stirred into his drink. And then he just sat there. He wasn't like all the other people that Ken had been watching who pulled out a cell phone and started yakking or pulled out laptops and started stuffing them full of little peckity-peck bits of information. Or even the occasional atavistic nut job who'd pull out an old-fashioned leather-bound agenda crammed with an entire hooray-we-landed-on-the-moon ticker tape parade full of remind-me notes. Nope. All Jeremy did was sit there and sip his coffee.

Ken didn't think that Jeremy was waiting for someone because he didn't do any of the telltale things that people do when they're waiting, like looking at their watches or paying a certain degree of attention to what's going on near the door. Ken buried himself back in the paper and tried to refocus on what he'd been reading, but for some reason all the letters in the articles seemed to have decided to go for a swim around the page. Hopeless. If he had a Walkman he could've plugged that into his ears and pretended to listen to music, which not only would give him something inconspicuous to do, but would also explain away the steady, rhythmic thumping sound that was emanating from his chest. Instead, nothing happened and a rare calm descended over the entire place, finally punctuated by the bony society matron parked next to the window across from Ken and Jeremy. The lady flipped open a cell phone, dialed a number, and then nothing happened for a while until she said, quite distinctly and quite loudly, with no preceding salutation—"Manhattan."

A pause. Then "Merck."

Then she didn't say anything else. She wrote something down on a piece of paper and flipped the phone shut, only to flip it right back open a few seconds later to repeat the same, strange procedure. "Manhattan." A pause. And then very distinctly, "Glaxo-SmithKline." She wrote something down again. "Manhattan." Tick-tock, tick-tock. "Schering-Plough." *Scratchity scratch scratch* went the Cartier pen.

"Excuse me," a voice said in Ken's ear and he nearly jumped out of his skin. It was Jeremy.

"Yes?"

"Would you mind guarding my spot for a moment?"

"I'm sorry?"

"My spot. They sometimes get a little too ambitious here in terms of clearing up the tables and I'm not done with this. I'll be right back."

"Oh, okay," Ken said. "No problem." He watched Jeremy disappear off toward the restrooms and then reappear just as quickly, making a beeline for the counter where the bored clerk handed over a tiny, little key chained to a huge wooden baton that looked just like a billy club—a jack-booted, union-busting billy club—and Ken thought, "Oh *right*, I was *wondering* what ever happened to union-busting goons."

"Manhattan," the rich bitch said. Ken swiveled around to look at her. "Bristol-Myers Squibb." He gave her a nasty look, which she registered, though not with enough offense to give Ken any sort of satisfaction, and then she jotted something down on her page and clicked her pen closed with what was surely some sort of exclusive, Cartier designed, Morse code equivalent of *"Fuck you."*

Jeremy had taken his backpack with him, so Ken didn't have to face the unpleasant question of whether he would've had the guts to take a peek inside (he wouldn't) and Jeremy didn't dillydally in the restroom either. Instead, he came striding back out, handed the jack-booted, union-busting billy club back to the bored clerk, and then came back to his seat. On the *way*, though, he paused near the door and flipped his own cell phone open and peered at it, evidently satisfying himself that he was getting reception.

"Thanks," he said, and Ken gave an encore performance of his tight-lipped smile.

The rich bitch evidently wasn't the type of person to beat around the bush. She wasn't the type of person who'd dial a number and then waste everybody's precious time by saying "hello" and asking if she might be permitted to speak with somebody in customer service. Please. Instead, she boiled the entire transaction down into two words—*"Customer Service"*—which she magically transformed from the hospitable, winsome nouns that they once were into the flinty, rigid imperative that they'd now become. And it seemed to work.

She started back up at the top of her list with Merck, and told the poor slob on the other end of the line who'd had the double misfortune of (a) being born; and (b) answering the rich bitch's call, that she wanted to know how many calories there were in their appetite suppressants.

There was a brief pause that corresponded rather precisely to the time it would take an underpaid slob in a beige burlap-lined cubicle at Merck to say, "I beg your pardon?"

"*Calories,*" the rich bitch said. "I believe you know what calories are, yes? Well, what I'm trying to find out is how many calories there are in the standard dose of your appetite suppressant. You know, Roche makes Xenical and Abbott Labs makes Meridia and you make one too, and what I want to know is how many calories there are in it?"

Another brief pause.

"Well, why *don't* you know that?"

A longer pause this time, and for some reason Ken found himself thinking about those segments on the news that they always had at the beginning of hunting season where people are out in a swamp somewhere at the crack of dawn and they point their shotguns toward the sky and blast a duck full of lead but the duck keeps on desperately, instinctively flapping its wings for a few more seconds even though it's already dead as a doornail and never really stood a chance in the first place.

"Listen, you're a *scientist,*" the rich bitch spat the last word out. "And what I'm asking you—what I am *trying* to ask you—is a *scientific* question, so I cannot fathom why you are making this so unnecessarily difficult. Everything has calories in it. Unless it's something like Diet Coke or sparkling water or something along those lines, right? And your fat-burning pills are made out of *something*, right? So unless your appetite suppressant is made entirely out of *Diet Coke*, which I very much doubt, then it has to have a certain number of calories in it, right? And what I want to know is how many. I don't think I can make it any simpler than that."

A tiny, little micro-pause.

"No! You may *not* ask me to me hold for a moment."

Forgetting all about trying to look inconspicuous, Ken caught Jeremy's glance and they both let themselves stare straight into each other's eyes for a split second longer than normal, the way New Yorkers do to mutually signal their unspoken subscription to the same point of view. To wit: *What a moron.*

"If you put me on hold," the rich bitch said, "I swear to God I'll—"

"You'll *what*?" This time the voice on the other end was loud enough to be heard.

And the bitch changed tactics. In the tried-and-true tradition of successful warriors since time immemorial, she simply opened a second front. She asked to speak to the Merck slob's supervisor.

There was a bit of mumbling from the phone, and then, quite distinctly, the Merck slob said that he was transferring the call to his supervisor, but in case they got disconnected, she should just call back and ask for the supervisor directly, and his name was *"Bite Me!"* And the line went dead.

Ken looked at Jeremy and Jeremy looked at Ken, and then they both looked over toward the counter where the clerk was sending a screaming geyser of steam up through a stainless-steel cup of milk even though there weren't any customers who'd ordered anything. The clerk's shoulders convulsed ever so slightly and he turned his back more resolutely on the rest of the room and leaned up against the machine and tried to turn the steam up louder and when even that didn't work, he gave up all pretense: he was laughing so hard there were tears running down his red, freshly steamed face.

The rich bitch didn't fare much better with GlaxoSmithKline, although she improved her argument by telling them that *Merck* had been able to furnish her with the information right away, and if *they* could, she didn't see why GlaxoSmithKline couldn't. She said that perhaps she should just bring her *custom* to Merck, but by that point Ken wasn't really following the proceedings any longer because Jeremy had gotten his own telephone call.

It was obvious that Jeremy's call didn't have anything to do with work because Jeremy didn't slip into that very distinctive, very businessy way of talking that Ken knew so well from his days at Leighton Fennell. Instead, Jeremy's voice was fairly soft and evenly modulated and he chatted with whoever was on the other end about everything and nothing at the same time. Everything because they really did cover everything—what Jeremy had done over the weekend (biking in the park; driving up the Palisades; hitting the junk shops on the way back down); what Jeremy had for dinner last night (penne with cream sauce and smoked salmon). And nothing, because he never once mentioned Iris even though Ken already knew that Jeremy had gone biking in the park with Iris, that he'd driven up the Palisades with Iris, that he'd trawled the junk shops on the way back down with Iris, and that it was Iris who had made the penne with cream sauce and smoked salmon while Jeremy cracked open the white wine and set the table because it was *Iris* who'd spotted the smoked salmon on special at the Fairway near the 125th Street exit on the way back into town and said that those sort of prices were too good to pass up.

Jeremy asked whoever it was on the phone if they were still on for Saturday night and then they said good-bye and he gathered his stuff up to leave. He smiled at Ken as he slipped out from behind the table and climbed into the harness of his backpack before he changed his mind at the door. At the door he hesitated, gazed out onto the street, and then unslung his backpack and held it up over his head as he dashed out into the deluge.

Chapter Ten. In Which Iris Finds
Herself Quite Uncharacteristically
Swept Off Her Feet

"How come stuff like this only happens to me?" Iris wondered. None of the Filipino drag queens gathered around her seemed to have the answer to that question, not even the one who was sitting in her lap with his arms around her neck making pouty eyes for the guy taking their picture.

"*Cheese!*"

When she came to the Warehouse, Iris was trying to be inconspicuous. It had been deliciously thrilling for her to pull open the door of a gay bar all on her own, but she reminded herself that she was there on a mission. She was there to bide her time until, she hoped, Brett and his home-wrecking friend came in and she got to spy on them. Instead, she found herself next to a group of Filipinos who'd somehow managed to convince the management that they weren't thirteen years old and, as a result, had managed to get themselves served. Quite well served, in fact.

Iris could say with some level of confidence that some members of the gang were unequivocally male and that others were unequivocally female, but the rest were anybody's guess, and no matter what else you could say about them—other than the impression they gave of having just escaped from the prom at a vocational high school for beauticians—the fact of the matter was that they were having themselves some fun. A *lot* of fun. Iris was intrigued by the fact that everything about them was somehow accessorized with various spare parts. The key chain plunked down in the middle of their table, for example, had a tiny stuffed koala bear clipped to it. And clipped to the back of the tiny stuffed koala was an even tinier stuffed panda. Even their drinks had little paper umbrellas or glowing swizzle sticks poking up out of the plastic lotus blossoms floating around in them. And then one of them tried to smoke and he got a quick lesson in New York's début-de-siècle antismoking laws and that put the kibosh on their cigarettes. For about ten seconds, because one of them found something better to do with the pack. He held it up horizontally in front of his face as if it were a camera and then clicked his lighter into a flame right next to it, mimicking a flashbulb going off.

The rest of the crowd blinked for a moment, and then the hilarity of it sank in—*he took our picture with his cigarettes!*—and they burst into screams of laughter. From there, pandemonium broke loose. Every single one of them had cigarettes and every single one of them had a lighter and they took pictures of each other in every conceivable pose and in every conceivable combination. And Iris didn't spot the inevitable until it was too late and she found herself being dragged into the undertow of their fun, and before she could say no, they were all piling around her until she felt like she was the lone, sane eye staring out of one of those pyramids on the back of a dollar bill, and they took their picture with her.

Hilarious.

A frozen, pastel-colored drink loomed up out of nowhere and landed on the table directly in front of her, and all that Iris could think was that it looked like a postapocalyptic ski resort: little avalanches of turquoise slush crossing paths underneath the burntout shards of these strange sticks that might once have been trees. "Nothing on God's green earth," she thought, "could make me feel any more conspicuous."

Until the waiter pulled out a lighter and lit the strange, barren stalks sticking out of the miniature nuclear winter in front of her and Iris realized that they were sparklers.

"I stand corrected," she thought.

Tracking down Brett was definitely not going to be easy.

In the first place, there was no way she was planning to set foot in *Sweat!* even though Ken had told her all about the place and said that Brett spent most of his free time there and that's where she'd be able to observe him most easily. Unfortunately, that was precisely the problem, because if she could easily observe Brett, then everyone else could just as easily observe *her*, and Iris didn't exactly warm to the idea of being stared at in that kind of place. She could just imagine the look she'd get from whatever nasty anorexic bitch was sitting at the front desk when she showed up. Still, Ken made it all sound so simple—all she'd have to do was go up to the front desk and smile and say hello and tell them she'd just moved into the neighborhood and was looking for a place to work out and let them vie for her business.

"*Vie* for my business? Are you serious?"

"Of course I'm serious," Ken said.

"Ken, nobody is going to *vie* for my business, least of all some über-snotty gym."

"Well, why wouldn't they? Your money is just as good as theirs, isn't it?"

"Do I really need to spell it out for you?" Iris asked. "Snotty gyms look for a certain type of customer, and I don't happen to *correspond* to that type of customer. As a matter of fact, I don't correspond to their second choice either or their last choice for that matter. And they're certainly not going to be enthusiastic about giving me a free day pass just to get my business when they don't want my business in the first place."

"Well, who cares whether they're *enthusiastic* about it, all that matters is whether you get in, and to do that, all you have to do is—"

"Ken, I'm not going to do it. End of discussion. No more *Sweat! Sweat!* is stricken from the list of acceptable subjects of conversation we're permitted to broach. Although speaking of which, what were you doing going out with someone who goes to a gym like that in the first place?"

"Goes where?" Ken asked.

"To *Sweat!*" Iris cried. "Jeez Louise, Ken, try to pay attention here!"

"But I thought you just said that *Sweat!* was off limits. You just said that—"

"Never mind what I said," Iris said. "Let's move on to Plan B."

Unfortunately, there weren't too many other bright ideas, although one thought that Ken had was for Iris to give Brett a taste of his own medicine.

"Meaning what?" Iris asked.

"Meaning we get you a clipboard and we make up a fake survey and you stand out on the street and wait for him to come by and then you pretend that you represent some charity and you're gathering data and you ask him if you can take ten minutes of his time and then we ask him anything we want."

"You want me to pretend to be from a fake AIDS charity, is that it?" Iris asked.

"Well, put like that it doesn't have quite the same . . ."

"The same what?"

"I don't know," Ken said. "The same *verve*. Whatever 'verve' is . . ."

They talked about it a little more and concluded that there was probably a very special, very uncomfortable place in hell reserved for people who impersonated AIDS charities, so they had to drop the idea.

And that's how they wound up with the very conventional plan of just following Brett around. Only unlike with Jeremy, the plan wasn't for Iris to lurk in the background and spy on Brett from a distance; the plan was to find a way for Iris to insinuate herself right into Brett's life. Watching Jeremy from a distance would explain what he was doing and with whom, but watching Brett from a distance wasn't going to shed any light on anything. To figure out what the deal was with Brett and Home-Wrecker, Iris would need to get inside Brett's head. She'd need to get inside his head and make herself right at home.

From a philosophical standpoint, it posed an interesting question— how do you insinuate yourself into somebody else's life? Should she just walk up to him during happy hour at some bar somewhere, the kind of place where they had trays piled high with free, iridescently red, spicy buffalo wings next to a big bowl of creamy blue-cheese sauce, and then tap him on the shoulder and say, "I'm Iris"?

And he'd say, "You've got a bit of tangy barbeque sauce on your chin there, Iris."

And she'd wipe it off with the free double-ply napkin that she had under her paper plate and throw back her head and laugh and say, "Well, there's plenty more where *that* came from. So where were we, anyway?"

Probably not.

People just don't do that. People have their friends and they're usually not looking for any more, even if those potential new friends are fun-loving people like Iris who are ready to tell amusing stories about the psycho cat lady who used to live upstairs from her who totally denied even *having* a cat even though Iris could clearly hear it scratching the floor around the same time every evening. It's as if some booming voice up in the sky somewhere had called out—"Okay, *time's up*"—and everyone on the playground was supposed to be friends with the people they were with right at that moment, and Iris was left there thinking, "But I didn't understand the rules. Can't we have a do-over?"

Sorry, no do-overs.

Iris sighed and decided that it probably didn't matter anyway. No, most people didn't seem to be open to making new friends, and no, they didn't want to hear her funny cat lady story, but that was basically okay because in the end, it was the lady upstairs who'd been right and it was Iris who'd been wrong. The lady upstairs wasn't in denial about having a cat; she was just a fussy woman who lived alone and combed out the fringes of her oriental carpets before going to bed, evidently under the impression that this would make them last longer.

How long is anyone's guess, because the catless cat lady didn't last very long herself. She went over to Mount Sinai for what was supposed to be a routine outpatient colonoscopy and just never came back. A social worker came over that night and packed a small bag for her, and then a few weeks later the same social worker came back and packed a huge suitcase, and then the next thing Iris knew the lady's apartment was being sold. Some renovation company showed up and clomped around up there raising Cain, and to save time, the workers loaded all the soft things—her clothes, the cushions from the couch, the pretty oriental rugs—into huge garbage bags and just dropped them out the window down into the dumpster waiting below.

They spiffed the place up a bit with a couple of quick coats of paint and then started showing the apartment to horrible people who turned up in droves, but by that point Jeremy was talking more and more about moving in together and how moving in would be the *right step* for them and Iris heard herself saying yes. And as the new upstairs neighbors began a full-on assault—knocking down freshly painted walls and tearing up recently waxed floors—Iris quietly moved out.

Iris licked her thumb and her index finger and *tzzzzisssttt*'d out the sparklers in her drink. Might as well knock it back before clearing out and reporting back to Ken that Brett and his home-wrecking pal never showed up. She fished around in her purse for something about the same size as a pack of cigarettes, and the best she could do was a package of Rite Aid's house brand of cough drop. Sugarless Honey-Lemon. "Well, beggars can't be choosers," she thought, handing it over to her Filipino drag queens so they could take her picture with *her* camera and then lifting her glass along with theirs. "Here's mud in your eye!"

Iris walked down Seventieth Street to the Santa Monica and rang the bell for Ken's apartment. "It's me," she said when the intercom crackled to life, and she planted her hip against the door to push at the very first sign of a buzz even though Ken was the kind of person who was overly generous in his estimated buzz times. She took the elevator to the fourth floor and walked through Ken's open door, shutting it behind her.

"You'll never guess who just called," Ken said.

"Especially if I don't even try," Iris said. "So who was it?"

"Jeff."

"Jeff the kid from class? The one who chucks computers at unsuspecting professors?"

"That's the one."

"What'd he want?" Iris asked.

"He said he was making spaghetti alla Bolognese, but he was out of tomato sauce."

"Well, that certainly warrants a call."

"I wasn't done yet," Ken said. "Anyway, he said that he *thought* he had a jar of tomato sauce somewhere because *everyone* has a jar of tomato sauce somewhere—it's some sort of rule—but he turned the kitchen inside out and he was one hundred percent out of tomato sauce."

"So?"

"Oh, so he wanted to know if you could use Bloody Mary mix instead."

"Well, what did you say?" Iris asked.

"I said I didn't see why not."

"I didn't know that you two were on telephone terms."

"We weren't," Ken said. "Until now, I guess."

"Wait a second," Iris said. "Did *he* say he was making spaghetti alla Bolognese?"

"That's what I just told you," Ken said.

"No, that's not what I meant," Iris said. "What I meant was, out of whose mouth did the words 'spaghetti alla Bolognese' come?"

"Well, mine," Ken said.

"*Ah-ha!*"

"He said he was making spaghetti with a meaty tomato sauce,

and spaghetti with a meaty tomato sauce happens to go by another name, which is to say, spaghetti alla Bolognese, so I thought that in telling you *why* he called, I'd just save some time and hassle and make things more clear and call it by its proper name."

Iris was enjoying watching Ken flail. "And how did it work out?"

"How did what work out?"

"All the time you just saved!"

"Just for that, I'm not inviting you over next time I make . . . *pasta*," Ken said, and they both laughed. It was so much fun catching Ken with his hand in the cookie jar, Iris thought, before she realized that that didn't make any sense at all.

Ken made room for Iris on the couch, and she briefed him on her less than successful foray into the Warehouse. When that wound down, they started paying more attention to the TV, which was showing one of those programs with cute amateur video footage of people fainting at weddings, babies vomiting into baptismal fonts, and kids falling into the orchestra pits during elementary school productions of *The Nutcracker*. That sort of thing. And Ken was eating it up. He had this well-oiled system of gently muting the annoying banter but then bringing the sound back up when they got to the good stuff. Even better, he seemed to be able to spot what was going to happen before anyone else. "Have you seen this before?" Iris asked.

"This show, or this episode?"

"This episode, what we're watching right now."

"No," Ken said. "Not that I know of." But the minute a grandmother in a tight, curly perm wandered into footage of a birthday celebration, Ken said, "That's flammable hair she's got there!" and sure enough, a few moments later, the grandmother had leaned in too close to the cake and everyone was trying to swat out the fire on her head.

But despite Ken's enthusiasm, Iris just couldn't seem to get into the show. It wasn't that she had anything against watching carefully decorated sheet cakes sliding off their trays at people's fortieth anniversaries or watching a bridesmaid getting her teeth kicked in by the bridesmaids who *didn't* catch the bouquet; that wasn't it. It was hard to put her finger on it, but it was the way that everything in the show was about couples and families. There weren't any hilarious videos showing some single person trying to stand on a rickety ironing board to put the star on a Christmas tree—plus the *hilarious* aftermath—for the simple reason that it takes two. It takes one person to fall off the ironing board and into the Christmas tree but it takes another one to *film* it. Not to mention that there's some unwritten rule out there that says single people aren't allowed to buy Christmas trees. It depresses the gas station attendants who sell them.

That was the thing. Being single stank. Being single meant being shunted off to the sidelines of society. Ken was back to being single and look at him—sitting on his couch bathed in the flickering blue glow of couples and families who were having fun. And with the way things were going with Jeremy, Iris was hot on his heels. She let herself drift backward in time, back to before she met Jeremy at Macy's. It hadn't been awful; it wasn't as if she cried herself to sleep every night, but by the same token, that whole period just seemed sort of flat and nondescript. Before Jeremy appeared on the scene, Iris was hard-pressed to recall what she used to *do* with her time.

And dating had been a nightmare. Dating had been disastrous. Dating had been one disappointment after another, which would've been easy enough to take except that those disappointments were . . . spaced . . . out . . . over . . . time . . . and it seemed to take forever just to get up to the plate only to have it all come crashing down. She remembered going out with one guy who literally pulled out the personal ads and started skimming them during their coffee together. She remembered going out with another guy who had this distant, distracted air that was kind of intriguing, right up to the moment when she asked him where he'd grown up and he'd answered, "Who, me?"

There were some guys out there who were clearly looking for a free maid and other guys who were vaguely looking for a second mother. There were guys who were morbidly afraid of commitment, and there were a few guys out there who weren't—guys who genuinely wanted to find a serious girlfriend—they just didn't want their wives to know about it.

Oh, and the exes! The staggering number of men Iris met who were wrapped up one way or another with their exes! She'd meet someone who was interesting and intelligent, and the only fly in the ointment would be this guy's penchant for going on and on about his ex-girlfriend Courtney who was a perfect size four and had the home number of the most gifted colorist in Manhattan and was a pathological liar, psychopath, and all-around menace to society. "But don't worry, I'm *so* over her," the new guy would say. "She is *so* not a part of my life anymore." And Iris would take him at his word and forget about it altogether until the fourth date when Iris would finally meet the new guy's roommate—a willowy young thing with gorgeous, blond highlights who, needless to say, answered to the name "Courtney."

Why was everybody still involved on some level or another with their ex? Whatever happened to just being single? Whatever happened to just being available without having a hideously complex network of exes and quasi-exes and all of *their* respective exes and quasi-exes milling around like a cross between a Greek chorus and an air-raid drill?

And that's one of the reasons that Iris was so happy to have met Jeremy—he came free and clear. There weren't any nefarious, though exquisitely coiffed, Courtneys lurking around his mind. Jeremy had friends he cared for and who obviously cared for him, but when the elevator got itself stuck at Macy's, Jeremy was as single as the day was long, and that's not something you see all the time.

Plus Jeremy was fun. Jeremy wanted to do things. Jeremy was always asking, "So what's the plan?" and then coming up with one if nobody else had any ideas. It made Iris smile to think about it, but when they'd been together for only a few months, Jeremy found these *wildly* inexpensive tickets to the Bahamas and he rallied Iris and some of the troops and said that tickets that cheap don't just turn up every day and that it would be *criminal* not to take advantage of the offer, so reservations were secured and arrangements were made, and when they arrived in Nassau, Iris quietly slipped the in-flight magazine that Jeremy had been reading out of the seatback pocket and into her bag. Jeremy had been working on the crossword puzzle in the back, and later that evening, while Jeremy was getting ready for dinner, Iris looked over the puzzle and found that Jeremy had correctly filled in the word élan just from the clue joie de vivre. And that was Jeremy, pure and simple—he had joy on the tip of his tongue.

Iris didn't really remember all that much about their whirlwind vacation in the Bahamas, other than sitting in a roadside café with everyone late one afternoon drinking beer out on the terrace, waiting for the sun to set. A rusty old jalopy spluttered up to the curb directly in front of their table, parked, and disgorged about eleven people, all of whom immediately evaporated, leaving just a miserable dog yapping away inside the empty car which was now blocking their view, meaning that the six of them were now sitting there in a loose semicircle staring directly at an unhappy dog whimpering in a pile of junk. And then there were only five of them, because Jeremy sprang into action.

Jeremy enlisted the owner of the bar and he enlisted some patrons from inside and when the dust settled, the car had been pushed a hundred yards farther along the road and the dog had been sprung from its clunker of a prison. They tied the dog up next to the bar where, in an unusual move for an animal that had *just* escaped death by dehydration, he waddled over to the closest table, lifted his leg, and unleashed a long, vigorous stream of urine. And that, in a nutshell, was Jeremy. Jeremy took charge. Jeremy got things done.

Iris noticed that Ken was starting to fade so she fussed around a bit with the cushions on the couch and then put her shoes back on and announced that she'd better be on her way.

"Already?"

"*Already?*" Iris said. "Sweetie, some of us work for a living."

"Ah, the lucky few."

"So I'll see you tomorrow in class?"

"That you can count on."

Iris undid the locks and rebuffed Ken's offer to walk her home and she walked up Seventieth Street to Broadway and was cutting through the little subway island in the middle of Broadway at Seventy-second when there—*bam*—right in front of her, was Brett! The same Brett from the photo Ken had shown her. The same Brett from the sneaker commercial. There wasn't the slightest doubt in her mind—it was Brett. It was Brett and some guy who seemed to be saying good-bye to two other guys at the entrance to the subway. Iris stopped right where she was and stared.

It was about as plain as the nose on your face that the two couples had been out together for the evening and that one of the couples was being dropped off for the long haul back home. And it was equally clear that everyone had had a good time. Brett and the guy next to him were rather couple-ish, not in the nauseating way where one person's hand always has to be on the other person's neck, but there was a certain complicity there. They didn't talk over each other, and it seemed, to Iris anyway, that when one of them said something funny, the other one seemed to build on top of it because the other couple kept laughing harder and harder and looking from Brett to Home-Wrecker and then back again.

Home-Wrecker was handsome and was probably the beneficiary of a very comprehensive dental plan, because the overall impression Iris was left with was his smile glinting in the night. Straight hair. Nice straight teeth. A little too old to be called preppy, but that was the look he was after. Clean-cut. Certainly not the monstrous image that Iris had been cultivating up to that point.

Iris moved in a little closer to try to listen to what they were saying, but that turned out to be a mistake because their entire foursome suddenly surged toward her to make room for some insane guy who came zooming along pushing a rolling garment rack that held, as far as Iris could tell, about two dozen space suits—all orangey and silvery with little accordion joints—and by the time it had all swooshed by, Iris found herself standing practically in the middle of their conversation, so she turned around to study one of the signs plastered all over the wall behind her and then tore off one of the precut tabs with the contact information just for a little extra credibility and stuffed it in her pocket.

She could hear the boys chatting and was just about to crane her neck around to get a better look when suddenly she felt herself jerked sideways. Iris was now staring at a *different* notice with *different* precut tabs and she couldn't figure how that had happened.

"What the . . . ?"

She reached out to steady herself against the wall, but then the tremendous jerking force came back and when it did, it ripped Iris and a handful of tabs sideways. *"Argghh!"* She couldn't do any better than that, and no matter how hard she struggled, her body just wouldn't stay centered over her feet. Her feet were there, back there, and her body was here, and that meant that she was falling but she couldn't seem to do anything about it or figure out why she was half falling, half being dragged somewhere, nor could she *say* anything about this new turn of events other than, *"Garrgh!"* Her hands went up to her throat and pulled down instinctively on something that felt like her own purse strap, and out of the corner of her eye she could see a weird swirl of orange and silver and, naturally enough, everybody gawking at her, and she finally realized that her purse was caught on a second garment rack following the first, and that the methamphetamine freak pulling the rack along didn't have the slightest idea of whether he'd gotten a wheel stuck in a storm drain, in which case a few more violent tugs should do the trick, or whether he'd hooked Iris, in which case a few more violent tugs would be the end of the fruitful relationship she'd had up until then with her own larynx.

"Garrrgh!"

Iris desperately tried to keep up with the rack but she stumbled amongst the slithery space suits and even as she fell and her hands splayed out in front of her, her knees never hit the ground and instead she found herself being dragged along and choked. "Hey!" she heard a voice say. It came from somewhere behind her, back from where her foursome had been. "*Hey!*"

Suddenly there were two hands on Iris's arms pulling her backward, and that was even worse because now she was being drawn and quartered, only it was some sort of low-budget drawing and quartering because she was only getting torn in half, and then the hands seemed to realize their mistake because a moment later they were grasping for the rack itself, and then other hands joined in and they stopped the rack, and Iris tried to stand up, but she was still all tangled up against the rack.

"Are you all right?"

Iris reflexively put her hand up against her windpipe, which was, broadly speaking, still where it was supposed to be. "I think so," she managed to croak.

"Don't get up," the voice said, which turned out to belong to Brett. He parked her on the curb and extricated her from her purse and then extricated her purse from the rack while the other guys started yelling at the meth freak who'd been pulling the rack along in the first place. "What the fuck's the matter with you?" Home-Wrecker's downtown friend seemed genuinely enraged. "Do you even look where you're going? Do you even have any idea of what you almost did? Do you see that woman sitting back there? You did that!"

The rack guy didn't care at all, which made Iris's defenders even madder. One of them was saying something about how people can't just go around running over other people, and the other was scanning the horizon in the hope of spotting a cop—sure, *dream on*—and throughout it all Brett stayed with Iris, crouching down next to the curb and, mercifully, shielding her a little from the crowd that had instantaneously gathered. Iris could barely take it all in. Brett was just as handsome as he was in the sneaker commercial, and despite the fact that he and his friends had been out all evening, he gave off this very fresh, very clean scent. He had his hand on her back and Iris just couldn't seem to put two and two together. How had Brett's hand ended up on her back? Why was she sitting on the curb? Was there a proper way to sit on the curb?

"Where do you live?" Brett asked. Iris had to think about that for a second. "Where were you heading?"

Oh, right. It all came back. Ken's house. Spying. The rack of ready-to-wear space suits. "Ken," she said, pronouncing it as simply and as clearly as she could. Brett looked directly at her and she realized her error.

"Can you give me a hand up?" she asked. "I think I'm fine now, I just had the wind knocked out of me."

"That's the least you can say," Brett said. "Just give it a few more seconds." He made her breathe slowly and then he made her stretch and flex each limb. The other guys reported back that the rack guy had taken off, and no, nobody got his license plate because garment racks don't *have* license plates even though they probably should and it was outrageous that people could behave like that and if Iris wanted, they could all serve as witnesses. Brett and Home-Wrecker helped Iris up and her head really did start to swim for a second, and they insisted that they walk her home while she insisted that she was fine. She got them to back down by agreeing to take down their numbers, and Brett pulled out a pen and asked Iris if she had any paper, and she pulled out the precut tabs that she'd pulled off the poster just moments earlier and passed one of them to Brett. He used his wallet to supply a hard surface and he flipped the paper over to its blank side and wrote down his name and number and then handed it back to Iris and then everybody thanked everybody and Iris went on her way. She still felt a little fragile and trembly, so she dutifully waited at each corner for the WALK sign to flash, finding herself amid this secret club of law-abiding people she'd never noticed before that was made up of old people and German tourists. Halfway home she pulled the paper back out just to make sure the whole thing hadn't been a dream, and there it was, "Brett Manikin" along with his address on Sixty-sixth Street and his number. She folded the paper in half again and only then thought about looking to see what those ads were all about in the first place, so she took them out of her pocket and read the notices. The first one said: "Enhance Your Anal Orgasm." The other one said: "Have You Seen My Son?"

Chapter Eleven. In Which Ken Learns to Embrace Failure

On his way down from City College, Ken's train got stuck in a tunnel—*naturally*—so he only barely managed to dash into Lucinda's classroom before the bell rang. He slipped into his seat, noticing that most of the class was glumly leafing through a handout entitled "Substance Abuse," whereas Iris looked positively electrified. She was bursting at the seams with *something*.

The whole first half of the lesson was devoted to substance abuse, mostly alcohol. But instead of dragging everybody down into the dumps by droning on about the evils of drinking, Lucinda took a different tack and talked up the benefits of *responsible* drinking.

Responsible drinking? That didn't sound too bad.

And it wasn't. Lucinda had all sorts of clever strategies worked out. She said to brush your teeth right after dinner and you'll be more reluctant to keep drinking on into the evening because it'll mess up all that tooth-brushing effort. She said to drink a lot of water right before you go to a party because then you'll feel like you're full and you won't drink as much. And as she ticked through her strategies, the mood in the room changed course like a school of fish turning in the water. When Lucinda was talking about strategies for a party, everyone got to imagine their own personal version of the party in question. Six-packs. Soirées. Coats thrown on the bed. Evenings saved by resourceful friends who knew how to open a wine bottle with nothing more than a nail and a fork.

When the break came, Ken was absolutely bowled over by Iris's report of the events that had occurred after she'd left his house the night before. He simply could not get over the fact that she'd met Brett, not to mention his entourage, and that she had his address and number.

"Well, some would say that the more salient point is that I was nearly killed," Iris said. "And for the sake of fashion, no less."

"Oh, sorry about that," Ken said. "I guess that must've been pretty awful?"

"It wasn't a walk in the park, I'll tell you that much," Iris said. "But it was basically over before I even realized what was happening."

"You could've been the next Isadora Duncan."

"Who's Isadora Duncan?" Iris asked.

"Who *was* Isadora Duncan," Ken said. "She's famous because her scarf got caught in the wheels of her car and it broke her neck."

"Yuck," Iris said. "Well, was she famous for anything else or just for the scarf thingy?"

"Oh. No, I mean, she was a dancer and already famous and all that, so I guess it's not a perfect analogy. Anyway, what did Jeremy say?"

"About Isadora What's-Her-Face?"

"No, about this," Ken said, tracing his finger along Iris's neck just above the collarbone where a faint, but distinct, bruise could be discerned.

"This what?"

"You've got a bruise here," Ken said. "It looks like a hickey."

"A *hickey*?" Iris laughed. "Did you just say 'hickey'? I didn't know that they still had hickeys. I thought that hickeys went the way of cod-liver oil and truancy officers."

"Well, I'm no expert, but I'd say that they're still around, and you look just like you have one. Jeremy didn't say anything about it?"

Iris was a bit more subdued than she'd been a moment before. "No," she said. "He didn't say a thing."

Ken had about a million questions for Iris, but they weren't getting anyone anywhere. "How did Brett seem? Did he seem, you know, *racked by regret*? Was Home-Wrecker awful? What did he look like? Did he have shifty eyes?"

"I don't even know what shifty eyes *are*!" Iris pleaded. "And I don't remember. I mean, I told you that it was over practically before it started, and he seemed, well, he seemed nice enough and he tried to help me; they all tried to help me, which is more than I can say for most people."

Ken didn't seem entirely satisfied. He tried another tactic. "All right, let's get back to the basics. You were saying that Home-Wrecker stank, right?"

"*Ken,*" Iris said. "If he'd stunk, you'd have been the first to know, but he didn't, okay?"

"And he didn't pick your pocket while you were unconscious?" Ken asked weakly.

Iris laughed. "No, and I wasn't ever unconscious, I was just rattled."

"So what you're saying is that he picked your pocket while you were rattled?"

Iris laughed again. "That's right," she said. "That *bastard*!"

After the break, Lucinda gave an overview of their remaining classes, which weren't very many, and then she passed out all the corrected homework that had been accumulating and collected the new batch. Then she divided the class into teams of two and handed each team a deck of cards and went on to explain the card game that they were going to play, which definitely kept the good mood afloat. "Except," she said, "you're going to write down what you're feeling as you play the game."

"I don't understand." That was Jeff.

"You don't understand because you haven't let me explain it yet," Lucinda said, passing out sheets of paper. "What you're going to do is to write down exactly how you're feeling at the beginning and end of each hand, okay? Whatever it is you're feeling." Everybody seemed eager to get the game under way, though Ken had taken advantage of the instructions and the distribution of the paper to actually count the cards in his deck. He'd had to do it at warp speed, but whatever the result was, it certainly wasn't fifty-two; that was for sure. Forty-four, maybe forty-five, but certainly not fifty-two. This game was rigged.

"Mr. Connelly?" Ken dropped his deck and scrambled to scoop the cards back up. "Are you planning to write something down or shall we just assume that you're not feeling anything at all?"

"Mea culpa," Ken said. He took out his paper and wrote, "I feel hopeful."

And then they started playing and, naturally enough, losing. Ken could see that the point of the exercise was to keep track of your feelings as everything goes wrong around you, as the world conspires against you, so he dutifully played along by noting down responses like "disappointed," "surprised," "incredulous," "*angry.*" Nobody else seemed to catch on that they were never going to win, and the results were themselves interesting, since some people laughed it off and other people took it very personally and got mad at each other until, inevitably, someone with a short fuse threw his cards up in the air and accused his partner of cheating. The partner countered with the time-honored defense that his accuser was a "fucking asshole," and Lucinda swept in and ended the game, gathering up all the cards and tucking them away inside her lumpy tote bag.

She gathered the sheets with everyone's feelings written on them and then tabulated them on the blackboard (after correcting for certain wide-of-the-mark responses like "Hungry"). And Ken's intuition had been good because his answers put him right smack in the middle of the pack. Lucinda then showed how, generally speaking, those who lost got progressively angrier even though the game was a game of *chance*, meaning that they had no control over its outcome, and the best they could do was to take their lumps a little more *philosophically.*

"A little more *what*?" That from the back of the room.

"Without losing your cool," Lucinda said.

"Oh."

"The point," Lucinda said, "is that good things happen and bad things happen and to a large extent, that's out of our control, but how we *react* to them isn't, that's *within* our control, so you can either let fifty-two little bits of paper put you in a foul mood or you can decide that fifty-two little bits of paper aren't worth that kind of negative energy. Not to mention all the consequences that go along with that kind of negative energy, you see?" Some did, some didn't, and some simply kept their own counsel. Lucinda returned the papers to their owners and then had everyone add the words "because of fifty-two little pieces of paper" right after the feelings they'd recorded. As in, "I feel *gypped* because of fifty-two little pieces of paper." "I feel *shitty* because of fifty-two little pieces of paper." "I feel *emotionally mortgaged* because of fifty-two little pieces of paper."

Ken thought it was perfectly brilliant and he was merrily marking in his paper when he saw Lucinda bite her lower lip, stand up, walk over to a guy in the back, the one who'd beaten up a bouncer, and pronounce the word "Hands." The guy paused, then held them out, and Lucinda's brow knitted and she looked down, without touching him, and then she turned on her heel and walked back up to her desk where she sat, very un-Lucinda like, with her arms folded resolutely across her chest until the clock struck nine and she let them go. Ken couldn't really say why he did it, other than a hunch and the strange, fleeting image of Isadora Duncan's long, swanlike neck snapping like a twig, but he practically knocked his chair over launching himself up out of his seat and off toward the back of the class. Iris and Jeff were just staring at him. "I'm Ken," he said to the guy in the back, sticking out his hand.

The guy looked at him with all of the requisite disdain that the situation warranted, but Ken just kept his hand stuck out there. A second ticked by, and then another, and just as Ken crossed the border from looking like a fool to *really* looking like a fool, the guy stuck his hand out and gruffly shook Ken's and mumbled,

"Darryl," and then cleared out. It'd taken a second, less than a second, but it was enough for Ken to get a single, fleeting glimpse of the guy's hand, and there wasn't any question as to what he'd seen—there was a cut on the knuckle.

It was Jeff who suggested that they go out and do some responsible drinking, although once they were installed in the Warehouse—Ken's choice of bar—Jeff went off on some bizarre tangent about thieves falling through skylights. Ken was so perplexed by this strange discourse that it took a full five minutes before it registered with him that Jeff had walked through the door of a *gay* bar with them and the bartender had looked up and said, "Hiya Jeff"—which put to rest any lingering doubts about which team Jeff played for. Way to pay attention, *Professor* Connelly. Iris, on the other hand, asked Jeff what the hell he was talking about.

"Thieves," he said. "And skylights. In law school, there are all these cases about thieves who creep along the roof of your house because they're trying to rob you or because they've already robbed you and now they're trying to get away, but the point is, you have a skylight, and as they crawl across it, it breaks and the thief falls through it and gets injured."

"I should think so," Iris said. "It's pretty hard to fall through someone's ceiling and *not* be injured."

"Exactly," Jeff said. "So the thief is injured and he sues you—"

"Wait a second. He sues *me*?"

"Exactly. He sues you and guess what?"

"You're not going to say he wins, are you?" Iris asked.

"Unfortunately, I am."

"Let me get this straight," Iris said. "He rips me off. *And* breaks my skylight while he's doing it. And he sues me and wins? On what grounds?"

"Ah, that's the thing, isn't it. Well, it would seem that you're supposed to keep your premises free of danger, even if the danger in question is only a danger to a thief crawling across your roof."

"Are you serious?" Iris asked.

"Dead serious."

"And you do realize, don't you, that it doesn't make any sense? It should be me suing him, not the other way around."

"Well, that's what you would think," Jeff said. "It's pretty messed up, isn't it? You sit around paying your taxes and trimming your hedges while unbeknownst to you, what you're *supposed* to be doing is going out and buying extra-strength, shatter-proof glass for your skylights just in case a really stupid thief comes along."

"And that's what they teach you in law school?"

"Yup."

"Does it have a name, this little gem of a principle?"

"More or less. It's called the 'duty of care.' "

"The duty of care," Iris repeated. "That's actually kind of a poetic name for something so stupid. And lawyers actually bring these kinds of cases? They stand up in court and say that their not-so-bright thief clients should be awarded a lot of money?"

"Apparently."

"And you wonder why people don't like lawyers."

Ken stayed lost in his own world while Iris and Jeff went on to debate whether it was necessary to specify that a lawyer was "unscrupulous" or whether, globally speaking, it would save time and energy and miles of typewriter ribbon to just silently incorporate the term "unscrupulous" into the term "lawyer," and then let that be the default position. And if for some unfathomable reason there was ever a lawyer who *didn't* warrant that label, they could call him an un-unscrupulous lawyer. So when Ken suddenly said, "You know what?" Iris was positive that he was about to point out that "un-unscrupulous" wasn't actually a word.

Instead, he told them about shaking Darryl's hand.

"Darryl?" Jeff and Iris said at the same time.

"The guy at the back of the room. The one who beat up a bouncer. I shook hands with him at the end of class, as I'm sure you noticed, and he had a cut on his knuckle."

"Which would mean?" Iris said.

"Which would mean that he probably beat someone up again," Ken said. "Wouldn't you agree?"

"Well, that would be one explanation, but there could be others," Iris said. "At a minimum, it would be jumping to conclusions, wouldn't it? I mean, I have a bruise on my neck, but that doesn't mean that Jeremy tried to beat me up." Ken looked at Jeff to see if he was following, but Iris caught him up by announcing that Jeremy was her boyfriend.

"So I gathered," Jeff said.

"Anyway," Ken said, "it's not just me. You saw Lucinda go over and take a look, so she must have suspected something, right?"

"But you don't know that either," Iris said. "He could've been cheating or sniffing glue or doing any of a million things that'd make Lucinda go over and see what was in his hands."

"Or what was *on* his hands," Ken said.

"Or what was on his hands," Iris admitted. "We just don't know."

"I guess not," Ken said. "But there's also the question of precedent. He's *in* the class because he beat someone up already, right? And I very much doubt that he got caught the first time he beat someone up for that matter."

"Why not?" Jeff asked.

"I don't know. Statistics. Nobody ever gets caught the first time they do something wrong."

"Except me," Iris said.

"And me," Jeff said.

"And me too, I suppose," Ken said. "Still, I can't help thinking . . ."

Iris filled Jeff in on Jeremy and told him all the nice, neutral things about him, like his job, and the way that waiters and waitresses always liked him and automatically assumed that he was in charge of the dinner or the event or whatever it was. Then she surprised Ken by talking about her suspicions and the fact that she'd enlisted Ken to help sort things out. To spy, in other words. It surprised Ken because telling one person something is one thing, but telling two people is something else altogether. Once two people know, it's impossible to go back, to retreat, to say, "Oh, never mind, it was all just a misunderstanding."

But there was Iris telling Jeff in an surprisingly even tone about the horrible, podium-hogging prosecutor and how the bland, utterly forgettable probation guy had managed to get his bland, utterly forgettable hands on her file—she had a file!—and how he'd lobbed the speeding ticket into the hearing as if it were a grenade because he couldn't just let sleeping dogs lie, and ever since then Iris had been dealing with the aftermath.

Then Ken took over and explained about seeing Jeremy during the downpour and the telephone call and the date that he made for—

"The appointment," Iris said.

About the *appointment* that Jeremy had fixed with whoever was on the other end of his cell phone for Saturday night.

"This Saturday?" Jeff asked.

"That's the one," Ken said.

According to Iris, Jeremy hadn't mentioned any plans at all for Saturday night. There was a huge fund-raiser scheduled that night for some lobbying group, but Jeremy had told Iris that all the work on his part—and there'd been a ton of it—was in the planning part and he wouldn't have to be there absent some sort of massive crisis.

"What kind of lobbyists?" Jeff wanted to know.

"It's the potassium hydroxide people," Iris said.

"There are *potassium hydroxide people*?" Ken asked. "Since when?"

"Since forever," Iris said. "They've always been there, you just don't hear much about them because they're shy. Or something. It's really called 'lye,' and it goes into everything, all sorts of products, but the potassium hydroxide people don't like the term 'lye' anymore. Just in case you want to be up-to-the-minute."

"Why not?" Jeff asked.

"Because it sounds too caustic," Iris said. "But that's not the point. The point is that Jeremy's working his behind off now, but he doesn't have to go on Saturday."

"Unless there's a crisis," Ken said.

"Unless there's a crisis," Iris slowly repeated. "And you're suggesting that there's going to be some sort of crisis?"

"Did I say that?" Ken asked.

"No, but that's what you think, isn't it?"

"It is, as a matter of fact."

"I have an idea," Jeff said. "Why don't you set something up yourself? You know, like make plans for the two of you that'd be hard for him to get out of. Like make a reservation at a really nice restaurant or get tickets to a play or something like that."

"How would that help?" Ken asked.

"Well, then it'd be harder for Jeremy to go off and, well, you know . . ."

"But the point is to catch him!" Ken said, and the two of them looked at Iris.

"I don't know what the point is anymore," Iris said. "I think I need three glasses of water."

"*Three* glasses of water?"

"Or a toothbrush," Iris said. "You guys decide. But either way, I'm about to drink a whole lot of booze."

An hour later, Ken and Jeff were deep in conversation whereas Iris had decided that she didn't want to talk about Jeremy or Brett or infidelity anymore; she just wanted to sit there and listen to the sweet sound of vodka swirling around ice cubes. "Did I ever mention," she asked, "that ice cubes are my favorite format for water?" She slid some stuff out of her briefcase while Ken and Jeff talked, and after she got bored with her pile of faxes and interoffice memos, she rooted around a little further and found a copy of this nifty health manual that one of her HMOs was giving away as a freebie to people who signed up for the plan. Iris clicked her pen a couple times and then she sketched a Hawaiian shirt onto the anatomical figure who was supposed to show you where your lymph nodes were. She made each little node the center of a bright, fresh flower. Then she put a nice, muted, argyle sock on a strained Achilles tendon, and added a nasty case of chicken pox to the emaciated but nonetheless D-cup bitch who was taking her sweet time plus no fewer than three different diagrams to do her long, luxurious, monthly breast examination. "I hope it itches, you slut."

"What was that Iris?" Ken was looking at her.

"Oh, nothing," she said, shifting around a bit so she could shield her work from view. She turned the page and drew a ring on the finger of some poor slob who was having a fishhook removed—Lord, did that look painful—when she suddenly recognized what she'd drawn. It was the exact same twisting, intricate, silvery signet ring from the ticket photo, and everything came rushing back at her, knocking the wind right out of her lungs. She flipped to the index and looked up shortness of breath, which didn't have an entry, so she looked up lightheadedness instead and the book said that she was supposed to put her head down between her knees. Fine. Unfortunately, the table stopped her—none too gently—so she just settled for that instead.

In the meantime, Ken found himself quite intrigued by Jeff. Earlier he'd heard Jeff talking with Iris about the law, so he assumed his professorial tone of voice and asked Jeff what the most important thing was that he learned from going to law school.

"Oh, that's easy," Jeff said. "That you shouldn't tie a mattress to the top of your car with speaker wire."

"Speaker wire?"

"Yeah, you know, the wires that go from the stereo to the speakers? You trip over them every so often? Without them the speakers are just big, wooden boxes with squishy, foamy fronts and *with* the wires they're big, wooden boxes with squishy, foamy fronts that blast out the Captain & Tennille whenever you want?"

"I actually know what speaker wire is," Ken said, "but was there some sort of case where somebody got killed doing that? Or fined? Or went to jail?"

"Oh, it's not a case," Jeff said. "It happened to me. You asked me what the most important thing was that I learned while *going* to law school, not what I learned while *attending* law school—you have to be precise with those of us in the legal profession—and *while* I was on my way to St. John's, I had my mattress tied to the roof of my mother's Oldsmobile Custom Cruiser wagon with speaker wire, which turned out *not* to be such a good idea because it flew off on the Long Island Expressway and I couldn't stop because I was in the middle of a highway and it made the car behind me swerve and he clipped the car next to him and they had to pull over and the mattress was still in the middle of the road and it blocked up traffic for hours and I got into a massive amount of trouble."

"I don't doubt it."

"I was even on the radio," Jeff said. "Eye in the Sky. They said some idiot threw a mattress into the middle of the Long Island Expressway, which was not the case. I didn't *throw* it; it fell."

"Point well taken," Ken said. "So what's the most important thing you learned while *attending* law school?"

"Oh, that's easy. Don't throw computers at people."

"You seem to have a habit of throwing things you shouldn't."

"Hardy-har-har. But you know, in all seriousness I really thought he was being attacked," Jeff said. "The professor. I didn't stop and think because there wasn't enough time to think. All I saw was these thugs barging in and roughing him up and I knew that the gun wasn't real, but the rest just happened before I had time to think. You know, if I saw somebody who was in the middle of the road about to get run over by a tractor-trailer, I'd push them out of the way, or at least I'd like to think that I'm the type of person who'd dash in there and push them out of the way. I just wouldn't expect to get in trouble for the pushing part."

"Well, I'd say that's normal," Ken said. "Do you think this whole thing is going to have ramifications further on in your career?"

"I don't know. I'm really not sure. I mean, I've been at Hofstra ever since the beginning of the semester and that's fine, but I suppose that when interviewing season rolls around I'll probably have to explain to employers why I transferred schools, and that could be a drag. And I suppose if someone ever wants to use it against me they can because the part where I almost killed a professor sounds pretty bad, and it takes a long time before you get to the part where it wasn't my fault, at all, where it was actually more *his* fault, but I'm not allowed to say that because it would demonstrate a *lack of remorse*, and I'm supposed to be *remorseful* and learning to control my anger. So yeah, I suppose it could come back to haunt me down the road."

"Which sucks," Ken said.

"Which sucks," Jeff agreed.

"But back to employers," Ken said, thinking about Crayton Reed and his ilk. "What sort of employers are you talking about? I've actually spent quite a bit more time than you might think in law firms."

"I thought you were a professor at City College?"

"I am. Well, I'm an adjunct professor at City College, and in this cold, cruel world, that's not actually enough to live on, so I've been known to offer my services to the occasional law firm here and there."

"Like?"

"Like Leighton, Fennell & Lowe. They're a big Wall Street firm."

"I know who they are," Jeff said. "And I don't think that they're the type of firm to be interested in me."

"Why not?"

"Well, for starters I'm going to graduate from Hofstra and not someplace a little loftier. But beyond that, I'm not sure that I'm interested in them, in that type of firm. I *thought* I was, since that's supposed to be the goal, but I don't know anymore. And sometimes I think that firms like Leighton Fennell can actually tell when you don't buy into their shtick, and they don't want that sort of subversive element around. I think they can sniff it out somehow. They only want associates who toe the line and bill lots of hours and sweat bullets over huge documents, and more and more I'm not sure that that's my style."

Ken was fascinated. This kid hadn't even set foot in a place like Leighton Fennell, yet he was starting to get it all sorted out more neatly than Ken had after almost ten years there. "So what kind of work do you think you'd like to do?"

"That I'm not sure," Jeff said.

"Well, what would make you happy?"

"What would make me happy? I don't know. I think I'd like to harmonize in the kitchen."

"You'd like to *what*?" Ken laughed. "And you're planning to get paid for this?"

"No, you didn't ask what I could do for *money* that would make me happy," Jeff said. "You asked what would make me happy, point-blank."

"And that would be harmonizing in the kitchen?" Ken asked.

"Yuppers," Jeff said.

"And can you sing?" Ken asked.

"Not yet."

"So we'll assume that you can't harmonize either? At least not yet, anyway?"

"Correctamundo." Then Jeff explained. He said that he was originally from New York City, that he was born on the Lower East Side while it was still the Lower East Side and before it went out one day like a surly adolescent and came back with its nose pierced and announced that from now on it would only answer to the name "East Village." And he said that his aunts—his mother's sisters—used to harmonize in the kitchen before his family moved out to Long Island, and that he really didn't have terribly many memories from the time they lived in Manhattan except for sitting in the front room after dinner watching his father in his recliner and listening to the clatter and laughter coming from the kitchen and feeling utterly sure of his place in the world.

"They sound wonderful," Ken said.

"Oh, they're just like anybody else," Jeff said, pulling a photo out of his wallet. "You know, they have their good points and their bad points, and they could drive a person crazy in just under five seconds if they really put their minds to it." The picture showed Jeff in a cap and gown standing almost a full head above his mother and father while three or four other adults were crowding around them in the picture. One of the women was holding an actual, honest-to-God, Kodak Instamatic with a rotating flashbulb stuck on top of it even though this could only have been what, four or five years ago, maximum?

"You have very nice posture," Ken said, just because he felt like throwing Jeff a curveball, but Jeff took it right in stride. "Oh, I had to," he said. "My cousin spilled a whiskey sour on my mortarboard the night before graduation and some loose papers ended up getting glued on top."

"Some loose papers?"

"Well, a loose paper."

"*A* loose paper?"

"It was a ShopRite coupon for twenty-five cents off my next purchase of a Mrs. Dash seasoning or salt substitute," Jeff said, and Ken heard himself burst out laughing. "And you couldn't get it off?" he asked.

"Nope," Jeff said. "By the time the whiskey sour dried, it was as if the coupon had been shellacked in there, so the whole day I had to go around with my head perfectly straight. And I didn't get the deposit back for the cap and gown, either."

"Well, at least you got to keep your mortarboard then," Ken said.

"Well, actually . . ."

"Oh, tell me you didn't!"

"Okay, I didn't," Jeff said. "But I did! I gave ShopRite the hat. And I got twenty-five cents off my next purchase of Mrs. Dash!" And Ken put his head down on the table next to Iris's and laughed until the tears ran down his cheeks.

Chapter Twelve. In Which Iris Contemplates the Mysteries of Avian Incarceration

Iris thought that perhaps she'd been turned into a battering ram. She dimly recalled being carried around like a log the night before, and on top of that, her head hurt, and the only explanation that came to mind was that Ken and Jeff must've pressed her into service last night as a battering ram. She thought ahead to next spring when she'd be filling out her taxes and how she'd have to remember to write "battering ram" in the little blank for her profession instead of "marketing."

No, hold on a second. That doesn't make any sense.

Then it all came back to her—the night out, the stumbly, swaying walk home supported by Ken on one side and Jeff on the other. Dropping her keys outside the door to her building. Dropping her keys outside the door to her apartment—which made an *ungodly* racket even though Iris had always adhered to a strict, essential-keys-only policy regarding her key chain—and then realizing that all that worry was for naught because Jeremy wasn't home yet. The answering machine was blinking, though, and Jeremy had let her know that he was still tied up at the office and was going to be burning the midnight oil there working on the potassium whatever-it-was affair for Saturday. Iris meant to take a shower and get the stale smell of beer and barroom floors out of her hair, but by the same token, she'd also meant to get out of her clothes and shoes and turn off the stereo, none of which she accomplished either.

When she woke up at about three in the morning, Jeremy

still wasn't there, and this time Iris made good on her resolution to actually get ready for bed prior to getting into bed. She brushed her teeth and brushed out her hair and tried to drink as much water as she could from the pitcher in the refrigerator before the evil light bulb in there got the upper hand and forced her to retreat. She got back into bed, but this time sleep didn't come rushing up on her like it had earlier. Instead, she lay awake listening to the very pleasant sound of almost nothing except some traffic off in the distance, and she tried to think through her evening with the boys.

It'd been fun, that much was clear. Walking—well, *sort of* walking—arm in arm with two other drunks and singing—well, *sort of* singing—just like happy, loudmouth drunks are supposed to. They'd left the Warehouse, that much she could remember, but they hadn't split up and gone home. Instead, they came up with a host of ideas, including taking a walk along the park, going back to Ken's place for a nightcap, or going over to Brett and Home-Wrecker's place and organizing a demonstration and getting on the local news and handing out colorful flyers that said that "Brett Manikin is a lying sack of shit." And then Jeff said something about getting sued for libel or defamation, and the only way they could protect themselves would be to state their opinion because opinions don't count for defamation, only facts do.

"So what does that mean in practical terms?" Ken asked.

"That means the flyers have to say, '*In our opinion*, Brett Manikin is a lying sack of shit.' That way it's not an assertion of fact, it's a statement of opinion."

"Well here's a fact," Iris chipped in. "I don't think we should be demonstrating in front of anyone's apartment building, not at midnight, and certainly not while we've been engaging in *substance abuse*. And some of us have criminal records which we're trying to get expunged, and they won't get expunged if we get into any more trouble, so sorry to burst your bubble, Ken, but we're not going anywhere near there tonight." And thus they lurched off toward Plan B, even though Plan B had yet to be defined.

They stopped to rest on the lawn on the north side of the

Museum of Natural History—if the city *really* wanted to keep people out they'd put in a taller fence—and Ken and Jeff got into this long debate over whether or not it would be defamatory to say, "In *my opinion*, the *fact* of the matter is that Brett Manikin is a lying sack of shit," and Iris just leaned back and closed her eyes. She found herself thinking about a trip she'd made to that same museum years and years ago and the fascinating exhibit she'd seen there. It was essentially a big Ping-Pong paddle stuck on top of a rod, and on one side of the paddle was a picture of a bird, and on the other side of the paddle was a picture of an empty birdcage. When you spun the paddle, though, you saw a bird in its cage. Not ten seconds earlier you knew as sure as you knew anything that on one side of the paddle was a perfectly empty cage and on the other side of the paddle was a perfectly free bird, and yet when you spun it, your eyes took the two images and overruled your brain and decided that the two different pictures went better together, and all of a sudden there was a bird in a cage, flittering and flickering in front of you.

Ken and Jeff had reached a lull in their debate, so Iris tried to tell them all about this strange phenomenon, but she only got as far as informing them that there was a *particularly* interesting Ping-Pong paddle in the museum behind them before she decided that it was all too complicated and gave up. They were all too drunk, and she decided to just lie there and let the world do what it did best—spin beneath her.

As far as Brett and the new boyfriend were concerned, Iris didn't pussyfoot around. She called Brett's number as soon as she got out of work on Friday and told him that she just wanted to thank him and his friends for helping her out the other night and actually, she was right in the neighborhood, so . . .

And Brett went right ahead and invited her over. It was as simple as that. She didn't need to wheedle or make up some long, elaborate story about needing a police report full of signed witness statements in order to qualify for disability. It was Friday evening and all Brett said was that he was home and he was expecting Neil fairly soon and they didn't have plans until later and if Iris didn't mind the mess, she could come over anytime she wanted.

"Including now?" she asked.

"Sure," Brett laughed. "Just ring Neil Loucks when you get here."

Brett's place was on Sixty-sixth Street just off Central Park West, and it seemed like a perfectly nice building. No doorman, but everything was in order, and judging from the faintly waxy, faintly alpine smell, whoever was in charge of cleaning the lobby actually cleaned it. She rang Loucks and Brett's voice came over the intercom, telling her that he was on the eighth floor and then he buzzed her in.

At his door there weren't any jerky, awkward, kiss-or-shake-hands seizures because Brett just sort of swept her right into the middle of the apartment and then disappeared into the kitchen, telling her to make herself at home and asking what he could get her, and Iris said just whatever was already open. She looked around and the overwhelming impression she had of the place was that it was just like any other apartment except that it had been put through a very strict, very successful diet, and it had emerged from all that privation with a sleekly elegant, though somewhat austere look. There were three jet-black, lacquered shelves fixed against a wall, for example, one of which held a fat candle with a white wick, meaning that it had never been lit, one of which held a single framed photograph, and the last of which held a matching hip flask and cigarette case that were made out of beautifully polished silver. Notable by their absence were the kinds of things that normally win the cutthroat battle for space on a Manhattan shelf: a pile of phone bills; an ashtray in the shape of Nebraska used to keep small change; movie stubs; library books; scotch tape; an unfinished, though blistering letter to the editor of the *New York Times*; the clicker to somebody's garage door opener; bobby pins; dry cleaner receipts; a papier-mâché avocado; a pamphlet on how to "season" cast-iron cookware; and then some regular, garden-variety crap.

Brett and Neil's apartment wasn't like that at all. Everything had its place, and everything that was particularly shiny or particularly valuable had its very own spotlight trained on it from the ceiling. "Dusting here," Iris found herself thinking, "must be a cinch." The magazines on the coffee table didn't have the telltale ripples of having served as coasters. And sharing the coffee table with them were four sparkling martini glasses, each filled with black sand and a single white tea candle.

Brett came out of the kitchen with a mixed drink of some sort in a surprisingly heavy glass and she thanked him again for saving her bacon, and he downplayed the whole thing and said that anyone would've done the same thing. He said that Neil was the real hero because he tried to chase the guy down and make him face up to what he'd almost done, and given how many lunatics there are out there, that was pretty damn brave.

"Have you two been together for a long time?" Iris asked.

"Oh, not that long," Brett said. "Not in the scheme of things, anyway."

Iris couldn't see herself pressing the matter by asking him *exactly* what he meant by "not that long," so she just wrapped up the gratefulness part of her visit and with that out of the way, she found herself surprisingly relaxed even though she knew that she'd be expected to report every single detail to Ken later. And Brett seemed equally happy to just talk to Iris about everything and nothing all at once. It was as if they'd both been invited to some cocktail party where they found out that they were the only two guests, but then found themselves in perfect agreement on everything from current events to the advisability of moving closer to the hors d'oeuvres. Iris asked Brett what he did, and when he said he was an actor, she asked if he meant the stage or the screen, and he said that he wasn't about to turn up his nose at *any* work so long as it was a paying job.

"Well, would that include commercials?" Iris asked.

"Funny you should ask—" Brett started to say when Iris clapped her hands and practically shouted, "I knew it! The running shoes. I knew there was something familiar about you. You know, the running shoes? *Just Get With It!* That was you, wasn't it?" And whatever restraint, whatever reserve was left on the part of Brett just evaporated. He was thrilled to be recognized, and it was just at that moment that Neil let himself in the door, and Iris couldn't have imagined a more perfect tableau as reintroductions were made and Brett fussed and clucked and waited the requisite ten seconds to go by in case anyone else had a subject that they might care to raise before he turned to Neil and said, "So, Iris has seen the commercial!" She was in like Flynn.

Iris wondered whether Brett had called Neil at some point and tipped him off to expect company when he got home, or whether they really lived like that. Which is to say, whether Neil really came home from work every day like that, because the grocery bags that Neil was carrying revealed not only some very high-end, low-utility food stuffs like water crackers, cilantro, and a little gumdrop-sized jar of something-flavored mustard, but also a single, sublime calla lily. Neil asked Brett what he thought, and Brett contemplated the flower as if it were a painting and then he said, "How about the twisting crystal?"

"I was thinking more a plain cylinder," Neil said. "Not etched because the stem is perfect."

"I think you're probably right," Brett said, and Neil went off to find housing for the calla lily while Iris got herself all tangled up in the math so that, in the end, the most accurate conclusion she could come to was that these people owned more than one vase.

When Neil rejoined them, Iris asked him what he did for a living, and he said he was a systems analyst for Deutsche Bank. Iris nodded thoughtfully and swirled her drink around even though she didn't have the faintest idea of what a systems analyst was or why Deutsche Bank kept one or more of them on call. "You really have a lovely place here," she said, but Neil seemed to be stuck back on the subject of careers. He went into a detailed explanation of how he was perfectly happy at Deutsche Bank but how you always had to keep an eye out to make sure there was room for advancement. He said that a person needs to step back and take stock of things from time to time, and if the results of that reflection are that the best course of action is to stay put, then so be it, stay put. But if there's something blocking your advancement—and this is without pointing fingers, mind you—then you need to take stock of that situation and examine your options.

He paused, but this time Iris didn't even try to steer the conversation elsewhere. "The point," Neil said, "is that blind loyalty will get you only so far. If climbing the corporate ladder requires that you zigzag a bit from side to side, well, then that's just life. And life's too short to be complacent." Iris had the impression that Brett had heard this speech before because Brett kept nodding approvingly at all the right moments, even those moments when a normally careful listener like Iris completely lost track of things because she was hoping that an analogy to the board game Chutes and Ladders would come up but, sadly, it didn't.

Neil turned the attention onto Brett and took him as an example. "This one here," he said, "this one acts. That's what actors do. But that doesn't take up twenty-four hours a day, seven days a week, so the question you have to ask yourself is what *else* are you doing to advance yourself, to increase your chances, to make sure that there's always some forward motion?"

Iris turned an expectant gaze toward Brett to see what he'd do now that he was in the hot seat, but Neil got there faster. "What Brett does, though, is far from resting on his laurels. He takes classes. Acting classes. He studies in seminars and in workshops. You see, you can't just rest on what you have, you have to be continually thinking of your next move and the move after that."

Iris said she saw Neil's point of view, and instead of leaving well enough alone, he announced that in his opinion, Brett should really consider applying for a Fulbright.

"A Fulbright!" Iris said.

"I'm serious," Neil said. "He's got the skills, the background, the credentials. All he needs is the motivation." He bent forward on the word "motivation" and kissed the back of Brett's neck as if that was the gentle push forward that Brett had needed all along, and

Iris smiled, looking from one to the other. Still, she couldn't help thinking about Jeremy and how Jeremy *loved* to make fun of this uptight lawyer acquaintance of theirs who actually got a Fulbright. This friend spent two years doing corporate law in a big white-shoe firm while slowly coming unglued from the mindlessness of it all, and by the time that his choices had been distilled down to having a standard, regulation-issue breakdown crouched down next to a photocopier or moving to Waikiki to design greeting cards, his application for a Fulbright came through and he got to skip out the door of the firm with no questions asked. Plus the firm assured him that the door would always be open if he ever wanted to come back. "A Fulbright is just an excuse to take time off," Jeremy always said dismissively and, perhaps, with just the slightest touch of envy. "It's a way to get out of the rat race for a while, only it's better than Club Med because they pay you to do it instead of your paying them. But the idea is the same. You disappear and it's for your own good but nobody holds it against you." Iris always loved what came next. "A Fulbright," Jeremy would say, "is the corporate equivalent of the Betty Ford Center."

Still, for better or for worse, that's how things had come to be defined in the Loucks/Manikin household. They were movers and shakers. They were going places. Brett had his feet on the ground and his head on his shoulders, and if you needed any more proof than that, he was thinking about applying for a Fulbright.

Iris tried to focus on her mission, but there really wasn't anything particularly negative that she could report back to Ken. Neil didn't seem slimy or fundamentally dishonest; on the contrary, he was perfectly nice to Iris and he made her feel welcome and surprisingly at ease. And Brett seemed fine. Ken would want Brett to look haggard and gaunt and to confess that he couldn't sleep because he was *consumed with guilt*, and then Neil and Brett would exchange a long, penetrating look before Brett would break away from Neil's stare and, ignoring his silent plea to keep his mouth shut, would pour out his guts. "There was this guy, you see?"

"A guy?" Iris would ask.

"That's right," Brett would say, collapsing into tears. "And I didn't do right by him."

Instead, Brett was just Brett, and there wasn't anything awful to report. The two of them, Brett and Neil, didn't excuse themselves to go into the kitchen to have a shouting match culminating in the distinct sound of one of them getting hit in the head with the Cuisinart after which the *other* one would emerge from the kitchen and blithely announce—"Oh, *by the way*, the blender seems to be on the fritz, so there's not going to be any more frozen daiquiris tonight."

True, the two of them were holding themselves out on display a bit the way a lot of couples did, especially new couples, but there wasn't anything bad enough that Iris could see that would satisfy Ken. "How did you two meet?" she asked, and Neil laughed and jumped up off his perch on the back of the sofa and said, "That's a story that requires a drink!" and Iris said that she really shouldn't, but Neil just said, "Objection overruled!" and everybody laughed.

Neil said that they met the old-fashioned way and let a long pause go by before delivering the punch line—"In a bar!" Then he turned the story over to Brett.

Brett said that he'd been all the way downtown at Inklings and it was freezing outside and he'd been outside all night—he'd get to *why* in a second—and he'd gone inside to get warm and it was packed, as usual, and he was carried along with the current to the back where he finally managed to stake out some space, and after a while he noticed this guy.

"A guy?" Iris asked. "And that'd be Neil?"

"Nope, though Neil was *there*. I just didn't know it yet. Anyway, there was this guy there in the middle of the aisle where the bartenders go by with their hand trucks full of beer bottles, and he had this crimson sweatshirt tied around his waist—the fact that it was crimson is important, so don't forget that—and he was pretty young, maybe twenty-one or twenty-two or something like that.

And he was good-looking. You know, boy-next-door look. Cute haircut. Plus the crimson sweatshirt tied around his waist, and it was tied so that the words 'Harvard Crew' were *splayed* across his ass." Neil was already giggling. "So what I'm saying is that he didn't just tie it any old way. He didn't just tie it willy-nilly and let the chips fall where they may. He tied his sweatshirt so that those words—'Harvard Crew'—were *emblazoned* right across his behind, and every so often he'd *check* to make sure that they were still in the right place. And he stood there blocking traffic, and every time one of the bartenders would come by with their cases of beer or come back in the other direction with the empties, Harvard Crew would be there and he'd look at the bartender and wonder what he wanted and then they'd *finally* make him understand that he had to move and he'd get out of the way and then wander right back into traffic again."

"But that wasn't Neil?" Iris said.

"Nope," Brett said. "Neil was the one who was watching *me* watch all this, and he came up and stood next to me and crossed his arms and said, 'You know, even a monkey could be trained not to stand in the way like that,' and I nearly blew the rest of my beer out through my nose. *That* was Neil!"

"Ah-ha!" Iris said, practically clapping.

"But seriously," Brett said. "It wasn't all fun and games because I was actually down there working for the Knowledge Project. You know the one?"

"The group that does . . ." Iris trailed off.

"AIDS prevention and education," Brett answered, saving Iris from having to profess ignorance. "That's what I was doing down there, and that's why I was frozen stiff when I went into Inklings to warm up. Later I corralled Neil on his way back out, which was easy because he'd already broken the ice inside."

"Ah-ha!" Iris said, though all of a sudden she didn't really see what difference any of it made. Brett and Neil met in a bar, and the story can be cute if you play up Harvard Crew's role, and it can be serious and civic-minded if you play up the outreach angle, but no matter how you work it, Brett was already with Ken when this happened, which means, a priori, that it shouldn't have happened.

They asked Iris about herself and whether she was with someone, and she found herself talking about Jeremy in a tone of voice that she hadn't used in what seemed like years—bright, upbeat, positive. Jeremy behind the wheel of anything with gears. Jeremy organizing a surprise party that actually came off as a true-blue, no-holds-barred surprise. And then for Neil's special benefit, the fact that Jeremy was such a hard worker and was, at this very moment, working his tail off for a fund-raiser tomorrow. And Iris wasn't just whistling Dixie. She liked Neil and Brett, despite everything, and, despite everything, she wanted them to like her and Jeremy.

"We'll have to have you both over sometime," Neil said, and Iris heard herself saying that she'd really like that.

Iris asked the boys what they were up to for the weekend, and the results were very *we*-centric. *We've* got a brunch on Saturday, and *we've* got to get up early even though the brunch isn't until one o'clock for sit down at two because *we've* got a million other things to get done. And afterward *we're* going over to a friend of ours because his co-op board—he's over on Eighty-third and Third—just let the Crate & Barrel downstairs out of their lease and he's hopping mad about it.

"He feels that strongly about Crate & Barrel leaving?" Iris asked. "Your friend?"

"Oh, not at all," Neil said. "He doesn't give a shit about Crate & Barrel. Nobody does. They just don't want the new tenant."

"A Sbarro's pizza," Brett added in a well-placed aside.

"What's so wrong with Sbarro's pizza?" Iris asked, genuinely perplexed given that some fried mozzarella sticks sounded wonderfully appetizing at that moment, particularly if they were just the prelude to a main course of cannelloni.

"Rats," Neil said.

"Rats?"

"Rats. That's right. Food stores and restaurants? They come with rats. No matter how much they promise that they'll be perfectly clean, the fact of the matter is that they breed rats, and Jason—that's our friend—Jason and the rest of his building don't want to have rats in their cellar, or anywhere else for that matter, so that's why they're trying to stop the board."

"So why did his board agree to this in the first place?" Iris asked Neil.

"Because they're idiots, I guess."

"Do you think he'll win? Jason that is?" Iris asked.

"*He* thinks so," Neil said.

"Well, good luck to him," Iris said. "Though if he loses, my advice would be to buy a cat for the laundry room and don't feed it."

Brett and Neil both laughed, and then Brett said, "Or a snake."

"Oh, God, that reminds me," Iris said. "The other day I was watching this program on Channel Thirteen, one of those nature programs? Did you guys see that?" Neither of them had, and even Iris found herself at a loss as to exactly when and where she'd seen that program. It definitely wasn't sitting on the couch with her feet in Jeremy's lap, though it seemed like it was just the other day. It was . . .

Oh, right. At Ken's house. *Duh.*

"Anyway," she said, "this program was all about snakes, and the photography was amazing because you could see every single scale slithering by and the tongue flickering around trying to find the right path to go wreak death and destruction all over the place. And then they explained how all the bones in this one snake's mouth came apart so that the snake could basically swallow a basketball if it really wanted to." Brett and Neil were gazing at her.

"This particular snake wasn't poisonous or anything like that," Iris said. "It just used plain old fang power to grab its prey, and then it'd work its strange mechanics with the bones in its face to swallow it, and here's the kicker—they showed it eating a rat and it swallows the rat *face-first*."

"Gross," Brett said.

"Believe you me," Iris said. "It just opens wide and slides its big, fat jaw around the rat, and a half hour later there's nothing more than a big rat-shaped lump in the snake's throat."

"Charming."

"But that's not the gross part," Iris said.

"It isn't?"

"Nope. They showed it catching a bat, and when it swallows a bat, it swallows it *feet-first*. It's got something to do with getting the bat's wings pointed in the right direction so that they'll actually go down the snake's throat," Iris said. "So the snake starts from the other end—feet-first this time—and then he slowly swallows the bat." She looked directly at Brett as she said the word "bat," but his face didn't reveal a thing. "What a thing to imagine," Iris said, "because they're still alive. The bats. The program was perfectly clear about that, that the bat is still alive as it gets swallowed. So ask yourself, which is worse, to get swallowed head-first and get it over with, or to get swallowed feet-first and live slightly longer, except you're aware of what's going on right down to the very last second?"

"Well, I'd just as soon not get eaten by a snake at all," Neil said, whereas Brett just laughed—perfectly naturally, perfectly neutrally—and told Iris, "You sound just like a friend of mine."

Chapter Thirteen. In Which Ken Attempts to Untangle Things, Only to Get Himself Tied in a Knot

Ken exploded. And what better place to explode than along the ramparts of an old fort? He'd been sitting with Iris on a bench in Fort Tryon just outside the Cloisters, pumping her for details, and when she'd finally started to run out of gas and realized that she had to lighten the load, she looked around, considered her options, and dropped the Fulbright bomb.

"*What?*" Ken said. It was a direct hit. "A *Ful*bright? For that little shit?"

"I'm just saying what they said."

"Wait a second, wait a second. The word 'Fulbright.' Did the word 'Fulbright' actually come out of Brett's mouth? Did he actually have the temerity to pronounce the word?"

"Well, actually," Iris said, "I think it was Neil who used the term itself. Brett just didn't disagree with him."

"What is he thinking? Is he under the impression that the Fulbright people have nothing better to do than sit around all day waiting for *his* application to come in and save the day? 'Oh, *woe unto us.* We've been sorting through piles of applications sent in by people with incredible credentials and wildly deserving projects and yet, somehow, we have the feeling that there's a pretentious shithead out there who *thinks* he ought to apply for one of our grants. We'd better race through all these vastly more deserving applications right now to make room for his. Better yet, let's just throw them away and *sit* here with our thumbs up our asses doing absolutely nothing at all until

Brett's application finally gets here so we're fresh and rested and able to appreciate the sheer magnitude of everything that little bastard's accomplished up to now. Which is nothing."

"Ken," Iris said. "I'm just the messenger. Messengers are a protected species, remember?"

"Oh, I know Iris. And I'm sorry. I just can't get over it. I mean, the nerve of it. The gall. The *hubris*. The idea that someone can take doing nothing and then somehow turn it into a virtue? Something that should be *rewarded*?"

"Well, I didn't say he'd gotten a Fulbright," Iris said. "I just said he was thinking about applying for one."

"God help us," Ken said. "Why doesn't he just run for president while he's at it?"

Ken had been meticulously thorough in dissecting—in trying to dissect—Iris's visit to Brett and Home-Wrecker's filth pit of iniquity, as he referred to it, but the results were less than satisfactory. Iris figured out right away that Ken didn't want any editorials or conclusions; he wanted the cold, hard facts from which he could draw his own conclusions—to wit, that Brett was evil and would one day be the holder of a nonrefundable, one-way ticket to hell. But even then, there wasn't very much for Iris to tell, and despite her best efforts, she found herself slipping into summaries like: "They seemed average enough," and, worse, "They seemed nice enough."

She trotted out every single detail she could remember—that there was one of those handheld electric mixers that don't splash all over the place sitting on the counter in the kitchen; that the phone didn't ring while she was there; that Neil was neither young enough to be a piece of fluff nor old enough to be a sugar daddy; that the floors were stained very dark and were actually quite free of dust for floors that dark; that they were invited to a brunch today—

"Oh, well *that* figures," Ken said.

"And then to some sort of party in the afternoon at Jason's."

"*Jason's!*" Ken blew the air out of his cheeks and said that that was just great. "You think you know who your friends are and then they go and do something like that."

"Something like what?"

"Invite Brett and his shit-for-brains new boyfriend to a party and not me."

"You know Jason?" Iris asked.

"Of course I know Jason," Ken said. He let a pause go by. "Well, *a* Jason."

"And what does your Jason do? Wait, scrap that. Where does your Jason live?"

"Now?"

"Of course now," Iris said.

"Well, that I'm not entirely sure of," Ken said. "But when he lived in New York, he lived on Thirtieth and First."

"When he *lived* in New York?"

"Yeah. He got a tenure-track spot in some god-awful place in the middle of nowhere." Iris just folded her arms and looked at Ken. "Does it help that his old apartment on Thirtieth and First cost almost nothing?" he asked weakly. "And was fantastic? Except for the noise from the helicopter ambulances going in and out of Bellevue?"

"Speaking of *Bellevue*, Ken. This Jason *lives* in New York. As in the present tense. He lives on Eighty-third Street. At Third Avenue. Where there used to be a Crate & Barrel. Is that the Jason you know?"

"Probably not."

"*Probably* not?"

"Okay, definitely not," Ken admitted.

"And if it's not your Jason, then why should you feel offended that you didn't get invited to his party?"

"Because it's my Brett."

"It was your Brett," Iris said softly. "Just not anymore." They both looked out at the Hudson, which offered up exactly zero explanations for this curious state of the world. Instead, there was just the slant of November afternoon sunshine and the coppery chop of exuberant whitecaps, which seemed about as appropriate to the occasion as going to a funeral on a pogo stick.

There was a method to her madness, though, because once Iris had let Ken vent over the nearly black floors ("Oh, *please*") and the shiny silver flask that got its own shelf ("probably stolen") and the thousand other details, he was too spent to mount a real counter-attack when she got to the heart of the matter and told him about the snake story.

"The thingamajig we saw on PBS the other night?" Ken asked.

"That's the one. I told them all about it."

"You did? Shall I ask why, or were you just feeling particularly expansive on the subject of reptiles?"

"Oh, it came up, actually," Iris said. "Or at least it wasn't out of context. Anyway, the point is that I told them about the snake swallowing some things one way and other things the other way, and Brett said, *in passing* I might add, that I sounded 'just like a friend of his.'" Iris stifled the urge to crouch down and plug her ears, but Ken didn't explode again. All gone.

"Those were his words?" he asked instead.

"As best I recall," Iris said. "I told them the story before I'd even thought about it because they were talking about rats—"

"The social class to which they aspire?"

"*Ken*. The subject of rats came up and I was trying to be inter-esting and I told them all about what we'd seen on TV and when I was done, Brett said that I sounded like a friend of his. And no, he didn't ponder things over and close his eyes and *ruminate* and then deliver that observation; he just said it and that was that."

"Do you think that it could've been someone other than me?" Ken asked gently.

"You tell me," Iris said. "Did you guys have other friends who are hooked on—well, let's just say who are *fans* of—the nature shows on PBS?"

"Not really," Ken said. "Not that I can think of."

"Well then, I suppose he meant you."

"A friend, that's what he said?"

"He said, 'You sound just like a friend of mine.' "

Ken thought this over for a moment. "I guess he couldn't very well say, 'You sound just like my ex-boyfriend who became my ex-boyfriend when I cheated on him right under his nose,' could he?"

"Probably not," Iris said. "Not in that sort of social situation."

"And how did Home-Wrecker react?"

"Neil?" Iris said. "He didn't say a thing one way or the other. It wasn't the kind of observation that called for a response."

"No, I don't suppose it really would," Ken said, though he seemed deep in thought. He let a few minutes go by before he asked Iris, again, "A friend?"—although this time he said it with a tone of resignation that made it clear that he was finished badgering her for details. She nodded and smiled and slid around a little so she could lean her head back against his shoulder. "It could be worse, I guess," Ken finally said.

"It could always be worse," Iris started to say, only before she could finish, her cell phone rang and *made that point* for her. Jeremy, it seemed, was really sorry, but he would have to go put out some fires at the fund-raiser tonight after all. From where he was sitting, Ken could hear what the brief conversation was about, and after it was done, after Iris told Jeremy not to worry about it and that she'd just rent a movie and stay in, Ken put his arm around her shoulder and they both went back to gazing at the river.

"You know what?" Iris finally said.

"What's that?"

"When I was a little girl, my mother told me there was a doll hospital and I believed her."

"Well why wouldn't you believe her? She's your mother after all."

"That's a good point," Iris said. "But in any event she told me that there was a hospital for dolls, and since mine happened to have fallen apart—and don't give me a hard time about having a doll. . . ."

"Look who you're talking to," Ken said.

"Oh, right!" Iris said and *almost* smiled. "Anyway, when my doll basically fell to pieces, she told me that she'd have to go to the doll hospital for an operation and she took it away in the car and she let me stay up late that night and make a card for her and she mailed it for me the next day, and the day after that she brought my dolly home from the hospital and it was as good as new. It was all bright and clean and I didn't notice a thing. I must've been what, fifteen or sixteen years old when I finally figured it out."

"That she just bought a new version of the same doll?"

"Bravo," Iris said. "You're a little quicker on the draw than I was. But I didn't care. I just thought that my dolly'd been to the hospital for her operation, and it made perfect sense to me that she'd come out of the hospital brighter and cleaner than when she went in, so what did I know?"

"Do you think she did the right thing, your mother?"

"Oh, I don't know. I suppose so. Why not? I certainly have absolutely zero fear of hospitals, that's for sure."

This time Ken laughed. "And you've probably been conditioned to think that people go into hospitals and eventually come out again, which isn't exactly the case anymore."

"No, I don't suppose it is," Iris said, letting that sink in. "I don't know, though. Maybe that's just it."

"Maybe what's it?"

"Maybe that's what's wrong with me," Iris said. "I grew up thinking that you could fix anything. I thought you could get dragged around by one arm, and have one of your eyes pop off, and let the padding around your heart slip out, and somehow it could all be fixed."

"And now?"

"And now I don't know anymore."

Ken and Iris sprang into action. Well, Ken and Iris found themselves slowly exiting the great state of inaction. Iris looked over at Ken and asked him, matter-of-factly, what he was doing that night, and he said, "What am *I* doing? On a Saturday night? Nothing, obviously."

And Iris said, "On the contrary, my dear. You're going to the potassium hydroxide fund-raiser."

"*I'm* going to the lye fund-raiser?"

"Yup. Do you have a tux?"

"A tux? I think you know the answer to that question."

"It was worth a shot," Iris said. "Do you know where you can get your hands on one?"

"Let me think for a second. Brett had one, though I guess that doesn't really help, does it?"

"Not so much."

"Oh wait," Ken said. "Scillat has one. The chairman of the English Department. He keeps his on the back of his door in case he ever gets invited to a faculty event at someplace *other* than City College. I know I've seen it there, and he's more or less my size."

"Can you borrow it tonight?"

"We'll find out if you let me borrow your phone." Ken took Iris's phone and called Maxine at home, which prompted a nice, neat pang to his solar plexus because he had to dig pretty deep to remember her number whereas before he used to dash it off without a second thought.

Maxine was delighted to hear from him, and from the sound of it, it seemed as if she were going through all the regular preparations for a nice, long chat—getting a drink of water from the faucet, kicking her shoes off and getting herself tucked into a position on the couch that was maximally conducive to gossip. She sounded a bit hurt when Ken said that he couldn't talk very long and he just wanted to know if Scillat's tux was still hanging on the back of his door and whether Scillat might be lurking around the department this weekend. And if he *wasn't*, how likely was it that Ken could borrow the aforementioned tuxedo and get away with it?

And Maxine was in perfect form. Yes, the tux was still there. No, there was zero possibility of Scillat creeping around the department this weekend because his wife was at some sort of holistic retreat—alone—and Scillat would be at home taking full advantage of the peace and quiet. And sure, go right ahead and borrow it so long as you have it back by Monday morning. And then she let this very expectant pause hang in the air. "Ken?" she finally said.

"Yes?"

"Are you going to tell me why you need Scillat's tux? Assuming that you're not just planning to get yourself dressed up with nowhere to go?"

Ken hadn't actually thought about how to handle this situation, so all he could think of saying off the cuff was, "Oh, well it's kind of this last-second thing."

"You don't say."

"I guess you noticed that. Anyway, it's no big deal, but it's this fancy schmancy fund-raiser thing that I got a freebie to at the last second."

Maxine seemed to brighten up at that. "You mean with lots of gorgeous, eligible men walking around in tuxes? And all for a good cause? I'm proud of you, Ken. This is just what the doctor ordered." Ken didn't really have the heart to disabuse Maxine of her misconception so he just let it go. "I'm giving you fair warning," Maxine said. "On Monday morning I expect you to produce at least one telephone number written on a cocktail napkin, and don't bother making one up to try and fool me—people have suffered greatly for lesser crimes."

"I wouldn't dream of it," Ken said.

And then the normally well-spoken Maxine paused again. "You know," she said, "this might not be the right time or place to discuss this, but I have a very strong feeling that you're going to be getting your job back at the reference desk." Ken knew Maxine well enough to realize that the *right* time and place to discuss this was in Maxine's office while she was there, as in the way they used to chew the fat for hours on end. This was a gentle reproach gift-wrapped in good news.

"This is something you have a feeling about, or something you know?" he asked.

Paul Schmidtberger

"This is something I know, but I don't know it officially yet, so neither do you. And I've *not* known it, officially, since *Wednesday*, which means that if I'd seen you around any time since *Wednesday*, I could've told you what I *don't know* and you might have been able to put yourself a little more at ease." Her tone softened up a little. "I mean, I don't think it's particularly easy for you to be living without a big chunk of what you used to earn." Ken's mind flashed back over the past few days to see if maybe he hadn't had any classes at all so he could tell Maxine that and he'd be off the hook. Unfortunately, he could distinctly remember going in on Thursday and harvesting the most recent batch of Lucinda's anger exercises. "I guess I could've been less of a stranger," Ken told Maxine.

"We'll talk about it," she said, "and not when you're itching to get off to your *glah*-morous event. But yeah, Ken. If you want my opinion, this kind of trouble isn't forever."

"No," he said. "But by the same token, you didn't get hung out to dry in a faculty meeting."

"I didn't say that I was talking about that, did I? I meant *all* this trouble. It's not forever. Any of it. That's what I'm saying."

"Do you really think so?"

"Have I ever been wrong before?"

"If you have, you've managed to keep it remarkably quiet," Ken said.

Recruiting Jeff was shockingly easy. "Hey, Jeff, it's Ken and I'm here with Iris and we were just wondering if you'd like to crash this fancy fund-raiser gig with me tonight so we can do a little spying on Jeremy?"

And all he said was, "Okay."

Iris drove Ken to City College where they found the English Department completely deserted. Scillat's office was locked, but Ken knew where Maxine kept an extra key—inside a bottle of rubber cement that'd dried out in the middle of the Johnson administration—and they let themselves into Scillat's private little universe of unlimited Scillatishness. Ken made a beeline for the tux, and with a simple, "Don't turn around," directed toward Iris, he started to get changed. Iris, evidently forgetting that you're not supposed to leave fingerprints in this kind of situation, picked up a framed photo of Scillat and what must be his wife and studied it. The wife had her hands clasped demurely together in plain view, as if to prove that *she didn't do it* in case her husband was found to have been murdered at the precise moment the picture was taken.

"Iris!" Ken hissed. "What are you doing?"

"I'm baking a pie," she said. "What does it look like I'm doing?"

"Shhhhh! Can you keep your voice down?"

"Why?" she said in her normal, everyday tone of voice. "There's nobody around for miles."

"Iris, just as a favor to me, could you tone it down? And don't touch anything."

"Oh, brother," she said, although she said it a lot more quietly and she stopped inspecting Scillat's desk and helped Ken with the cufflinks and the studs and then quite cleverly concealed a tiny spot of brownish blood near the front collar with some Wite-Out. The bow tie, unfortunately, was a real one, which neither of them had counted on and which neither knew how to tie.

"How come you can't tie a tie?" Iris asked.

"I *can* tie a tie," Ken said. "Just not a bow tie."

"Well, you'd think they'd come with instructions or something if it's so complicated."

"Well, they don't. And I don't know whether it's complicated or not; all I know is that *I* don't know how to do it." He'd worn a real bow tie exactly once before in his entire life and Brett had tied it for him. Of *course* Brett had. Ken tried to push away the memory of Brett's arms reaching up around his neck to tie the tie and the smell of his recently brushed teeth. Or at a minimum he vowed to stop taking it out on Iris. "So what do we do now?" he asked.

"We don't panic, that's the first thing," Iris said. "I suppose you could wait outside the fund-raiser and then ask someone wearing a bow tie to help you?" Ken visibly cringed. "I'm not saying it's ideal," Iris said. "It's just an idea. It's just *one* idea."

"Okay, so what's our second idea?"

"Well, we could go with the free-spirited, I-can't-be-hemmed-in-by-a-tie look. It might fly."

"I don't know, Iris. I don't think I'm the right person to pull that off, and the whole idea is to blend in, not stick out like a sore thumb."

"What about Maxine?"

"She lives in Leonia."

"What about Jeff?"

"Jeff? I don't think he seems like the type who'd know how to tie a bow tie."

"Well, I don't think what he *seems* like really matters," Iris said, picking up her cell phone and hitting redial. The entire conversation took all of twelve seconds, most of which were devoted to pleasantries (Jeff's inquiry as to how Iris was and her response—*fine*—plus her counterdemand as to the state of his well-being—also *fine*), and that left only about two seconds for the meat of the matter: did he, or did he not, know how to tie a bow tie?

"Sure, no problem."

"Great," Iris said.

She flipped the phone shut and told Ken, as if he hadn't already guessed, that Jeff could indeed tie the tie and that they'd better be skedaddling. On the way out the door, though, she told him that he underestimated people: "And you get that," she said, "from doing it to yourself."

Iris got behind the wheel of her car and they zoomed all the way down the Henry Hudson, and she swung over to a stop at the corner of Forty-fourth and Tenth to pick up Jeff, who was easy to spot because he was the only one in the Local 638 Steamfitters Union picket line trudging around the corner in a tuxedo. He gave his sign back to somebody and climbed into the backseat, all elbows and shins everywhere, and Iris asked him what they wanted.

"Justice," Jeff said.

"And when do they want it?" Ken asked.

"That would be now, from what I could gather."

"Yeah, well, *good luck*," Iris said, peeling out, which made Jeff tip all the way over in the back. It was more for effect than anything else because they weren't in a hurry at all since the International Photography Something or Other, which was where the fund-raiser was being held, was only a few more blocks away. Jeff righted himself and tied Ken's bow tie from the backseat as if he were one of those hit men in the movies who rubs out the guy in the passenger seat by choking him with a piece of wire. Iris didn't drive them all the way up to the building so that they wouldn't be spotted, and as he got out, Ken pressed her hand and told her to hang in there. Then he thought—*ah, screw it all*—and he leaned over and hugged her as best as you can hug somebody who's strapped into a boxy piece of Swedish steel. "Get yourself on home and we'll call you later."

Outside the building, Ken launched into a lengthy speech about how they were going to have to just "breeze" right by the table where the badges and the registration things would probably be, and Jeff just said, "Like this?" He turned on his heel and strode in the door, leaving Ken no choice but to rush in after him, and boom, just like that, they were inside. There was a bright, friendly buzz to the place, and it took Ken a few moments to get his bearings. And once he got his bearings, his first thought was that the enormous photographs on the walls were more likely to get people to bring up their lunches than to bring out their checkbooks. The huge photograph he was standing directly in front of looked like an aerial shot of some concentration camp somewhere taken in the middle of winter—the roofs of the dark, rectangular barracks forming a strange, and strangely familiar, circular pattern in the snow—with a huge, shadowy footprint superimposed over one whole part of the camp. He read the little blurb to try to figure out what the point was, but the title of the photo was, naturally enough, "Untitled." The sign did, however, note that the photo had won a prize in England.

Jeff appeared out of nowhere with two gin and tonics and said, "I didn't know you were into manhole covers."

"Into what?" Ken asked, whirling back around to take a second look at the photograph. "Oh, for Pete's sake."

They surveyed the crowd and nothing seemed terribly out of the ordinary. It basically seemed like what it was—an event where people with dinero parted with some of that dinero in order to hobnob with other people who were willing to part with some dinero in order to hobnob with *them*. In short, it was buzzing. There were bars everywhere and they were well staffed and there were still tons of glasses turned over in row after row on linen-covered banquet tables behind the bars that gave off this glittery feeling of possibility. The music was actually kind of pleasant, and the flower arrangements around a pillar in the middle of the room were spectacular. All of which was vaguely troubling because, try as he might, Ken could spot no signs of a crisis serious enough to warrant Jeremy's presence.

"So what's the plan?" Jeff asked.

"The plan is we wait and see," Ken said.

"And would sidling over to that tray of little puffy pastry things be *inconsistent* with that plan?"

"The answer to that would be no," Ken said, happy to have a definite course of action, even if that definite course of action would only cover the next three seconds. "Let's do it."

Jeff turned out to be quite a natural at cocktail parties. He seemed to be able to insinuate himself easily into other people's conversations and, unlike Ken, he was equally able to extricate himself from those conversations without having to make up some utterly noncredible lie about needing to go schedule a dialysis appointment or something like that. It was a curious experience to tag along after Jeff and get introduced to total strangers by him and then talk to them and joke around with them and gradually realize that the more urbane of those total strangers were just assuming that Ken and Jeff were *together*. That's why people would ask questions like, "So where do you guys live?" and then turn to some other subject after only one of them, say Jeff, had answered, as if the location of Ken's residence was irrelevant. As if nobody cared that he lived on West Seventieth Street right next to the single most misguided piece of construction since the Leaning Tower of Pisa architects said, "*Oh, plans schmans.*"

Ken kept an eye out for Jeremy, who seemed to be missing in action, while Jeff's job was to keep their social standing afloat. Jeff could break the ice with someone just by asking how that person was doing, a gambit that Ken couldn't have imagined doing in a million years. Jeff would turn to someone at his elbow and introduce himself and from there the conversation would take off. And if it didn't, that was no big deal either. Ken would be trying to think up something clever and witty to say, and meanwhile Jeff would take charge and just ask people what they'd done earlier in the day. And he seemed genuinely interested in their responses, even though a lot of them were from out of town and had evidently spent the day doing touristy things that weren't as interesting as regular New York things, like ransacking the local five-and-dime in search of a really inexpensive salad spinner because it doesn't make a lot of sense to spend good money on something that just rotates leaves.

Ken tuned back in to the conversation and this woman with a very precise haircut and a husband who followed everything attentively but never piped up himself, was asking Jeff in return what *he'd* been doing all day and he said he'd spent the day reading. He said that he'd been rereading *Mansfield Park* and he'd almost been late tonight because he was just at the part where the shit hits the fan, and the lady with the precise haircut paused for a moment and looked at him uncertainly and then threw back her head and laughed.

The lights dipped for a moment and a hush spread through the crowd and then everyone was turning and shifting and trying to pinpoint whoever it was who was tapping on a microphone and asking for everyone's attention. It was a short, red-faced man standing behind a podium who thanked everybody for coming and then turned things over to the first of many speakers, and Jeff seized control of the situation by steering Ken over to the closest bar under the guise of getting themselves into a better position. The vantage point was ideal, because by the time the woman who was introducing the keynote speaker got to reason number six, subsection (c) of what a privilege it was to make the introduction, Ken had spotted Jeremy.

"That's him," he whispered to Jeff. "Jeremy's behind the speaker. Straight back from the microphone. See the sweaty guy with the gut? Shiny forehead? Go one, two, three people to the left—"

"Including Sweaty?"

"No, number one is the guy next to Sweaty, then two, then three, see him?"

"With his arms folded?"

"That's him." Jeremy was standing there in the back with his arms folded, listening carefully to the speaker. Jeremy was dressed in a way that was more or less work-ish, though he didn't have any immediately evident attributes of officialness. No clipboard. No walkie-talkie. He didn't even have one of those little earpiece microphones fixed to his head, the kind that let important people stay in permanent communication with other important people.

Wait a second, Ken thought. *Jeff was rereading Jane Austen?* And then Jeff nudged him.

Blabby had finished her exhaustive introduction of the man who, contrary to all prior evidence, needed no introduction, and while all eyes were on him with high hopes for a hilarious opening zinger and a mercifully short speech, Ken and Jeff watched the woman walk back to the wall and take the place next to Jeremy, who clearly wasn't adverse to this intrusion given that he scrunched over slightly to make room for her, only not all that much room because their shoulders were touching.

Ken used the keynote speech to study Blabby. She was probably in her early thirties and nothing about her appearance or demeanor screamed "Adulteress." She was slim and had dark brown hair that was parted on the side and neatly cut to reach just above the shoulder of the black suit she was wearing. She had trendy glasses with black plastic frames, but the overall effect wasn't that of harshness or severity; instead, she had the same kind of wholesome, professional appeal that you only ever see in optometrist ads—the glasses look great and the person looks great and the fact that the two don't really go together doesn't bother anybody.

As soon as the speech was over, though, Jeff moved in and Ken had to scramble to keep up, ditching his glass and the handful of crackers he'd just grabbed, each of which featured three perfect salmon roe marooned in a blob of pink salmon paste—which suggested some complicated oedipal issues on the part of the caterer. Jeff strode toward Jeremy and then changed course at the last possible second, extending his hand to Blabby instead and congratulating her on her speech. But even as he introduced himself to the Blabmeister, he smiled at Jeremy and Jeremy was brought into the return introductions, and Ken arrived just in time to get swept in too.

"And this is my friend Ken," Jeff said. Jeremy looked directly at him but his expression didn't reveal a hint of recognition from the time they'd spent at Starbucks hiding from the rain. On the other hand, Ken had the feeling that Jeremy's long, unbroken look was designed to size up (a) Ken's donating capabilities, and (b) his donating inclinations, an inquiry that ground to a halt after the negative assessment of Ken's cash flow. Then Ken was afraid that Jeremy would rush off to accomplish various administrative tasks but he didn't; he stayed put at Blabby's elbow—she turned out to be named Alicia—while Alicia was getting deeper and deeper into a conversation with Jeff about stage fright. "Normally," Alicia said, "I don't ever have to speak in public, and that's a very good thing because even the thought of getting up in front of people makes me sick to my stomach."

"Well, if that's true," Jeff said, "you certainly had us fooled because it seemed to me that you were perfectly at ease." He told her that he wouldn't have been surprised if she spoke in public all the time, and she laughed and said, "Oh-ho, no no no!" She said she hadn't been able to take advantage of any of the hors d'oeuvres because she'd been so nervous she was afraid they'd wind up stuck in her throat. And Jeff took that as an invitation to talk about how stressful and nerve-wracking law school could be and how he could feel all that bile churning away inside of him. He said it left a bitter, metallic taste in his mouth in the morning, and when he told the nurse practitioner at the infirmary at St. John's about it, she said that people who were under constant stress should raise the heads of their beds up to keep all that bile down where it belongs and not allow it to wash back up.

"You're at St. John's Law School?" Jeremy asked, entirely missing the more interesting point about bile bubbling away in stressed-out people's stomachs.

"I was," Jeff said. "I'm doing my third year at Hofstra." He paused, which Ken thought was a bold (and stupid) move since it gave Jeremy the chance to ask *why* he was doing his third year at Hofstra, but instead it was Alicia who spoke up. "So, did you try it?" she asked.

"Propping the head of my bed up with a few books?" Jeff said. "I did. And no, it didn't make a difference."

"What books did you use?"

"Actually, that was a difficult choice," Jeff said. He said that his contracts book was one of the best candidates because it was the thickest. Though he didn't want to give short shrift to his Constitutional Law book which, while slightly thinner, was definitely the source of a lot more *anxiety*. . . . And that's when Ken cut him off and copied a move he'd seen earlier. "So," he said, looking from Alicia to Jeremy and back again, "where do you guys live?"

Jeremy looked at him oddly and said, "New York," and then turned to look at Alicia. She said, "Washington, D.C. Which I think I mentioned during my speech. Twice. In fact."

"Oh," Ken said. "That's right."

And then a nice, toxic pause settled over the four of them while Ken racked his brain searching for a way to undo the damage and get things back on track. He was about to resort to desperation tactics and make a comment on the utterly unremarkable weather, but Jeff jumped in ahead of him and picked up Alicia's hand as if it had been sitting there on a platter and he was planning to eat it. Instead, he brought it up close to his face and said, "That's really beautiful."

"Well, thank you," Alicia said.

"And so distinctive too. You don't see rings like that every day."

Chapter Fourteen. In Which Iris Leaves a Lamp Burning While Events Unfold Around Her

Ken and Jeff held an emergency summit in the men's room and settled on a strategy: divide and conquer. Jeremy and Alicia had given them the slip a few minutes earlier with nothing more than a polite, "Will you excuse us?" from Jeremy, and now the boys needed a plan for weaseling their way back into Jeremy and Alicia's orbit to pump them for information. Ken kept coming up with unhelpful things, like how he could go ask Jeremy for directions somewhere—he did say he's from New York—but Jeff kept a level head and rejected each idea. "The key," he said, "is to step into the shoes of someone whose job it is to wriggle information out of people, and then do whatever *they* would do."

"Like tie them up and shine a spotlight in their eyes?" Ken said.

"No, that's not what I had in mind," Jeff said. "I'm thinking more like a principal. Say a high school principal knows that somebody was smoking in the girls' room because the smoke alarm went off and four girls emerged in a cloud of smoke. What does he do? He separates them and talks to each one separately to see how their stories match up. You know, who was standing where, what were they talking about and so on. And once you catch them in little lies, like where so-and-so's Abercrombie & Fitch casual canvas tote bag was, then it's easy to confront them with their big lie, like who was smoking and how did they get their hands on a pack of Virginia Slims Menthol Lights in the first place?"

"Okay, so who gets whom?"

"I'll take Alicia," Jeff said. "And you take Jeremy."

"Roger," Ken said. "Roger Dodger."

Alicia and Jeremy were still together, but Ken managed to break them up by going out to the lobby and calling Jeremy's cell phone from a pay phone and then crumpling an ATM slip directly into the mouthpiece to supply some of the crackle and garble that you normally get for free. Jeremy went from saying, "Hel-*lo*?" and plugging his other ear to saying, "Hold on a second," and dashing out of the room. And then Jeff swept in.

He brought Alicia a glass of white wine and she just seemed grateful for the booze and the conversation. She didn't seem to be part of any of the larger, more organized delegations that Jeff had started to notice. "Potassium hydroxide lobbyists seem to travel in packs," he thought.

In short order, Jeff found out that Alicia loved New York but didn't think she could live there; that she'd recently bought a set of plain, pine shelves for her CDs, only when they said that the assembly was easy, they were lying because she nearly jammed a Phillips-head screwdriver through the palm of her hand; that she was going back to D.C. tomorrow; that no, she didn't have a lot of friends in New York, but the friends she had here were good friends; that she wasn't sure that her hairdresser had a coherent, long-term goal for her, because he once said that he was trying to get enough length to do an early Jean Harlow and another time he mentioned, without being asked, that if she could hold out for say four months between cuts, he could get enough raw material built up to go for a cascading Rita Hayworth in *Gilda* look, but in the end she felt pretty comfortable in his hands and she certainly didn't want to argue with him in any event.

"Why not?"

"Because he got me a free jacuzzi."

"Your *hairdresser* got you a free jacuzzi?"

"Well, his friend did," Alicia said. "I was telling Kurt—that's my hairdresser—that the ceiling fan in my bathroom was broken and I needed to get somebody to fix it, and he said that his boyfriend, who's some sort of designer, was really good at handy stuff like that and he could do it for next to nothing, and anyway, Jordie—that's Kurt's friend—came over and borrowed a ladder from the super and he climbed up and was fiddling around with the fan when he fell off the ladder and ricocheted off my sink and then the ladder itself fell right through what *used* to be my shower door. I mean, *right* through it. And it was made of glass."

"Oh, my God, was he hurt?" Jeff asked, although given Alicia's sly little smile, it didn't seem like she was beholden to her hairdresser just because she'd killed his designer boyfriend.

"No. It was a miracle, but he was pretty much fine."

"So how did you get from that to a jacuzzi?" Jeff asked. "You're going to have to connect the dots for me."

"Oh, that. That's easy. It had something to do with the insurance. Like instead of saying that my shower door got shattered in an accident, he said that my *tub* got broken, that it was ceramic or porcelain or something like that and once it was broken it couldn't be fixed, and then together with the discount he gets as a designer, I ended up with a bubbly new shower-jacuzzi combo for nothing."

"And what about the ceiling fan?" Jeff asked. "Still broken?"

"Dead as a doornail," Alicia said, and they both laughed. Then Jeff changed subjects and asked Alicia what she did, and she said that she was a lawyer with the Department of Agriculture in Washington, which shouldn't be surprising, she said, because *everybody* was a lawyer in Washington. And then Jeff reminded her that he was midway through his third year of law school at Hofstra and the *real* bonding began.

Meanwhile Ken was having a little less luck with Jeremy. He intercepted Jeremy on his way back into the party without any strategy at all other than trying to *insinuate* that he had tons of money, no heirs, and a charitable bent that would make Eleanor Roosevelt look like Ebenezer Scrooge. You know, *before* he realized the error of his ways and lightened up and leaned out the window in his nightshirt to wish everybody a Merry Christmas?

Yeah, well, easier said than done.

Instead, Jeremy seemed like he was looking for a way to extricate himself from Ken, so, without even thinking, Ken said, "You know, you really remind me of someone—and it worked. Jeremy stopped edging away and looked at Ken and was curious to know who.

Think, Ken. Think think think *think*.

"A friend of mine," he said. Well, so much for thinking.

Jeremy was still gazing at him so he plowed on. "I don't know what it is, but there's something about you that reminds me of him. He's . . ."

"Incredibly good-looking?" Jeremy offered, and Ken laughed.

"Right!" he said, and once at ease, he was able to talk to Jeremy without sounding like a buffoon or a pedant or anything between. He asked Jeremy what he did and Jeremy said he was in "consulting" without saying what kind of consulting it was and without mentioning any official involvement in the current proceedings. But Ken played it cool for once in his life and just kept putting the ball back in Jeremy's court. Did he find consulting to be rewarding? Was it difficult to go from one project to another? Was this the kind of thing where clients called him up at four a.m. because the clients were in Australia and didn't care that most people in New York want to sleep at four a.m., with the possible exception of everybody's upstairs neighbors?

"Fascinating," Ken thought. "The less I talk, the more interesting I am."

Jeremy was perfectly at ease and chatted away with Ken. He knew exactly where the Santa Monica was and, even better, he saw absolutely eye to eye with Ken as far as the Trump debacle was concerned. He said that he wouldn't want to be in a building that touched the Trump house of horrors, and when Ken said that they didn't actually touch—the Trump building was actually a whopping eighteen inches away but that a gray fiberglass *building zipper* had been used to make the two look flush out at the sidewalk—Jeremy said that even if they didn't touch, the Trump building probably had stray *molecules*, and those stray molecules probably went out and tried to take over other buildings and ruin them too.

"You got that right," Ken said.

Jeremy asked Ken if he was going to stay in the neighborhood, and Ken heard himself saying that he wasn't sure, which was definitely odd since right up to the moment that those words left his lips, the idea of moving hadn't crossed his mind. He said that, well, actually, he'd been living in the Santa Monica with someone and that, uh, unfortunately their relationship had ended somewhat abruptly—let's just say more abruptly than he'd anticipated—and for the moment he hadn't quite figured out what to do. A curious look passed over Jeremy's face, but all he said was that he was sorry to hear that.

"Yeah, well, me too."

"Actually," he said, "if you want to know the truth, I thought you were with your friend there, Jeff, I think his name was." And Ken blushed. And *as* he blushed, he thought—well, *so much for a career in espionage*—but all he said was, "No, he's just a friend." Jeremy looked straight at him and he felt compelled to go on. "Plus he's like eleven years old or something."

And Jeremy said, "Are you trying to convince yourself, or me?"

"It's not that simple," Ken said, steeling himself for Jeremy to say that yes, of course, it was that simple. Instead, Jeremy just smiled and backed down and agreed with him. "You're probably right," Jeremy said. "Nothing ever is."

And then before Ken knew what was happening, it was over. The lights came up and the people who'd been discreetly removing dirty glasses from behind the bars started openly removing them in these big green plastic tubs, and there wasn't any way to mistake the obvious—the party was over. Jeff and Alicia appeared, and

Alicia already had some sort of businessy raincoat draped over her arm and a purse strung over her shoulder. The two pairs stood there and told each other that it had been really nice to meet each other, and Alicia reminded Jeff to look into some something or other that sounded like a lead on a legal job, and that was that. They moved out toward the street together, and on the curb Ken asked Jeremy and Alicia which way they were heading, and that provoked a moment, just a moment, of hesitation before Jeremy took control and half answered, half dodged the question by saying that they'd need only one cab. Ken selflessly let them have the first cab and then grabbed Jeff by the cummerbund and leapt into the next taxi that pulled up.

"Follow that cab!" he shouted, and they peeled out into traffic. "*Go!*" Their taxi zoomed right up to the back bumper of Jeremy and Alicia's cab where the two of them were clearly visible in the backseat; then the driver eased off a bit before neatly taking a corner right after the first cab.

"Jesus," Ken said to Jeff. "What kind of info did you get?"

"Not much, what about you?"

"Not much? You were talking to Alicia forever. You must've gotten something."

"Well, when I said not much, I meant that I didn't get anything definitive, like that she's here in New York to break up somebody's relationship."

"Well, I didn't mean *that*," Ken said. "Nobody's going to come right out and say that. But you must've learned something about her?"

"Oh, tons," Jeff said. "For starters, she's a lawyer."

Ken groaned as the cab swung onto Lexington and followed the other cab downtown. "Oh, Lord help us."

"And I don't think she lives with anyone," Jeff said.

"Why not?"

"Because the ceiling fan in her bathroom broke and she had to call somebody to get it fixed."

"She told you that?"

"No, I just made it up. Of course she told me that," Jeff said.

"No, what I meant was that you guys were talking about the fixtures in her bathroom?"

"Among other things, yes," Jeff said. "And it proves, well, it *indicates* that she lives alone because if she lived with somebody, that somebody would've fixed the fan for her."

"That's your logic?" Ken asked.

"That and the fact that she never mentioned anything about living with someone else."

Ken was about to complicate matters and ask if the ceiling fan was one of those combo deals that doesn't just suck moisture out of the air but also supplies heat when Jeff spotted the first cab pulling over to the curb about fifty yards before the front of a small hotel down near Gramercy Park. They pulled over too under the shadow of a sweet gum tree and waited, but nothing happened. Zero. Jeremy and Alicia appeared to be talking in the backseat and their cab stayed where it was, crimped up against the curb, so Jeff told their own driver to cut the headlights.

"What are they doing?" Ken asked.

"Now how would I know the answer to that?" Jeff said.

"Do you think they're fighting?"

"I don't think so. Why would they be fighting?"

"Maybe the stress of all that cheating got to them?" Ken said.

"Well, they're not cheating yet," Jeff said. "Besides, maybe she's not his cup of tea. Or vice versa. In fact, maybe she's not even straight," he said, halfheartedly grasping at straws.

"Did she *say* she was gay?" Ken asked.

"No, but she has a gay hairdresser. If that helps."

"It doesn't."

"I didn't think so," Jeff said. "I did get her card though."

"Oh my God, you did? Let's see it!" Ken grabbed it out of Jeff's hand and read it out loud. "Alicia M. Kosewic. I wonder what the *M* stands for?" he asked before changing gears and interrupting himself to congratulate Jeff on successfully worming Alicia's card out of her.

"It actually wasn't that hard," he said. "We were having a really nice chat. I mean, she seems like a perfectly nice person."

"Yeah, well, they usually seem nice until they steal your partner right out from under your nose."

"If you say so."

"What do you mean, if I say so?" Ken asked.

"I don't know. I mean, I thought that Alicia was really nice, and actually Iris said the same thing about you. About your situation."

"You mean about Brett and Home-Wrecker?"

"Brett and Neil, that's right." *Iris had been talking to Jeff about Brett and Neil?* Could that possibly be a good thing? "Anyway, Iris said that she really wanted to hate them both on your behalf, you know, just on principle. And especially Brett because he's more at fault. Only she found them both to be pretty likeable guys."

"Well, they sort of saved her life," Ken said. "That tends to predispose you to liking someone. Did she mention that part?"

"Yes, Ken, she told me that. All I'm saying is that Iris was ready to hate Neil, but she didn't—and don't tell her I told you that—and if she were to be a hundred percent honest with you, she thought that Neil was probably more your speed than Brett was."

"*Neil* was more my speed than Brett?"

"I'm just saying what she said. All she said was that of the two of them, Neil was a little bit more serious and had his feet planted a little more steadily on the ground and that if she were putting together a big, gigantic jigsaw puzzle that fell out of the sky and you and Brett and Neil were three pieces of the puzzle, she would've tried to put you and Neil together rather than either of you with Brett, because it's the two of you that match the best."

"Oh, now there's a laugh," Ken said.

"All I'm saying is what Iris said. She said she almost felt sorry for Neil because on some level he'd probably end up like you. . . ."

"Oh, well *thanks*."

"No, not that, but you know what I mean. That he and Brett aren't made for each other and that maybe it'll last, but probably it won't, and when it doesn't, her bet was that Neil would come out holding the short end of the stick."

"Good," Ken said.

"You don't mean that," Jeff said.

"Yes, I do," Ken said, even though everyone present could tell that he really didn't. Everyone except the driver, that is, who was diligently rooting around in his ear with the cap from some long lost pen.

Finally there was some movement. The cab up ahead nodded down slightly toward the curb and then the vague shape in the back split apart like a cell in a biology textbook and Alicia got out. She bent over and said something inaudible into the cab and then straightened up and shut the door, waved, and walked into the hotel.

"We keep following?" Jeff asked.

"We do," Ken said, and they took off after Jeremy as his taxi made a beeline north and they followed it all the way uptown. When they turned down Eighty-fifth Street after Jeremy's cab, Ken made the driver slow down to a crawl and then stop, and they watched Jeremy pay, get out, and go up to the door where, instead of taking out his keys and letting himself into the foyer, he paused. He walked back down the steps and out into the street and looked up at his own windows which, unlike the rest of the building, were still lit, and then he walked back up to the top of the stoop and sat down.

"What's he doing?" Ken whispered.

"He's sitting down," Jeff said. "It's one of the many wonderful things you can do with your butt."

"I can see that," Ken said. "But why?"

"How would I know? Call him up and ask him."

"Oh, that'll help."

"So what do we do?" Jeff said.

"We wait," Ken said, and then he leaned forward and asked the driver to kill the lights and the engine, and they went back to watching Jeremy sitting on the top step with his elbows on his knees.

Then Jeff brought up a complication. "I asked Alicia about the ring," he said, "and she said it was her brother's."

"It was her what?"

"Her brother's. She said it was her brother's ring. I asked Alicia where she got it and she told me that it was actually her brother's ring, but given its size and style, it could just as easily pass for a woman's ring."

"How's that a complication?" Ken asked. "Why should we care whether it was a gift from her brother or whether she bought it at Bloomingdale's or Bergdorf's or wherever people go when they give up on the idea that someone's going to buy them jewelry and they just decide to buy it for themselves?"

"Because something about the way she phrased it—that it *was* her brother's ring—struck me as odd."

"Was, as in maybe he's not around anymore?" Ken asked.

"That's the impression I got, and before you ask me if I *know* this for a fact, I don't. It's just an impression. Just from the way she said 'was.' Plus the fact that she seemed reluctant to talk about it." They watched Jeremy for a few minutes, and it was as if he had become as much a part of the hardware of the street as the wrought-iron railings and the hydrant and the dumpster in front of the restaurant supply store that had finally made good on its decade-long threat to go out of business.

"It was my brother's ring," Ken said, trying out the phrase a couple different ways. "Wait a second," he said, "what about Pennsylvania?"

"What about it?"

"Did you find out if she'd ever gone off to Bucks County, Pennsylvania, for a passionate, though secretive, weekend?"

"Well, no," Jeff said. "Obviously I didn't."

"What do you mean, 'obviously you didn't'? That's what we're trying to find out, isn't it?"

"I know what we're trying to find out," Jeff said. "It's just that there wasn't any moment where it would've made sense for me to blurt out a question like that. You know, given the context and everything."

"The context," Ken echoed. He didn't sound convinced. "Well, couldn't you have found a way to make it come up? You know, say you were just talking about Pennsylvania *in general*. Or something Pennsylvania-ish, just to break the ice. Like the Liberty Bell."

"The *Liberty Bell*? You're telling me that I should've brought up the Liberty Bell?"

"Well, not *per se*. I'm just saying that maybe you could've used it as a trap for getting her to talk about her romantic weekend with Jeremy."

"Speaking of which, how come you didn't?"

"How come I didn't what?"

"How come you didn't ask Jeremy the same things. If it's supposed to be so easy, then why didn't you ask *Jeremy*?" Jeff said, and they both reflexively looked over to be sure that Jeremy was still sitting on the stoop with his elbows on his knees, only he wasn't. He was still there, that much was clear, only now his face was buried in his hands and his shoulders were shaking convulsively and there just wasn't any mistaking what was going on—Jeremy was crying his heart out.

Dawn the next day was one of those moments that helps explain why one and a half million otherwise rational people choose to live on a not particularly welcoming chunk of rock lodged between the Hudson and East rivers; it was an exquisite, achingly clear fall morning. Iris was aware that Jeremy had come home late—very late, in fact—and that he'd slipped into bed next to her, but all that was hours and hours ago. Jeremy had settled into a deep, exhausted sleep while Iris, on the other hand, hovered just under the surface of wakefulness. She dreamed that she was driving her Volvo with Jeremy at her side, which meant that it was still very early in their relationship because Jeremy would later wrest control of the wheel away from her even though she was actually a very good, very deliberate driver. They were heading back to the city, and from the looks of things, it had snowed quite heavily the night before and traffic was creeping along, which didn't bode well for the moment when they got to the entrance to the George Washington Bridge and all ten billion lanes merged down to one.

But get there they did. One lane merged with the next, and Jeremy squeezed the back of Iris's neck as they inched along, and then Iris let a car go in front of her even though it had taken five minutes for that bit of space to open up, and Jeremy had looked over at her and said, "I think you're more generous than I am."

"Because I let that guy in?" Iris asked.

"That and other things as well," Jeremy said, and Iris just smiled at him, but deep down she felt unsettled. Deep down she felt like a fraud, because Iris hadn't let the car cut in front of her out of the goodness of her heart; she'd just gotten tired of the car that *had* been in front of her before then, the one with the horrendous couple in it who were having a bitter argument. Iris wasn't kind and forgiving. Iris just wanted to fob those two off on somebody else, which worked like a charm.

Jeremy stirred next to her and Iris pulled him closer as he slept. When Jeremy was tired enough to sleep on his stomach, he basically turned into a rag doll that you could pull and bend any way you wanted. Iris settled herself down as close as she could, but then remembered that she was supposed to be watching the snowy road or she'd get everybody killed, and then she just as quickly remembered that that had all been years and years ago and they'd eventually gotten over the bridge and the streets in Manhattan had been plowed and she'd loosened up a bit and driven home, glancing over every so often at Jeremy and the locket that swung back and forth between them.

Oh, the locket.

Iris just couldn't understand how that could be, how two realities could exist side by side like that. In version one, Iris is kind and considerate; she's the type of person to let another car cut in front of her even though the people in that car were probably revolting assholes from the Upper East Side with a Hungarian maid who used to be a chemical engineer back when Hungary had an economy, and they take advantage of her by making her help the family's brats with their science homework, only they still pay her a regular, minimum wage maid's salary.

And in a different reality, Iris is petty and easily annoyed and she slows down when she should be speeding up and she tricks some unsuspecting driver into zipping out into traffic and wedging himself behind the most annoying couple on the face of the earth where *he* can have front-row seats as they bicker and hurl accusations at one another and literally break up just as the sun sets and the twinkling lights on the George Washington Bridge finally loom up overhead.

So which one is right?

On one side of the Ping-Pong paddle the bird is as free as . . . , well, *as a bird*. And on the other side there's a cage. An empty cage. Unoccupied. For rent. Won't last long. Rare in this neighborhood. All-electric kitchen!

And when you spin the Ping-Pong paddle and you look at the blurry result, neither is right anymore. The bird's in the cage and you were wrong. Wrong, wrong, wrong. How did this happen? How did everything get so mixed up? And why is an all-electric kitchen a good thing? Why do all-electric kitchens always merit an exclamation point? Do people *like* waiting forever for the burners to get hot? She'd have to ask Jeremy, she thought, settling back down and letting herself slide into a deep, deep sleep. Jeremy knows all about that kind of stuff.

Chapter Fifteen. In Which Ken Evaluates Matters and Draws Certain Conclusions

On Sunday afternoon, Iris picked up Ken and they drove down to the flea market in Chelsea so they could poke through other people's stuff in search of things that, were the price to be right, would change hands and officially become their stuff. In a definite break with tradition, though, Iris was running at the mouth. In fact, ever since the Volvo swerved over to the curb at the corner of Seventieth and West End and Iris had commented on what a glorious day it was and ordered Ken to hop in, she hadn't shut up. She went through a long litany of dreams she'd had the night before, and then she launched into a long discourse on how sweet and cuddly Jeremy had been all morning and how Jeremy must've really tied one on last night because his eyes were all swollen and how it had been almost impossible to give him the slip to come meet Ken because he was acting all clingy and cuddly at the same time. Is there a word for acting all clingy and cuddly, and if there isn't, shouldn't somebody make one up? How about "cluddly"? And how the only way Iris could get away was to make something up about having to go review a restaurant all on her own and get seated at a table for one and stand up for herself and send something back even though she didn't have a table full of friends around her to back her up.

"And he bought that?" Ken asked. If he didn't know better, he'd say that Iris wasn't talking in order to *convey relevant*

information to him, but more to put off the moment when he'd tell her everything he'd learned the night before.

"Bought what?"

"Never mind," Ken said, picking up a porcelain doorknob contraption and looking at it closely enough to try and figure out how it worked, but not closely enough to arouse the owner of the stand's attention so that they could all go through a big, useless debate about the relative merits and demerits of a complicated porcelain doorknob contraption that he didn't need in the first place. "Iris," he said, "we really have to talk."

He told her about the evening, from beginning to end. He said they knew exactly who the ring belonged to—a certain Alicia M. Kosewic of Washington, D.C.—and that the ring had previously belonged to Ms. Kosewic's brother who had definitely been alive at some point in the past but may or may not be alive today. Alicia lives in D.C. and she's a lawyer and she's probably single because she had to have somebody over to do some handy work around the house and no matter how you slice things, there's some sort of *emotional charge* between her and Jeremy because they talked forever on the way home and afterward Jeremy cried while sitting out on the stoop.

"An emotional charge," Iris repeated slowly. "How long did it take you to think of putting it that way?"

Ken laughed. "Believe me, a long time."

"And you do realize that that's an interpretation?" she said, smiling despite herself. "When I had to give you all the details about Brett and Neil's place, you practically bit my head off if I didn't stick to the cold, hard facts."

"I guess I must've been pretty awful," Ken said.

"Well, you weren't exactly a picnic," Iris said. "But awful? No, I wouldn't say so."

"So does this Alicia person mean anything to you?"

"You mean do I know her or have I ever heard of her?" Iris asked. "If that's what you're asking, then no. Doesn't ring a bell. Doesn't mean a thing."

"Well, is Jeremy particularly prone to D.C. or D.C.-related events."

"Prone to D.C.-related events?"

"Yeah, you know," Ken said. "Is he always looking for a reason to zip off to D.C.? Like the way that businessmen are always getting sent to meetings and conferences and when the trip is to South Bend, Indiana, everybody tries to get out of it and make somebody more junior go, and when the trip is to Miami or San Francisco, nobody ever tries to get out of it. So what's *Jeremy's* vibe as far as D.C. is concerned?"

"I don't think you have a very realistic view of how the business world works," Iris said. "And in any event, no, Jeremy's not particularly for or against D.C. He's against everything D.C. *stands* for, but that's neither here nor there." Then she paused and said the word, "Alicia."

"Well, at least he wasn't cheating with her, last night anyway," Ken said.

"I guess not."

"You don't seem thrilled," Ken observed.

"Well, I'm not," Iris said. "In an ideal world I'd have never heard the name Alicia, and Jeremy would be here with us instead of parked on the sofa at home with his swollen eyes—and I believed him, by the way, when he said they were swollen because they'd really laid into the sauce last night. In an ideal world, Jeremy would be here with us and he'd be chatting up the stand owners and he wouldn't be afraid to ask them what anything costs and he'd know how to make something all creative out of a useless piece of junk like, like . . ." Iris was casting around for a particularly germane example, but the fact of the matter was that it was *all* junk. It was all this useless, sad-sack junk. Ken wrapped her in his arms and let her cry, and he just stood there with his chin in her hair while people walked around them. Finally Ken gave Iris his hankie and held her around the shoulder and started steering her away, telling her that everything was going to be all right, but before he could finish, he got drowned out by the incredulous voice of some guy behind them. "You got to be kidding," the guy practically screamed. "You want how much? For *half* a fish poacher?"

Monday was a little less exquisite, as Mondays tend to be, but Ken steeled himself and packed his briefcase with papers that needed grading and went into his office at the department for the first time in a long, long time. And on the way in, he found a thick, creamy envelope in his slot from Scillat, which gave him a moment's pause since it was the kind of stationery that the department usually used to reject grossly overqualified candidates for any and all posts. Instead, there was a brief note inside which said that, *upon* reflection and *upon* proper completion of his anger management class, Cohen Library was prepared to offer Ken his old post at the reference desk. Indeed, Ken should see the director of human resources at Cohen at his earliest convenience to make the necessary arrangements. Scillat was confident, the note said, that everybody could put the final punctuation on this unfortunate chapter and leave it all behind them.

"Hey Maxine," Ken said, barging into her office.

"Hey stranger," she said. "Methinks you've seen the good news?"

"Well, *me*thinks that you probably typed this particular piece of good news, unless Scillat's suddenly learned to type all on his own, so you already know, don't you?"

"Very clever of you."

"So what's the deal?" Ken asked. "How did somebody as bad as me get so lucky?"

"They couldn't fill the post," Maxine said. "It's as simple as that."

"They couldn't *fill the post*?" Ken asked. "People are desperate for jobs in this city. Everybody's out of work or looking for more work even if they already have a job. How could they *not* be able to find somebody?"

"Oh, they found people, that's for sure," Maxine said. "They just didn't find the right people."

"What do you mean?"

"Well, the first guy stank, in the sense that his body gave off an offensive smell, as opposed to the sense where his reference work wasn't up to snuff, which it wasn't, by the way, so they had to get rid of him. And then they got another guy in there but they had to let him go before his probation period was up because he was some sort of fundamentalist kook and he's convinced that the whole world came into being a few thousand years ago—lock, stock, and barrel—and he wouldn't give anybody any reference materials that said otherwise. You know, like a *dictionary*."

"What's wrong with the dictionary?"

"It has the words 'Pleistocene era' in it."

"Ah," Ken said. "Which was approximately one bazillion years ago and would contradict the idea that the world's only been around for a couple thousand years?"

"Exactly."

"Oh, brother," Ken said. "How can they be that wrong and not know it? I mean, how could anyone possibly think that we could've screwed the world up as badly as we have in just a paltry couple thousand years?"

"Actually—" Maxine started to say.

But Ken was already answering his own question and, not surprisingly, agreeing with himself wholeheartedly. "I can't believe that I'm getting my job back because the only person they could find was so spectacularly unqualified that he wouldn't hand over the reference materials."

"Oh, that's not actually the case," Maxine said. "There was someone else after him. Somebody in Human Resources got the bright idea of using a work-study student to fill the post, and that kid had the place *hopping*. Suddenly *everybody* was lining up to use the reference desk, and the people in Human Resources were thrilled."

"Except?" Ken ventured.

"Oh, except he was selling pot. The work-study student. That's why everyone was suddenly so interested in reference materials."

"*Drugs?*" Ken asked.

"Well, pot's still a controlled substance," Maxine said, "so yes, he was selling drugs. I believe it's called 'dealing.' Apparently his marketing angle was consistent quality at reasonable prices."

"Good Lord," Ken said. "And let me ask you this. Did he get sent off to some farce of a class where he had to learn to *control his anger*?"

Maxine looked directly at Ken for a long moment before answering. "No," she finally said. "He didn't. They fired him from his job but they didn't want it going any further than that, you know, in terms of the police or publicity or what have you. And it's not clear whether he'll lose his financial aid, which probably wasn't very much to begin with, but was probably a lot to him, but no, he didn't get sent off to anger management. *Like you did*. And no, it's not fair. But you know what? Life's not fair."

"Life's not *fair*?"

"Nope, it isn't," Maxine said. "And besides, you probably learned a thing or two in those classes. Not to mention that none of this is really about the reference desk at Cohen Library. You didn't just disappear off the face of the earth for the last few months because of something that happened over at Cohen. You disappeared because of what happened with Brett. Am I right or am I right?"

"You're always right."

"*Ken*," Maxine said. "I'm trying to be serious here."

"Well, I am too. And I just don't understand it. You knew Brett. You liked Brett, didn't you? Either that or you were fooling everybody all those years. So tell me, were Brett and I wrong for each other? And if so, why didn't you tell me earlier? And if we *weren't* wrong for each other, then why did he go out and cheat on me? And not just a little, either. He's living with this new guy, did you know that? They have an apartment with more than one vase and they're living together."

"More than one vase?" Maxine asked.

"It's a long story," Ken said.

"Well, what do I have but time?" Maxine said, and Ken shut

Maxine's door and sat down and told her all about meeting Iris in his class. He told her how they'd put their heads together to spy on each other's partners and how the whole thing seemed to be blowing up in their faces because Iris was sad enough to cry in the flea market and all that Ken had found out was that Brett seemed perfectly happy without him.

"And that's what I don't get," Ken said. "And you know what? You'd like Jeremy too, just the way that you liked Brett. Most people would like Jeremy. But look what he's doing to Iris! And I don't see how Iris is going to get over this when it all comes out."

"Well, we don't know that yet," Maxine said. "Not that I'm making excuses for Jeremy. Or for the Bretts of this world either."

"Let me ask you this," Ken said. "In all honesty, did you see this coming? I'm not talking about Iris and Jeremy, obviously, but about this thing with Brett. Did he seem all slimy and sleazy and prone to cheating to you?"

"No," Maxine said, but she drew the word out to show that she was still thinking it over.

"Well, did you think that we were right for each other?"

"I don't think that people are necessarily right or wrong for each other," she said. "Obviously at either extreme there are people who definitely should *not* be together, but extreme examples aren't very helpful for everyday situations. You know what I'm saying? But other than those couples out there who *definitely* should not be together, and I suppose a few who definitely *should* be together—you know, the type of couple who has their wedding album displayed on its own little table in the living room and it's plunked down on top of some antique lace and has dried rose petals sprinkled around it that *somebody else* is paid to dust around every week—maybe that kind of couple is truly meant to be together, although probably just to spare the rest of us. But beyond that, no, I can't say that you and Brett were meant to be together. Or that you were necessarily right for each other—that is, beyond the time you had together."

"You're sounding very relativistic," Ken said. "You're not going to start strumming a guitar, are you?"

Maxine laughed. "Not unless someone teaches me how to play one," she said. "But seriously, the point is that no, I didn't think that Brett was somehow perfect for you and that the universe had somehow decreed that from the beginning of time forward, you two were meant to be together. But I didn't think you were wrong for each other either."

"I always thought that something had to be right or it had to be wrong," Ken said. "You know, two plus two equals four. Period. Not five. Not three. Four. So I don't see how two people can be neither right nor wrong for each other. Especially if they love each other. Or *say* they love each other."

"Just because you love someone won't make them love you back," Maxine said. "Think of it as a design flaw."

"A what?"

"A design flaw. You know, like how sometimes a company will make some really great product and everybody's happy with it and then little by little they figure out that there's a problem with it that nobody anticipated."

"Like what?" Ken asked.

"I don't know. Like the Pinto," Maxine said. "The Ford Pinto. Everybody was all excited about it when it came out because it was so little and zippy and it got great gas mileage and that kind of thing was important back then because Jimmy Carter was sitting around the White House in a woolly cardigan sweater freezing his ass off like the rest of America, and the Pinto was just the thing. Except that the geniuses at Ford put the gas tank under the back axle, and whenever anyone got hit from behind—say at a red light or something like that—the whole thing blew up. Sky-high. No chance of surviving. In short, the design was great. But not perfect."

Ken let out a long, low whistle. "That's quite a little error they made there."

"Right. But that's the way things are. And I don't really see how we, as humans, are any different. We're an absolute *miracle* of design. We come in all these fun shapes and sizes and we're designed to last for a good long time, and we can survive all sorts of hardship and mistreatment and be as good as new the next day—try pouring a bottle of bourbon down your toaster and see just how well *it* works the next day—but the design's not perfect. Nothing is. And just because you love somebody won't make them love you back."

Ken thought about that for a moment. "And just because you love somebody won't necessarily prevent them from cheating on you."

"Exactly," Maxine said.

"What a world," Ken said.

"It could be worse," Maxine said. "At least *we* don't explode on impact!"

As Ken had been telling her the entire story, Maxine kept making mental notes to get back to one point in particular, and now she remembered it. "What about this Jeff person?" she asked.

"What about him?"

"Well, you know. Is there some sort of click there? Between the two of you?"

"With *Jeff*?" Ken said. "Maxine, he's two years old. He's in *diapers.*"

"Ken, he's not two years old. You said he was in law school, which means he's no longer an undergraduate, which means he's got to be older than twenty-two, not that undergrads have ever been off limits for any number of your straight colleagues, so how come it's okay for them and not okay for you?"

"It's *not* okay for them just like it's not okay for me. Besides, who's to say that Jeff would be interested in me anyway?"

"Well, *Jeff* would, that's who. Have you dropped any hints?"

"Nope."

"Are you planning to?" Maxine asked.

"I don't know. Maybe."

"Maybe as in 'get off my back' or maybe as in 'maybe I'll get up and dust myself off and go out and actually give it a try'?"

"Maybe as in I love you dearly, Maxine," Ken said.

"Oh, thank you, sweetheart, but that's not the point. The point is that it really is time to move on. You realize that, don't you."

"I do, actually. It's just not as easy as you'd think to let it all go and start over."

"I don't think it's easy," Maxine said. "But it's not as hard as you think either."

"Can you guarantee that?" Ken asked.

"Nope. There are no guarantees. And no free lunches."

"And what if I'm scared stiff?"

"Of what?"

"Of everything, Maxine. Of rejection. Of making a fool of myself. Of never finding anyone and dying alone in my apartment and nobody'll know about it until the cable company gets pissed off about the unpaid bills and the city will come and break down my door and the last thing that'll ever be said about me will be said by an underpaid social worker who's on a flex-time schedule until her psoriasis sorts itself out, and she'll observe that if I'd only had the consideration to lie around rotting on the kitchen floor instead of in the living room, then they wouldn't have had to go through all the trouble of changing the wall-to-wall carpeting, *hideous though it may be*. That's what I'm afraid of."

"Well that's good," Maxine said. "Fear is good."

"Why is fear good?" Ken asked.

"Because it proves that you're human."

Everybody in the class was on pins and needles waiting for Lucinda to show up with the final exam. Everyone except Ken, that is. Ken was waiting for something else, something he usually dreaded—the student evaluations. He wasn't sure when it had happened, but at some point *after* he'd gone to college but some point *before* he started teaching, student evaluations had suddenly become all the rage. Suddenly administrators were falling all over themselves to draw up these ghastly forms for students to fill in where they could *anonymously* say whatever they pleased.

"I think Professor Connelly's course was OK except I don't agree with multiple-choice quizzes on account of how they don't encourage creativity."

"I didn't like it when the red pony died."

"Professor Connelly should definitely not wear his summer khaki suit anymore. Olive is not for everyone and it's doing him no favors."

"Too much homework!"

"My stomach hurts."

The responses were simply amazing. And what was even more amazing was how seriously the administrators took this exercise. Students could snore through an entire semester and wake up just in time to drop a depth charge on the teacher—"I think Professor Connelly is mostly nice except when he starts acting like a major A-hole"—and somebody in the administration would actually take it seriously. And if you didn't turn in your stack of evaluations the second they were filled out, the administration, who'd been comfortably ignoring your three dozen requests for a piece of chalk all semester, would hop right on it and send you urgent notes and call you at home to find out what happened to your manila envelope full of constructive criticism.

Now the tables were turned and Ken was practically rubbing his hands with delight as Lucinda announced that they'd be getting to the final exam in just a few minutes, but before that, there'd be the evaluations to do. Only to his great surprise, Ken couldn't bring himself to even the cosmic score a bit and just toss in any old crap. Instead, he read the questions and genuinely thought about his answers.

"What did you expect to get out of this course at the time you enrolled?"

That couldn't be easier, Ken thought. He wrote down, "Absolutely nothing."

"And what, if anything, did you get out of this course?"

He thought about it for a few moments and then wrote down that he thought he had a better grip on his emotions than he'd had when the course began. Then he went back and changed the words "grip on" to the words "awareness of." Then he said that he'd also gotten some friendships out of the experience and that, in this day and age, that was nothing to sneeze at. He said that he felt a little less wound up and a little more comfortable with himself—Kenneth Connelly—and he printed his name on the bottom of the sheet and signed it for good measure. He looked over at Iris to smile some encouragement her way, but she just feigned offense and whispered, "No copying!"

The exam itself wasn't nearly as bad as Ken had imagined it would be. There were different sections with their point value clearly spelled out, which always appealed to Ken, and the scenarios were actually kind of amusing: (1) You get cut off on the FDR by a souped-up Acura Integra with Quebec license plates and a "Je-♥-Jesus" bumper sticker. What do you do? (2) You're at a family reunion and your evil sister-in-law is there, as usual, only this time she's carrying around a pad of paper and she's taking notes on everything anyone says, especially you, just so she can "keep the record straight." What do you do? (3) You come home to find that your husband/wife/partner has dyed your favorite dog black so that his stray hairs won't be quite as noticeable on your plum-colored couch. Note that your dog was, up to this point, named Whitey whereas your plum-colored couch had no particular name. What do you do?

This is going to be a cinch, Ken thought. Until he read the last question: "Your ex-husband/wife/partner is throwing a casual, sort-of-brunchy, sort-of-afternoonish kind of party next Sunday, and for the first time since your breakup has invited you along. What do you do?"

And there, Ken was stumped. He looked over at Iris but, no surprise there, she was the type of person who read a question and then methodically answered it and only then went on to the next question without ever skipping ahead to see what sorts of horrors were lying in store for her. Where was the fun in that? He had to crane around to try to get a look at Jeff behind him, but Jeff was fully absorbed in the test, and Ken couldn't keep looking much longer without attracting Lucinda's attention.

Well, what *do* you do? Accept the invitation—with relish—and then poison the punch bowl? With what? Drano? New, improved Drano? Hemlock? Where do people buy hemlock these days? All right, forget about poisoning them. So do you get someone really good-looking to go with you and get your teeth bleached and your hair cut and make dazzling conversation all afternoon, even when the topic is something you know absolutely nothing about like mutual funds or Dame Margot Fonteyn? And then everyone will comment on how much better off you are without your ex and how you've positively *bloomed* in his absence as if, unbeknownst to you, you were really some sort of human tulip bulb?

Probably not.

So what do you do?

Ken went back and wrote three brilliant essays for the first three questions and then sucked it up and tried to tackle the last one. The trouble was that Brett had pulled the rug out from under him. Brett had led him to believe one thing and then turned around and did another. And Brett did it in a way that was so abrupt and so brutal that they'd never even had a chance to talk about it. Brett was there one day and gone the next. They never got to have it out—the long, time-honored tradition of having a shouting match filled with bitter accusations, flat-out denials, subtle swipes, and lumbering broadsides. One moment there was Brett and the next moment there was the absence of Brett. So why should he go to Brett's stupid party, which was neither a brunch nor a cocktail party, but some stupid in-between kind of thing? Why should he go and act as if what Brett had done to him was somehow normal or forgivable? When it wasn't.

He looked up and found that Lucinda was staring right at him.

She cocked an eyebrow and he just kept looking at her, sort of confused, so she pinched the fingers of one hand together and gestured as if she were busily writing away an answer and he got it—oh, *right*. The test.

Ken decided to skip the party. He was better off without Brett. In his essay, Ken said that he would politely decline. He said that he'd leave a message when he was reasonably sure that Brett—the ex, that is—wouldn't be home, and the message would say that he was glad they'd invited him, but unfortunately he'd have to decline because of another commitment. And then here was the kicker: he really would go out and find himself something else to do. He'd go for a long walk with Iris up at the Cloisters or down along the piers. Maybe they could convince Jeff to come along too. It didn't matter that this other commitment came into being *after* he declined Brett's stupid, half-baked invitation; all that mattered was that it existed. People can do some amazing things—they really can—but they can't be in two places at once, so he'd just have to decline.

But hey, *thanks for thinking of me*.

Ken put his pencil down and laced his fingers together behind his head, a gesture that earned him a wave of dirty looks from the back of the room, so he settled into a posture that announced—a bit more subtly this time—that he was all done.

The final meeting of the class was a week later and, in comparison, it was almost a letdown because Ken only got to stay for the first half; everything after the break was for one-on-one exit interviews with the judicial diversion people. In the first half of the class, they went over the test together, and then Lucinda handed out the corrected tests along with these nifty certificates attesting to the fact that a certain Ken Connelly had duly completed his course in anger management to the satisfaction of the Board of Directors of the Continuing Education Program of the Y. Lucinda had given Ken an A minus, and next to his last essay she'd marked a little smiley face in red ink.

Somebody passed a sheet around for people to list their addresses and phone numbers in case anyone wanted to keep in touch, and while the pluses and minuses of that were vigorously debated, the idea was born for organizing a celebratory dinner. The non–judicial diversion crowd retired to the café just down the street from the Y to work out the details, and Ken and Jeff went along for the ride, but mostly to have a place where they could wait for Iris while she and her various triplicate forms got processed and stamped and ker-chunked through the system.

At the café, Ken and Jeff found themselves a bit apart from the others. They were debriefing the results of the exam and shooting the breeze when Ken suddenly realized that without the class, they wouldn't have a built-in opportunity to see each other anymore. Neither Jeff nor Iris. And with Iris it would be quite complicated because of the Jeremy factor. With Jeff, on the other hand . . . And that's when Ken realized that he knew almost nothing about Jeff's personal life. He shook himself out of his thoughts just as Jeff was saying—"There's a right way and a wrong way to destroy compromising negatives"—and he butted in and asked Jeff if there was someone in his life.

"In my what?" Jeff asked.

"Someone in your life," Ken repeated. "You know, a person. Who's in your life?"

Jeff looked at him curiously and then said no. He put it just like that, with no editorial. No bit about how he'd been in a relationship and that it had tanked and now he was on the market. No comment about how he was perfectly happy being single or how he'd really like to change that. Just no. Just the facts.

The next day Ken bit the bullet and went to see Scillat. All must be well with the world, he thought as he walked in the door, because Scillat was in his usual foul mood. Indeed, the only thing that was vaguely off kilter was this faint, though distinct smell that Ken noticed.

Ken said that he wouldn't be needing more than a moment of

Scillat's time, but he surprised himself by taking a seat anyway—uninvited—in one of Scillat's black, polished Chippendale side chairs. He pulled out his certificate of completion and handed it over to Scillat, who looked at it as if he'd just been handed a parking ticket.

"I believe you'll find that it's all in order," Ken said.

"This would be . . . ?"

"It certifies that I've completed the course you recommended," Ken said. He was going to add—"in anger management"—but he decided to let Scillat figure things out on his own.

"I see. And tell me, did you find this course to be, how shall I put it, helpful?"

Ken didn't have any interest in being patronized by Scillat, so he just said that it was more *illuminating* than helpful, and while Scillat—not to mention Ken—was trying to figure out what that could possibly mean, Ken stood up to leave. "But like I said, I didn't want to take more than a moment of your time."

Scillat looked at him evenly and then put the certificate in the black leather-bound box where he tossed all the filing for Maxine.

"Actually," Ken said, reaching over and taking the certificate back out, "I think it's best if I keep that. I don't think it's the type of material that would be particularly useful to have in my file." Where *had* he smelled that smell before? And why was he suddenly thinking about fish sticks? "And in any event, the course is over, as you can see, so as far as I'm concerned, this is the last we'll ever need to visit this subject." He looked directly at Scillat who was doing a fantastically accurate impression of a doe in the headlights. Ken couldn't believe what was about to come out of his mouth next, what was actually coming out even as he vaguely thought of slamming on the brakes and trying to stop it but it was already too late. "Do we understand each other?" he asked Scillat.

And Scillat just nodded his head. Scillat said *yes*.

Unbelievable.

"Good," Ken said. "I'm glad we had a chance to sort this out." He turned to leave and as he opened the door, he asked Scillat in a jaunty, collegial tone if he wanted the door open or shut, and that's when the faint smell was suddenly at its strongest. It wafted up Ken's nose and it launched a series of microscopic chemical reactions that flashed all around the inside of his skull before they focused on a single neuron and assigned it the grave responsibility of creeping over to a cage—the kind of cage where they keep bulls at rodeos—and yanking it open and letting out a thought that would burst into the open and buck and twist itself around until it was either free or exhausted. And the thought was: *Salmon roe on salmon paste.* From the fund-raiser. Sweet tears of Christ! When he'd scrambled to keep up with Jeff, he'd stashed the hors d'oeuvres in the breast pocket of his tuxedo, *which was actually Scillat's tuxedo*, which was now hanging on the hook behind the door.

"You decide," he heard Scillat saying.

"Oh, we'll leave it open in that case," Ken said.

Then he fled.

Chapter Sixteen. In Which Iris Goes Too Far Without Getting Off the Couch

Things were definitely easier the second time around. For starters, Iris already knew exactly where the courthouse was and how to get there. Even better, this time she had a one-way ticket to freedom safely tucked into her briefcase: an official certificate of completion signed by Lucinda. And just in case that wasn't enough, she brought Ken and Jeff along for good measure. She felt like a pro.

They found the right courtroom and it was just like it was the last time, with the exception that the impossibly pregnant woman at the check-in desk was gone—thank God for small favors. She'd been replaced by a woman with a grown-out perm who was wearing a tan synthetic uniform with a stripe down the side of her pants who looked like she would've been more at ease on the highway patrol. In fact, on closer inspection, that was a gun that she had in the shiny black holster clipped to her belt. When Iris got to the front of the line and announced that she was Iris Steegers, as in *Defendant* Iris Steegers, she was hoping that the grown-out perm woman with the gun might do something in keeping with Iris's desperate, unpredictable status, like letting her hand hover over the holster or unlocking the safety on the gun. Instead, all she did was smile and take the certificate of completion and make two copies of it and slip one of them into a manila folder which she kept. Then she told Iris to give the clerk's office the other copy.

"The clerk's office? Aren't *you* the clerk?"

"No, I'm the bailiff," she said, rocking back on the balls of her heels and *almost* cracking her knuckles for the effect. "The clerk's office is one floor down." So they all trooped downstairs and stood in line there, and the guy at the window just snatched the paper out of Iris's hands and stamped it with this *humongous* medieval stamping contraption and threw it in a wire basket on the counter next to him.

"Is that it?" Iris asked.

"Is what it?" he asked.

"Is that all I have to do?"

"I don't have the faintest idea what you have to do," he said, "but that's all *we* do here, so that's all you're going to get."

"Well, that works for me," Iris said, and everybody went back upstairs to the courtroom to watch the show.

As per standard operating procedure, the door in the back opened and somebody bellowed that court was now in session and everyone stood up and then settled back down and waited for the bailiff to call the cases forward, one by one.

Jeff was positively fascinated by the proceedings. He followed all the legal jargon, even the less than interesting moments when Iris and Ken's eyes glazed over and even the stenographer started to yawn, which she had to do in full view of everybody because she couldn't take her hands off her strange, postmodern spinning wheel where she took all those stray words, those endless interruptions, and those sudden outbursts and braided them all into one long, soft, silent tail that would've been perfect for a kite drawn aloft on a swell of hot air.

It was all smooth sailing until the prosecutor in one case kept asking for an order to be made nunc pro tunc, and every time he said that, the bald defense lawyer went ballistic and turned purple and said it was shocking. Ken leaned over toward Jeff and asked him what nunc pro tunc was.

"It means 'now for then,' " Jeff whispered.

"Who for what?"

"Now for then," Jeff said. "It means the court takes something that happened in the present and then it goes back in time and says, okay, it *really* happened way back then."

"Which would explain why baldie over there is turning purple," Ken said.

"Exactly."

Amazing, Ken thought. I'd turn purple too if my opponent had that kind of power over time and space.

Think about it. Think what he could do if he had the power to go around rearranging things in time. But the funny thing was, the more Ken thought about it, the *less* he could envision using those magical powers to go backward in time to fix things so that he'd never even met Brett. You know, simply not opening the door when Brett's blood-curdling scream had ripped down the hallway that night. Or he could go back even further in time and pick the apartment that he'd really liked up on Riverside instead of picking his apartment in the Santa Monica. The apartment on Riverside had gorgeous views and was *practically* in move-in condition, the only exception being the team of tough-looking DEA agents camped out in the living room listening to the drug-dealing going on in the apartment next door. No, the more that Ken thought about it, the more he'd say that he *wouldn't* go back and just erase Brett from his existence. And that realization was, well . . . what was the word?

"Shocking!" the bald, purple-faced lawyer said.

Something along those lines, Ken thought.

And then all of a sudden the bailiff was calling Iris's case and she was striding up to her podium, and before anyone had a chance to say anything, not even good morning, the prosecutor started complaining. "Your Honor, I've only been handed this about a minute ago," he said, waving Iris's certificate of completion which now reappeared stapled to the inside cover of a manila folder.

The judge waited until the grown-out perm bailiff gave him a copy too, which he studied, and then looked over his half-glasses at the prosecutor. "And is there a reason that you would need *more* than a minute to review this?"

"No, but in the orderly administration of—"

"*Good*," the judge said, cutting him off. "Case No. SDNY20048 is hereby dismissed with prejudice. So ordered." The prosecutor gathered his papers and turned around, making the kind of eyes that are usually made behind the backs of substitute teachers, and then he sat down, leaving Iris all alone at her podium. "Your Honor?" she ventured.

"Yes?"

"Do I get to say anything?"

"If it's quick," the judge said.

"Actually," the prosecutor popped back up. "We would object on the grounds that there's no subject matter jurisdiction for Miss Steegers to address the court. The case is over."

"Then how come he gets to talk?" Iris asked.

"Yes, tell us, counsel," the judge said. "Why exactly are you still talking?"

"I'm not *talking*," the prosecutor said. "I'm *objecting*, and what—"

"Oh, why can't you just shut up for a change?" the judge said. And then, turning to Iris, he told her to go ahead.

"I just wanted to say that I didn't do anything wrong," Iris said. "That's it. I didn't do anything wrong and I actually paid quite dearly to get the certificate that I just gave you. And I might have to keep paying for a long time to come. How or why doesn't concern you, but I want you to know how much this cost me. How much this is still costing me. That's all I had to say. I just wanted to say that to you and let that woman over there type it all down in her machine. And now I've said it."

"So noted and so ordered," the judge said before the prosecutor could start bawling all over again. "Next case!"

And Iris walked out of court a free woman. She'd walked *into* court a free woman, but that was beside the point. The point was that she was free to do as she pleased.

. . .

Iris had thought long and hard about what to do next. What to do about Jeremy, that is. She thought about writing him a long, poetic letter explaining everything that she'd learned and asking Jeremy to reflect, to examine his conscience, and then to respond to her once his heart was clear. Take all the time you want.

And then she ditched that approach in favor of the element of surprise.

"Jeremy," she said, quite matter-of-factly, as Jeremy came out of the bathroom the next morning with nothing more than a towel around his waist.

"Yes?"

"Who's Alicia Kosewic?" Iris asked, turning to look straight at Jeremy, who stopped dead in his tracks.

"How . . . ?" Jeremy tried to say but what came out was mostly breath. That was now fixed in stone—Jeremy's first word was "how." Not "what," as in maybe he didn't hear the question. Or "who," as in who the hell are you talking about. But "*how*."

"Alicia Kosewic," Iris said evenly and then just left it at that.

"She's a friend of mine." The "just" that should've come right after the word "she's" was noticeably absent.

"A friend of yours?"

"That's right," Jeremy said, recovering a bit more of his composure. "Why do you ask?"

"Oh, well, I ran into a friend of mine and it was actually kind of funny because we were talking and it turned out that he'd gone to the fund-raiser thing on Friday night for the potassium people, and he saw you, well, he said he wasn't sure whether it was you or not, but anyway, he said he saw you there and you were there with Alicia Kosewic."

"Who are you talking about?" Jeremy asked. "Which friend of ours?"

"More a friend of mine," Iris said. "Actually."

"Well, then how does he know me?" Jeremy asked. "And who is this guy anyway? What's he been saying?"

"He's not been saying anything. He just told me that he saw you there on Saturday night with a girl named Alicia and that he was a little surprised because I wasn't there and he thought that, I don't know, you seemed particularly friendly with Alicia."

"Friendly? In what way?"

"He didn't say."

Jeremy paused and then exhaled a long, uninterrupted wave of annoyance. "Listen, I don't like listening to insinuations from somebody I don't even know."

"I'm not making insinuations!" Iris said. "I just asked you who Alicia Kosewic was. If she's such a good friend of yours, why haven't I ever heard you talk about her before?"

"She's not necessarily such a good friend," Jeremy said. "But that doesn't change the fact that I don't like being cornered with some sort of accusation when I haven't done anything to deserve it. Unless your *friend* has something else he'd like to accuse me of."

"Who's accusing you of anything?"

"You are."

"Of what?" Iris asked. "What am I accusing you of?"

"I don't know. Of forgetting to mention that I have a friend, that I *know* somebody named Alicia Kosewic. Which I do, but big deal. I don't know everybody you know, *apparently*, so why should you know everybody I know?"

"That's not the point."

"Actually, I think it is," Jeremy said. And then he made the first movements toward getting dressed for the day. "Listen, I don't want to argue about this, and I especially don't want to argue about something where there's some sort of accusation being lobbed at me from behind my back from somebody I don't even know. But yes, I know somebody named Alicia Kosewic and she's a lawyer for the Department of Agriculture and she lives in D.C., which is probably why I've never mentioned her to you before. And yes, I saw her at the gig on Saturday night and it was perfectly nice to run into her again. *And* she introduced the keynote speaker, just in case you're wondering what she was doing there."

"Oh."

"And afterward we shared a taxi home," Jeremy said. "Is that a crime?"

"No, and I didn't say there was any kind of crime here. I just asked who she was because I'd never heard you mention her before, and I was curious because my friend said that he thought there was some sort of . . ." Iris paused. "Some sort of *emotional charge* between you and Alicia."

Jeremy snorted. "Oh, like I had the hots for Alicia and this guy just picked right up on it? Is that what you're saying? You don't think that's a little insulting, Iris? Somebody I don't even know comes running to you saying, 'Oh, Jeremy was just drooling all over this poor girl while working on a Saturday night—I was there to *work*, I might add—and then you legitimize it by ambushing me and asking me what the deal is. Well, there is no deal, that's what the deal is. Alicia's a friend of mine, and no, there wasn't any sort of *emotional charge* between us."

So Jeremy's strategy was going to be the categorical denial. "But now that we're on the subject," he said, "what about you?"

"What about me?" Iris asked, mystified.

"Well, I don't think it's any secret that you've been acting a little cool and distant for a while."

Had Iris been acting cool and distant? Was Iris so hopelessly out of the touch with things that she'd actually forgotten to keep track of *herself* this time?

"I don't *think* that's the case," she said. "At least I haven't meant to. Not purposefully anyway. And if I have, then I apologize. I didn't realize that I'd been"—she searched for the word—"distracted."

"And just who is this guy anyway?" Jeremy asked.

"What guy?" Wait a second. Had Iris just apologized to Jeremy? How did *that* happen? How come that always happened?

"This friend of yours! The guy who knows all and sees all and went running back to you to tell you everything about the potassium thingy."

"He's just a friend of mine," Iris said.

"What's his name?" Jeremy asked, looking straight at Iris.

"I'd rather not say."

"You'd *rather not say*?" Jeremy repeated, incredulous. "What's that supposed to mean?"

"It means I'd rather not tell you," Iris said weakly.

"Well, since when do we keep things from each other?" Jeremy asked.

"I don't know," Iris said. "Since forever." Suddenly she was exhausted and the day had hardly begun. "Everybody keeps something from somebody," she said, "so what's the difference?" Jeremy just shook his head in a slow mix of disappointment and disbelief.

Iris met Ken for a crisis management session at lunch. He was planning to rake her over the coals for going off half-cocked and approaching Jeremy without having a clear strategy plus a fallback strategy in case the clear strategy encountered unexpected resistance and tanked. And for doing it without backup support—meaning Ken—who'd be there at the ready and could fling himself in front of any stray bullets if necessary. In short, he was just peeved that she'd gone ahead without him. But when he saw her sitting there looking so thoroughly forlorn, he changed course and slid in next to her on her side of the booth and squeezed her hand and asked her what happened.

"He denied it," Iris said. "And then he turned the tables on me and said that I was being cold and distant. Oh, and he *really* didn't like the idea that there was somebody at the fund-raiser who was reporting back to me."

"Did he figure out who it was?"

"No, but I don't think it'll take him very long."

"So how did you leave it?" Ken asked.

"We didn't. I asked him who Alicia was and he said that she was a friend of his from D.C. and it was crystal clear that my question threw him for a major loop and he said that the whole *emotional charge* thing was ridiculous."

"Oh, I'm sorry about that. I guess that term is kind of my fault."

"That's all right," Iris said. "It made sense when you said it to me; just not when I said it to him. Anyway, like I said, he got his back up right away, as in the instant I asked him who Alicia was, and it stayed that way and in the end I was the one in the wrong because I was being all accusatory without revealing my tattletale source—sorry, sweets—and he said that he was disappointed in me. That's how we left it."

"Well, you know what that is? That's that strategy in sports where you defend by attacking. I forget what it's called."

"The best defense is a good offense?" Iris offered.

"That's it! That's the one. That's what he's doing. He's diverting all the attention away from the real issue and attacking you instead. You see that, don't you?"

"I see that I'm being attacked. Or at least I feel it anyway," Iris said. She took a drink from her Coke and then put the glass back down on the table. *Next* to where it used to be. Then she stared at the little ring of water on the table for a minute before pulling a napkin out of the shiny chrome napkin dispenser, which she plopped onto the ring of condensation. Then she lowered her forehead onto the napkin and slowly moved it back and forth, which actually worked surprisingly well.

"Iris?" Ken asked gently.

"Yes?"

"You're not planning to spill any ketchup are you?" And poor Iris almost smiled.

Ken didn't want to seem like the argumentative prosecutor who always had to have the last word, but he reminded Iris that he'd been there that night at the fund-raiser and Jeremy had *definitely* not been working. Unless work for him meant hanging on to Alicia's every word and just leaving at the end of the evening as if somebody else was supposed to do all the official things like count the broken stemware and argue with the caterers.

And all Iris said was that Jeremy could be very convincing.

"And did you mention the ticket?" Ken asked. "From Pennsylvania? From Yardley? What did he have to say about that?"

"I didn't bring it up," Iris said. "I didn't have any kind of excuse for knowing about that. All I said was that I bumped into a friend who'd been at the fund-raiser and he'd given me the rundown on the evening."

"Hmmm."

"What's 'hmmm' supposed to mean?" Iris asked.

"Nothing."

"Well, it doesn't mean *nothing*," Iris said. "Otherwise you wouldn't have said it."

"I don't know. I'm just thinking that Jeremy denied it because he could. And my guess is that he'll continue to deny it."

"Why do you think that?"

"I don't know. Look at it this way. Let's say that I hadn't caught Brett cheating on me. Say that horrible night never happened. I didn't get fired and I didn't come home early and catch my boyfriend in bed with a home-wrecker named Neil. But let's say that, by the same token, I'd started to get suspicious for some reason or other—it really doesn't matter why—but the point is that I decided to confront Brett and ask him if he was cheating on me. What do you think he'd do?"

"I think he'd probably deny it," Iris said.

"Well, so do I, and that's what I think Jeremy did and will continue to do."

"Well, what about this," Iris said softly. "What if he's right? What if there isn't or wasn't anything going on between him and Alicia and she's just a friend like Jeremy said? If that were the case, then he'd deny it too. So no matter what, he denies it. How are we supposed to know what the truth is?"

"Are you saying that you believe him? That you'd be willing to believe him?"

"I don't know what I'm saying anymore," Iris said. "Maybe what I'm saying is that maybe I should just take his word for it. I asked him a question. He answered it. And then I take his word for it."

Ken thought about that for a while. "Is there a difference," he finally said, "between believing him and taking his word for it?"

"Sure," Iris said. "Believing him is out of my control. I can't make that happen or not happen. I don't know whose control it's *in*, but it's certainly not in mine. Taking his word for it, on the other hand, that's something I could probably learn to do. That sounds like the kind of thing that partners are supposed to do for each other."

Ken was there in his official capacity of supportive friend, so he *didn't* smack her over the head with a pleather-bound menu and tell her to come to her senses. Instead he just said, "Probably," and left it at that. "Do you want dessert?" he asked even though he already knew the answer because dessert, by definition, is what people eat *after* eating the main meal, and sad, troubled Iris hadn't been able to eat a thing.

Unfortunately, Iris never got the chance to try to just close the subject because she was only *half* of the equation. Jeremy was the other half, and once he'd gotten over the initial shock, Jeremy couldn't *stop* bringing Alicia up. As far as Jeremy was concerned, Alicia was now a subject to be fleshed out in minute detail—just so that future misunderstandings of the type they'd just weathered could be avoided.

Jeremy was very even-keeled about the whole thing. He'd think up an additional point and put it out there—Did I mention that Alicia's a lawyer with the Department of Agriculture and we've actually done a lot of work through referrals from them?—and then that bit would get added to the overall picture of Alicia which was slowly coming into focus, hovering somewhere within the walls of their apartment. The only trouble was that there seemed to be a slight, though noticeable *delay* between the time when Jeremy would provide some information about Alicia and the time when Jeremy would then slightly revise that information. For example, when Iris asked Jeremy if Alicia was married—practically to be polite since Jeremy kept bringing her up—Jeremy first laughed and said he had no idea. That night, though, he said he'd been *thinking* about it and now that Iris mentioned it, Alicia wasn't married, but he thought there was a boyfriend in the picture, but of course who could be sure?

Okay, Iris would think, *duly noted*. But a day later the story would get slightly tweaked and reworked. "Actually," Jeremy might say out of the blue, "come to think of it, they might be engaged."

"Who might be engaged?" Iris asked, utterly perplexed.

"Alicia. Alicia and her boyfriend, silly. Now that I think about it, I think she once mentioned that her boyfriend's really her fiancé, only it's one of those situations where there's no date set yet."

"Oh," Iris said. Jeremy is rewriting history, she found herself thinking, only not exactly. He's making a little change here and some corrections over there, and he keeps trying out different versions to see which one works best, and the *net* effect is to come up with a more coherent, more credible story. That's what Jeremy was doing. Jeremy was *copy-editing* history.

In the meantime—and quite confusingly—Jeremy had also become extremely solicitous of Iris. Iris *had* been distant and distracted for a while now, and Jeremy intended for them to work through this. The working-through-it part wasn't too taxing because it mostly consisted of Jeremy talking about how Iris had been distant and distracted—in any of the three billion ways in which that particular concept could be phrased—but in practical terms it meant that Jeremy started acting extra warm and generous toward Iris. In short, Jeremy was there to help, and the road to recovery was filled with gentle, soft words written on Post-it notes that Jeremy started leaving on the mirror for Iris in the morning.

And Jeremy wasn't just emotionally present. He was *physically* present. He was simply always there. But it wasn't exactly the same Jeremy as before, the same Jeremy who used to organize evenings of drinks with various people. Now it was much more likely to be a quiet evening at home, and to the extent that there were events on the outside, Jeremy would work through all these complicated logistics and find a reason why it made sense—God only knows how—for him to swing by Iris's job and pick her up so they could go out together.

And once they were at the Alco-hole or the Broadway Brewery, it wasn't quite the same routine that they'd had down before. Now Jeremy kept pulling Iris into the conversation or, more accuritely, shining the spotlight of the conversation over onto Iris and the corner of the table where Iris used to be able to let her mind wander in relative peace. Jeremy would point out something admirable that Iris had done, or something noteworthy that she'd said. People would look over and smile and nod, and it began to feel like Iris was being permanently introduced to somebody's disapproving parents as a potential in-law who only *seemed* like she wasn't up to snuff.

What was strange about all this was that up to this time Iris had never thought of Jeremy as someone who didn't fight fair. And that, she realized, was because up until now they'd always been on the same side. Jeremy had *always* been a formidable opponent. Most people—cab drivers, landlords, the entire staff of Verizon, the people who hung out in front of the Off-Track Betting joint on Seventy-second Street—realized this right away. And those who *didn't* were usually treated to a display of firepower that would crush them quickly and mercilessly. And throughout it all Iris had always been supportive. Iris admired Jeremy because Jeremy stood up for himself, and when he did, he didn't seem whiny or petulant; he seemed like a person to be reckoned with. Someone who was used to convincing other people of the error of their ways.

Now, though, Iris wasn't quite so sure. Iris wasn't sure that Jeremy's tactics were entirely fair. When Iris first brought up Alicia, Jeremy bit her head off and put the fear of God into her as far as ever bringing up Alicia again. But ever since then, Iris had been forced to listen to Jeremy as he undertook this strange, slow process of *retooling* Alicia. And no matter how you slice it, that wasn't fair.

And these strange machinations with Alicia—with the whole *idea* of Alicia—were themselves troubling. It was just undignified to watch Jeremy doing this, to listen to him say something about Alicia and then grant himself a do-over to make the story a little better. The fact of the matter was that over the past few weeks, Alicia had been transformed from a concrete figure into some sort of blank slate who magically fit all sizes and situations: Jeremy knew her originally through work connections, but they were on the same wavelength in terms of socializing, so it's hard to say whether she was really a work friend or a regular friend. Alicia was a sports fan, but given that she wasn't from New York, Jeremy couldn't name any teams that Alicia rooted for because they hadn't *registered* with him when Alicia mentioned them, what with them not being New York teams and all. Alicia was in a long-term committed relationship unless of course everything had gotten shot to hell and come undone and she was now single. Or had always been single.

"Does Alicia have a brother?" Iris asked this one evening while they were watching a television series about a hauntingly beautiful district attorney who always solved crimes and won her cases, but had never been able to solve the mystery of her own enigmatic past. Then Iris added, "Apropos of nothing," but purely because she'd always wanted to say "Apropos of nothing."

Jeremy looked stricken. "A brother?" he asked.

"Yeah."

"You mean like does she have any brothers and sisters?"

"That's right," Iris said, even though she wanted to scream, "*Get your ears cleaned.* I asked if she had a brother. Not any brothers."

And the response wasn't particularly edifying. No, Jeremy wasn't sure because Alicia wasn't on very good terms with her family because they lived far away. Or actually, the fact of the matter was that she was on quite good terms with her family, but since they lived so far away, she didn't see them very often so one could get the *impression* that she wasn't on very good terms with them when she really was. So far as Jeremy knew.

"I see."

"You see what?" Jeremy asked.

"Nothing," Iris said. She was watching the young, hauntingly beautiful district attorney getting stuffed into the trunk of a drug kingpin's car. "I bet she finds a way out of that," Iris thought. "She's gotten out of tighter spots than that."

"No, seriously, what did you mean by that?" Jeremy pressed.

"I didn't mean anything," Iris said. "I was just asking about Alicia's family."

"Oh, *okay*." Sarcasm from Jeremy was a most unwelcome development.

"Okay what?" Iris asked.

"Nothing," Jeremy said. "Just like you said."

"Look, do you want to watch this or do you want to argue?"

"Well, you're the one who got all huffy just because I don't know every single thing you want to know."

"I'm not huffy," Iris said. "And I haven't scratched the surface of what I want to know." And just like that, she'd gone too far. *Way* too far.

"What's that supposed to mean?"

All right Iris, that's your cue. "Did you go away with Alicia?"

"*What?*" Jeremy asked, completely taken aback. "When?"

"Whenever!" Iris said. "It doesn't matter when. So did you?"

"No, I didn't. What kind of crazy question is that?"

"It's a regular question, just like this is—did you go away with Alicia to *Bucks County*?"

Jeremy looked straight at Iris and his lower jaw, which had been jutting out just like it had in the dreamy, blurry picture from the radar camera, slowly slid in as if someone were shutting the drawer of a cash register. "Why on earth would you ask that?"

"Because I think you did," Iris said.

"Who told you I did that?" Jeremy demanded.

"The same person who told me that it was last January, right around the time that your aunt was dying up in Holyoke. So is it true or not?"

"Why are you attacking me?"

"I'm not attacking you, Jeremy. I'm asking you a question and you're not answering it. You went away with Alicia to Bucks County last winter, didn't you?" On TV the beautiful district attorney was using a lighter to survey her circumstances and analyze her options, which was ridiculous because everybody knew she didn't smoke so why would she carry a lighter?

"No, I didn't!"

"Yes, you did."

"I can't believe you're accusing me of that. I don't understand how you could take my friendship with Alicia and twist it around and make up stories, and I don't know who is whispering things in your ear but he's going to regret it when I get my hands on him."

"Jeremy," Iris said. "Did you go away with Alicia to Pennsylvania when you were supposed to be in Massachusetts? Last January?"

"Who told you that?"

"Nobody told me that. It's just something that I *think* happened. And what I want to know from you is whether it did or didn't. I don't think I can make it any simpler than that." Iris couldn't believe that she was having a fight with Jeremy—*a terrible fight*—and yet here she was in complete possession of her faculties. "Well?"

"I'm not cheating on you, Iris."

"That's not what I asked you, Jeremy. I asked you if you went away with Alicia last year. And you said no, didn't you?"

"That's right," Jeremy said. Finally, a question he could answer.

"But that's not the truth, is it?"

"Yes, it is," Jeremy pleaded.

"No, it isn't." The hauntingly beautiful district attorney now had the drug kingpin's head clamped inside the jack from the trunk. Iris decided that she hated the DA.

"What, were you following me that weekend? Because you've got it all wrong."

"No, I wasn't following you Jeremy. I just happen to know that you were in Pennsylvania with Alicia when you said you were in

Holyoke, Massachusetts, and I *still* don't know why and I *still* don't know why you're lying about it and—"

"Oh, so now I'm a liar?"

"Well, you're not telling the truth, Jeremy. Wouldn't that make you a liar?"

"What are you trying to do here?" Jeremy practically screamed. "Are you trying to push me away? Is that what this is about?"

"Did I say that?" Iris asked. "I'm trying to get you to tell me the truth and you won't do it! So who's pushing whom?"

"This is ridiculous," Jeremy said. "I don't have to sit here and listen to these kinds of accusations when you won't tell me where you're getting them from."

"I already told you that it's something that I *believe*, and all I want you to do is to tell me I'm right."

"Well, I'm not going to tell you you're right when you're wrong," Jeremy said.

"So you deny it?" Iris said.

"Stop saying that! I *already* denied it. I didn't go out to Pennsylvania when I was supposed to be up at my aunt's funeral." Jeremy looked petrified. He was too panicked to figure out if this was the moment when he was supposed to bolt and change course and make a desperate dash for safety. Instead he just blindly held his ground.

"Yes, you did."

"*No, I didn't!*"

And Iris thought, "If I say, 'yes you did,' one more time, he'll tell me to prove it. That's exactly what Jeremy will do. I know Jeremy like the back of my hand." So she said it. Iris said, "Yes, you did."

And Jeremy said, "*Prove it.*"

Ken was holding office hours at City College, and, for once, he actually had a customer. It was a girl from one of his composition sections, but instead of complaining about her grades, she said she was there to complain about gay porn. "I see," Ken said slowly. "What's on your mind?"

"Well, the thing of it is, me and my friends rented a gay video from the video place over on St. Nicholas Avenue, over by where they closed the McDonald's? You know, for laughs? And they showed this guy who's, you know, *doing it* with this other guy which I guess—*duh*, it's gay porn—but anyways my friend Pattie zoomed in on this one guy because he was the cutest and he had this tattoo on his arm, and we froze the picture and kept zooming in until we could read the tattoo."

"And?"

"And it was a heart with the word 'Kathleen' written inside it."

"Kathleen," Ken repeated. "Are you sure?"

"Oh, believe me! We saw it for like an *hour*. And it said 'Kathleen.'" She let a long pause slide by. "Which is a *girl's* name." Another pause. "In fact, it's *always* a girl's name."

"I think I can agree with that," Ken said. "Although it doesn't strike me as the kind of name that you see tattooed on *anybody's* arm. It seems a bit too, I don't know, ecclesiastical."

"*What?*"

"Never mind. So what's the problem?" Ken asked. He wasn't sure where all this was leading. Was it an elaborate joke? Was it an elaborately disguised plea for information—any information—from a sympathetic ear? Or was it just another gambit to sniff out some personal information about Professor Connelly that would finally make him gossip-worthy?

"*What's the problem?*" she practically shrieked. "He's *gay*. And Kathleen probably doesn't know it! Does that sound *fair* to you?"

"Well, if we were to step back and look at all the various possibilities *dispassionately*," Ken started to say when his door burst open with no knock, which usually meant Scillat, but this time it was Iris. It was a wild-eyed Iris, and she'd either been up all night or she'd gotten run over this morning by an Entenmann's delivery truck—repeatedly. She stood in the doorway for a moment before Ken realized that it wasn't just good manners that kept her from butting in any further; she was on her last legs.

"Oh, *Ken*," Iris said. "Thank God you're here."

He leapt up from his chair and dragged Iris over and onto it and started to apologize to the undergrad—telling her that he was afraid they were going to have to adjourn their meeting—but the undergrad didn't seem to mind at all. She stared at Iris and then gathered up her backpack and hightailed it out of there with a distinctly carnivorous gleam in her eye. Professor Connelly has a deranged lady friend with no dress sense who barges into his office; the hunt for fresh gossip had been successful.

"What on earth happened, Iris? Are you okay? Do you want a glass of water? A cup of coffee? A *drink*? Maxine knows where Scillat keeps the good stuff."

"No, just close the door," Iris said. Ken didn't want to leave Iris unattended in his swively chair, so he wheeled it with her still in it over to the door, closed it, and then wheeled her back to his desk and wedged the chair where it couldn't slip loose from its moorings and let Iris drift away altogether.

"Okay, first things first," Ken said, getting Iris a glass of water and fussing and clucking while she drank it. "Did you call in sick or are you just AWOL?" he asked.

"I called in," Iris said. "I told them that I ate something that didn't agree with me."

"And what'd they say?"

"Well, my boss said that having a *tummy ache*—his words—wasn't the kind of thing that most people find *disabling*, so I had to tell him I had diarrhea shooting out of my asshole faster than lies coming out of a Republican National Convention. And then I *thanked him for caring*."

"You didn't!"

"I sure did," Iris said. "Screw him anyway. I work my butt off for him for three hundred and sixty-four days a year and he hands me that kind of shit the one day I'm sick?"

"Well, in all fairness, you're not actually sick," Ken pointed out.

"Oh, I don't know about that," Iris said. "I'm feeling sick to death."

"Of?"

"Of everything."

Iris told Ken all about what had happened with Jeremy. How Jeremy kept pushing at her and needling her until she lost her cool and let the cat out of the bag and accused Jeremy of gallivanting around Bucks County when he was supposed to be in Massachusetts and how Jeremy just denied it.

"So what did you do?" Ken asked.

"I told him about the picture."

"*You told him about the picture?*" Ken asked. "What'd he say?"

"Well, first he wanted to see it, but I told him that it was at work, which was true. I told him that I'd gotten a letter from my insurance company raising my rates and I'd thought it was just some kind of mistake, so I called them up and they said I had a moving violation and I said what on earth are you talking about and they told me all about it. And then they sent me the file. And I told Jeremy that there was a picture of him in there, so he *was* in the Borough of Yardley when he said he wasn't."

"Bravo, Iris. But what'd he *say*?" Ken pressed.

"Well, he admitted that he'd been out in Bucks County."

"*Finally.*"

"Yes, finally, but he swore that nothing happened."

"So why did he lie about it?" Ken asked.

"Well, it makes more sense when he explains it, but—"

"Iris!" Ken interrupted. "You're not going to tell me that you believe him, are you?"

"I don't know what to believe," Iris said. "I'm just telling you what he said and that it makes more sense the way he says it."

"All right, what'd he say?" Ken folded his arms across his chest.

"He said that yes, he'd been out to Bucks County, and that yes, he should've told me all about it instead of trying to keep it from me, but that no, nothing happened between him and Alicia, and the only reason he didn't tell me about it before was that he didn't want to get me all upset."

Ken looked at Iris and then prompted her. "*And?*"

"And that's that."

"Did you ask if Jeremy had seen Alicia on any *other* occasions that he didn't tell you about either?"

"Actually, I did," Iris said. "Although it took me a lot longer to think of that question than it just took you."

"And what'd he say? No wait, let me guess. He said no. He said that this was the only time and he shouldn't have done it in the first place, obviously—not without telling you—but he didn't want you to get all worried and upset about nothing and it was the only time so there's nothing else to worry about. Am I right?"

"Yes, you're right," Iris said slowly. And then in a supreme concession to the idea that a person should tailor her discourse to fit her audience, she added, "That's his story."

So that was the broad outline, and from there they went on to fill in the details. No, Jeremy did not have any kind of explanation as to *why* Iris would've been upset if he'd mentioned that he wanted to zip off to the country with some innocuous friend named Alicia.

Nor did he have an explanation as to why he'd lied and denied it when Iris first asked about Alicia.

"You realize that's exactly the way somebody who's cheating would be expected to act?" Ken said. Iris just made a gesture to indicate that she'd *heard* Ken's words without pronouncing upon her inclination to agree or disagree with them. "Why else would he have kept this from you? Why else would you have been upset if he went away for the weekend with a friend? Do you get *upset* when he goes to work every day without you? Do you get *upset* when he goes to lunch without you? Do you get *upset* when he goes to the movies without you?"

"Jeremy never goes to the movies without me," Iris said softly. "He's the type of person who prefers to organize a crowd."

"*Iris,*" Ken said, and Iris finally admitted that she saw Ken's point. Jeremy was going to deny everything except where there was photographic proof that he was lying. And even then the story was that he'd just lied to spare Iris's feelings, which, so far as we know, were never in danger of being hurt in the first place. "Does that about sum things up?" Ken asked.

"I suppose it does," Iris said.

"And how does that sit with you?"

"How do you think that sits with me?" Iris responded.

"Actually," Ken said. "You don't seem too bad. You definitely don't seem too great, don't get me wrong, but you don't seem like you're about to, I don't know. . . ."

"Stick my head in the oven?" Iris offered.

"Exactly."

"Well, my oven's electric," Iris said. "Not to mention broken. But you're right. I don't feel like I'm dying. I just can't eat. But beyond that, no, the sky hasn't fallen down on me."

"You know, on the eating thing, we could start you out on some bananas and some toast and some flat Coke just to see how it goes."

"Ken, the diarrhea was just an excuse. I can't eat because my stomach is in knots, and my stomach is in knots because I don't know what the hell Jeremy's done or is doing or is going to do. I don't know anything anymore."

"Well, actually, what Jeremy is going to do is a good point, and I want to get back to it in a second, but before I do, I *realize* that you don't have explosive diarrhea, Iris. And for that I'm grateful. But the bananas and toast trick works for heartache too. Believe me."

"Oh, sorry," Iris said. "I sort of forgot."

"Well, I didn't."

"Well, you should. You two are better off apart."

"Not that I have any choice in the matter," Ken said. "But that's what I wanted to ask you. What does Jeremy want to have happen?"

"What do you mean?"

"Well, does he want to stay together? Judging from what he's saying, he sounds like he's making a case for the two of you to stay together."

"I hadn't thought about it like that," Iris said.

"Well, I think he *has*," Ken said. "And what do you want?"

"I just want everything to go back to the way it was," Iris said. Ken cracked open the can of RC Cola he'd unearthed way in the back of his drawer and set it on his desk where they both stared at it for signs that it would do as expected and slowly go flat. "I just want my appetite back," Iris said.

Jeff came over to Ken's house that night—ostensibly because he was "thinking about buying a citrus zester and had a couple of questions"—but Ken steered the conversation around to what was going on between Iris and Jeremy and how Jeremy reflexively denied any wrongdoing and how none of it made any sense. And Jeff pointed out that in a court case, everybody always denied everything, which was indeed true, but this was not, mercifully, a court case. And then Jeff asked all sorts of questions about the documents that Ken used to proofread at Leighton Fennell—which surprised Ken because he hadn't thought that his stint as a proofreader at

Leighton Fennell had particularly registered with Jeff—but apparently it had. And Ken explained about the cases and the teams of lawyers who worked on them and how they made the junior lawyer on the team run down to pick up pages from the nether reaches of Word Processing even though the firm paid these scary people in blue smocks to do nothing else but *rush* desperately urgent interoffice mail from one cluttered desktop to another.

"And why do they do this?" Jeff asked.

"Do what?"

"Well, rush around like chickens with their heads cut off, all over nothing?"

"I suppose for the money," Ken said. "They're actually rather well paid, for headless poultry."

"Hmmm," Jeff said. He wasn't entirely convinced.

"Actually, who cares why they do it," Ken said. "The lawyers, that is. They get paid *barrels* of money. But they barely have the time to spend it and they're always in a bad mood and they're always at the firm even though they hate it. So they get what they deserve."

"Do you think that's how they see it?" Jeff asked.

"Oh, Lord no. They think they're martyrs to some sort of worthy cause. They think they work hard. They're always *swamped*."

"But that's not what I meant," Jeff said. "What I meant was do they actually have a *reason* for working that kind of a job which, apart from the money, doesn't sound very fulfilling? Or maybe it's just that the culture in those kinds of firms puts a premium on, well, working in those kinds of firms, and the idea of just getting up one day and leaving wouldn't occur to them. You know, a corporate culture with an *insular* perspective?" Astute little Jeff.

Now it was Ken's turn to say, "Hmmm." "Maybe," he said. "But I'm going to stick with the they-have-their-heads-up-their-butts theory."

Then Ken changed gears and asked Jeff if he'd ever tried to deny anything as shamelessly as Jeremy was trying to do, and what *he* thought was going through Jeremy's head. Did Jeremy think he could get away with it? Did he simply feel like he had no other choice? Was he mental?

And once again, Jeff seemed to have already thought things through. He said that generally speaking it was much easier to admit to the truth in most circumstances because the truth was easier to keep straight. He said that the truth is stored in an immediately accessible part of our brains whereas everything we lie about is tucked away underneath various locks and obstacles that we put into place to make sure the lie stays safe. So then, every time you need to *refer* to that information, it takes all this extra time to access it and *that*, that moment of hesitation, is how people can spot a liar.

"So you would never just flat out deny everything like Jeremy did. Or is doing?" Ken asked.

"Oh, I didn't say that. Actually, I think I learned my lesson in college," Jeff said. "My parents used to drive me up to school at the beginning of the year, just like everybody else, and I'd kind of gotten into the habit of, let's see how to put it, *appropriating* some of their booze in the last weeks of summer, which they suspected and which I denied. Vigorously. Fast-forward to a week later and we're unloading the car and my mom's being utterly non-helpful because she's gotten the idea into her head that I absolutely *must* have an African violet for my room and she's standing around holding it in her hands like she's one of the three kings and it's a pot of frankincense or myrrh or something and my dad is getting pissed off because he's doing all the work and he's up on top of the roof of the car unloading my stuff and he holds up a white laundry bag and says, 'Anything other than clothes in this?' and I have absolutely no choice but to say nope and he tosses it down onto the parking lot and we all hear a distinct *crack* followed by the unmistakable scent of wasted gin. *Their* gin. Ooops."

"Ooops is right," Ken said. "What kind of sentence did you get for that?"

"Lighter than you'd think. They couldn't very well ground me given that they were dropping me off at college and the instant their taillights were out of view I could do absolutely anything I wanted to, with the possible exception of having a gin and tonic, so actually they didn't really do anything. And in some ways that was worse, because getting punished equals the score whereas my stupid lie just stayed out there. It's still out there. Just kind of hanging around in the air."

"You're not saying that they're still mad about it?"

"No, obviously not," Jeff said. "Believe me, I've done plenty of things since then to disappoint them worse than that. And I've probably done a few things here and there that've made them proud too. No, what I'm saying is that standing there in a puddle of Beefeater-soaked jockey shorts was when I decided that it didn't make any sense to cross my arms across my chest and say, '*I didn't do it!*' whenever I got caught doing something wrong. That's when I thought that it was time to start owning up to things."

Ken tricked Iris. He said he was giving her some flat root beer, which he did. He just didn't mention that he was also going to plop a scoop of vanilla ice cream into it to make—ta-dah!—a rudimentary root beer float. He told her she didn't have to eat it if she didn't want to, but he gave her a long, slender spoon, and as the pale rays of afternoon sunlight that *hadn't* gotten all hogged up by the Trump buildings fell through the windows of the Santa Monica, she dipped the spoon into the melty, swirly ice cream and licked it. And then did it again. Iris was eating.

After that, it was just a question of finding things she could get down. Fried won tons, for some mysterious reason, worked quite well. As did sweet-and-sour soup. Regular meat and potatoes still wasn't feasible, but Iris had lost that twisting, trembling feeling that she was slowly starving to death.

Iris told Ken that things on the home front had settled into a sort of strange equilibrium. Iris seemed to be waiting for Jeremy to explain what had really happened while Jeremy seemed to be waiting for Iris to pronounce whatever sanction might be in the works.

And in the meantime they went to bed at night and set the alarm clock for the next morning and went to work and came home again. And when nothing happened, it was Jeremy who blinked first. Jeremy started to change the story.

It was probably inevitable because it just didn't make sense for Jeremy to have behaved the way he did if Alicia were just a friend, so Jeremy began to touch up that part of the picture. He admitted that he had a certain kind of bond with Alicia.

"A bond?" Iris asked.

"More of an affinity," Jeremy said. And from there, the affinity became not so much an *affinity*, but more the type of situation where Jeremy had confused feelings for Alicia.

"And would Alicia have confused feelings for you?" Iris asked.

"Oh, no!" Jeremy said. "Not at all."

"Maybe," Jeremy said the next day.

"Just between you, me, and the goalpost," Jeremy said the day after that, "I think she probably does."

And that's how Iris and Jeremy went from being a regular couple to being a couple who were *having problems*. Jeremy had conflicted, confused feelings for Alicia, who reciprocated in kind, and because of these conflicting, confused feelings, Jeremy's judgment had been clouded and he'd foolishly kept the innocent trip out to Bucks County secret and he deeply regretted doing that and still, no sanction fell.

Ken didn't buy it at all. "I hate to say that I'm right," he said.

"So don't say it," Iris snapped, and then immediately felt bad about it. She reminded herself that just because she'd recently discovered how much fun it was to interrupt, lecture, and otherwise terrorize her boss, it didn't make it okay to walk all over everybody else. "Oh, okay, if you really want to, you can."

"Thanks," Ken said. "I was right." But somehow being right just wasn't as much fun as it used to be.

That night Iris swung by City College and picked Ken up and instead of going somewhere safe like the Warehouse or to Ken's apartment, she drove straight to the Broadway Brewery, almost as if to dare someone she knew to catch her there and report back to Jeremy on the strange company she'd been keeping. Fortunately or unfortunately, the place was pretty dead, which left them ample time to discuss Iris's newfound tolerance for ambiguity. To wit, Iris announced that she *didn't* think that she would go rifling through Jeremy's papers or his credit card bills or anything else like that in the future. Nor would she spy on him. Whatever way things shook out, Iris was not planning to devote the rest of her life to letting doubt eat away at her.

And before he could formulate a measured response, a thought suddenly swung back and forth right in front of Ken's eyes. "The pendant," he said. "What did Jeremy say about the pendant? The one with the nail polish on it to make it look cheap and plasticky? How does he explain that it's *not* in the picture? It was in the car when the car left New York and it was in the car when he got back, but it's not there when the picture was taken, which means that . . ."

"I know what it means, Ken. *You* wouldn't know what it means unless *I'd* already told you what it means, which I did, so obviously I already know."

"So what did he say about it?" Ken asked.

"He didn't."

"He didn't as in he didn't have any explanation, or he didn't as in you didn't ask him?"

"I didn't ask him," Iris said. Ken treated her to a long, unblinking look. "I just didn't see what good it'd do," she said.

Ken was perfectly well aware that misery loves company. If he had to suffer the indignity of losing his boyfriend then it made sense to take a very hard line with all the other cheaters out there. It made sense for Ken to rake Jeremy over the coals. But what he *hadn't* realized was that misery doesn't just love company, it *craves* it. It'll do anything for it. It'll sit up late at night and swallow its pride and dial long-disconnected numbers in order to sniff out someone else in the same miserable boat so they can be miserable together. For better or for worse, Ken was aware of this tendency on his part and he tried to rein it in as far as Iris was concerned. Iris was a big girl who could make her own decisions, even if her decisions were ones that she would surely regret, like *not* tossing Jeremy out on his behind and then tossing all his things out the window right after him. Ken tried to picture Jeremy's pajamas floating down over West Eighty-fifth Street while some heavier, more gravity-centric objects like his electric toothbrush and his hockey skates rained down around him. But that fantasy stayed a fantasy; Ken tried not to egg Iris on any more than he already had, which was probably more than he should have.

"I see your point," he said. Which was true. He just didn't agree with it.

Ken and Iris sat back against the banquette and just watched the world of the Broadway Brewery go by. On one side of them, two very young women were having a spirited argument about whether or not a mutual friend of theirs had highlighted her hair. The friend in question had apparently admitted to the fact that some of the strands of hair framing her face had indeed been altered—okay *lightened*—through the application of chemicals. However, her position was that she'd been using hydrogen peroxide–based acne cream for her face and had accidentally gotten some of it onto her hair and it had lightened it a little bit as everyone knows peroxide will do. So without any actual *intent* to do so, she'd inadvertently colored her hair. *Slightly*.

And despite the fact that the word "argument" implies that one person advocates a position while the other person advocates an opposing position, Ken and Iris's two neighbors were actually very much in agreement: it was *bullshit*. Their friend was full of shit. Why couldn't she just have some balls and call a spade a spade and admit that she colored her hair?

" 'Cause she's a liar," one of them said.

"More like a lying sack of shit," the other one said.

"I just can't believe she's trying to get away with this," the first one said.

"Oh, believe me," the other one said. "She'd try *anything*."

"She thinks she's so big," the first one said.

"I can't believe she thinks she's so big," the second one said.

And that reminded Ken of something. "Hey, Iris?" he asked.

"Hey, what?"

"Has anyone noticed that you've lost some weight?" Ken asked, and instead of looking pleased at the compliment, Iris looked more like she'd just been caught cheating. In a poker game. At a convent. Which was an odd way to react because given everything she'd been going through, she really did look pretty good. People who really knew her might be more inclined to focus on the dull-ish tinge that'd taken over the healthy glow she used to have; but if you *didn't* know her well, you'd never guess that until very recently a much more *imposing* figure had been occupying that body. "What's the matter?" he asked. "Nobody noticed?"

Iris slowly shook her head back and forth.

"Then what is it?" Ken asked. "Who noticed and why aren't you happy about it?"

"I am happy about it," Iris said, looking anything but. "But you won't be."

"And why's that?"

"Because it was Brett," Iris said. "Brett noticed."

And Ken said, "Oh," even though he felt like the air had been punched out of him.

"You're not mad at me, are you?" Iris asked, reaching over and putting her hand on his.

"Of course not," Ken said. He wanted to add something about how this is a free country and that Iris could do whatever she wanted without getting some sort of *permission slip* from him, but no matter how he composed the phrase in his head, it sounded arch, prissy, and bitter. "And why would that be?" Ken thought. "Because you're arch, prissy, and bitter. There. *Glad we got that cleared up.*"

Paul Schmidtberger

"No, I'm not mad," he said. "What was the occasion?"

"No occasion, really," Iris said. "We were home the other night and Brett called and he said he knew it was last minute but they were having some people over for drinks and could Jeremy and I make it? And I didn't particularly want to go but Jeremy was actually all for it."

"Any idea why?"

"Not really," Iris said. "Not beyond the idea of meeting new people and getting a chance to start all over, even on a microscopic scale. You know, to be charming and get them to like him. I think Jeremy likes to be liked."

"Don't we all," Ken said.

"We do," Iris said. "But I think Jeremy's more willing to do something about it. Anyway, I said yes and we brought a bottle of inscrutably priced Chilean wine so as not to come empty-handed but at the same time not to spend too much on that *low-life bastard Brett. . . .*"

"Thanks for that one, sweetie."

"Oh, it's nothing," Iris said. "Anyway, Neil was there, and yes, before you ask, they seemed happy enough, just like the last time, and everyone else there was a couple and one of the other couples was straight and that might've had something to do with why we got invited too, you know, so the straight couple would have somebody to play with. And they were nice enough too."

"What do they do?" Ken asked, just to show that he was genuinely interested in those aspects of the evening that *didn't* involve Brett and fantasies of shattering Brett's vertebrae.

"The guy's a sales rep for somebody and the girl's a financial planner. Does that ring a bell with you?"

"Nope," Ken said. "Were they at least interesting?"

"They weren't boring."

"Did you like them equally?" Ken asked, a bit out of the blue. "Or maybe you liked one a little more than the other?"

"About the same," Iris said. "Although I suppose I preferred the guy a little. The girl kept phrasing all these questions in the negative, and that got my back up for some reason. 'Oh, honey, are you sure you wouldn't feel a little more at ease with a coaster under that?' I hate it when someone asks a question in a way where a simple yes or no won't make any sense. But I mean, she was all right. The guy was funnier, though. He said he used to live right across the street from Secular Sushi, down in the Village, and he said that when the line would get really long, the waiters would give people free cups of sake and sometimes when he saw that the line was out the door he'd just go downstairs and stand in it and get himself a free glass of sake."

"Which is rather resourceful," Ken said. "Did Jeremy like them?"

"Yup."

"And they liked Jeremy, I take it?"

"They loved Jeremy."

"And what about Shithead and Neil, they must've liked Jeremy too?" Ken asked. "This would've been the first time that they've met him, right?"

"They loved him too," Iris said.

"Well, let me ask you this," Ken said. "You've been to Brett and Neil's place alone, and you were there the other night with Jeremy. Do you think they prefer you as just you, or as a part of Iris and Jeremy?"

"As a part of Iris and Jeremy," Iris said slowly.

"Well that just shows how little they appreciate your finer qualities," Ken said to take a bit of the sting off this realization. But then he found himself going ahead and asking the next question anyway. "And what about *you*," he asked. "Which do you like more, you as you, or you as part of Iris and Jeremy?"

Iris closed her eyes so she could think for a moment, kind of the way that a computer has to shut down all its secondary, nonessential functions when asked to do something really, really hard. "The latter," she finally said. "Even I like myself better when I'm with Jeremy."

Extraordinary. How did she end up cast as an understudy in her own life?

. . .

The celebratory graduation dinner was set for Nourriture, one of Manhattan's snootiest restaurants and one that commanded a striking view out over Bryant Park. At first Ken was shocked that Lucinda would pick such a fancy—read expensive—place as opposed to something a little more accessible. But Lucinda let it be known that an unknown donor in the class was underwriting the entire cost of the meal as a *healthy* way of working through her anger and, not insignificantly, as a way of spending as much money as possible before the court order making her ex-husband responsible for her expenses ran out. Jeff collected Ken and then the two of them collected Iris and they took the subway down to Forty-second Street so that, according to Jeff's logic, if Iris had too much to drink, then they'd only have to carry her home as opposed to carrying Iris *and* her car home. Jeff himself was actually quite well turned out for the occasion. He had on a suit and a tie and had obviously gotten his hair cut quite recently because the back of his neck was all razor-fresh and inviting.

Nourriture was very chic, very dark, and it had lots of polished wood surfaces with tiny, impossibly thin bud vases on them that were just begging to get knocked over. In a sea of confusion, the only thing that was clear was which of their classmates was responsible for pulling a Helena Rubenstein and generously underwriting the evening—it was a woman from the front of the class who was all decked out in a strapless red dress with a poofy crinoline skirt complete with a humongous velvet bow across her butt. The only thing missing, Ken thought, was a tiara.

June, the benefactress, grabbed on to the three of them as if they'd all been best friends ever since tunneling out of a political prison together. She literally squealed with delight at how slim Iris was looking, taking her by the wrists and holding out her arms as if Iris were a Diane Von Furstenberg wraparound dress and June was thinking about trying her on. She told Jeff that he was looking "sharp" and then she looked at Ken and said, "And Ken!" without quite knowing what was to follow, but she recovered quickly enough and said that she was just thrilled they could make it.

They weren't all at one huge table; instead, there were four small, separate tables, each set with a dizzying array of long-stemmed glasses and intricately folded napkins, and at the center of each of their four tables there was a beautiful flower arrangement featuring pennyroyals, which meant that June must've done her homework because pennyroyals symbolize peace. Their classmates were hovering around, unsure as to the protocol, and it was June who organized the seating and shepherded people to their assigned tables. And after years of having to sit at the gay table at wedding receptions—usually off in the Himalayas of the banquet room—Ken was positively shocked to find that he, Iris, and Jeff had actually been assigned the best table in the place. Together with a poetess from the front of the classroom, they were seated at a table for four in the center of everything, with a stunning view of Bryant Park, which at some point had been festooned with all these tiny, twinkly lights for the holiday season.

The cocktail order was long and complicated, and the regular ordering was even worse. With all his years of Latin and Greek, Ken could generally take each item on the menu and assign it to some fairly accurate place in the food chain. But beyond that, the ordering was chaotic and drawn out, and it didn't help matters that each dish came with various accompaniments, each of which was in turn accompanied by at least several dependent clauses supplying extraneous and confusing information as to the origins and pedigree of the food in question or the cooking processes to which it had been subjected: Gigot of pré-salé roasted with wisteria honey and slow-braised red currants. Still, they eventually got everything ordered and the drinks finally arrived and the mood lightened noticeably.

Iris wanted to draw the poetess into their conversation, but when Iris asked her how she liked having her Monday and Wednesday evenings free again, the poetess just sighed and said that freedom was a very *subjective* construct. She let that thought percolate for a few moments and then said, "A leaf that falls from a tree," looking around the table. "Can we consider it to be free?"

Where'd *that* come from?

"A leaf so perfect, so pristine, so carefully sculpted by the twisted hands of time. When it falls from the tree, can we say that it's truly free? Picture it as it falls. Does it land in the gutter next to a lost mitten that nobody realized is missing? Or does it slip through the railing and down into the sewer like the dreams an insomniac never had? Or does its fluttering, tumbling beauty momentarily blind a driver who slams into the car in front of him?" And that made something tug in the back of Ken's head, but before he could say anything about it, Jeff asked what happened to the cars in the accident. Was anybody hurt?

The poetess gave Jeff the same look that people normally use when they find a hair in their soup—a hair still attached to the skull of a dead rat—but then she went on, looking from face to face. "Three autumn leaves," she said. "You tell me which one is real."

But Ken had a better idea. The poetess had reminded him of his conversation with Maxine about exploding gas tanks and design flaws in the human condition, and he explained it to the table and was eager to see what they all thought about it. Jeff picked up on the mechanics of the concept right away. He said that all through his first year of college, he had an alarm clock with a button on it that you press so you can sleep for ten more minutes.

"The snooze?" Iris offered.

"Exactamundo," Jeff said. "And it had this *other* button on it that you could press which turned the alarm off and reset it for the exact same time the next morning. You know, for people who have a *job* or something where they always have to get up at the same time."

"And?"

"And the two buttons were *right next to each other*," Jeff said. "So when people thought they were hitting the button to buy themselves ten extra minutes of sleep, they were really resetting the alarm for the next morning."

"Which means they're screwed," Iris said.

"Exactly. And the same thing goes for those freaks who want to set tomorrow's alarm when they're barely finished getting up today. They hit the button and go for their eighteen mile jog and *while* they're running up and down the suspension cables on the Verrazano Narrows Bridge, their snooze function is driving everyone else in their building nuts."

"And which were you?" Iris asked.

"*Moi?*" Jeff said. "I was more the type to try and hit snooze and get the wrong button and then miss class altogether. The dean made me buy a new alarm clock, and when I told him that my credit card was maxed out, he said, and I quote, 'tough shit.' "

"But you all see the point," Ken said. "It's not an error, intrinsically speaking, to have a snooze button and it's not an error, intrinsically speaking, to have a doodad that resets the alarm for the next day. The problem is with the *design*; they just shouldn't be together."

Holy moly. Had he just said what he thought he'd said? Sometimes things just don't belong together? Could it really be as simple as that?

The poetess was trying to make a point about the futility of trying to divide something indivisible, like time, into units of ten minutes, but more and more her discourse was getting drowned out by a distinct, and distinctly displeased voice floating in from the antechamber where the maître d' held court. "No, that is *not* acceptable," the voice said, cutting off all further debate. Clipped. Demanding. Female.

The din in the dining room dropped down a bit but June rushed in to bring it back up the way a conductor can make an orchestra play louder just by putting his palm out and lifting it up. Iris, though, didn't seem to be paying attention to the conductor.

She had the most curious expression stretched across her face. "I *know* that voice," she thought. "Where do I know that voice from?"

And before they knew what was happening, the maître d' had materialized next to their table and he was leaning over and whispering something about being terribly sorry but there'd been some sort of mistake and he was *frightfully* embarrassed to have to do it, but would they mind moving? And even as he was supposedly *asking* them, his henchmen were already expropriating their drinks and their cutlery and the pitcher of ice water with the linen napkin tied around its handle, and worse, the poetess was already sighing and getting to her feet and Ken suddenly heard himself say, "No."

"I beg your pardon?" the maître d' said.

"I think we'd prefer to stay here," Ken said. He felt the color rising in his cheeks. "Right where we are." But the maître d' was launching into this long thing about how it was all a *mistake* and of course it was all the house's fault and the house was ever so sorry and it wouldn't ever happen again and there was a party of *this* who'd been expected and in fact it was a party of *that* and the only way to accommodate them was for Ken's table to move so everything could all be rearranged. The poetess had already evaporated and Iris was standing in the middle of the room, exactly where Ken knew she hated to be, while Jeff was stuck sort of halfway in and halfway out of his chair. Out of the corner of his eye he spotted June starting to extract herself from her table so she could come over and sort things out—she may have a big bow on her butt, *but thank God for the cavalry!*—but it was just too late. Some things can stay in limbo for a long, long time, and some things can't, and Ken didn't have any choice other than to fold. He picked up his drink and followed the waiter who showed them to their new and crappier table while the maitre d' supervised the swarm of busboys and waiters who undertook the complex machinations necessary to ready their old table for its new occupants.

And no, they didn't dismantle the table and spirit away little bits of it to be added onto other tables to make them incrementally larger. And no, they didn't wheel out one of those huge, plywood wagon wheels and plop it on top and cover it with a tablecloth to magically turn a square table for four into a round table for eight. And no, they didn't pack in a bunch of little extra tables to create one of those complicated banquet arrangements that would give even Emily Post a headache (*See* Suppers, Last, Seating Arrangements, Apostles Who Are *Not Speaking*). Nope. They didn't do anything. They stripped off the linen and they reset the table *for two* in about ten seconds flat and then a waiter frowned and swiped indignantly at some imaginary crumbs before the maître d' showed an ostrich-faced man and a bony woman with clunky Cartier shackles on her wrists to the table. "Oh, God, no," Ken croaked while Iris slowly slid down in her chair. *"I know him,"* he hissed.

"And I know her," she replied.

And it was true. It was Helvetica Carlyle, née Fahrtstaller. And Crayton Reed.

It was Iris who first recovered her ability to speak. Drawing on a full semester's worth of fake lessons in the art of restaurant criticism, she thought things over and put her imprimatur on the situation. *"This place stinks,"* she said.

Chapter Eighteen. In Which Iris Runs in a Circle but Discovers the Point

Looking back, Iris wished she'd done something wild and dramatic, like hitting Helvetica in the face with a slice of Boston cream pie. Unfortunately, no such opportunity presented itself because everything Helvetica ordered was utterly devoid of the least trait of creaminess or splatterability. Her appetizer appeared to be five or six green beans which the chef had tied into a neat triangular stack using a single strand of chive. And even then Helvie didn't really eat it; she mostly just pushed it around her plate suspiciously as if it might detonate at any moment.

In short, the celebratory dinner was left in shambles. Iris had chosen one tack, hiding, and Ken another, confrontation, but neither had been particularly satisfactory. Iris had slunk down in her seat and she'd eliminated all unnecessary movement and cursed herself for not wearing something made out of beige linen with eyelet hemstitching which would've blended in better with the tablecloth. Ken, on the other hand, was positioned so that he could fix his stare straight at Crayton Reed and he was trying to make it come off as a *Boy oh boy, have I got your number* kind of stare. Except it produced no effect. None. Helvie and Crayton were there to celebrate a bazillion-dollar initial public offering that they'd evidently inflicted on the world, and Ken's stink eye didn't register in the least. In short, Crayton didn't seem to remember or care who Ken was.

Leaving the restaurant was the worst. Both Iris and Ken were terrified that at some point June might get up and give a speech, which would be very much June's style, and there was simply no way that any such speech could be delivered without divulging the *reason* that this particular group had been assembled, and that was the last thing that either of them wanted Helvie or Crayton to know anything about. But in the end there wasn't any speech, and there weren't any awards or consolation prizes, and as the dinner went on, Iris and Ken's table moved through their courses more quickly than the other anger management tables because all conversation at their table had become impossible, what with Iris hiding and Ken staring and the poetess delivering a surprisingly tender meditation on how lonely it must be to be a *single*-malt scotch. Jeff kept offering to rush over and give Helvetica or Crayton the Heimlich maneuver. "Nobody needs to know that they weren't actually choking," he said, but his offer didn't find any takers. The dinner was ruined and all Ken and Iris wanted to do was leave.

And leave they finally did. Ken bit the bullet and went first, staring at Crayton the whole way. But the burning indignity that he had trained directly on Crayton's cerebral cortex was evidently less captivating than the cognac that Crayton was swirling around in this positively *huge* snifter, which had probably been conceived and born with a view to serving as the tip jar on top of a baby grand in a gay piano bar. Instead it had Crayton Reed's ostrich-beak face stuck into it vacuuming up any stray molecules of cognac that might have otherwise escaped. *It figures.*

Ken got closer and closer and thought—it's now or never—and as he passed by, he swung his hip and knocked the back of Crayton's chair. It was harder than just brushing by, but it wasn't hard enough to send Crayton crashing forward onto the table where his head would whiplash directly *into* the outlandishly huge brandy snifter and get stuck inside it. It was a minor bump and Crayton extracted his beak from his brandy snifter and looked up over his shoulder, vaguely curious as to the origins of this minuscule intrusion on the integrity of his person, but his look at Ken didn't register even the slightest bit of recognition. He simply looked up over his shoulder as if Ken were any old klutz who couldn't get his ass from A to B without bumping into the back of somebody else's chair, and as he looked, Ken felt his mouth opening and the words coming out and it was already too late to stop himself. He *apologized*. "Sorry about that," he mumbled.

Aw, *shit*.

In the weeks following the graduation dinner, Iris started to do a lot of thinking. She'd taken to getting up an hour earlier than normal to go for a jog in Central Park before leaving for work, which actually turned out to be the source of quite a few discoveries. First, she discovered that there were all sorts of crazy people who got up an hour early to run around the reservoir despite the cold and the gray half-light of those wintry mornings. Every morning they were out there in force, in all shapes and sizes, in getups that varied from snazzy, *up-to-the-second* ensembles to shapeless, gray sweatsuits that were already out of fashion when they were originally stamped with an EAST LANSING UNIFIED SCHOOL DISTRICT DEPARTMENT OF PHYSICAL EDUCATION logo in the midseventies. People with sleek, little radios strapped onto their biceps and people with huge, complicated radios clamped onto their heads who looked like they were on their way to their jobs out at the airport where they waved glow sticks around and helped jumbo jets park. People with leg warmers. People with dogs. People doing short, explosive exercises. People doing long, slow, oriental exercises. A few people doing push-ups. And one guy who skipped rope with all the skill and determination of someone who learned to skip rope in a prison yard as a way to steady his nerves and focus his attention while plotting revenge against the rat fink who'd double-crossed him and got his ass shipped off to the hoosegow for five to ten years in the first place. In short, there were people everywhere. Which led Iris to discovery number two: you don't have to have existential anxiety or chronic heartache in order to get up early on a winter workday to go running in the park to clear your head. Anyone can do it. No questions asked.

So she ran in the mornings, and she tried to sort things out in her head, and there never was a moment of inspiration when everything suddenly became clear to her. Instead, she plodded along and with time she began to develop a better stride and she began to make it all the way around the reservoir without resting, and then she began to do it a little faster, and then there was the moment when she first passed somebody else, as opposed to always being passed. Granted, the guy was about ninety and was tying his shoe when Iris overtook him, but still. Iris jogged and she didn't keep track of her declining weight, slightly out of fear of jinxing herself, but mostly because she didn't really care. She'd buy new clothes in the spring when it made more sense to buy new clothes, and for now she just belted stuff that didn't need to be belted before and she let her wristwatch get itself all catawampus because the usual hole for the strap wasn't tight enough anymore and she just left things like that. None of that was really important.

What *was* important, though, was what to do about Jeremy. That's what Iris thought about as she ran around the reservoir, letting Jeremy float in and out of her head. There was Jeremy taking charge in the elevator at Macy's, back when they first met. And there was Jeremy sitting next to her on the flight down to the Bahamas, getting the two of them into the stewardesses' good graces and cleverly holding Iris's hand by folding up the armrest and making it go away—a trick that fascinated Iris given that up until that moment, the armrest had only ever served as the last line of defense in a slow, losing battle with somebody else's corpulence, somebody else's body odor, somebody else's drool-geyser offspring, or the weepy, nose-blowsy story that somebody else just *had* to tell her about love gone down the toilet.

"*The shitter,*" her weepy neighbor would've said.

And so Iris went jogging in the mornings and Jeremy came flitting through her head. There was Jeremy clowning around on the tennis court and mugging for the camera. And there was Jeremy bringing shy, unassuming Iris into the conversation at the Broadway Brewery, telling everyone the story about how Iris's parents changed her name when she was little and how if it had been something like changing from *Liza* to *Lisa*, then maybe that was something he could've understood. Or even *Eliza* to *Elizabeth*, for crying out loud. And there was Jeremy behind the wheel of Iris's car a few weeks before Christmas, dropping a none too subtle hint about how much he'd like to have a pair of driving gloves someday. Not just any old Isotoners that you happen to be wearing while you're driving; he was talking about gloves that were *made* for driving. Like people used to have. Sleek, form-fitting gloves that were custom-made for directing horsepower and nothing else.

And *that*, that was definitely odd.

It was odd because it *never happened*. Jeremy had never sat at the wheel with Iris next to him on a freezing day in early December and commented—as if Christmas *weren't* just a few more weeks away—on how much he'd always wanted to have a pair of authentic driving gloves. And yet Iris could picture the scene perfectly clearly: they were at a light and they'd just gotten started because the inside of the car was still freezing cold and their breath was billowing out in clouds and Jeremy was loath to tightly grip the wickedly cold wheel, but he had to because he was Jeremy and that's the only way that Jeremy knew how to drive. And he turned toward Iris while the light was still red and said how great it would be if he had a pair of those tight, old-fashioned driving gloves, the ones that people always used to have in the movies. And Iris thought, "*Ho-ho!* Could this be a *hint*?" but she played it cool and didn't say anything for a few moments until she looked out the window and said, "It's green," and they drove off. *And none of that ever happened.*

And if that hadn't happened in the past, Iris thought, then that just leaves the future.

Unbelievable. She could still see a future with Jeremy.

Iris closed her eyes and replayed the scene one more time in her head. There she was in the freezing car with her breath billowing out in clouds, and a voice next to her dropped a little hint about wanting driving gloves for Christmas, and Iris played it cool and just watched the light change, and then she *turned to Ken* and said, "It's green."

Fascinating. It was up to *her*. She could make it happen any way she wanted it to. She tried putting Jeff in the driver's seat and re-played the scene and that worked. And then she dumped all the passengers altogether and pictured herself at the light thinking, "Maybe it's high time I bought *myself* some gloves." And that worked too. She could see a future with or without Jeremy. She didn't have to wait to see what he wanted to do or to see how things would "shake out." She had the power to do whatever *she* wanted to do.

Now all she had to do was figure out what that was.

She knew that Jeremy had fallen in love with Alicia. And from all the available evidence, the converse was pretty likely as well. Whether it was purposeful (probably not) or accidental (proba-bly) paled in comparison with the simple fact of the matter— Jeremy had, for some period of time beginning in the past and continuing to a point in the more recent past or to the present, been in love with Alicia, which is to say, in love with someone *other* than Iris. That much Iris knew. That and the fact that Jeremy had gone to great lengths to keep this a secret from her. Whether the two of them had actually slept together was less clear. Some evi-dence suggested that they probably had; other evidence suggested that they might not have. But that whole issue was like one of those supercomplicated questions on a tax return that you don't have to answer because you got nailed by an *earlier* question, and when that happens, you get to skip ahead to the end and sign and date your return. Jeremy had been in love with Alicia. That was bad enough. That was all that Iris needed to know. That's the point from which things couldn't get any lower.

And if things can't get any lower, Iris thought, then they can only get better. That or stay the same, she thought, silently crediting Ken and his firm belief that sloppy reasoning, like polio, could one day be eradicated from the face of the earth. From her perspective, Jeremy seemed to want to stay together; that much was clear. Jeremy was essentially on pins and needles around Iris. Jeremy wanted to *work things through*, as if being in love with someone were some sort of gigantic geometry project that would take forever to finish and they'd have to sit down to it every night after dinner and get out their pencils and their protractors and neatness would count and they'd have to *work*.

That was one option. But there'd have to be some changes if they stayed together.

In the first place, there would be no more Alicia. Alicia might be the nicest person on earth or she might not be. According to Ken, she was a depraved slut from the crappy part of hell who spent her time defrauding insurance companies whenever she wasn't busting up couples. But according to Jeff, she was a perfectly nice lawyer from D.C. who got a free jacuzzi in some sort of complicated transaction where, just *unlike* reality, everybody came out ahead. So maybe one was right and the other was wrong. Or maybe they were both a little right. Who cares? The point was that Jeremy would not be seeing Alicia anymore. No trips, no phone calls, no letters. Jeremy could speak to Alicia enough to communicate this new game plan so that, from Alicia's perspective, Jeremy didn't just fly off the face of the earth one day, which isn't a very nice thing to do to anyone—not to mention how it clutters up outer space—and then that would be the end of Alicia.

There would have to be some other changes too. For one thing, Iris didn't want the locket hanging from the rearview mirror anymore. Yes, they'd trafficked it to make it look plasticky and worthless, but the fact of the matter was that it *wasn't* plasticky and worthless; it was worth a lot. And if it's worth a lot, Iris thought, then it belongs inside and out of harm's way. Somewhere nice, like on top of the mantelpiece.

And since they didn't have a fireplace, much less a mantelpiece,

Iris decided that they'd probably have to move. It was high time anyway. When they'd first moved in together, Iris had been fleeing from the new upstairs neighbors who'd replaced the dead, catless cat lady. It had been Iris who'd moved into Jeremy's apartment, and to a certain extent, that subtle nuance had remained unchanged. Well, they could change that. They could spread out the paper and pore through the ads and call unscrupulous brokers who'd swear that the garden-level apartment had ORIGINAL VICTORIAN WAINSCOTING when in point of fact it had the *remnants* of where the original wainscoting *used* to be, which, on closer inspection, weren't even that; they were just the traces left over from the high-water mark when the whole place flooded back in 1972.

Iris wasn't particularly sure where she wanted to go, but there were plenty of options. She definitely imagined a bigger apartment with at least two walk-in closets, but probably in a building that was still on the small side so that it would be manageable and there wouldn't be any doorman-tip-at-Christmas debates and people would actually say hello to each other.

Something like the Santa Monica.

Except that was a tricky issue. Iris had sorted through a lot of scenarios, but she hadn't quite figured out how Ken or Jeff would fit into the picture if she stayed with Jeremy. To introduce Ken or Jeff to Jeremy would mean backing up, backing *way* up, and saying, "Oh, *by the way*, remember that whole thing about being interested in learning about restaurant criticism and disappearing for two evenings a week for the past few months? Well, that was just a big ruse to throw you off the scent while I went to court-ordered anger management classes—*long* story—and *while* I was in anger management, I recruited a cabal of gay men to spy on you. Jeremy, this is Ken and Jeff. Boys, this is . . . Actually, I think you guys already know each other."

Not so likely.

And that, in a nutshell, was the problem. Patching things up with Jeremy seemed to mean *unpatching* them with Ken and Jeff. And not just because Ken's own relationship had blown sky-high and he'd lost the ability to see any shades of gray in any debate regarding infidelity. The real problem was that Ken and Jeff were mixed up in all this right up to their eyeballs. They'd spied on Jeremy and crashed his fund-raiser and asked him all sorts of unusual questions and, shortly thereafter, Jeremy had been busted, and Jeremy wasn't stupid. He was a lot of things but he wasn't stupid, and there just didn't seem to be any practical way to work Ken or Jeff back into the picture if she stayed with Jeremy.

Nor did she want to preempt things and fess up to Jeremy that she'd been lying too. When all this blew up, Iris had told Jeremy that she'd gotten a letter from her insurance company saying they were going to jack up her rates and *that's* how she found out that everything wasn't copacetic at 119 West Eighty-fifth Street. If she confessed now, she'd be pegged as a liar too, merely a bit player to be sure, but at the moment, the shame of being a liar belonged to Jeremy and to Jeremy alone. Jeremy was the one who'd done something wrong, something very wrong, and Iris wasn't going to have that diluted by letting Jeremy turn the tables and accuse her of doing something wrong too. There's wrong and there's *wrong*, and Iris considered herself a shining example of the former.

All this seemed like it would need a little more thought, she told herself. Some fine-tuning.

Iris was clear on one thing, though. If she stayed with Jeremy, this was going to be a once-in-a-lifetime offer. In other words, a reconciliation was not going to be an invitation for Jeremy to lose his way again, safe in the knowledge that Iris would always take him back. That would be an incorrect interpretation—a *very* incorrect interpretation. If this happened, it would happen once and it would never happen again. Ever. Iris even thought that she might get to end the discussion of that particular term by saying, "*Capiche?*" Iris had always wanted to end a conversation by saying,

"*Capiche?*" Only now, now that she actually had the chance to do it, it felt more like a chore than anything else. Something about it felt all wrong.

Iris cocked her rifle, held the scope up to her eye, and thought, "Let's just see if my new mascara really is smudge-proof in *extremely demanding situations* like the commercial said it would be." Her boss was making a desperate, flailing dash to the right and Iris squeezed off a shot to the ground a few feet ahead of him and, like magic, he stopped moving in that direction. He turned and scrambled and scrabbled on the buffed, linoleum floor in the office break room and when he finally caught some traction, he tried to run in the other direction. Iris calmly raised the gun again and fired a round to the other side, stopping him in his tracks. "When would be a good time for us to talk?" she asked him.

Iris hadn't been planning to use her boss for target practice; it had just turned out that way. She still didn't know what she was going to do about Jeremy, but once she realized that she had the power to write her own ticket, wherever that ticket might lead her, it put her in a very strong negotiating position. You figure out what you want and if you don't get it, then there's no deal. That's how it works. And while she was still thinking all that through on the Jeremy front, where it mattered, she tested the theory on the job front, where it really didn't matter.

And the results were *most* encouraging. If you fire a bullet in the direction in which somebody is heading, 99 percent of the time they'll turn around and head in the opposite direction. Why? Because for a variety of personal, political, economic, and physiological reasons, they *don't want to get shot*. So when Iris approached her boss with her new idea, to wit, a little more responsibility and a *lot* more money, she saw where he was going and she aimed and fired in that direction—calmly putting the idea out there that the market might place a higher value on her services than he currently did—and the effect was as beautiful as it was predictable. He stopped where he was heading and he *turned around*.

Paul Schmidtberger

From there, it was child's play. She didn't whine and say she wanted a raise, she said that she wanted him to start thinking about a raise. And he had to say yes because nobody says no to just *thinking* about something. And later she said that she'd like to get him thinking about the *timing* of her raise, which meant that "her raise" had suddenly gone from being a vague, primeval concept to a foregone conclusion. And every time he tried to escape, she headed him off. There'd be more responsibility. And there'd be a lot more credit in front of the clients for work if it had been hers and hers alone. And the salary would have to be commensurate as well. "Needless to say," she added.

He looked her straight in the eye and Iris didn't blink.

"Of course, as part of those increased responsibilities, or should I say *consistent* with those increased responsibilities, I'd be happy to help you work through the details and figure out the best way to get this pitched so that it flies with the suits upstairs." Confusion. Consternation. Inability to sort conflicting data. Offers to help are automatically accepted whereas requests for raises are automatically denied. Pressure rising. Circuits overloading. Crash imminent. Warning issued. *Warning* . . .

"Why don't you give me a memo?" he said.

"I'll have it on your desk in the morning," Iris said.

Iris called Ken at the English Department to tell him that they had some celebrating to do that night, and she was a little disappointed when he said he'd *try* to make it.

"*Try* to make it?" Iris said. "You have to come. Did you not just hear me say less than a minute ago that I'm going to be making more money soon? You realize what that means, don't you?"

"You're going to move out to the Hamptons and sue your neighbors over every little thing?" Ken asked.

"*Ken*. It means I'm paying!"

"Oh, well in that case, yippee! Count me in."

"Good. Meet me at the Broadway Brewery," Iris said.

When he got there, Ken found that Iris was already there with

Jeff, and there were three drinks on the table. "I'm supposed to be demonstrating more initiative," Iris said, pushing one of the drinks toward Ken and plumping the place next to her on the banquette. "Not to mention forward thinking."

"Well, I'm all for that," Ken said, and they all toasted and congratulated Iris, and then Jeff went back to telling this story he'd been in the middle of. He said that he'd been at Our Lady of Solace in Brooklyn earlier in the day and even though it's neither here nor there, the fact of the matter is that *while* he was there, he checked out the baptismal font and get a load of this: it's this gorgeous old marble baptismal font and the thing's probably two hundred years old or even older if it came from Europe, which it could've since the whole idea of baptizing people came from Europe in the first place. Unless, of course, you think of the sixteen or seventeen centuries that Christianity spent in Europe as a kind of *layover* while it was on its way from the Middle East to America. But the point is that even though the marble font is super-old, in the middle of it there's this rubber stopper on the end of a little beaded chain. The kind of beaded chain that you see in banks when they don't want people to walk off with their pens even though their pens never work in the first place.

And Iris got to delegate for the very first time. Iris gave Ken a look and Ken turned to Jeff and said, *"And?"*

"Oh, and I just thought that it was really weird. You know, to see such an old, such a stately, such a . . . I don't know—*holy*—thing mixed up with something as commonplace as a little rubber stopper on a beaded chain. Like you'd find in Sears or at the A&P or someplace like that."

"Well, it's got to come from somewhere," Ken said. "And in any event, the juxtaposition of the sacred and the profane actually has a long and rich tradition in literature."

"The *whobitty whatiddy*?"

"Never mind," Ken said.

"No, tell us," Iris said. And she looked genuinely interested. So

Ken explained the theory and some of the supporting evidence and he got to give examples without worrying about the notes that might come flooding in the next day from offended parents or, in the case of parents who were lawyers, *shocked and offended* parents. And Iris got it right away. She said that it was sort of the same idea as when two people get married or got hitched or *whatever* it is they do to get themselves attached to one another for all eternity; the fact of the matter is that they still have to get up the next morning and when they do, one of them will probably still leave inexplicable amounts of his curly, golden hair all over the sink. Or he'll take forever in the bathroom and then even longer getting dressed, but he'll magically disappear when it's time to make the bed. Or maybe he'll be feeling nice and generous and he'll make the bed while the other person's out *jogging*. Or even better, he'll get the coffee started because the one thing the jogger hates more than anything else in this world is to extract yesterday's soggy filter and throw it away.

Ken and Jeff were looking straight at her, but only Jeff seemed merry and amused.

"But the point," Iris plowed on, "is that life goes on. All on its own. It's what it's programmed to do. It's what it wants to do, and there's no use trying to stop it. Something very good can happen or something very bad can happen, and that doesn't change the fact that the next morning you're going to have to get up and put your *panty hose* on one leg at a time, just like everybody else."

"Actually," Jeff said, "you can put your pants on *both* legs at a time if you sit on the edge of the bed." Now it was Iris's turn to look at Jeff. "I mean, that's the expression, isn't it? 'He may be a billionaire fifteen times over but he's got his head on his shoulders and he puts his pants on one leg at a time just like everybody else.' Well, not so fast. Just sit on the edge of the bed and you can do both legs at once."

"Jeff," Iris said.

"I'm serious," Jeff said, balancing on the edge of his seat and demonstrating. "Look!"

"*Jeff*," Iris said. "That's not the point."

"It's not my fault that conventional wisdom doesn't make any sense," Jeff said.

"Well, conventional wisdom is for conventional people," Ken said to Jeff. "And you are anything but."

"Actually, I'm quite average," Jeff said. "Almost uniquely so."

"My foot," Ken said.

"I really am."

"Baloney."

"No really," Jeff said. "Other than being a little taller than the average American male and slightly thinner, I'm squarely in the middle of everything else. As a matter of fact, if you asked one of those police artists to draw somebody, you know, like a suspect or something, but then didn't give them any details? They'd draw me."

And Ken said, "I don't think that's how I'd describe you to a police artist."

And Iris thought, "*Uh-oh.*" There'd been a faint, but distinct quality in Ken's voice that Iris hadn't heard before.

And Iris realized what was wrong—they'd veered out onto thin ice. They'd gone too far and there wasn't any clear path back to safety because *Ken was making a move.* Ken had finished dillydallying and hemming and hawing and he must've figured that now was about as good a time as any and he was making a play for Jeff's affections and it wasn't the right thing to do because Jeff was wonderful, Jeff was great, *Jeff beaned a law professor in the head with a laptop computer*, but Jeff didn't like Ken that way. Iris had figured it out and Ken should've figured it out too, but apparently he hadn't, and the last thing Ken needed was a little more rejection to fan the flames. If Jeff were interested in Ken, he'd reply, "Oh? So how would *you* describe me to a police artist?" and Ken would step up to the plate and tell Jeff how handsome he was— put better of course. If Jeff were interested in Ken, he'd never pass up such a golden opportunity to know what Ken thought about him.

Instead, Jeff just let it pass and turned to Iris with a thoughtful expression on his face and asked why she didn't like emptying the old coffee filter. Why she always wanted Jeremy to do it. "That's what you were talking about, right?"

"What?" Iris asked. She didn't dare look, but out of the corner of her eye she could see Ken, and Ken was following along as if nothing had happened, as if nothing more than gravity and the late hour were behind the slightly more pronounced slump of his shoulders.

"The coffee filter? Remember?"

"Oh, *that*. Well, given its small size and its light weight and the fact that it's slightly squishy, plus the fact that you have to carry it really delicately so you don't spill anything and you can only touch it by the edges so you don't get your hands dirty, it sometimes makes me feel as if I were throwing out a dead bird."

"*A dead bird?*" Jeff said.

"Well, you're the one who asked," Iris said.

"And knowing how you feel about it, does Jeremy always empty the filter?" Ken asked.

"He does the best he can," Iris said, imparting exactly zero information, and from there they all went back to talking about everything and nothing at the same time. And throughout it all Iris kept an eye on Ken, but Ken was holding his own. Sure, Jeff would've been the perfect solution for him. Jeff was so young and so fresh and so unburdened by what other people thought. Jeff was good-natured and fun loving and he'd been plopped down into their laps out of the sky—which was apparently Ken's modus operandi in terms of finding a boyfriend. But Jeff didn't like Ken that way; that was the only hitch. If Jeff *had* liked Ken that way, then everything would've been so easy. Brett would fade into a distant memory as Ken and Jeff became an item, and Ken would start to wonder what all the brouhaha had been about with that Brett character.

"Brett *who*?" Ken would say with a laugh on those rare occasions when Brett came up.

But 'twasn't to be. Not with Jeff, anyway.

"Wait a second," Iris suddenly heard herself saying. She'd let her mind wander and instead of going for a gentle, meandering stroll around the neighborhood, it had tugged at its leash and then dragged her straight back into the past, back four, five, maybe six weeks ago, back to the moment when Iris had been sitting in Ken's office in the English Department and Maxine had put through a call from Jeff. "He says it's a Mr. Mandel-*buns*," Maxine had said over the speakerphone, trying to stifle a laugh on the off chance that it was actually true. Jeff's last name was Mandelbaum.

"Hey, Mr. *Mandelbaum*," Iris said. "What were you doing in Our Lady of Whatchamacallit anyway? Apart from examining the plumbing?"

"What's that?" he asked.

"Our Lady of Solace," Iris said. "It's a church? One God, divided by three, but still equals one? As in not Jewish. What were you doing there?"

"Oh. Well, I was going to tell you. . . ."

"But?"

"But I didn't want to count my chickens before they hatched," Jeff said.

"Let me see if I understand this correctly," Iris said. "You've decided to raise chickens in the *churchyard* of Our Lady of Solace? Don't you think that's the kind of career decision that should get bounced off your friends first?"

"Very amusing," Jeff said. "And actually, my friends—meaning you two—did play a pretty big role in making my decision, which wasn't easy, by the way."

"You're not seriously talking about entering the . . . ?" Ken asked.

"No," Jeff said. "No need to panic. There's a community law clinic at Our Lady of Solace, and it's actually affiliated with Brooklyn Law School and not mine, but I applied anyway and I've been through two sets of interviews and like I said, I don't want to count my chickens before they're hatched and all, but it's beginning to look like it's going to be a done deal."

"Oh, Jeff, that's great!" Iris said. "At least I think it is. Or rather it must be since you wouldn't have applied if you didn't want it." She paused. "But what does a community law clinic lawyer do?" she asked at the same moment that Ken said, "I don't remember helping you apply for that job."

"It's not that you helped me get this *specific* job," Jeff said. "It's more that you helped me sort through what was so wrong with the direction where I was headed. You know, the whole law firm deal. That's what they tell us we want and that's what we're supposed to want, and I suppose I'd have gone along with the crowd too—and why not, when going along with the crowd means earning so much money—but something didn't sit right and I'd never been able to put my finger on it."

"Until?"

"Until I met you," Jeff said.

"But what do clinic lawyers *do*?" Iris asked.

"Oh, a bit of everything," Jeff said. "They help people who are getting evicted and they help people who are getting hounded by creditors and there's a domestic violence clinic that walks you through the process of getting a restraining order and they help people apply for food stamps or benefits that they might not even know about and there's help with immigration questions and—"

"In short, they help people," Ken said to Iris, based on a statistical analysis of the frequency with which the word "help" had left Jeff's mouth over the past twenty seconds.

"They stand up for people who can't stand up for themselves," Jeff said.

"I like the way you put that," Iris said.

"But I don't see what that has to do with me," Ken said. "Or with Iris either."

"Well, think about it," Jeff said. "Before I met you, I didn't have any opportunities to get inside a law firm or a courtroom even though, at least for the latter anyway, they're open to the public and any bum can just stroll right in. Which is what I did when I came with you guys for Iris's hearing. And as far as law firms go, I just listened to Ken talk about his experiences at Leighton Fennell. You know, most people at school would give their left *anything* for a chance to work at a place like Leighton, Fennell & Lowe."

"But not you?" Iris asked.

"Sure, yes me. Or maybe me. I don't really remember what I was thinking at the time. But not after listening to Ken. Ken was all I needed to convince me that Leighton Fennell was not the right place for me.

Fascinating, Ken thought. He was actually *listening*. But all he said was, "Well, I'm just glad that my constant complaining finally came in handy. Not that you wouldn't have figured out how crummy a law firm can be all on your own. Say after about five minutes."

"Maybe," Jeff said. "And then again, maybe not. But you know, life is short, and if you save somebody some trouble along the way, whether it's five minutes or five years, you've done them a bigger favor than you might think."

And that left clever Kenneth Connelly without anything to say.

Jeff gave Iris and Ken a rundown of all the details—how he was supposed to pass the bar next summer on the first try and if he didn't, he'd be put on probation at the job; how he could start coming in one afternoon a week right after the holidays because they were going to tap into some grant to pay him in the short term; how he'd be in court all the time right from the get-go instead of sitting in a high-rise prison in the financial district crushed under a collapsed stack of boxes full of documents that urgently needed to be reviewed and nobody would find him for weeks and the firm would commission an official autopsy and everyone would pause and think—oh, *our mistake*, I guess the firm really *did* care after all—until they realized that the partners just wanted to bill the client right up to the precise moment of death.

And thanks to them, Jeff would be spared all that.

It was supposed to be a celebration, what with Iris getting a promotion and Jeff taking the first steps toward charting his own course in the world, but Iris thought she noticed a slight touch of melancholy about Ken, despite his best efforts to put up a good front. Just the slightest minor chord playing around the edges of his smile. But look what he's losing, Iris thought. He's not going to end up with Jeff, and not only that, Jeff would soon be off on his crusade and wouldn't have as much time for Ken in the future, even as a regular friend.

And what's worse, Ken's afraid he's going to lose me too, Iris thought. Ken was no ding-a-ling. Ken knew that weeks had gone by since everything had blown up and that I haven't thrown Jeremy out on his keister. I haven't thrown Jeremy out and the other shoe hasn't dropped yet, and if it hasn't dropped by now, he thinks it never will. He thinks that Jeremy and I are going to soldier on and try to salvage things—and maybe that's what we'll do—but that will leave Ken by himself as the lone hawk in the war on infidelity. He'll be right, she surprised herself by admitting, but he'll be alone.

Chapter Nineteen. In Which a Thought Tumbles out of the Sky and into Ken's Head

The art of letter writing might be long dead, Ken thought, but nobody had told Chase Manhattan Bank because they faithfully dispatched missive after missive to him. And he was equally faithful in his reaction—he tossed them, still unopened, into a shoebox that he kept on the shelf in what used to be known as his side of the closet. Unfortunately, all good things must come to an end, and as the shoebox started to overflow, one thing became clear—it was time for Ken to sort things out.

He really hated dealing with his finances because, for one thing, it reminded him of just how little he earned. Second, even the most basic financial planning forces a person to make an honest assessment of the likelihood that he's going to spend the rest of his life alone or not, and where's the fun in *that*? It's one thing to stroll through the home furnishings section at Bergdorf Goodman's and think, "Gee, wouldn't it be *swell* if one day I found someone and we fell madly in love and we loaded up on expensive bone china and we got to send smug, self-satisfied notes to the alumni newsletter?" Okay, it's nice if it happens, but if it doesn't, no harm done. It's another thing altogether to be strolling through the home furnishings section at Bergdorf's and think, *"How am I going to support myself in my dotage?"*

Still, Ken was determined to do his best. He dumped out all the letters from the bank and organized them by date and then assembled a highlighter, a calculator, a stapler, and a letter opener, although the letter opener was actually a metal swizzle stick with a little tennis racket on top and, confusingly, the words GREETINGS FROM ALASKA! stamped beneath it. Ken lost at least ten minutes of prime accounting time puzzling over that little gem before he realized that it wasn't a tennis racket at all; it was supposed to be a snowshoe.

The accounting news, on the other hand, wasn't as bad as he'd thought. First and foremost, all the letters and the statements seemed to be regularly generated communications. Which is to say, there weren't any letters addressed to him in particular to let him know that his account was woefully overdrawn, that they'd be suing him shortly, and that they'd be sending people over to repossess all his belongings.

Instead, he was operating in the black. It wasn't by much, but he was in positive territory, and Ken couldn't figure out how that could be given that he was working only one of his three jobs. Plus Brett used to pay half the rent, so Ken had just assumed that his financial situation was now desperate and that at any moment the bank machine was going to swallow his card and digest it and rearrange its molecules and then spit them back out some other orifice in the form of a mean, registered letter informing Ken that he was impoverished and that life as he previously knew it was officially over and that he'd have to go stand in a bread line somewhere.

So how did this happen? True, Brett's portion of the rent had always been a little late—depending on your willingness to consider three weeks as a *little late* when compared to an overall period of one month—but it always got paid in the end, so how could Ken still be solvent without Brett's half of the money? Ken hadn't been particularly frugal since Brett left because a financial free fall was still a financial free fall; flapping around a little bit wasn't going to change the end result, which is to say, the fact that he was going to go *splaaaat* when he hit the ground.

But apparently that wasn't going to be the case. He'd still have to get another job—that much was obvious—but outright disaster would be avoided. Ken opened still more statements, slowly moving backward in time until he figured out that yes, Brett had been contributing half the rent, but Brett had also been *really* expensive. When Ken reached the statements where there'd still been a Brett in the picture, the evidence was shocking. Back then, Ken went to the cash machine every other day; now a single trip lasted three times as long. And the checks—to *Sweat!*, to the Learning Annex for acting seminars, to the photo studio that did Brett's headshots, to the *other* photo studio that did his *other* headshots, to the voice coach, and then the *whopping* big check written out to the Kiehl's skin-care store, which might as well have been a down payment on a Mercedes-Benz, fully loaded, *natch*. So much money and for what? For itty, bitty pots of miraculous skin-care cream which, now that he thought about it, really had worked because Brett's nascent wrinkles actually had disappeared—right out the door with Brett.

And that's to say nothing of the credit card statements. Good gravy, look at the difference! Ken's statements now fit onto one page whereas before they'd gone on and on and on. Restaurants. Barney's. Bloomie's. Brett's MetroCard. And *those* were the things that Ken could figure out; there were plenty of obscure charges that were real enough when you had to pay them, but didn't offer any clue as to what had actually been *acquired* in the transaction. What the hell was Amsterdam Avenue Associates and how on earth had they dropped $91.13 on them in whatever fleeting amount of time existed between the small fortune they spent on drinks at Sheer Bar and the king's ransom they spent on dinner at Akushû? Ken could remember that night perfectly well. He'd come straight from City College and joined Brett and two of his actor friends for cocktails at Sheer Bar and then they'd *walked* to Akushû at Columbus Circle, which meant that the ninety-one-dollar charge *couldn't* be related to a car service or a private helicopter or some other form of fantastically expensive transport that Brett had heard about at *Sweat!* and was dying to try himself.

How does a person spend more than ninety-one dollars during an eleven-block walk?

Ken had an entirely different shoebox where he stored credit card slips and receipts, and he got up on his tiptoes and tried to pry it out from the back of the shelf but something was blocking it. "I could get the chair from my desk, which is all of seven feet away from here," he thought. "*Or* I could jump up and neatly dislodge the box during that fleeting moment when I hang in the balance forged between my own athletic prowess and the pull of earth's gravity."

Well, that's a no-brainer.

Ken jumped up and swatted at the box and smashed his elbow into something that *really* hurt, and the box of receipts didn't pop loose and fall into his arms, which was what he'd been expecting; instead, the box itself exploded and stayed where it was, but produced a blizzard of paper. Chits and slips and fleeting, fluttering bits of paper, all of which spread themselves out over the bedroom floor. Nice going.

He got down on his hands and knees and started sorting through them, arranging them into piles by year, then by month, and then finally by date, and when he was done and he'd zeroed in on the mysterious Amsterdam Avenue Associates charge, he couldn't believe his eyes. It was a newsstand. It wasn't anything more exotic than a newsstand. And as he sat there it came back to him: they'd been walking toward the restaurant and Brett had said something along the lines of, "Hang on a second," because they'd passed a newsstand and Brett had been looking for some magazine or other. It was probably one of the thick, glossy magazines that he was partial to, the kind of magazine that was filled with advertisements where you couldn't figure out what was for sale—like an ad featuring a man with razor-sharp cheekbones and a sullen, methadone-induced stare who was surrounded by deerhounds and had apparently decided to lounge, half-undressed, on a log in a forest somewhere while on his way to an eighteenth-century hunt. Anyway, Brett ducked into the newsstand and came back out with his magazine plus a few others.

And they'd cost ninety-one bucks?

Good Lord in heaven. Ken worked in a *library*. Ken's *third* job was in a library, a place where patrons, not customers, could come and read whatever they wanted to. For free. Ken was working three jobs, including one in an establishment that lent books to readers, for free, and for what? So that Brett could blow ninety-one bucks on slick, glossy magazines in the blink of an eye? Now that, *that* was seriously messed up. He gathered the slips back up and tried to keep them in order in case he ever decided to go through his accounts with a fine-tooth comb—which he already knew he'd never do—and then he tried to pry their shoebox free, but something that wasn't supposed to be there kept blocking it. He knuckled under and got his chair and stood up on it, and then he remembered—the box of stuff from Leighton Fennell; the box he'd used to carry his meager possessions home from his former job. He'd stuck it up there for lack of any other bright ideas as to what to do with it.

Well, now he had one. It was a big, sturdy box, and it was much better than his shoeboxes, and he decided that it would now become the hub of his new accounting system. It would be the *nerve center* for his new, hands-on approach to financial planning and life management. He dumped out the Leighton Fennell box and then dumped the contents of all his shoeboxes into it: the one with the statements; the one with the receipts; the one with the ATM slips. All of them. *There.*

And that just left the little pile of Leighton Fennell stuff to deal with, which wasn't too taxing because most of it was junk and richly deserved to go straight into the trash. For example, during those few minutes that he'd had to gather up his stuff before leaving Leighton Fennell, how could he have possibly thought that someday he'd need his copy of the internal phone directory? And even the things that were truly his, like his sandwich-sized Tupperware tub, probably belonged in the garbage given that the remnants of his last tuna salad on rye had now festered in hermetically sealed peace for the past four months and would surely gas him and all his neighbors to death if he ever tried to open it. Straight into the trash.

What stopped him in his tracks, though, was a photo he found in a thick, beige, Leighton Fennell envelope—a picture of Brett. Brett smiling at him out at Jones Beach. The picture that had been in the weird three-sided frame that Maeve from the day shift had bought for the three of them to share, *sort of* as a joke. He'd pried it out of its frame and taken it with him and now, sitting there in his thoroughly de-Brett-ified apartment, there was Brett gazing out at him from Jones Beach, and it took his breath away. He could remember taking that picture as if it were yesterday. They were still so new together and they'd gone out on the Long Island Railroad and hiked all the way down to the far end of the beach and they were almost there and when they got to the last point of commercial civilization, they stopped to buy water and junk food and to rent folding lawn chairs. And that's when Ken took Brett's picture.

Brett had just loaded himself up with a folding lawn chair on each arm, pushed up toward his shoulders as if they were bizarrely designed water wings, and Ken said, "Hey Brett?" And Brett turned and saw the camera and smiled, broadly and beautifully, and Ken took the picture, and as he took it, he had a feeling that it was going to be a good one. But all Brett did was laugh and tell him that he was wasting film and that he should wait until they were settled on the beach before taking pictures.

The day went on and they ate their picnic and they dozed for a while and they asked the people next to them to watch their stuff while they went for a long, lazy swim that wasn't like anything that Ken had ever experienced before—touching Brett's beautiful body through the sensual, slimy prism that is the Atlantic Ocean; the strange contrasts of cold water and hot body; the salt against the sweetness of his lips. But just *before* they'd gone for their swim, Brett had run his fingers through his hair and then reminded Ken that if he wanted a really good photo, now was the right time.

So Ken got the camera back out and took a few pictures of Brett glistening in the sun, and then the neighbors who were willing to mind their stuff for them, though evidently less willing to mind their own business, got into the act and volunteered to take pictures of Ken and Brett together, which felt vaguely discordant because the neighbors were so obviously interested in Brett and not Ken. But be that as it may, Ken and Brett hammed it up for the camera and then they went for the long, lazy swim that Ken would remember for the rest of his life.

The thing, though, was that when the pictures came back, they didn't have the slightest trouble dividing them. This was long before the hedge-fund guy went off on his permanent vacation, which meant that this was back when the two of them still lived in separate apartments, albeit on the same floor of the Santa Monica. But as far as the pictures from Jones Beach were concerned, Brett wanted the shots that Ken took of him on the blanket on the beach, whereas Ken wanted the goofy shot of Brett that he'd taken just before they staked out their spot on the beach. The one where the underarms of his shirt were still wet from riding the train; the photo of him with a folding lawn chair pushed up onto each shoulder as if he were some sort of clunky, clattering butterfly, some sort of overloaded angel. That's the picture Ken wanted, and that's the one that he slipped into the half-joke, half-serious frame that somebody named Maeve once bought for three strangers who shared one pointless job.

So how did they all get from there to here?

Ken's idea for the final exam in his composition sections was so wonderfully simple that he was genuinely surprised when it met with wails of protest from his students. "But you made us write about *anger* all semester. Remember? How are we supposed to write an essay about *happiness*? It's not fair."

Fair or not, though, that was the assignment. "You have two hours. You can have all the blue books you want. You should write on only one side of the page, and if your handwriting is atrocious—

and you know who you are—then double-space your answer to make it easier to read." It would be hard to imagine happiness existing anywhere on this planet with so few constraints.

"Question!"

"Yes?" Ken said.

"How are you going to grade these?"

"How am I going to *grade* them? Your tests? With a red pen. How else would you like me to grade them?"

"No, I meant on what *basis*. You know, the happier the essay, the more points you get? Or do we get points for having a topic sentence and making references to all the reading that you assigned, which was a lot in case you don't remember."

Yeah, *sure* it was.

"There's no formula," Ken said. "I'm giving you happiness as a *topic*, so there's no right or wrong answer. The essay will be graded on its quality. Period. That, and whether it demonstrates that you actually learned any of the things I taught you this semester."

"Question. Like spelling 'accommodate' with two *c*'s and two *m*'s?"

"Get started," Ken told the class. "Time's a-wasting." And then even though he wasn't supposed to, he left them alone. He told them that he could be reached over at the English Department in case of emergency—meaning a *real* emergency—and that he'd be back when the spirit moved him or at the end of the exam, whichever came first. He knew that he was supposed to watch them to make sure they didn't cheat or annoy each other or make or receive phone calls, but Ken thought that they were mature enough to mind themselves. And if they weren't, then they needed to learn to be.

He went over to the department and was glad to find that Maxine was there and hadn't been roped into proctoring one of Scillat's exams. On the other hand, he was more than a little surprised to find that she was hanging from the long, fluorescent light fixture as if it were a trapeze that had lost its steam and had slowly come to a halt. "Oh, hey there Ken," she said.

"Hi Maxine. What's new?"

"We'll get to that in a second," she said. "But in the meantime, do you think you could do me a little favor and get that step stool set back up?"

"This one here?" Ken asked, walking behind her desk and righting the little stepladder that had fallen over onto its side and helping Maxine back down onto it and then back down onto solid ground.

"That's the one," she said, rubbing her elbows and stretching a crick out of her back. "You know, I think my arms just got longer."

"Wouldn't surprise me," Ken said. "So what were you doing up there anyway?"

"Oh, we're going to be having a holiday party and I wanted to get going on the decorations. There was something about it in your mailbox, which, if you'd been a good boy, you would've read."

"I don't remember anything about a holiday party."

"That's because we're not allowed to say 'holiday party,' " Maxine said. "In the memo I called it a 'gathering.' "

"A gathering for . . . ?" Ken asked.

"A gathering, period. That's it. It's not a Christmas party, it's not a Hanukah party, it's not a pagan feast or an Alternate Side of the Street Parking party. It's a *gathering*."

"I thought the memo was talking about some sort of departmental meeting," Ken said. "Only more horrible than usual because the word 'gathering' made it sound like we were going to have to sit around talking about our feelings and stitching together a quilt."

"Well, it'll be just like a departmental meeting only less horrible than usual," Maxine said. "Because there'll be booze."

"Count me in."

"I already did," Maxine said. "On the othe hand, *however*, I didn't know whether you'd be accompanied or not." Maxine crossed her arms and looked at Ken expectantly.

"No," he said. "I'm sorry to disappoint, but I'll be on my own."

"And what happened with that young man you were going on so effusively about a ways back? What was his name again?"

"Jeff," Ken said. "And ten bucks says that you didn't forget his name, you're just trying to play it cool."

"Touché," Maxine said. "But that doesn't answer my question."

"Well, it didn't work out. And yes, I tried, and no, he just wasn't interested. And before you say anything else, *yes*, I made an honest effort. He just wasn't interested in me that way."

"That's his loss," Maxine said. "I hope it wasn't too, what's the word . . . ?"

"Awful?" Ken volunteered. "Devastating? Humiliating? No, it wasn't. It was about the gentlest rejection I've ever had. Which doesn't change the fact that it was a rejection all the same, but at least he had the decency to do it gently. Not that I would've expected any less from him. He really is a good kid."

"That's what I'd gathered from the way you were talking about him," Maxine said. "I guess you win some and you lose some."

"Winning seems like a pretty distant memory at this point," Ken said.

"Oh, there'll be others," Maxine said.

"But that's just it," Ken said. "I don't want there to be others. I'm not saying that I can't live without Jeff; I'm just saying that I just don't want to go through any of this anymore. With *anyone*. I want to buy a cat, or lease one, or do whatever it is that lonely people do these days. Call it quits. And that's what I don't get, because no matter how much I tell myself it's all useless and it's all a waste of time and energy, there just doesn't seem to be a way to *stop* myself from looking for the right person. You know? From looking at every face on every escalator that's going up while I'm going down and wondering whether the right guy for me just went by. Where's the emergency brake here? How do you get off this ride? Why isn't there a fuse box somewhere that I can go peer at with a flashlight until I find the fuse with "Heart" written underneath it and then throw that switch and let the rest of them keep humming merrily along and just, I don't know, *opt out* of the whole thing?"

"Oh, Ken, I wish it were that easy."

"I know, Maxine. And don't think that I don't appreciate your concern, because I do, and I really am doing better—I'm not the train wreck I was at the beginning of the semester—and that's in no small part thanks to you. And to Iris. And Jeff, for that matter. Even so. But don't you see how much easier it could be? If there were some sort of pill I could swallow that would make me wake up tomorrow and simply stop looking for somebody despite the fact that, intellectually speaking, I know it's hopeless, I'd take that pill. I'd take a handful of those pills. And gladly, too."

"But that's not how it works," Maxine said.

"I know. It's like a toy. It's like getting a little yellow metal bulldozer for Christmas when you're a little kid and you switch the bulldozer on and it creeps forward. You switch it off, it stops. And sooner or later you turn it on and your mind wanders or it's dinnertime or any one of a billion things happens to grab your attention and you forget about it and the little yellow bulldozer creeps across the room and it eventually runs into a wall somewhere and it bounces back a fraction of an inch and goes—*grrrrnn*, *grrrrnn*—and then it tries again, and it runs right into the wall again, and then bounces back again. Again and again and again. Until the batteries are dead. There's no *override* button in there that says, okay, after the fifteenth or sixteenth, or, who knows, the twentieth failed attempt, we're going to conclude that this is useless and we're going to shut ourselves off and preserve what's left of our battery life and wait for a more, I don't know, propitious opportunity."

"So what you're saying is?"

"What I'm saying is that it's a crappy system," Ken said. "The yellow bulldozer. The human heart. Both of them."

"You're trying to say that there's another design, flaw," Maxine said. "You're saying that there should be a way to shut off whatever that thing is, that thing inside us that makes us keep trying to find someone even though everything's stacked against us and it all seems so useless."

"You took the words right out of my mouth," Ken said.

"Well, then I'm going to have to stuff them right back in," Maxine said, "because you're wrong."

"I'm what?"

"You're wrong," Maxine said sweetly. "That's the part of the design that's most right."

"But—"

"But nothing. Now why don't you help me make some nonsectarian decorations?" Maxine said, fiddling with something that looked like a high-tech version of a laundry wringer.

"Like what? And what is that anyway?"

"It's Scillat's new paper shredder," Maxine said, feeding an interoffice memorandum into one end which came out the other end in long, thin, spaghetti strips. "It's actually quite satisfying."

"Can I try?"

"Sure, shred this," Maxine said, handing him a stack of brightly colored flyers advertising a colloquium called "Sic!—Grammatical Errors in Bomb Threats, Ransom Notes and Blackmail Attempts" that had come and (thankfully) gone. "I thought I'd shred a bunch of useless paper that I had lying around and then tie them into pom-poms or something festive like that," she said.

"Works for me," Ken said. Maxine was right; it *was* fun to clear out some of that extra garbage. "Give me some junk and keep it coming."

At the appointed hour Ken went back to his classroom, paused outside the door, and was relieved *not* to hear the sound of femurs shattering and desks collapsing. He cleared his throat, pushed the door open, and called time, provoking a chorus of groans mixed with relief. He gathered up the blue books and erased the topic from the blackboard and answered a few questions from the students who, for some reason, didn't evaporate the *instant* the class ended like they usually did. Instead they were hanging around him, getting underfoot and asking questions about when the exams would be graded, what he was doing for the holidays, where the grades would be posted, was there going to be a curve, what was he teaching next semester, which of his two composition sections was full of idiots, us or them? It was fascinating. The little monsters didn't want it all to end just yet.

"All right," Ken said, laughing and leading them out the door. "These exams aren't going to grade themselves."

So what light did his students shed on the question of happiness? Quite the spectrum.

One young woman argued, quite convincingly, that happiness was the state of not being aware of any current annoyances.

Another said, "Happiness is what I had before my boyfriend slept with Caitlin."

"Happiness is when I turn twenty-one because my *real* mother put aside this money for me that she got from my grandmother before she died (my grandmother) and for whatever reason, I can't touch it until I'm twenty-one."

"Happiness, as a term, is fine. But it's nothing compared to the word 'benign.' "

"Happiness is coming from a family where the police don't have to break up your niece's first communion party. And where your cousin doesn't ask you to testify for him and swear that he *didn't* kick out the back window of the squad car and that it was your other cousin who punched it *in*, but the fact of the matter is that the broken glass from the police car window was all over the driveway, so—*paging Sherlock Holmes*—he did kick out the window. Oh, and even though my cousin has a big butt to go with his big mouth, the squad car was very roomy and was able to *accommodate* his big butt."

"Happiness is just like anger, except nobody ever slowly counts to ten before exploding in happiness."

And then one student said that happiness is what happens when you go to bed on the hottest night of the summer, a night so hot you can't even wear a tee-shirt and you sleep on top of the sheets instead of under them, although *try* to sleep is probably more accurate. And then at some point late, late, late at night, say just a bit before dawn, the heat finally breaks and the night turns cool and when you briefly wake up, you notice that you're *almost* chilly, and in your groggy, half-consciousness, you reach over and pull the sheet around you and just that flimsy sheet makes it warm enough and you drift back off into a deep sleep. And it's that reaching, that gesture, that *reflex* we have to pull what's warm— whether it's something or someone—toward us, that feeling we get when we do that, that feeling of being safe in the world and ready for sleep, that's happiness.

Ken felt a lump take up residence in his throat. A lump that he'd thought had skipped town *years* ago. But there it was, back again. He gathered up the blue books and put them in his briefcase to go over more carefully later. But even as he did, he realized that he'd been wrong earlier in the day. He'd been wrong when he told the class that there were no right or wrong answers, because there was at least one very right answer. Happiness was having somebody *he* taught sit in a cold, bare classroom in the middle of December and write so beautifully, so longingly, so lovingly about a warm summer's night.

Ken had some serious thinking to do. He was sitting by the window in his living room watching workmen tie big, cheerful bows onto all the poles, ledges, and miscellaneous outcroppings belonging to the Trump complex. They used a long telescoping ladder so the bows would be out of reach, one would suppose, of bow-stealing marauders. After each one was securely fixed into place, a different worker climbed up the ladder wearing a backpack with something snaking out of it that looked like the drapery attachment to a vacuum cleaner. Only instead of sucking dust and dandruff and broken paper clips *into* itself, this strange attachment shot *out* a blast of sparkly white powder that settled and dried on top of the bows to look like some very fake snow. They'd been at it for at least an hour and they weren't even halfway around Ken's side of the building.

What would happen, Ken thought, if I were to run into Brett?

Correction. What will happen *when* I run into Brett?

Because the simple fact of the matter is that New York City is not all that big. And that's before you consider the fact that people tend to move in certain circles and do the same sorts of things and that makes running into each other all the more likely. Ken could go out to Yankee Stadium every night for the rest of his life without worrying about running into Brett, but Ken didn't *want* to go to Yankee Stadium—that night or any other—other than on the off chance that the city finally and rightfully converted the stadium into the world's largest wall sconce and rare opera recording emporium. Basically, when he thought things through, he realized that sooner or later he'd run into Brett and it was much better to be prepared than to leave everything to chance.

So what was the protocol here? Ken let himself imagine the possibilities.

Let's say he spotted Brett somewhere but Brett didn't spot him. Let's say Ken was just coming out the door of a drugstore and the beeper thing went off, so Ken opened up his bag for the guard who checked his receipt and saw that Ken *hadn't* simply appropriated his Mennen Speed Stick antiperspirant (Deep Sea Blue). And with that Ken walked out the door.

But that little holdup, that brief moment of hesitation that slipped by as Ken was accused of, tried for, and acquitted of theft, that was enough time for Brett—*Brett!*—to walk by the door. So what do you do? First you panic. Then your heart pounds in your chest. Then you're momentarily distracted as you think, "Why on earth would an antiperspirant market itself as Deep Sea Blue? *Was there anything wetter than the middle of the ocean?*" But then you shake that thought away and remind yourself to stay focused. *Think.* Brett is walking down the street and he doesn't know you're behind him. What do you do?

You follow him. You sneak up behind him and push him from behind and he falls, cracking his skull open on the sidewalk. You pull out the roll of quarters you've been carrying around—*must remember to stop doing laundry and start saving quarters*—and you wrap your fist around them and as Brett rolls over face-side-up, you sock him right in the kisser, fracturing his jaw, although not badly enough to prevent him from whispering his dying words: "I'm sorry I was such an asshole."

But what if it was the other way around? Say the beeper thing didn't go off and Ken just left the drugstore and walked right smack into Brett? They'd each stop because it's second nature to stop when you bump into someone you know, and by the time that reason and history kicked in, it would be too late to change course and try to charge on by without stopping.

So the two of them would stop and say hello, and even from this far away Ken hated the archness, the cattiness, the recriminations in his voice that came through so clearly even though he'd only said two little words—"Hello, Brett."

"Hey, Ken."

God, he hated the way Brett made him sound.

And that thought just dropped out of the sky. He hated the way Brett made him sound. That thought gathered itself into a raindrop and it came plummeting straight down toward earth and it went through whatever metamorphoses were necessary to go from being a simple raindrop to becoming a huge, icy hailstone and it dropped down like a piece of lead out of the sky and smashed into Ken's skull. *I don't like the way Brett makes me sound.* I didn't ever like the way Brett made me sound. Brett doesn't bring out the best in me, and while he's at it, while he's *not* bringing out the best in me, he's making up for it by bringing out the *worst* in me. To the point where I can say, without the slightest hesitation, that I don't even like the way he makes me *sound.*

It was shocking. "Brett and I weren't right for each other," Ken thought. A single, baseball-sized hailstone on an otherwise crystal-clear day. Who would have ever imagined?

The first order of business would be to normalize relations with the enemy. There wasn't any rush, and Ken certainly didn't intend to forgive Brett for any of his trespasses, but that being said, the time was right to call off the cold war. Bring the troops on home for the holidays. Ken didn't need to waste his time or energy worrying about what would happen when he ran into Brett or, even worse, when he ran into Brett and what's-his-face. Neil. The two of whom would no doubt be on their way home from the christening of their most recent godchild. Instead, Ken would devise a way of conveying the message to Brett that he wished to speak to him. Privately.

And from that meeting, from that coffee at a diner up near City College—let the little twerp come to me—things would slowly smooth themselves out. Ken wasn't planning on ever setting foot in Brett's house, and Brett was definitely still persona non grata at the Santa Monica. But it would be nice to know that the coast was clear in terms of anyone else's parties. Someone they knew in common could throw a Christmas party and Ken could go and Brett could go and even Home-Wrecking Neil could go and nobody would wind up getting talked in off a ledge and nobody would wind up in the emergency room with a hand-painted nativity scene rammed down his throat.

So Ken would tell Brett that he wanted to speak to him and get some things sorted out. And who knows, perhaps Brett would say, "Sorry, not interested." After all, while it may take two to tango, it definitely does *not* take two people to fight. One person can easily carry an entire dispute on his shoulders for years and years while the other one forgets about it and takes night classes in small business administration and applies for a real estate license. So maybe Brett had moved on and would rebuff Ken's overtures, in which case more power to him, but the benefit to Ken would still be the same. Which is to say, putting it all behind him.

Besides, Ken knew Brett and Brett wouldn't say no. Brett always wanted people to like him. It's what made him try so hard at acting—he always wanted everybody's approval and everybody's praise and everybody's attention. And if the word "everybody" included Ken, which it ought to since it's hard to get yourself booted out of a group as undiscriminating as *"everybody,"* then logically

Brett wanted Ken's approval too. Or at least he *didn't* want Ken to be out on the highways and byways of Manhattan explaining to anyone who'd listen what a terrible, low-life, rotten person Brett Manikin was. Brett couldn't predict the future any better than anyone else could, and who's to say that at some point in the future Ken wouldn't bamboozle an otherwise discerning casting director into sleeping with him and then, over coffee the next morning, Ken would slowly hypnotize the guy and indelibly ink his brain with Brett Manikinisms:

"Brett Manikin bad."

"Brett Manikin ruin your film."

"Brett Manikin cost you *mucho* in postproduction voice-overs."

So Brett would say yes and they'd meet up at a diner near City College and they'd talk, and they'd avoid getting into anything overly painful; that wasn't the point. The point was to normalize relations *out* of the state of war and hatred—which takes energy— and *into* the state of calm indifference, which conserves energy. And all would be quiet on the Upper West Side front.

The phone rang and Ken involuntarily looked at his watch before answering it. If it was still regular work hours, there was some chance that it could be Iris; if it was after work and she was home with Jeremy, she wouldn't call. But it was Dina Marghosian, his old supervisor from Leighton Fennell. "Dina, what a sight for sore ears. Or sound for sore ears," Ken said. "Something like that. But you know what I mean."

"I do," she said laughing. "How've you been doing?"

"Good," he said, feeling surprisingly *not* like a liar. "There have been some ups and downs, but on the whole, I'm fine. At least I certainly can't complain."

"Oh, I'm glad to hear it," Dina said. "Listen, I only have a minute but I want to ask you one thing and then ask you to *think* about another thing. Just think about it, okay?"

"I'm all ears."

"Okay, first things first. The firm's having its Christmas party which, as I'm sure you'll recall, can be quite a bit of fun, and this year should be no exception, and I would personally be delighted if you'd come. And, as I'm sure you'll recall, retired staff are always welcome."

"I think I was more fired than retired," Ken said. "As far as Crayton Reed is concerned."

"Oh, who cares what he thinks," Dina said. "And I'll get back to him in a second. But seriously Ken, nobody down here has seen hide nor hair of you in months, and we need to set eyes on you every once in a while too, you know."

"Well, what are you going to do about Crayton?"

"That actually brings me to my second point. We're desperate here and I can't get anyone in and the lawyers are breathing down my back and I actually had to go to the Executive Committee and I told them that I can't provide them with staff if *lawyers* keep firing the staff I hire, so basically, to make a long story short, you can have your job back. *And*, in the interim, it would really, really get me out of a jam if you could pick up a few extra shifts between Christmas and New Year's. Both proofing and some word processing."

A long pause.

"Ken?"

"I'm still here," Ken said. "I'm just a little surprised."

"You didn't think I'd forgotten about you, did you?"

"No, no," Ken said, even though the answer that had been generated by his brain, formatted for human dictation, and dispatched to his lips was clearly "yes."

"Well, what do you say?"

"Really, I don't know, Dina."

"Pretty please," Dina said. "I am desperate here. I'm on my knees!"

"When's the party again?" Ken asked, and Dina gave him all the details. Unfortunately, it was the same night as the English Department's entirely ecumenical, wholly random assemblage of its members and their guests, so Ken had to pass on that one. "But you can put a slice of cake in the break-room fridge for me," Ken said.

"Oh, does that mean you'll come back?" Dina asked, already whooping it up.

"Actually no," Ken said, and the whooping noise abruptly disappeared.

"*No?*"

"Not entirely no," Ken said. "I can come in between now and the end of the year *if* you really need me to. As in you have no other choice *and* they're holding a gun to your head. But I'm only coming in for as long as it takes you to find someone else, you know, somebody full-time," Ken said. "And you really have to look, okay?"

"You know I won't find somebody between now and New Year's," Dina said. "Other than somebody who just got out of jail. Or worse."

"No, I know that," Ken said. Things suddenly felt so clear. "But I don't want to get sucked back into all that. I'll come in if it's to get you out of a jam. You Dina, not you Leighton Fennell. But only for enough time for you to find someone if you try. Can you give me that?"

"Word of honor."

"Okay, then we have a deal." Dina had backed Ken up when it mattered to him and he would back her up when it mattered to her.

"You know," Dina said, "we should've never let you go. I told them that way back when. I told them that we'd never find anybody as careful and as conscientious as you were, and it was like talking to a brick wall."

"That's the problem with people," Ken said. "They never listen."

"People," Dina sighed. "The problem is they never listen."

And that left just the picture to get rid of—the picture of Brett gazing at the camera out at Jones Beach from back when they first met. Ken had ticked through quite a few ideas as to what to do with it. He could take it to the photocopy place and get one of those technological whiz kids who seemed to be everywhere these days to make it into a flyer and print out a billion copies of it and it would say *"LOST: My sense of morality,"* and Ken would have them put Brett's phone number on it all along the bottom with precut tabs so that helpful citizens could tear off a tab and lend a hand in the search.

Then he thought he could tape it to the bottom of his shoe, face-side-down, and walk around not caring if he stepped in gum or doggy-doo and let it slowly wear apart and disintegrate into nothingness.

Or he could just make it into a paper airplane and throw it out the window.

He'd thought of tons of ideas, but that was then.

Ken got up from his place next to the window and went over to the kitchen table and picked up the picture. He took it into the bedroom and dislodged the nice, sturdy banker's box that now held his pile of financial records: the bank statements; the receipts; the letters assigning him complicated secret codes he hadn't asked for; and a truly mystifying series of letters from some sort of financial institution informing him that people who "work hard and play right" like Ken—neither of which was currently true—were their clientele of choice.

The chances that Ken would go back through all that stuff were slim. *Very* slim. But they weren't zero. There was always the possibility that some sort of bank mix-up would happen someday and it would force Ken to get up and go sift through this box of financial flotsam. If it happened sometime in the next decade while Ken was still relatively young and stupid, he'd just drag a chair over and pull down the box and go through it. And if it happened two decades from now, he'd probably have turned into the type of person who prudently kept a rubber-soled, nonslip step stool in the house so that he wouldn't fall and break his neck every time he changed a light bulb. And if it happened even further in the future, then Ken would probably have to ask somebody—and who that somebody would be is anybody's guess—to help him get the box down. But once it was down on the ground and opened back up, once Ken had gotten the chance to sort through all that stuff, he'd probably stumble across Brett's picture and he'd hear himself saying, "Oh, that's *right*. I kept that."

"Kept what?" the person who helped get the box down would ask.

"This. This picture," Ken would say, showing him.

"And who's that?"

"Oh, that's just somebody I used to know," Ken would say.

Chapter Twenty. In Which Peace and Tranquility Are Restored to the Good People of Manhattan, with Certain Noteworthy Exceptions

"Hey, Iris?" Ken said.

"Hey, what?"

"What was your doll's name?"

The two of them were pretending to browse through books in Kinokuniya, a Japanese bookstore near Rockefeller Center. Their original idea had been to go skating, but the rink was way too crowded, and their follow-up idea, which was to visit Saint Patrick's Cathedral, got scuttled when they discovered that nowadays one is expected to stand in a long line and open one's bag for a security guard before entering a cathedral. They'd patiently done so, only Ken couldn't stop himself from mentioning that he was really there to *lay bare his soul*, and not his bag, and the security guard just told him that there was no smart-mouthing allowed. The fallout, and their subsequent ejection from the House of the Lord, was entirely predictable. Plus it was captured on more than a few handheld video recorders. Kinokuniya offered warmth and refuge, and Iris scored extra points for being perceptive and discovering that Japanese books begin at the end and go backward toward the beginning. It gave their "browsing" a more authentic edge.

"My what?" Iris asked. "Is this some sort of trick question?"

"Not at all," Ken said. "Remember when we were sitting up at Fort Tryon, up near the Cloisters, the day of Jeremy's big fund-raiser? You said that when you were little, your mother told you there was a doll hospital and she pulled a fast one on you because she took your dolly in and came back with it a few days later and it was all bright and clean."

"Yeah. Not to mention brand-new," Iris said laughing. "I remember. But what makes you think of that now?"

"Oh, just something I read recently," Ken said, showing Iris the book he was thumbing through. The text was obviously incomprehensible, but there was a photograph of a Japanese housewife who'd just opened her refrigerator to find her husband sitting cross-legged inside it holding a red bowling ball in his lap, although on closer inspection the bowling ball turned out to be a goldfish in a bowl. The goldfish's face was hugely distorted and enlarged by the curve of the bowl, and coming out of a corner of the fish's mouth was a cartoon thought bubble showing what the fish was thinking. Whatever he was thinking was *jammed* full of exclamation points.

"*Ken,*" Iris said.

"I don't know," he said. "I guess I was just wondering."

"Well, you already know what her name was."

"No I don't."

"Yes, you do. You just said it."

"No I didn't," Ken said. "I just said what *you* said back when we were sitting up by the Cloisters when it used to be warm enough to sit outside. You said your mom told you there was a doll hospital and she took your dolly there and she helped you write a letter to her in the hospital to tell her to get well soon."

"Exactly," Iris said.

Ken's brain went tick-tock, tick-tock. "So wait a minute, your doll's name was *Dolly*?"

"Bingo," Iris said.

"Dolly Doll?"

"No, Dolly *Steegers,*" Iris said. "Obviously. And what's wrong with the name Dolly? There's Dolly Madison, first lady extraordinaire. There's Dolly Parton. There's Dolly Levi, famous for . . . , well, famous for being Dolly Levi." Iris paused in thought. "And for giving Carol Channing the role of a lifetime."

"I didn't say there was anything wrong with the name Dolly," Ken said.

"Well, you seemed a little surprised is all," Iris said. "Besides, what was I supposed to name her? Kate? Deborah? Or how about Chadwick? This was a long time ago, Ken. This was before people started naming their kids stuff like Chadwick or Logan or Logjam or whatever it is people name their kids nowadays."

Ken was laughing. "I didn't say a thing!" he protested, although he still felt the same slight flush of embarrassment that people get when they're caught with their hands in the cookie jar. And it wasn't over something trivial like teasing Iris about her *inspired* choice of doll names. No, he felt a little caught because if Iris was going to make things work with Jeremy, then Ken would have to fade out of the picture, one way or another. And fading out of the picture gets harder the better you know someone, right down to the name of her long-gone doll. "Come on," he said, re-shelving his book. "I want to go somewhere warm where we can talk."

"What do you want to talk about?" Iris asked.

"Oh, I don't know," Ken said, scratching his head to symbolize deep thought. "How about Dolly's *middle* name?"

Actually, Ken really did have something on his mind as he and Iris slid into a booth in the Skylight Diner and ordered open-faced turkey sandwiches over steak fries. Ken had an idea and he wanted to bounce it off Iris.

"I've decided to give Brett a Christmas present," he said, and Iris did that thing that people do in movies where the surprised person spits out whatever she just drank in a big, misty, fire-hose blast, only Iris did the more considerate version where she only *pretended* to hose him down in surprise. "You decided to do *what*?"

"To give Brett a Christmas present," Ken said. "Although to be a bit more precise, *you're* the one who's actually going to give it to him for me."

"Hell no I'm not," Iris said. "I've had enough trouble with the law. There's no way I'm going to bring him an exploding whatever. What have you made that explodes?"

"Relax," Ken said. "It's a legitimate present. Or let's just say it's a good thing. It's something that he should appreciate and it's something that Neil—and you'll note that I just called him 'Neil,' as in plain, old Neil, and not 'that shithead home-wrecker Neil'—it's something that Neil will *definitely* appreciate. And it's legal. It's perfectly legit."

"Try me."

"Okay," Ken said, "I've found him a job."

"You found a job for Brett?"

"Ta-dah!" Ken said. "And you're going to give him all the details. And, if you don't mind, you're also going to make very sure that *Neil* knows all the details too so that Brett can't wriggle out from under it."

This was the deal. Ken was willing to bail Dina out of an emergency situation down at Leighton Fennell, but he wasn't going to let himself get dragged permanently back into all that. Which left one job desperately needing to be filled. And Brett would be perfect for the job because, for all his abundant flaws, he was well educated and able to concentrate for long periods of time. People can't memorize the dialogue for a two-hour play (*Margaret Mead—The Musical!*) unless they have the proven ability to concentrate. So what if the play opened and closed on the same night? Brett was an actor. Brett's only constraint was that he needed to be free during the day to go on auditions, and with this job he would be. It was a perfect match, and, as icing on the cake, Dina would probably hire Brett on nothing more than Ken's recommendation and a typing test.

The genius, though, was that there wouldn't be any way for Brett to say no. Ken had lived with Brett for five years and he knew exactly what sort of tune Brett liked to sing—how Brett wanted to get a job and pull his own weight, but didn't want to cut off his nose to spite his face in terms of his acting and blah blah blah.

That was the drill. Brett was ready, willing, and able to work, but the right job never seemed to come along. Until now. Even better, Ken would come off as magnanimous and forgiving and Dina would get out of the jam she was in and all would be well in the world.

Except for Brett, who'd finally have to work. Brett would have to get up and haul his cute, sculpted behind down to an office to slave away just like everybody else. Brett would have to stop sponging off the world. Brett would have to sit through performance reviews and get 2.5 percent raises and be expected to smile and say thank you. Brett would have to nod sympathetically when people complained about the weather in the elevator on the way up to the cafeteria even though there's no weather in the basement. Ever. Brett was going to have to think about whether holidays fell on Saturdays and Sundays and became worthless or whether they fell during the week and actually counted for something. Brett would have an in-box with a steady stream of memos about nothing and then follow-up memos complaining that nobody'd paid attention to the first memo and, accordingly, Draconian measures would be implemented.

And Brett would have to brush his teeth in the men's room. And *while* he was brushing his teeth, there'd be somebody in the stall behind him who just didn't *feel* like waiting the twenty-five seconds it takes the average human being to brush his teeth, and that somebody would take a raucously loud, severed-aorta type of spurting, splattering dump. And while Brett stared in utter disbelief at the mirror—his toothbrush frozen mid-stroke—in that split second that followed the launch but preceded the first whiff of the *lethal* smell that would suddenly permeate every square inch of the bathroom, in that split second of clarity after the shock of the first attack but before the gagging, scorched-earth devastation of the second, the author of the gruesome crap would go "*Ahhhhhhhh*" as if he were genuinely satisfied with what he'd done, with what was surely the first tangible thing accomplished that day at the firm.

Paul Schmidtberger

Ken could hardly believe how neatly it would all work out. Brett's gravy train was about to grind to a halt. Permanently.

"Hey Iris?" Ken asked. "Are you going to finish those fries?"

"Nope. Knock yourself out if you want," she said, sliding her plate over to Ken, who used the fries to ladle up what remained of the gravy.

Brett was going to have to grow up.

People say that revenge is a dish best eaten cold. Maybe, maybe not. But what they don't tell you is how *good* revenge tastes, even the tiniest bit of it. Because in the scheme of things, that's all Ken had gotten when he'd figured out how to saddle Brett with the perfect job that he'd always dreamed of *not* getting—a tiny, insignificant piece of revenge. So how come something so small and insignificant still felt so *good*? Sitting with Iris in a warm diner on a cold winter afternoon, that's what Ken couldn't quite understand. He'd spent all those months coming to terms with what had happened, with the havoc that Brett had wreaked on his life, and he'd done a pretty damn good job of it too. And despite that, this little, symbolic piece of vengeance gave him *immense* pleasure. But not pleasure in the generic sense, as in something that feels good like the smell of a bakery or having somebody else shampoo your hair. It was more the kind of pleasure that you get when something is properly completed. If he had to describe it, it was more like the pleasure you feel when a cup of coffee appears at the end of a really good meal.

So this is how Ken's reasoning went. For every action, he thought, there's an equal and opposite reaction. That's what he'd learned back in Mr. Massiello's science class in high school, before he got banished for excessive enthusiasm. So when Brett fooled around with somebody else, that was an action—at least one action—and that action can't just sit around without a reaction. And that's not just Professor Ken Connelly talking out of his asshole, that's the laws of physics, the laws of nature talking. Action, reaction. You can't have one without the other—the universe doesn't like it. So even if the reaction was more symbolic than any-thing else—handing Brett over to the soul-leaching world of gain-ful employment—it was what was necessary to restore order to the universe. And *that's* why it felt so good.

Ken thought it over. The universe, he decided, always tries to right itself. The universe is like one of those tall, inflatable punch-ing bags with sand in the bottom that you can punch and it'll swing over toward the ground, but then it'll right itself. On just about every level, from the molecular to the interplanetary, it seemed that the principal driving force in the world was the urge to return to an equilibrium. When a person cuts himself, the brain snaps out of whatever it was doing (usually watching *Jeopardy!*) and it turns itself into this amazingly efficient logistics center that starts conscripting platelets from here and dispatching clotting compounds from there and it organizes armies of hundreds of thousands of cells to push the assault back and set things right. And when millions of years of ice gouged deep, jagged fjords into a coastline, the earth turned around the very next day and it started sending in dandelion seeds borne on the breeze to colonize the torn, barren land and slowly begin the process that would eventually spread forests across the gashes to smooth over the edges. And if the earth can push back so stoically, so staunchly, to make things right again after such a deep wound, Ken thought, then so can I.

Here, today, Ken thought, there were tiny, little loose threads floating around the universe and that's just not the way things are supposed to be. He looked across the table at Iris and told her that he had an interesting theory to try out on her.

"I'm all ears," she said. Ken explained the whole thing, and she let herself think it over for a while before she asked her first ques-tion. "So what you're saying is that until we even the score, cosmi-cally speaking, we'll be at odds with the universe?"

"All I'm saying is how good it felt to even the score, however in-finitesimally, with Brett."

"Hmmm," Iris said. "And what do you think Lucinda would say?"

"In my opinion," Ken said, giving it some genuine thought, "Lucinda would be loath to meddle in the workings of the universe. That doesn't strike me as her vibe. If you pitched it as just getting revenge, I don't think she'd approve. But if we're talking about respecting order in the universe, then I'd say she'd be okay with it. She's of the school of thought that says that every stream flows where it's supposed to."

"I'd have to grant you that," Iris said.

Ken started writing on a napkin. "What are you doing?" Iris asked.

"I'm trying out for the Harlem Globetrotters," Ken said. "What does it look like I'm doing?"

"It looks like you're making a list."

"I am."

"And what, pray tell, is going to be on that list?" Iris asked.

"Just some people who need to learn a lesson."

So it was official. Iris and Ken had just formed a gang. They didn't have a tough-sounding name or a secret handshake or even distinctive gang colors. And they were only going to last until the end of the year and then dissolve, but they were still a gang. They were going to make things right.

It was Iris's idea to program the gang's demise for the end of the year. New Year's is always a time for starting fresh, and Ken could see her point—that no matter how fun or innocuous all this was, they probably shouldn't let it carry over into a brand-new year. Still, on a certain, bittersweet level, Ken couldn't help thinking that what Iris *really* meant about the New Year and starting over fresh was that she'd be starting over fresh without him, but if that's what it took for Iris to get her life back on track with Jeremy, which seemed to be what she wanted, then that's what it took. Besides, his own era of idle, free time was coming to an end. He was already picking up a few shifts at Leighton Fennell, and after the holidays he'd have his old job back at the reference desk. So if ever there was a time and place for getting down to brass tacks, it was here and it was now.

So, whose hash needed settling?

"Well, there was the pushy flight attendant who got me into trouble in the first place," Iris offered. Ken put her down on the list as "Ax, Battle."

There was the mean, podium-hogging prosecutor.

"There was—" Iris started to say when Ken cut her off, laughing. "Slow down," he said. "I can't write that fast!"

Their very first order of business was to recruit Jeff, and once again, it was as easy as one, two, three: "Hey Jeff, it's Iris. Ken and I are forming a gang to get revenge on everyone who got us into trouble. You want in?" A slight pause. "Great." Another pause. "I'll ask him." She covered the receiver and said Jeff wanted to know if they could have turf wars with rival gangs, but Ken just laughed and shook his head. "Sorry, honey," Iris said into the phone, "but you're still in, though, aren't you?" A pause. "Okay, see you in a few!"

To find out who Battle was, Jeff suggested that they go back to court, only this time they went straight to the clerk's office one floor down, and Iris asked if she could see the file for a case called the United States of America versus Steegers. The guy at the window told her that she wasn't going to see "no nothing" without a case number, but when Iris said "Oh," and looked dejected and said that she didn't know what the number was, the guy softened up and told her not to worry. He said that all she had to do was go over to this ancient computer terminal on the public side of his window barrier, type in the names, and the case number would pop out.

And as easily as that, they had the file in their hands. *Anyone* could look at it. And inside the file, amongst all this confusing paperwork, there was an affidavit from a certain Anne-Marie Wyatt, the affidavit that tattled on Iris, the one that said that Iris had used foul and abusive language and disregarded crew instructions. It also said exactly where Anne-Marie Wyatt lived. Right there, in black-and-white.

Battle lived in Hoboken and Ken, Jeff, and Iris hopped into the intrepid little Volvo and zoomed off in search of supplies. They had to go to three different bookstores before they found a translation of Charroux's *Rudeness and the Social Construct of Stupidity*— bought with cash—and then Jeff wrote out the card in case someone ever tried to trace Iris's handwriting. "Thanks for the demonstration!" it said. And they left it in Battle's mailbox and crossed her off the list.

The court file held another choice piece of information—the name of the mean, podium-hogging prosecutor. He was no longer just a screechy, impossible-to-satisfy pain in the neck with a receding chin who'd gotten Iris (sort of) sent up the river; now he had a name. Mitchell Quinlan. And guess how many Quinlans there were in the New York City phone book?

Answer: who cares? Because that's not what they did. Instead, Ken asked the bored clerk what the name was of whoever was in charge of the prosecutor's office.

"Meaning what?" the clerk asked. "We don't take complaints here."

"It's not for a complaint," Ken said. "We just wanted to know who the big boss is for the prosecutors. You know, just to know?"

"Oh, well, in *that* case," the clerk said, and he told them what they wanted to know. Not that they couldn't have gotten the same thing by just calling the U.S. Attorney's Office and saying they wanted to *fax* some *flowers* over to the big kahuna and could they please have his name? Ken called the U.S. Attorney's Office from a conference room at Leighton, Fennell & Lowe and said that it was Merit Lowe himself on the phone and that he wanted to speak to the boss. Then while some secretary looked around for him, Ken shoved the phone into Iris's hands.

"What am I supposed to do with this!" she hissed.

"When he gets on the line, just say 'One moment for Mr. Lowe,' and then don't even wait for an answer. That's what all the really big egos do."

"Ken!" But before she could protest any further, Quinlan's boss got on the phone and started to say hello and what can I do for you, and Iris put on this marvelously pinched voice and cut him off, saying, "One moment for Mr. Lowe, please." Ken had to hold the phone between his knees until he stopped laughing. He got on the phone and said, "Merit Lowe here!" and then he said how much he appreciated the prosecutor giving him a moment of his time and how he just wanted to get a brief reference concerning a certain Mitch Quinlan.

"Mitchell Quinlan?" The big boss sounded confused.

"That's right," Ken said. "He's applied for a position with us here at Leighton, Fennell *and Lowe*, and I was hoping you could shed a bit more light on his skills. His potential. His sense of integrity. His sense of *loyalty*."

"Oh."

"My father"—Ken pronounced it *fah-thaa*—"used to tell me never trust a man with a weak chin, but this Quinlan character seems all right to me I'd say, wouldn't you?"

And that was all it took to sow the seeds of doubt in the mind of Quinlan's boss. "And as I'm sure you can appreciate," Ken said as they wound things up, "this conversation never happened."

The restaurant couldn't have been easier. Jeff called Nourriture up and blithely told them—as if the restaurant staff were supposed to know what he was talking about—that he was the ambassador's *social* secretary. "Not his administrative assistant," he paused. "Who *types*. But his social secretary. There's a difference."

"And what can we do for you?"

"Well, there's the question of a little holiday banquet that we're putting together on very short notice," Jeff said. And then he poured it on thick. What could they do in terms of a set course menu? Weren't there any appetizers *with* truffles? Don't dishes incorporating dabs of foie gras taste even *better* when they incorporate great big *slabs* of foie gras? Discretion was a must. Eight seats, but other than the ambassador, no names for the moment. "Oh, and by the way, ambassadors are addressed as, uh . . ." He looked over at Ken and Iris, but they just shrugged. "As Your Eminence," he said. "No, wait! As *Your Serene Eminence*," he said. "He got promoted. Not that you'll be addressing him at all; the ambassador has enough headaches without any more intrusions on his time." Ken and Iris were simply in awe. "And no press!" Jeff barked into the phone before telling whoever was on the other end to read everything he'd just written down back to him. "That's right, that's right," Jeff said. Then a long pause. "Ambassador Scillat," he said. Then he spelled it and gave them Scillat's number at the English Department. "That's right," he said into the phone. Clipped. No nonsense. Efficient. "We'll see you on Saturday night, then," and he hung up.

"In your dreams," he added.

It was time to shift into overdrive. Time to pick up the pace. By this point the days couldn't get any shorter, and that didn't leave very much time for taking care of the last two people on the list: Helvetica Carlyle and Crayton Reed. It was the day of the English Department party, and the plan was for Iris to pick up Ken after his shift at Leighton Fennell and drive him uptown to City College where they were meeting Jeff for the party. Despite having picked up three different shifts already, Ken had yet to cross paths with Crayton at Leighton Fennell. He *had*, however, noticed one of Crayton's precious works-in-progress in the little wire intake basket for Word Processing one day, and even though it was earmarked for somebody else, Ken decided—"Oh, *why not?*"—and ran the whole shebang through the photocopier and kept the copy for himself.

True to form, it was a mess. There were riders written on scraps of yellow legal paper which were supposed to be inserted somewhere—one would presume—but didn't indicate where. There were scribbles. There were scrabbles. And there were cross outs. There were edits written right off the edge of the paper where Crayton evidently hadn't realized that his paper had ended and he'd been writing on some *other* piece of paper underneath it, and all his edits just abruptly plunged off their own personal cliff into nothingness. It was a big, scritchy-scratchy pile of urgent, unpleasant words. And that gave Ken an idea.

He called Iris on her cell phone and asked her to try to park and come inside instead of meeting him out on the corner. And when she got there, he was momentarily distracted from the task at hand by how beautiful she looked in this gray and silver dress with a very fitted bodice. Ken changed into his suit in the bathroom and by the time he'd come back to his cubicle and drew another chair up next to Iris, she'd already made quite a bit of progress in cutting out words. And there was so many to choose from! With the way that Crayton Reed went through words, they could've pieced together *anything*—no manifesto too long; no screed too convoluted; no dissertation too arcane. In the end, they only had to physically doctor one word—the word "dictum"—and that didn't bother Iris at all because she didn't know what it meant in the first place. "It's something a court says but doesn't mean," Ken explained.

"Come again?"

"It's something that a court says but doesn't really mean," Ken said. "Or at least that's how the lawyers use it. They're always writing something like, 'Oh, yes, sure, in such-and-such a case, the court did say this and that, but the court didn't really *mean* it. It was just *dictum.*'"

"You got to be kidding," Iris said.

"Do I look like I'm kidding?"

"No, I'd have to say you don't," she said, handing him a bottle of Wite-Out and a nail scissors. "You have my permission to tear that word apart." Ten minutes later they'd pieced together a doodled note, all in Crayton's uniquely loathsome handwriting, that said that Crayton should get paid twice as much as the other partners because, unlike them, he didn't have his head up his *rectum*. They used the Word Processing intake form to lift a copy of Crayton's signature and then ran the whole production through the photocopier for a few generations to give it that nice patina of a long-forgotten, scratch pad note.

Then Ken slipped the note into a crisp, new, interoffice envelope, one out of a box of about a hundred new envelopes he'd gotten from the supply room, and then he put the envelope back somewhere in the middle of the box and brought the whole box back to the supply room and told them that his eyes had been bigger than his stomach. Or something like that. So here you go. Oh, and happy holidays!

Ken and Iris had to hustle a little bit, not because they were late—the department's gathering wouldn't begin for another half hour—but because they had an errand to do on the way. Needless to say, though, they got stuck in traffic. As far as Ken was concerned, merrymakers who clogged the sidewalks in front of high-priced toy stores marketed toward high-end parents of high-maintenance kids were one thing—and easily avoided—but merrymakers who clogged all of lower Manhattan were another thing altogether. But instead of complaining, he just commented on how strange life was sometimes. How he never would've believed it last summer if someone had told him that he'd be going to the English Department's holiday *amalgamation* this year without Brett, but on the arm of a beautiful woman.

"And with a beautiful young man waiting for us there," he said. "Just to be precise." They stared out the window at the festive human flow surging across the crosswalk despite the bitter cold. "Explain to me," Ken finally said, "why that guy there, the one just about to reach the curb, explain to me why he's wearing that hat."

It was a huge, felt, four-leaf-clover novelty hat that was clearly intended for a Saint Patrick's Day party. A ghastly Saint Paddy's Day party in hell.

"The green hat?" Iris asked, sounding somewhat distracted.

"Exactly."

"Because it's freezing cold?" Iris offered.

"Iris! It's a green, *four-leaf clover hat*! It's as if the whole world recently decided that you can just mix and match holidays and if the point is to celebrate, then any celebratory holiday will do. I mean, that's a Saint Patrick's Day hat. Period. Not that Saint Patrick's Day automatically entails the donning of a big, oversized, foamy, four-leaf-clover hat. Not the last time I checked, anyway."

"Well, when was the last time you checked?" Iris teased. "Speaking of?"

"It's just a figure of speech," Ken said. "You know what I mean." Iris finally got through the intersection and Ken went back to studying the crowds on the sidewalks for other signs of inter-holiday leakage. He didn't come up with anything for the first two blocks, but on the third block there was a pair of women in their late twenties who were both wearing fuzzy black earmuffs with long glittery antennae built into them that hovered above their heads, wobbly-bobbling as they strode along. "Halloween," Ken announced. And then, just as an afterthought, he said, "Or New Year's Eve."

And *that* made him think and he turned and asked Iris what she was doing for New Year's Eve. And even though her face didn't betray a thing, not the slightest thing, he saw her hands tighten around the wheel. She's doing something with Jeremy, Ken realized. *Obviously* she is. "Some A-list Eighty-fifth Street party with all the A-list Eighty-fifth Street people?" Ken offered, rushing to answer his own question so that Iris wouldn't have to be the one excluding him.

"Something like that," she said, laughing, and then she went back to carefully surveying the road, which probably wasn't all that necessary given that they were moving so slowly.

"Hey, Iris?" Ken asked.

"Hey what?"

"It's okay, you know?" Ken said.

"What's okay?"

"You, me, and Jeremy. You know? How one of us is not like the others, and how that one would be me?"

"What do you mean?" Iris asked.

"You, me, and Jeremy," Ken repeated. "And Jeff for that matter. There really isn't any way for us to all get along, is there?"

"Not that I've been able to think of up till now."

"And you've probably been giving it some pretty careful thought?" Ken asked.

"I didn't say that," Iris said.

"But you don't deny it?"

"I don't remember what the question was!"

"*Iris,*" Ken said. "Listen, I'm not utterly devoid of the powers of perception. If you hang out with Jeff and me, you have to explain to Jeremy what you've been doing, and that creates a lot of trouble because you don't want him to know that we were your spies. Am I correct?"

"You sound like Quinlan."

"Iris, I'm trying to be serious here."

"And I'm trying to get us through traffic here," Iris said. "So there."

"Listen, Iris. All I'm saying is that I understand what the problem is and I'm on your side here. And if I need to bow out of the picture," Ken paused to pick his words carefully, "bow out for the greater good that is, then I'm willing to do it. I don't want your friendship with me to cost you your relationship. There's already been more than enough heartache to go around."

"Just shut up and let me drive," Iris said, which, Ken noted to himself, was *not* the same thing as categorically refusing his offer. "I'll think of something," she said, but she said it so softly that it wasn't clear who she was trying to convince.

. . .

They drove up Park Avenue and glided by Helvetica Carlyle's building and then Iris turned left onto the first cross street and, miracles of miracles, found a parking spot right away.

"Well, *that* never happens," she said.

"What never happens?"

"That parking spot right there! When was the last time you just found a parking spot like that?"

"Iris, that spot is blocked by that double-parked Jeep Grand Cherokee. Which shows no sign of moving."

"But that doesn't change the fact that it's still a parking spot," Iris said. "That just affects whether or not we can get *into* it, which we can't." Iris parked in front of the Jeep Grand Cherokee and Ken got out and dashed back around the corner to Helvie's building.

What to do about Helvetica had been a tough question for Iris and Ken. From everything they could gather, she was the big boss where she worked so there wasn't any point in trying to get her in trouble with her boss. Nor did she seem to present any vulnerability on any of the other fronts that most human beings have, like an appeal to her sense of shame or her sense of humility. Plus even the most rudimentary surveillance showed that she didn't give a rat's ass what her neighbors thought about her, so their idea of sending a mass mailing to Helvie's building with a hard-hitting exposé on what a unredeemable slattern she was went right out the door. Helvetica, it seemed, required a more direct approach.

And that's just what they'd decided to do. Ken went instead of Iris because Helvie might remember Iris from the plane, and Ken strolled in the door with his wool cap pulled down low and tight and announced that he was Crayton Reed and that he was here to see Helvetica Carlyle. Ten seconds later, he was standing, just like he planned, right outside her door ringing her bell. However, just like he *hadn't* planned, he was holding some dry cleaning for her that had just been delivered. "Would you mind killing two birds with one stone and bringing it up?" the doorman had asked. "*Thanks a mil,*" he said, without waiting for an answer or bothering to look up. He just handed Ken the slithery plastic and nodded toward the elevator bank.

When Ken rang Helvie's bell, she threw him further off track by hollering "It's open!" from somewhere deep within the apartment. It threw him off because his plan had been to stand there at the door and tell her exactly what he thought of her and then turn on his heel and march away. Now, though, he was inside her apartment and it shifted all the dynamics around in a slightly creepy kind of way.

"You're not Crayton Reed," Helvie said, suddenly stopping midway down her immense marble-floored entrance hall.

"No, I'm not," Ken said. "But I think you'll find that this is your dry cleaning, nonetheless."

"Put it on the table," Helvie said, pointing toward this thin, fantastically expensive and fantastically impractical Louis XV console table against the wall.

"Put it on the table *please*," Ken said, surprising himself.

Helvie eyed him carefully for a long time before she spoke. "Put that down and get out of my apartment," she said, calmly and distinctly.

"Fine," Ken said, dropping the cleaning onto the floor. "But before I go, there's something I'd like to say to you."

"I don't care what you want to say to me," Helvie said. "Who are you anyway? No, wait, who cares who you are. You're going to get out of my house this instant or you're going to regret it for a long, long time."

"I'm leaving," Ken said. "But I just thought you should know that you're a horrible human being. If you're even human. That's what I had to say. What do you think about that?"

"I think you were just leaving," Helvie said, turning back toward the other end of the entrance hall. "Oh, and *Crayton*," she spat the word out. "On your way out, would you let the doorman know I'll be needing a cab shortly?"

"I will if you say please," Ken said.

. . .

Design Flaws of the Human Condition

Meanwhile Iris had been lost in thought. She actually didn't have any specific plans for New Year's Eve; she just figured that she'd do what she always did, which was leave everything in Jeremy's very capable hands. But still, it had gotten her to thinking.

What if this year she said no? What if this year she put her foot down and said, "Whatever you want to do, the answer is no"? Say Jeremy wanted them to go to some great party whereas Iris wanted them to stand on their heads on a filthy sidewalk on Skid Row? Iris would get her way. And *why* was that? Because what Jeremy had done with Alicia was so wrong. What he'd done was so wrong that Iris could have her way on virtually *anything*, and all that contrite, abashed Jeremy could do would be to go along with it.

And that was the problem, because Iris didn't *want* to impose her will on Jeremy. Nor vice versa. She didn't want to hold the whole Alicia thing over Jeremy—lord it over him; in fact, she'd just as soon have never heard the name Alicia. It would be degrading to go through life getting her way just because nobody wanted to raise the specter of Alicia.

And that's when it hit her. "I don't think this is going to work," she thought. "Jeremy and me. It's not going to work out. I want someone who only wants me."

She sat there and let the thought sink in. It was eerily calm for such a cataclysmic development. Of course, she'd give Jeremy the chance to tell his side of the story—that much she owed him—but *only* if he was planning to be honest this time. One hundred percent honest. But even then she couldn't really see herself changing her mind. "I'll listen with an open heart and an open mind," she thought, "but unless I hear something pretty damn revolutionary, he's going to have to go." And she could wait until after the holidays before the axe fell—if that's what decency demanded—but fall it most likely would.

Jeremy. She'd loved Jeremy, but that hadn't been enough. And before she'd loved Jeremy, she'd been so—what was the word?—so *grateful* to him for choosing her. And on a certain level, she still was and probably always would be. She tried to think about Jeremy at his best. Not the Jeremy who came looming out of a blurry gray fog into a traffic photo in Yardley, Pennsylvania. She thought about the other Jeremy. Jeremy in the elevator at Macy's. Jeremy holding her hand on the flight to the Bahamas. Jeremy clowning around on the tennis court and holding his hand up behind his back the way players do when they're going to poach, but playfully giving the camera the finger. Fun, fresh Jeremy. But even then, Iris thought, Jeremy didn't really need to signal that he was going to poach; when Iris was his doubles partner, he *always* poached. He was always coming over onto her half of the court because . . .

Because why?

"Because he doesn't think I'm good enough," she realized.

What a thing to discover! If she were Sir Isaac Newton, she would've glued the apple right back onto the tree because she didn't *want* to know what she'd just figured out. But there was no going back. He didn't think she was good enough. "Well, I've got news for you," Iris thought. "I *am* good enough, and that's good enough for me."

Besides, she'd changed too. For better or for worse, the Iris sitting there next to a teasingly free, though inaccessible parking spot wasn't the same Iris who'd driven home from Newark Airport all those months ago after getting the Very-Insignificant-Person treatment from that horrid airline. This Iris was more confident. This Iris was more self-assured. *This* Iris was the type of person who'd steal a NEIGHBORHOOD CRIME WATCH sign from a street in Rego Park, Queens, *sneak* it into the classroom building at St. John's Law School, and then attach the sign to the door of Jeff's former professor's classroom. The sign had a very stylized graphic of a watchful eye on it, and when they were first stealing it, it had been *Iris's* suggestion to drape her fake pashmina shawl over it so that if anyone asked what they were doing, they could say that her shawl had blown off onto the sign and these two knights in shining armor had come to her rescue.

She smiled at the thought of their gang. Ken, Jeff, and Iris. Making things right.

In the rearview mirror she could see Ken trotting toward the car so she started the engine back up. There aren't any guarantees—not in this life anyway—so maybe she'd find someone someday and maybe she wouldn't. If she did, though, he'd have to love her for being her. Period. End of story. Or rather, the beginning.

Ken tapped on the window and Iris undid the lock and let him in, asking him how it had gone. "As well as can be expected," he said. "Nice apartment, though."

"I bet it was," Iris said, letting out the parking brake and pulling back out into traffic and none too soon, given the sirens and the commotion that were swelling up behind them because traffic *just wasn't moving slowly enough already*. Ken filled her in on the details and in the end they had to agree that it was a good effort on their part, even if people like Helvetica Carlyle were pretty much immune to anything that Ken and Iris could possibly dish out. "How do you think she got to be that way anyway?" Iris asked. "Do you think she was born like that or do you think that one day she just tried being rude and obnoxious and discovered that it fit her like a glove?"

Ken laughed. "That's a good question," he said. "Which came first, the rude chicken or the insufferable egg? Somebody really ought to apply for a grant and research that."

"I suppose," Iris said. "Although in the end, the result is the same. She's obnoxious and she inflicts her obnoxiousness—in *very* generous portions—on everybody around her. I say good riddance."

"And I say *Amen* to that." Ken said. "So long, Helvie. We hardly knew ya!"

"But what we knew was more than enough!" Iris added gleefully, gunning the motor for emphasis as she zipped her faithful little Volvo across Sixth Avenue where, mercifully, things finally seemed to be thinning out a bit. But even their upbeat farewell to Helvetica couldn't quite shake the little tinge of melancholy that the two of them had somehow picked up and brought along for the ride. And it wasn't just Helvetica and how hard it was to truly get back at a person like her because Ken and Iris were right—good riddance. It was something else, and the more Ken thought it over, that something else seemed to be the impossibility for them, for Ken and Iris, to keep their friendship going forward, at least without Iris having to lie or craft elaborate excuses or sneak around behind Jeremy's back. To Ken it felt like he was going to a bright, festive party with Iris on his arm and Jeff waiting for them there, but that afterward, it would all be over. It was the opposite of a wedding, he thought, because there'd be a big, fancy party with flushed cheeks and drunk great-uncles, but afterward, instead of everyone's lives coming together, they'd all go their separate ways. The holidays were right around the corner and then the new semester would get going and since Iris couldn't tell him to get lost, which was what she needed to have happen, then maybe he'd have to do it himself.

"Iris?" he asked.

"Dah-link?" she said in a fake, Russian spy accent.

"Don't you think that a friendship can sometimes run its course?"

"A friendship?"

"Yeah. Any given friendship," Ken said. "Say for example ours."

"I don't think friendships come with expiration dates," Iris said. "If that's what you're asking."

"Iris, you know what I'm saying. Think about it this way. At any given moment, I could get a job offer, *a tenure-track offer*, at the University of God-Help-Us-Nowhere and I'd have to pack my bags and leave. You know? We'd have to go our separate ways."

"Well, have you gotten an offer from them?"

"From whom?"

"From the University of Stop-Talking-Nonsense, that's who. This job offer is just an idea, right? Not a reality. Okay, so what? So someday you get an offer for a job that's not horrendous and off you go. What's that got to do with here and now?"

"Well, nothing," Ken said. "I'm just using it as an example. Sometimes friends stay together and sometimes they don't. Sometimes the friendship runs its course and it's done. You know, the people have finished telling each other everything they have to say."

"And that'd be us?" Iris said.

"If that's what it takes, then maybe so," Ken said. Somebody honked and Iris jerked the car forward and then braked a bit too roughly. "I'm just saying it's something to think about."

"Oh, I'm so tired of thinking," Iris said.

"Yeah, well you and me both," Ken said with a sigh, tabling the whole subject for the moment.

Only not quite.

Not quite because a few minutes later Iris asked whether he really thought that friends could run out of everything they had to say to each other.

And Ken said, "Sure, I guess so."

And Iris said, "Let's see." She said she'd like to make him a bet. She said that he should look at his watch and give her a signal and then let two minutes go by and they'd see if they didn't have anything new to say to each other. "And it has to be new," Iris said. "Nothing about inappropriate holiday hats or Jeff's *guileless, radiant smile* or anything else we've been over before."

"Fair enough," Ken said.

"And if we *don't* have anything new to say,"—Iris gave Ken a sly, little glance and then went back to studying the traffic light—"then maybe I'll take your ridiculous offer to call it quits a little more seriously."

"Also fair enough."

"Well, I'm ready when you are," Iris said, and Ken held up his hand like he was a traffic cop and then blinked four fingers, three fingers, two fingers. "And go!" he said.

Unfortunately, they didn't get to go anywhere because the light was still red, but when it finally changed, Iris popped the clutch and swung hard to the right and neatly went around the worst of the traffic waiting to go all the way west toward the West Side Highway. "This is my patented shortcut," she said.

"Doesn't count," Ken said. "You told me that when we were

coming home from somewhere or other. The flea market or something."

"So I did," Iris said. "But try to keep it a secret anyway, since I don't want all the riffraff using my shortcut."

"Your wish is my command," Ken said as Iris edged her car back into traffic at the tip of Fifty-seventh Street, the last chance, dagnabbit, final opportunity for getting on the highway at the point where it stops being a street and starts being a highway. They shot up the ramp and Ken said, "Oh."

"Oh, what?"

"Nothing. I don't know. Did I ever tell you that I almost got killed right there?"

"You did?" Iris asked. "Well, then they really need to do something about that spot because I almost got killed there too."

"You did?"

"Sure did," Iris said. "Some buffoon was sitting in the right lane, just parked there as if it wasn't a major highway and instead there was a big, fat sign that said 'Rest Stop' or 'Scenic View' or 'Pull Over *Here* If You Don't Have Anything Else to Do.' "

"No joke?" Ken said.

"No joke. And it really made my day, because it was *while* I was on the way home from the airport after a certain flight that ended up costing me rather dearly."

"So it was back in the summer?"

"Mmmm, more or less," Iris said. "Labor Day weekend."

"Right around when I got fired," Ken said. "And this guy was just sitting there in the right lane?"

"Yup."

"And that's what happened to your front fender?" Ken asked.

"Exactly," Iris said. "And I'll be getting it fixed when the insurance cuts me a check, which will be approximately never." She glanced into the rearview mirror to be sure nothing so untoward was about to happen to her tonight. "And what happened to you?"

"Oh, me? I was in a car service car one night that got its sideview mirror blasted off by some crazy bitch driving like a bat out of hell. Driving her *sky blue Volvo* like a bat out of hell." Ken had an unfair advantage because he didn't have to look at the road so he was able to turn sideways to watch the news slowly sink into the top of Iris's head and then seep down and spread and swirl and bloom into a wide smile.

"A Volvo?" she asked.

"That's right," he said.

"And this was a car service car? The one you were in?"

" 'Twas."

"Black, boxy town car?" Iris asked.

"Black and boxy, yes. Side-view mirror, not anymore."

"Something tells me we have quite a bit left to talk about," Iris said. She could barely speak for the size of her smile. "Wouldn't you agree?"

"Oh, I'd say that's about right," Ken said, watching the trail of red taillights winding and blinking their way up one side of Manhattan while the cold, quiet Hudson slipped by the other way. "I don't think I could've put it better myself."

Epilogue. In Which Loose Ends Are Tied Up and a Toe Tag Is Tied On

As far as the police could tell, Helvetica Carlyle, née Farht-staller, fell off her balcony. That's not a particularly common occurrence, especially on Park Avenue, and especially when you consider the fact that Helvie was getting ready to go to a party where, by all accounts, she was going to have a great time—the hostess was terrified of her and that was the kind of party that Helvie just loved. But sometimes people get dressed up and go to parties and sometimes they get dressed up and fall off their balconies.

In any event, there weren't any particularly noticeable signs of foul play.

According to the neighbors, Helvie occasionally went out onto the balcony to smoke, and it wouldn't have been unusual for her to have been out there for a cigarette without a coat on, even on such a cold night. And she occasionally took her cell phone out there when somebody on the other end of the line needed to have his head bit off, long-distance. The only slight hitch being that Helvie wasn't carrying her cigarettes or her cell phone when she executed her flawless swan dive down onto the roof of a taxi seventeen floors below.

Strange.

Helvie had just gotten something delivered from one of the soulless drones at Leighton, Fennell & Lowe, but that was par for the course because nights and weekends were Helvie's favorite time for making her lawyers work overtime. But by the same token, the delivery itself seemed to be missing in action.

Very strange.

In any event, the police report kept coming back to one particular theme; that is, how every element was consistent with several different theories. For example, the report noted that there was slight bruising around Helvetica's right wrist which could've been the result of her clunky Cartier bracelet rattling around at the moment of impact. Though it was *equally* consistent with her being yanked sharply by the wrist and dragged across the room.

Likewise, there were neighbors about midway down who testified to hearing an unusual *Ohhh* sound as Helvie dropped by their dining room window. They were absolutely sure because this unusual *Ohhh* sound—not to mention the extremely unusual sight of Helvie plunging by—happened in that moment of silence just after they'd all bowed their heads to say grace. "That's strange," they'd thought, abandoning the prayer in order to gawk. "Helvie never says *anything* to her neighbors." But in any event, the police report duly noted the distinctive *Ohhh* sound and concluded that it was very much the type of sound that a person might make as she accidentally slips and falls and realizes that nothing stands between her and the irresistible pull of the earth's gravity. Nothing except seventeen floors. *Although*, the report noted, the sound was *equally consistent* with a person yelling, "No!" Somebody out of earshot who bellows "No!" and then holds that note as she comes closer, passes by, and then heads on down to meet her maker.

So who knows?

There was one little bit of evidence that helped explain how she lost her balance, though. There was some dry cleaning that had slipped onto the floor of the entrance hall and at some point Helvie must have accidentally stepped on it, because the spiky heel of her right shoe had punctured the plastic, and that punctured piece of plastic had stuck to the bottom of her heel, following her from the entrance hall to the living room, from the living room to the balcony, and from the balcony to the roof of the cab that was pulling up downstairs.

Oh, well.

At least Helvie got her cab. And she got it without having to say please.

Acknowledgments

I would like to express my heartfelt gratitude to Andrew Corbin at The Doubleday Broadway Publishing Group. I would also like to thank the following people for their willingness to read the first draft of this book; if there's more wheat than chaff, it's thanks to Mary Heslin Schmidtberger, Loren Francis Schmidtberger, Sophie Schlondorff, and Bill Prendiville. For their support, encouragement, and invaluable assistance, I would like to thank Karen Hwa, D. Vander Hooten, and Joni Lachman.

Finally, I owe a debt of gratitude to my agent, Marly Rusoff, who has the gentlest voice I've ever heard, even when it reaches all the way across the ocean.

PAUL SCHMIDTBERGER was born and raised in Schooley's Mountain, New Jersey, and currently lives in Paris. He is a graduate of Yale College and Stanford Law School, and is a member of the California State Bar. This is his first novel.